He wanted to stay out of the conflict, but now he had no choice...

Slater closed the school early, went home, took a shower, and changed his clothes. Carlos and Maria would arrive at any minute and he longed to see her again. He hoped that she would have dinner with him and then talk until the sun faded into the trees behind his house.

He heard a car and looked out the window. It was Casey but Maria and Carlos weren't with him. He stood on the porch while Casey emerged from the vehicle. "Where's Maria," Slater said.

Casey's thick eyebrows narrowed and he squinted against the sun. "Something's gone wrong, Jim."

Slater stepped off the porch and the two men shook hands. "What do you mean?"

"We think Maria's in El Chipote. Alberto betrayed her."

"No," Slater said. "What happened?"

"We don't know. This is all conjecture but we think Alberto turned her over to the Sandinistas and they took her to the prison. He told Carlos he was going to the camp but I saw him in Managua. He told me he was going to see his family but he probably betrayed Maria. One of our sources mentioned a heavy military convoy was being sortied from the base north of Managua. I suspect Perez is mounting a counterstrike against us and time is running short. Carlos, Luis, and Raoul are in the process moving the camp to a new location. They are going to radio me when they have found a suitable site. You still have your short-wave radio?"

Slater ignored the question about the radio. "What about Maria?"

"Most likely she's being interrogated by professionals. God help her."

Slater could not swallow and he wiped droplets of sweat form the back of his neck. Maria was right. The consequences of their romance were beginning to plague them. He no longer felt like an innocent bystander.

The steamy mountain jungles of Nicaragua provide a sanctuary for ex-US Marine Jim Slater as he struggles to build a schoolhouse for a rural community ravaged by the country's civil war. Haunted by demons that have followed him from Vietnam, Slater only wants to be left in peace. But that peace is shattered when the beautiful contra fighter, Maria Martinez, pulls him from a pub just before the rebels blow it up. When a plot to assassinate an important Sandinista colonel fails, and Maria is taken prisoner, Slater is propelled into the conflict, determined to rescue the woman he loves. With the help of a local CIA operative, Slater embarks on a harrowing journey that will change his life forever...if he even survives.

KUDOS for *Blood of Brothers*

In *Blood of Brothers* by Richard Edde, Jim Slater is a Vietnam vet, suffering from PTSD. He goes to the mountains of Nicaragua to build a schoolhouse and teach the children of the war-torn country. He stays out of politics and doesn't get involved in the violence. All he wants is to live his life in peace. But when the beautiful contra fighter Maria Martinez saves his life, and then is later arrested, Slater realizes he can no longer remain neutral. Determined to save the woman he loves, he teams up with a local CIA agent and begins a journey that will change his life forever. The book is very well written, with vivid scenes, believable characters, a strong plot, and plenty of bite-your-fingernails tension. Be prepared for a long reading session, because once you pick it up, you won't want to put it down. ~ *Taylor Jones, Reviewer*

Blood of Brothers by Richard Edde is the story of a man torn between his need for a quiet peaceful life and his determination to do what is right. Jim Slater is a US ex-patriot, a veteran of the Vietnam war, and a good man with PTSD. Unable to fit in with "civilized" society in the US, Jim heads to the mountain jungles of war-torn Nicaragua to build schools and teach the children of the rural farmers. But as hard as he tries to stay out of the conflict exploding around him, it becomes a moot point once Maria Martinez, a pretty rebel fighter pulls him out of a pub, just before it blows up, and saves his life. Maria and her friends are passionate about their cause, and Slater finds himself being drawn into the fold. But when Maria tries to assassinate a powerful colonel and is betrayed by one of her own, Slater is determined to free her before she is executed, committing himself fully to the rebel cause and putting his life in grave danger. *Blood of Brothers* has a ring of truth that makes me think the author has either been there or knows someone who has. His detailed descriptions of what must be a truly beautiful country, and his understanding of how the rebel view their cause, pulls you in and makes you feel like you're right there with Jim and Maria as they fight for freedom from tyranny. A powerful, thought-provoking, and enlightening read. I highly recommend it. ~ *Regan Murphy, Reviewer*

BLOOD

OF

BROTHERS

RICHARD EDDE

A Black Opal Books Publication

GENRE: THRILLER/SUSPENSE/ROMANTIC ELEMENTS

DEDICATION

For Frank
Gone Too Soon

Save you, Nicaragua! On your soil
The sound of the cannon echoes no more;
And the blood of brothers no longer stains
Your glorious blue and white banner.

~ Nicaraguan National Anthem

CHAPTER 1

High in the mountains of northern Nicaragua, an early morning mist hung like a dense mantle over the village of San Rafael while the heavy air deepened the shadows in Jim Slater's cluttered bedroom. Pulling the pillow over his head could not drown out the sound of his neighbor's crowing rooster—the stupid critter was up especially early. It was one of those mornings, when time refused to loiter and allow him a few minutes more of much-needed rest. Sitting on the edge of his bed, he shook out his shoes, relieved that nothing scampered out. He pulled them on and headed for the tiny bathroom, remembering the first lesson of jungle living—check your shoes before getting up because anything could have found its way into the primitive, whitewashed house during the night.

Slater bent over the cracked porcelain sink, took a sip of bottled water, and brushed his teeth. Fighting through the early morning mental fog, his attention slowly focused on a loud commotion outside and a heavy banging on his front door. A scream pierced the confusion while cries for help erupted from San Rafael's main street. Jolted awake, Slater crossed the sparse living room, opened the front door, and found his friend, Francisco Velasquez, standing on the front porch, out of breath. Francisco's eyes were wide and they darted furtively between Slater and some of the town's residents who stood behind him.

"Please, Senor Jim," Francisco said, as he reached through the doorway and grabbed Slater by a bare arm.

"What's the matter, Francisco?" Slater said.

Deep furrows etched Francisco's tanned face, made leathery from years of farming. Slater pulled a shirt off the back of a chair and followed his friend onto the wooden porch. The mist had ended and a weak sun glinted through low-hanging clouds.

"Something horrible, Senor Jim. Please hurry."

Francisco pulled Slater into the street where a crowd of tearful, angry men and women greeted them with panic etched on their dirty faces. The men, clad in their field clothes, thrust clenched fists into the muggy air and shouted angry words that Slater could not identify. The women walked a short distance behind the men, weeping and consoling one another. Whatever happened had shocked the entire village.

"Slow down, Francisco, you talk too fast for me." Slater held up a hand to emphasize he needed Francisco to speak slower.

The man wrung his gnarled hands together while he continued to talk with three of the men who had crowded around them. The cacophony had risen to a high pitch.

"It's Ileana's cousin who lives in Ocotal," he shouted above the noise and confusion.

"What happened?" Slater's attention darted between Francisco and the loud confusion behind him but, with his basic Spanish, could not make sense out of the chaos. Francisco again grabbed him by an arm and pulled him away from the shouting trio.

"Ileana's cousin! He's been killed in Ocotal. By a big explosion. He's still lying in the street up there. The bank, also, has been destroyed. His son, Pedro, ran the news to us. Please, Senor Jim, we need to lose no time to get there. Pedro says that there may be more dead. We should help—there could be survivors. Your truck, senor, does it still work?"

Slater nodded. Before he could pry more information from Francisco, a dozen men ran to the side of the whitewashed house and jumped into the back of his rusted, vintage pickup.

"Anyone else injured?" Slater grabbed his baseball cap from the seat. Glad that the keys were still in the ignition, he cranked the engine.

"*Si,*" Francisco said. He spat out the word and his eyes filled with tears. "Two CDS officials were killed as well. Enrico and Jose. You knew them, Senor Jim?"

"Yes," Slater said. His stomach churned and acid bile rose in his throat. He knew all three men well.

He gunned the engine. The truck sputtered to life then careened down the road to Ocotal. Now and then, the truck would hesitate and backfire, a fact that further agitated the men in the rear. Their shouts became a continuous roar. He shot a quick glance in the rear-view mirror and wondered at their wild gestures. The men of San Rafael were a simple but emotional bunch, typical of Nicaraguans. They provided for their families by farming beans and corn, spending most of the day tilling the rock-infested limestone soil. It was a difficult task but their patience and perseverance usually yielded enough to keep them a few steps ahead of starvation. He pulled on the choke, the engine grunted to life again, and they left San Rafael behind them.

Ocotal was located ten kilometers north of San Rafael on a winding, dirt path that functioned as a road, which was punctuated by large potholes. People normally traveled to the village by mule or on foot, rarely a car or truck. In fact, Slater's pickup was the only vehicle on the entire mountainside. While they bounced along the narrow lane cut through the jungle, Slater fought to keep the truck from hitting a deep rut while maintaining a heavy foot on the gas pedal. The path was barely passable when dry. In the rainy season the resulting mud made it all but impossible. He struggled to hear what Francisco was saying over the engine's roar and the arguing in the rear of the truck. He was talking about Ileana's cousin and that he had worked at the coffee plantation. From what Slater was able to discern, the bank was rubble and the flying debris from the blast had injured many. Enrico and Jose were the government's representatives from the Sandinista Defense Committee that operated the coffee plantation. They kept the books

and paid the workers after harvest. The rest of Francisco's rapid explanation remained unintelligible. Except for one word—
contra. And Francisco kept repeating it—*contra, contra*.

A hundred families lived in Ocotal, and most were standing
in the road when Slater sped into the town. Francisco pointed
out the window and Slater plowed through a field until he
spotted what was left of the bank in the distance. Pieces of
brick, wood, and glass shards lay scattered about the area
where more villagers stood, gawking, crossing themselves.
Slater brought the pickup to an abrupt halt. The men jumped
to the ground and began chattering with the villagers. Slater
pushed his tall frame from the driver's seat and walked with
Francisco to the body.

The dead man lay face down in the dirt amidst a pool of
dark blood, his legs askew. Francisco knelt and turned the
corpse over. The man's face was gone, his shirt covered in a
thick, dried gore. Splintered bone protruded through the plaid
shirt. Francisco crossed himself then touched the gold ring on
the man's little finger.

"I drank many a tequila with him," he said, wiping tears
from his sunburned cheeks. "He was a good *hombre*."

A man with a gaping wound in his shoulder limped toward
them. Fortunately, Slater noticed, the bleeding had stopped.
Dazed, the man begged Francisco for help while another man
joined the discussion and babbled on about the explosion. The
best Slater could make out in the confusion was that it had
happened before dawn and the villagers suspected the culprits
were contras. He turned to Francisco.

"Any other damage?" he asked.

The man nodded at Francisco's question and pointed to the
west. The man ran through the tall grass with Francisco and
Slater close behind.

"The CDS office," Francisco said, prying his way through
the weeds. "It's over this way."

They pushed through the crowd to a small side road that
was overgrown with grass and cactus. Slater noticed the now-
silent crowd following them, a short distance behind, then everyone stopped at the CDS office—or what was left of it. The

front of the building was gone as well as its roof. The other walls were half-standing and the smell of cordite hung in the air. Slater picked his way through the rubble and entered what had been an office only hours earlier.

All that remained was a pile of charred wood and bricks. Mangled metal filing cabinets lay overturned with their doors open allowing official papers to scatter over the scorched, wooden floor.

An occasional jungle breeze blew them into the street where a few of the children tried to chase them down.

A bloody arm protruded from beneath a pile of black rubble. Kneeling, Slater felt for a pulse and, finding none, he rose and picked his way through the debris only to recognize from a distance that there was a third victim. He was covered with dust, wore black tennis shoes, and faded blue jeans.

"Shit," Slater whispered. He turned to the man who led them to the office and put an arm around his shoulders.

"How did this happen?" Slater asked.

The man shrugged and answered in rapid Spanish. Slater fought to keep up.

"Early this morning," the man said. "My wife was cooking my breakfast of *gallo pinto* when the explosion occurred. It woke me up. I ran to the bank and found Ileana's cousin dead. The CDS office was gone. It was them. We have seen them in this area the past few weeks."

"Who?"

"Contras," the man said. With the word, *contra*, he stared at the ground and lowered his voice. It was as if he did not want anyone to hear him speak the word.

"You think the contras blew up the bank and the CDS office?" Slater said. "Why would they do that? I thought the CDS makes sure you farmers have a market for your crops. They actually help you."

"You are right, Jim," Francisco interjected, dropping the Senor title in obvious excitement. "Don't get us wrong. We are patriots like the contras. But when they blow up a bank, not only do they steal money from the National Directorate, but from us poor farmers as well. Now there will be no money to pay for the harvest. And there will be government reprisals, sure enough. You can bank on it."

Slater was struck by Francisco's unintended play on words and walked back to his pickup. The ruling Sandinista government created several organizations that were responsible for indoctrinating Nicaraguans into the party's belief system regarding the revolution and for reporting critics of the revolution as counter-revolutionaries. Typical of the government's political and ideological reach were Sandinista Defense Committees, *Comités de Defensa Sandinista*, or CDS, which served as the eyes and ears of the revolution.

"These men need burying," Slater said, his pulse pounding and his stomach heaving. "Can you get some men together, Francisco, to pull the dead from this place and take them to the church? Maybe the padre in San Rafael can see that they get a funeral and proper burial. Also, send someone for bandages and antiseptic. The mayor can set up a first aid station at the church as well. If you can get the men working, I will drive back to San Rafael and talk to the padre."

"I want to go with you, Senor Jim." Francisco shouted orders at a group of men, who were standing around the rubble, and they began to pull two other bodies from what was left of the bank. Slater climbed into the pickup with Francisco beside him and the two men began the drive back to San Rafael. Francisco continued their earlier discussion through the dust that filled the cab.

Slater's six-foot-two-inch frame sat at an awkward angle behind the wheel but his blue eyes were fixed on the road ahead of them. Periodically, he raised a deeply tanned hand to slow Francisco's speech so he could follow.

"Like I said, Senor Jim. It's not that we don't hold the same views as our contra neighbors. Most of us are just trying to survive, to feed our families. This, I think you know, already. The Sandinistas, they do not help us much. Yes, there is the school in San Rafael and there is the CDS, but what else? Even most of the profits from our coffee plantation are sent back to the National Directorate in Managua. We get very little for our crops and remain poor as ever. The Sandinistas, for all their good words, have forgotten their promises."

Slater had heard all of this before during his year in San Rafael. Under Anastasia Somoza Debayle, the most brutal of the Somozas who tyrannized Nicaragua for half a century, most of the peasant farmers owned the land they tilled. In spite of the brutality, they still were landowners. After the revolution and Sandinista victory, all the farmland was confiscated by the government and turned into cooperatives. Many of the people, now working for the government instead of themselves, had grown lazy—their crops suffered as a result. No longer proud landowners, the farmers grew discontent with the Sandinistas and when the counter-revolutionary forces were organized, the contras received a lot of emotional, if not outright tactical, support from the peasants.

"You know how I came to be here?" Slater asked.

"No, senor," Francisco said.

"I came to San Rafael as part of the Sandinista literacy program. You remember when I came a year ago?"

Francisco nodded.

"And you remember that with the help of the government and the people of the village, we built the small school?" Slater didn't wait for Francisco to nod. "Well, now it has thirty students. Most of the children come because their parents force them. But in the long run they will benefit from the education they receive in San Rafael. The Sandinistas frown on parents who keep their children toiling all day in the fields. They understand the value of the schools."

"You have done much, Senor Jim. We all respect the way you care for us. Our children are learning to read because of you. But do not try to convince me that the National Directorate cares about us as you do. We poor farmers will never believe it. They took our land away, remember?"

"You are not better off than you were before?" The pickup swerved as Slater avoided a huge rut in the road.

Francisco smiled at Slater. "We make about the same selling our beans and corn to the CDS as we did before the Sandinistas took away our land. Many of my friends have become lazy as a result of the confiscation. They sit around and complain about not having much money to spend on tequila or to shoot the dice. No, senor, we have become soft."

San Rafael was a village located in northern Nicaragua and was supported by the area's main economy, the coffee plantation. It was run by a governmental cooperative, and the income derived from their labors assured all able-bodied men the opportunity to feed their families. In addition to the plantation, most of the areas inhabitants farmed small acres of corn and beans and sold them to the government as a way to supplement their income from the plantation. Of late, more of San Rafael's young men were dissatisfied with their wages and a growing number of them had moved south to Managua and the more profitable black markets in the city. Slater knew that if the town kept losing their young eventually there wouldn't be much left of San Rafael and the coffee plantation would close down. The area couldn't afford such a catastrophe. The people were near starvation as it was.

After a moment of silence, Francisco tapped Slater on the arm.

"The army will be up here in a matter of days, looking for the ones who did the bombing. We know their ways to make a person talk. I am afraid, Senor Jim. For myself, I do not look forward to their questions. After terrorizing Ocotal, they will most surely come to San Rafael. When they do, will you help us?"

Slater feared Francisco was right in this prediction but couldn't see what help he might lend. However, he assured Francisco that he would try. Mostly, he wanted to stay out of the country's politics, remaining neutral in the civil war that was consuming Nicaragua.

They drove to the side of his house where he parked the pickup. A woman dressed in a ragged cotton dress leaned against a pole that supported the roof over Slater's porch; Francisco put his arms around her. The embrace touched Slater as Ileana buried her head in Francisco's shoulder while she sobbed. His gut wrenched at the sight of the couple who had become family during his year in San Rafael. Embarrassed, he left them alone, entered the house, and flipped on the small fan. He sank into his wicker rocking chair and let the fan's cool breeze ease the tension that gripped his neck and shoulders. He closed his eyes and remembered a past life almost forgotten.

A knock sounded at the door. Slater looked up, saw Francisco on the porch, and waved him in.

"Pardon," the man said.

"It's all right, Francisco. I was just thinking that I never expected to find myself in the middle of a revolution. I thought I left all that behind in Vietnam."

"I know Vietnam. I read about it in a book years ago. You were there, Senor Jim?"

"Yeah," Slater said. "And it was not a very nice place. Now look at me. It seems I'm going to be in the middle of another war, after all. My poor mother, she must be sick with worry."

"You have mentioned your mother before, *senor,* but I have never heard you speak of a wife. You never married?" The wrinkles in Francisco's somber face began to disappear.

"Once," Slater said. "Years ago, although now it seems like an eternity. I worked at an advertising agency in New York. You have heard of New York?"

Francisco nodded and smiled.

"Well, after a while, I couldn't stand it any longer. The stress of always worrying about losing a client and the incredible pace of the daily grind were killing me and I wanted out. In the end, my wife left and later divorced me. I guess I didn't have either the fortitude or inclination to make it in a world of scheming and half-truths. When she left, she got the house, the savings account, the car, and most of everything. I got an easy chair and lots of bills. I worked as a bartender for most of a year to pay off those bills."

"It causes you much pain. Maybe the more you talk about it, the easier it will be to put it behind you."

"I doubt it, but maybe. I went to Vietnam straight out of high school and fought at a city called Hue. I lost many friends in that battle and I still replay it in my dreams and nightmares. But I was one of the fortunate ones who made it out alive.

There's guilt in there somewhere, too, I guess. Can you understand?"

Francisco nodded.

"So now I find myself, it seems, in the middle of more fighting and killing—more bloodshed. It didn't make sense back in Vietnam and it sure doesn't make any sense here in Nicaragua."

Francisco's face lightened and he smiled at Slater. "Do you write your mother?"

"Now and then. After coming home from Nam, she wanted me to go to an Ivy League university but I had other ideas. I wanted to go to Cornwall, a small, liberal arts college in central Virginia. We had a very heated discussion about it."

"What happened?" Francisco asked.

"I went to Cornwall."

"You didn't obey your mother?" Francisco asked, obviously troubled by Slater's disobedience.

Again Slater laughed then threw his hands into the air. "No, I didn't. But it was at Cornwall that I fell in love with Latin America. Quite by chance, I had enrolled in a Cultural Anthropology course and I became fascinated with what happened to the Maya. To my surprise, I found that the Maya were still here, not extinct like the Incas or Aztecs. So, I majored in history, joined the Peace Corps, and spent two years teaching English and sanitation in Costa Rica. After the divorce, a friend told me of Nicaragua's nation-wide literacy campaign and I thought it sounded like a great opportunity. Another grand adventure. I wanted to be of help somewhere, to really fit in and make a difference. I hoped that here in San Rafael my life would finally amount to something. But I still have nightmares about Vietnam."

"You didn't know about the Sandinistas?"

"Not really. The events you know, of course. When Somoza resigned his presidency and fled to the US in 1979, there was elation that American interests were out of Nicaragua and hope that the new government would restore human rights and allow the people to determine their own future. After being denied asylum, Somoza took refuge in Paraguay but the Sandinistas found him and killed him. That was when I first heard of them. Initially, the government was hesitant for Americans to see what they were doing, but when a Catholic priest learned of my work in Costa Rica, he persuaded them to give me this post. It's been only recently that I learned of Secretary Rivas's two offices—one for regular work and one for meetings with American religious groups. In the office he uses for the Americans, I hear he has photographs of children, gilded, carved crucifixes, and a Bible or two. Up here in San Rafael, I thought I could stay out of the political fray, just do my job. But now with these bombings, I have to admit, the war is moving closer to home and it's getting more difficult to remain neutral."

Francisco waved an index finger in Slater's direction. "The National Directorate is extremely suspicious of most outsiders, especially Americans. In fact, most of them have separate offices they use when Americans or missionaries come to our country. Most Americans, both Christian and non-Christian, seem to feel that a few weeks' visit will make them experts on Nicaragua and the Sandinista government. They have no idea, however, how easily deceived they are."

Francisco left and Slater walked through the undersized schoolhouse next door. How he loved this place. Only a small patch of ground overgrown with weeds when he first arrived, it had been transformed into a tiny schoolhouse by his naïve zeal and boundless energy. At first, the locals gathered around, curiously watching him, gossiping, pointing, and giggling. As the days stretched into weeks, some offered help, unwilling to stand by without contributing. When the walls were up, he posted a small sign in front, declaring that a school for all the children would open soon. A school where they would learn arithmetic, English, and history.

The adults sought him out, asking numerous questions about the school and why he was there. Mostly, he thought, they wanted to know if he was for real, if he planned to make San Rafael his home. He sensed they wanted to know if they could trust him. It had taken two months but he'd been able to convince the adults of San Rafael that he was not a government official, just a schoolteacher wanting to teach their children.

With time, the independent, hardworking, conservative farmers of the area came to trust him. The school grew to thirty students and soon it would be necessary to add another room and find another teacher. In return, Slater learned a valuable lesson—when you care about a child, their parents will care about you. They will give you a most important gift—the gift of trust. It had been a slow and arduous process but his effort at winning their hearts had paid off and the events of the day proved it. When they needed help, the villagers sought him out and it felt good to be needed.

Slater opened the door on his ancient refrigerator and grumbled. Only two beers left. He opened a bottle, returned to his rocker, and let the refreshing liquid quench his parched throat. He pressed the cold bottle to his aching forehead. The parallels were there between Nicaragua and Vietnam. The senseless killing, the murdering. The helpless people caught in the middle of a war they did not understand. Pawns in an endless struggle for power and control over their lives. He could feel the malevolent forces that conspired to destroy Nicaragua begin to swirl about his village, and he sensed it was only a matter of time before he was sucked into its vortex of violence and bloodshed. What was he to do? In his heart knew he must do something—either assist the people he came to help, or rationalize the violence and leave the country. Remaining apart and neutral was going to be a difficult, if not impossible, feat. The pounding in his head intensified and a voice kept nagging him. *Vietnam. Nicaragua.* The horror of those days in the jungles, fighting an unseen enemy, returned in nauseating detail. He could not let himself get drawn into the madness. Yet, an unseen force was pushing him to the edge of a cliff and he didn't know how to end the nightmare.

All the while, he knew Francisco was right—it was only a matter of time before the Sandinista army came calling.

CHAPTER 2

The shade on the north veranda of the National Palace revived Colonel Ramon Perez, the army *commandante* in Nicaragua's Sandinista government. He stood stiffly under a slowly revolving ceiling fan and gazed out over the rolling verdant hills and streets of Managua where, in the distance, Lake Managua shimmered under the sweltering, oppressive sun. The humidity felt higher than usual so he loosened the collar of his heavy, khaki uniform. While he paced, he retrieved a large bandana from his pocket and methodically wiped his wrinkled forehead. He knew his large frame was the cause of his heat intolerance, a peculiarity that set him apart from his countrymen. His light complexion gave people who met him the impression that he was not a native of Nicaragua. But he was definitely Spanish, not Indian. What little indigenous blood he had inherited from his mother, he had disavowed long ago. Not only was he a Nicaraguan, he was a Sandinista at heart. Since the Triumph of the Revolution, he had risen from the ranks of a guerrilla leader in the FSLN—Sandinista National Liberation Front—obtaining the status and recognition as the government's most brilliant army commander.

Perez adjusted the large diamond ring on his left hand and continued his pacing. His balding head was oval and contained fiery, brown eyes that could reduce most men to silence. His right earlobe was missing, blown off during an encounter with one of Somoza's *Guardia*. The scarred ear served as a constant reminder of the former dictator's ruthlessness. Perez touched his waxed black mustache, stroked it gently, and wondered for the third time why he had been summoned to the palace. When Rivas called, he sounded angry, not at all his usual, jovial self. His request was short and curt—come immediately.

Fernando Rivas was a Sandinista who loved the power he'd commanded since the revolution. A member of the Group of Twelve who formed the anti-Somozan coalition in the early years after the revolution, he now consulted with the National Directorate. As Minister of Defense and responsible for the Nicaraguan Army, he was Perez's superior. Usually, the orders from Rivas came directly from the president. Perez knew the friendship between the two men was a close one, born out of years of guerrilla fighting and endless nights discussing Nicaragua's future over warm beer. Rivas and the president had been bloodied in the August 1978 Sandinista capture of the palace where, for days, they had held fifteen hundred officials and citizens inside until Somoza paid a $500,000 ransom. Perez again wiped his brow. What was keeping the minister? It was not like Rivas to keep a *commandante* waiting.

Colonel Perez poured himself a glass of water from a crystal pitcher that sat on an antique brass table and sipped while he took in the view from the veranda. Set high atop a hill, the National Palace was the home of the FSLN and the Chamber of Deputies. Here, men like himself translated the edicts of the president into laws and action.

As Perez set the glass back on the table, the door to the veranda opened and Rivas entered, hand extended. "*Buenos dias,* Colonel," he said.

The men shook hands and embraced for a brief moment.

"Good of you to come on such short notice. Please have a seat. You don't mind if we sit out here, do you?" Perez shook his head and Rivas continued. "I love this view of Managua and the lake in the distance. We are privileged to live in such a beautiful country, no?"

Perez ignored the question. Rivas's scarred face always intimidated him. "I came as soon as I could, Mr. Secretary. I trust the president is in good health?"

"He is, Colonel. He extends his best wishes to you and your family." Rivas snapped his fingers. A palace servant attired in a stiffly starched, white jacket appeared and bowed slightly.

"*Chichas?*" he asked. Without waiting for Perez to reply, the Minister of Defense turned to the servant. "*Dos chichas,*" he commanded.

As the two men waited for the servant to return with their drinks, Perez studied his boss. In contrast to himself, Rivas was a small man, wiry in stature with a scarred face, which he acquired when a barrel of gasoline exploded during the last days of the revolution. The jagged scar extended to include his left eye and accentuated the man's ferocious look. His full head of hair was heavily streaked with gray and he wore thin, wire-framed spectacles perched on the end of his nose. The man's left arm, which Perez never saw him use, was carried close to his side. Perez was familiar with Rivas's extreme anti-Somozan and pro-Marxist philosophy, a fact that explained his fanatical obsession with the contras. Rivas was instrumental in changing the structure and content of *La UCA,* the University of Central America. Originally, a Jesuit institution for the rich and wealthy of Nicaragua, Rivas's Marxism forged a curriculum adapted to the new Nicaraguan reality. Before the revolution, much of the faculty's teachings were identical to that of the United States. Now, they emphasized Nicaraguan history and culture.

The drinks arrived and the two men toasted each other. Rivas settled back in his chair and lit a cigar. He was attired in a light-tan business suit and blue shirt. As he blew the acrid smoke over the veranda's railing, he tapped a finger on the table.

"Nothing like a homemade brew, hey, Colonel? Where I grew up, this drink was all we had so I never acquired a taste for bonded whiskey, although I do enjoy an occasional Kentucky bourbon." Rivas frowned and stopped the tapping. "Now, to business. It's the contras," he said. "They struck again up at Ocotal. Blew up the bank and the CDS office. Two government officials and several farmers were killed."

"When did this happen?" Perez asked.

"Early this morning. The president wants action. And he wants the perpetrators by their balls. That's where you come in, my dear friend."

Unnerved by the use of the word, *dear,* Colonel Perez shifted his corpulent frame in his chair and stared at Rivas. The minister smiled and rubbed the scar around his eye. From his daily intelligence reports, the *commandante* knew the contras were getting bolder by the day, forging into new government-held territory. This attack on Ocotal was their most daring to date. The problem with what to do with them, however, was a complex one and Perez prayed that Rivas would not demand the impossible. "Give me the details," he said.

Rivas took another puff on the cigar and a long pull on his drink. "The bastards swooped into the village before dawn, coming from over the Honduran border and striking while everyone was asleep. For months now, we have suspected them of having an American-financed training base in that country, maybe even an airbase somewhere nearby. Unfortunately, our Honduran neighbors have not been very cooperative. They have given the president little to go on. US lackeys in all likelihood. They took out the bank and CDS office with a grenade launcher and killed a farmer with the burst of an M-16. The poor man had stumbled out of his house to investigate the noise and was cut down like a dog. Three others were killed as well. The Sandinista Defense Committee reported the attack to me early this morning before I briefed the president. These little skirmishes are starting to grate on him."

"An American M-16, sir? Are you sure?"

"Reasonably so," Rivas said. "We have suspicions that the American CIA is supplying the bastards."

"The farmer was the only casualty?" Perez said.

"No. As I said, there were two employees of the CDS office who were killed also plus one other bystander. Many were injured."

"The buildings were blown away?" Perez asked.

"Yes, reduced to nothing but rubble. New CDS officials will have to move to another village. God knows when the bank can be rebuilt."

"Any money missing?"

"No word on that yet. But what do you think? I'm sure those bastards ran off with a great deal of cash. I'd give my left nut to be able to find just one of them."

"Yes, Mr. Secretary, I understand. I take it then I'm to find these traitors and arrest them?" Perez knew it would be no easy task.

Rivas stood and eyed Perez for a moment. The secretary's menacing stare caused Perez's bowels to loosen. He squirmed in silence.

The Defense Minister smiled a sardonic grin. He leaned over and patted Perez on the back. "No, Senor Colonel. Your assignment is to find the bastards and make sure they never can do such an act again."

Perez rose slowly from his chair, finished his drink, and hugged Rivas. He felt the minister stiffen with his embrace.

"Let me guess," Perez said. "My job—"

Rivas interrupted. "Let me be perfectly blunt, Colonel, so there will be no future misunderstanding. The president is tired of the army's inability to deal effectively with these rebels. Your mission is to exterminate these hooligans and as many of their fellow anarchists as you can find. Exterminate, period. No leniency. We need to nip this insurrection in the bud before it gets out of hand. Eradication is what is called for now." Rivas lowered his tone to one more informal and pointed to the French doors on the veranda. "It's hot. Do you mind if we finish our discussion inside under the air-conditioning?"

Rivas led the colonel into a spacious living room decorated with grand paintings of the president and the Group of Twelve. On the far wall hung posters of Marx, Engels, and Lenin

Once ensconced in an overstuffed, velvet chair, the minister continued. "We have suspicions that the CIA is surreptitiously aiding the contras by providing them with weapons and advisors. As I said earlier, most likely they have a training base inside Honduras. In fact, our secret police have pictures of what purports to be the beginnings of an airstrip being constructed. Without question, we need to rid our country of these pests. If we could produce evidence that the United States is behind these raids, it would blow the lid off the whole affair. It would mean an embarrassment for America and a great public relations victory for our Sandinista Government. The world would know, in spite of their rhetoric to the contrary, that the Americans are exporting terrorism to Central America. The president would love to throw a little trouble their way. The US President is angry that our brand of democracy is aligned with Cuba and the Soviets. With all their condemnation of Middle Eastern countries funding terrorism, wouldn't it be sweet if we could prove that they were engaged in the same kind of activity?"

"When Ronald Reagan took office," Perez said, "Nicaragua and the Sandinistas abandoned all hope of being able to live peacefully with the Americans. They set out to destroy us."

"The Americans believe we are Marxists. Well, what of it? You understand then. That is good. Somewhere, across the border in Honduras there are contra bases and supply depots. I'd guess there might even be a CIA agent or two. Let there be no misunderstanding, Colonel—those renegades must be stopped at all costs. Totally eradicated. The president thought that, when we arrested their leader, this Carlos, the insurrection would dry up, but it hasn't. There must be others, who have taken over the leadership since we threw that bastard in El Chipote. So find them, Colonel. In addition, if you can get evidence that the United States is behind these contras, so much the better. It would be a significant feather in your cap, one that would almost certainly lead to your promotion to general."

The palace servant reappeared but Rivas waived him away. The archaic air-conditioning system in the palace did not prevent the droplets of sweat from running down the back of Perez's neck. But it wasn't the mission that was causing him to sweat—it was the thought of going back into the damn jungle.

For the foreseeable future, he would be living in that infernal maze of green and heat, a place he detested. No longer the eager lieutenant, he was too old for such maneuvers and preferred the city with its soft bed, nightlife, and beautiful women. It would take him away from his newfound diversion and the long, erotic nights he spent with her. If there was to be peace in Nicaragua, he knew the contra insurrection needed to be put down forcibly but he wasn't going to be happy with the forced absence from Maria.

Like the dutiful soldier he was, Perez rose and saluted Rivas. Rivas returned the salute and embraced his *commandante*.

"It's my pleasure to serve Nicaragua, Mr. Secretary," Colonel Perez said. "Tell the president that I shall do my best to bring the outlaws to justice."

Rivas nodded and escorted the colonel to the door. "I'm sure he will be pleased with your professionalism and determination to do your duty. He has a great deal of confidence in you, Ramon. If anyone can succeed in this undertaking, the president knows it is you. Please report to me before you leave and then again when you are encamped in the field. I have instructed the CDS office to afford you all the information they have on the last known whereabouts of these contras. You will, I assume, head for Ocotal first?"

"I need to first interview the eyewitnesses to form some idea as to where they were headed after the raid, Mr. Secretary. I think the best way to approach the search is with a small contingent of men, maybe a platoon of volunteers. When we find them, I'll send for re-enforcements from my regiment here in Managua. With luck, I will uncover the identity of their leader and will then strike, and strike hard. Cut off the head of a snake and the body dies. You're familiar with the northern jungles, I know. You can believe it will be rough going. A small band of men can disappear and subsist a long time without being spotted. Captain Salazar—You know Captain Salazar, Mr. Secretary?"

Rivas nodded.

"Captain Salazar was born and raised in San Rafael. The town is not far from Ocotal and he has intimate knowledge of the area. If there's a band of contras up there, he should be able to sniff them out. Tell the president not to worry—I know what to do when I find them."

"Take a camera, Colonel," Rivas said. "When you capture them, pictures of the American involvement would be proof beyond denial. But be careful, Colonel. Stay out of Honduras. We don't need an international incident."

Their meeting adjourned and an army sergeant, dressed in a khaki uniform with white boots, escorted Colonel Perez to the front portico and his waiting Mercedes. For a moment, the brutal sun caused the perspiration to flow again and forced him to use the bandana while he climbed into the rear seat of the automobile.

"Main CDS Office," he commanded the driver.

The car sped away from the palace with its Sandinista flags flapping on the front bumper.

Perez settled into the sedan's thick, leather upholstery. He hated meetings at the palace. With each visit, he felt increasingly out of place. Maybe it was his childhood, growing up in a poor ghetto, coupled with the fact that he was not as educated as his acquaintances but functions at the palace were painful, unbearable. The Sandinista patricians who attended palace parties spoke flawless Spanish, almost Castilian, while his own language and vocabulary skills were born in the streets of the peasant village of his youth. He respected Secretary Rivas, but the two men were not of the same social class. The Minister of Defense was educated, having spent time during the sixties at Yale, studying agronomy. He understood world politics and economics, fields in which Perez was grossly ignorant. The colonel, on the other hand, came from peasant stock and developed skills using his fists on the boys in his village. His sixth grade education seemed woefully inept in the presence of the palace elite.

In spite of his reservations about maneuvers in the jungle, he was pleased with the mission given him by Rivas. True, it would take him away from Maria, possibly for months, but it was his path to respectability among the president's inner circle. Since the dreadful night in Masaya when contra guerrillas set fire to his grandmother's neighborhood and she died without medical help, he had pledged himself to avenge her death. These contras would serve his political ambitions and enlarge his circle of influence. Who knew what might happen after a promotion to general? He might possibly be invited to join the Group of Twelve. If that happened, no one could ever say again that Ramon Perez was just an ignorant street kid who loved to fight. No, it would be different then—people would extol his name. Tonight, he would treat Maria to the best dinner Managua had to offer and take her to bed. In the morning, he would brief Captain Salazar.

CHAPTER 3

Pueblo Salto was a sleepy town located high in the densely forested mountains a few miles from the Honduran border. The lush greenery covered the mountainsides in all directions, making travel in the area slow and, sometimes, difficult and dangerous. A few coffee plantations dotted the region but most of its Nicaraguan residents were farmers who quietly tended their crops of beans, coffee, and potatoes without any involvement in politics or the insurgency. Main Street was a dirt affair interspersed with gravel carried from the river that flowed through the gorge nearby. The road then stopped short of the border with Honduras. Years earlier, the road had been cut through the vegetation, and since only one person in the village owned a vehicle, it got no traffic and now served as a meeting place for the town's residents. The usual collection of pigs and chickens foraged the roadside in search of morsels of food, leaving in their wake, stinking piles that, when combined with the burning garbage, lent an unusual odor to the village. Pueblo Salto's women tended their children, did the laundry, and cooked their family's meals. Wooden shacks, whose once brightly painted exteriors had faded to a dull color, were interspersed along the road. Their rusted tin roofs no longer acted like large mirrors in the sweltering sun. Each morning at dawn, the women swept their dirt floors, prepared a simple breakfast, and watched their husbands leave for the fields. The mornings were always quiet as families went about their business like sullen, sleepy automatons. The men never kissed their wives before leaving and the women never scolded their children. Mornings were the quietest part of the day.

Located at a higher elevation, Pueblo Salto's weather was perceptibly less hot and humid than the capital city of Managua. However, the sun still beat down with a fierceness known only in the tropics and the men who labored over their crops were inclined to take long *siestas* each afternoon. There was one automobile in Pueblo Salto and it belonged to the town's mayor, Armando Ruiz, who owned and operated the only café. He was a wealthy man by peasant standards.

Located at the end of the dirt road, Armando's Café Central was cramped but tidy. It sported a covered porch and a large ceiling fan stolen from a van in Managua. Since the revolution, life for the café proprietor was one of shrinking revenue. There was no meat. The butcher shop in nearby San Rafael opened at nine in the morning but the line outside started to form around four-thirty. Before the Sandinistas, there was plenty of milk but they had reduced the number of dairies to three and most of the children in the rural towns and villages went without. In the beginning, he had been a Sandinista at heart, happy when the Somoza regime was overthrown and the dictator hustled out of the country. Now things were decidedly different and he realized that the Sandinista National Directorate was failing in its efforts to modernize the country.

In addition, the Sandinistas confiscated all the land owned by Somoza which amounted to over half of the farms, roughly two million acres. They confiscated all the former dictator's assets, including one hundred corporations. When they nationalized the banks, they discovered that Somoza had taken all the money with him to Miami. Farm output had plummeted. Armando knew this from reading *La Presnsa,* the newspaper he smuggled out of Managua. An anti-Sandinista newspaper, *La Prensa* was full of what had gone wrong with the revolution and its bombastic rhetoric placed it on an endangered list. Soon, Armando thought, the paper would be shut down altogether.

While Nicaragua's economy struggled to stay afloat, most

of Pueblo Salto's residents were no longer able to afford his café. Most of the time Armando spent his days alone in the tiny kitchen serving the occasional visitor. His only source of steady income was the small band of young men and a woman who frequented the café several afternoons a week. They sat on the porch during in the heat of the day, drinking *chicha* and cold beer while they argued the current state of governmental affairs. They appeared to be unemployed but always paid their bill, never asked for credit. He suspected they were contras but they weren't dressed in the usual guerrilla camouflage and carried no weapons. Where they lived or what they did, he never inquired as long as they paid their bill, which they did in cash. If they were contras, his heart was with them, but he didn't want to know the truth. For someone living in the mountains near Honduras, knowing the truth could be dangerous to one's health.

Armando returned to the café after his *siesta* and found the group sitting at the round table on the porch. He smiled and a man wearing boots and a broad-rimmed hat stood to greet him.

"Armando," the man said. He slapped the café owner on the shoulder and laughed. "Do you have cold *cerveza?* We are in need of something to quench our terrible thirst. Our mouths are dry and full of cotton."

Armando nodded and fumbled with the keys to unlock the café's door.

"You're always thirsty, Raoul. Name me a day when you weren't."

"Oh, *senor,* you put the knife between my shoulders," Raoul said, feigning being stabbed in the back. "We pay for the *cerveza,* do we not?"

Armando entered the café, returned with six bottles of Victoria beer, and set them in front of the group. There were five men and one woman, who, by their dirty sweat-stained clothes, looked as if they had trekked all morning through the jungle.

"I did not say you sponged my beer, Raoul, only that your thirst was never quenched."

The group laughed at Raoul and dug into their pockets producing enough *cordobas* to cover the drinks. Armando bowed short and disappeared into his café. Raoul took a large gulp of his beer and removed his tattered straw hat.

"Where is your friend, Carlos?" Armando called from the doorway.

"He is not well," Raoul said. He wiped his face with a tattered bandana. "Feeling a bit under the weather, I'm afraid."

The others in the group exchanged glances and waited for Armando to go inside.

"We did well this morning folks, but I confess I don't feel very good about it," Raoul said.

Julio set his bottle down and stared at Raoul.

"Why?"

Julio's clothes matched the ones Raoul wore, a pair of dirty dungarees and a tan, cotton shirt soiled around the collar and cuffs.

"Blowing up the bank and CDS office may have been a mistake. They worked there to help our people. In spite of the office being a government building, it did run the farm co-op that fed a lot of families. Besides, one of the men Luis shot supplied us with food and hid our weapons in his chicken house."

"I feel terrible, but there was no alternative," Luis Santana said. "He shouldn't have been up so early and in the dark I couldn't make out who he was."

Raoul lit a cigarette and leaned forward, his elbows resting on the table. "The fact remains," he said, "the man sympathized with us. I'm afraid that these mistakes isolate us from our fellow countrymen. They will find it difficult to help in the future if we continue to kill and maim our own people. Frankly, I'm surprised at you, Luis. I thought you might grieve a little over this blunder. How can we justify this among ourselves? In the future, we need to be more careful, our targets need to have greater tactical importance. Strategically, we cannot afford to make these kinds of mistakes."

Maria Martinez reached into her boot for a knife and began honing its blade on a leather strap. She had straight, black hair that was pulled into a ponytail and her round eyes glittered as she looked at Luis. "Raoul is right, of course," she said. "The only thing we have on our side at the moment is moral superiority because we certainly don't match the government in firepower. This moral superiority gives us the trust of most of our people. Without it, we are doomed. In order to keep this trust and support, we need to conduct ourselves beyond reproach. There are too many widows and orphans already in Nicaragua for us to be adding to their numbers. The enemy is our president and his band of cutthroats and criminals who rape and pillage our country. Instead of blowing up banks and co-op offices, we need to concentrate on bigger targets. Ones that target the oppression"

Alberto Montalban, the group's quiet member, listened to Maria then spoke. "Like the president himself?"

Raoul waved a finger and continued. "Fat chance of that ever happening, Alberto. No, Maria is right. Our fight is with the bastard Sandinistas. We need to make sure that our tactics involve those government organizations that carry out their Marxist proclivities. Killing a poor Nicaraguan farmer is unacceptable."

"It was an accident," Luis repeated. "For the love of God, Raoul, I couldn't have known he'd be up there so early. These things happen—I've heard Carlos say as much."

"I know, Luis. Accidents do happen. It's just that this sort of thing leaves a sour taste in my mouth. These poor farmers have suffered so much for so long. We all know this from personal experience."

Raoul knew his eloquence could never match that of their leader, Carlos Mendoza. Carlos had an electric way with words and the ability to charm and influence anyone who listened to him. Sadly, he was in the El Chipote prison in Managua, having been apprehended and arrested a week earlier, following their raid on an army supply depot.

Raoul was six feet tall with slender, muscular arms. His face betrayed a sense of humor, his large eyes and crooked nose posited above his ever-present smile. His teeth were victims of years of neglect, a fact that did not seem to bother him in the slightest.

"That farmer was an accident, Raoul," Luis said. "You know it. The man just happened to be walking by the bank but I thought he might discover the explosives. I had to kill him. If he had stumbled into the office, who knows what might have happened?"

Raoul held up a hand and smiled.

"I know," he said. "It's been a long time since something like this happened. Carlos has warned us of the penalty, physically and psychologically, that we must endure to bring about our goals. I'm terribly upset about it but I know you did your best, Luis."

"What about the CIA?" Maria interjected.

"That's our next big problem," Raoul said. "That and how do we get Carlos out of El Chipote?"

"Those damned bastards," Julio chided. He hollered at Armando for another round of beers. After the drinks arrived, he waited for the café's proprietor to return to his kitchen before continuing.

"What about the CIA," Julio said.

Raoul was about to answer when a herd of braying pigs invaded the porch, eager for a handout. Everyone jumped up from the table as Armando appeared with his broom and smacked each pig on the back.

"Out of here, you stinking fools," he yelled. The pigs screeched and waddled off the porch and Armando followed, waiving his broom in the brilliant sunlight.

Alberto let out a whoop. "Go get 'em, chief." He returned to his chair as the rest of the group resettled around the table.

They again focused their attention on Raoul.

Leadership wasn't something that came naturally to him. From the time he had been in grade school, he had deferred to his more charismatic and forceful friend, Carlos. Carlos's heroes were the soldiers of the American Revolutionary War and Nicaragua's own Augusto Sandino had especially fascinated him. Sandino, Nicaragua's first legitimate revolutionary, led a six-year military campaign in the early 1930s that had decisively shaped Nicaragua's political history. But Sandino was more than a mere political figure. By successfully waging war on the United States Marines, who were there to protect American interests, he reshaped the consciousness of his country. In fact, Sandino's base had been in the village of San Rafael where Carlos attended school. Sandono's tactics were so effective that even though they were outnumbered and even though the marines were technologically superior, Sandino's army was never eliminated. The marines finally left the country, leaving behind a Nicaraguan Army that was then known as the Nicaraguan National Guard or *Guardia*. When Sandino publicly challenged the constitutionality of the national guard, he was given an audience with Somoza. Sandino was invited to a gala by Somoza. After arranging a compromise of ceasefire, Sandino accepted the offer. On the road, in Managua, soldiers of the national guard intercepted Sandino's car. The soldiers then escorted Sandino and two of his generals to a place where the hero and his men were brutally shot to death. Later, Anastacio Somoza Debayle, the elder's son, assumed the presidency and continued the dictatorial repressive and devouring regime.

Initially, after the Triumph of the Revolution that forced Somoza to flee the country, Raoul and Carlos supported the new government. They joined thousands of guerrillas and civilians on the Plaza de la Republica, in the old center of Managua, and celebrated the fall of the Somoza dynasty. It was a national celebration and the opportunity to create a new Nicaragua. During the ensuing months, however, they became frustrated with the slowness of progress. The Sandinistas ordered the nationalization of all banks, credit agencies, insurance companies, and export businesses, along with the mining and forestry industries. They got shiploads of weapons from Cuba, North Korea, Czechoslovakia, and the Soviet Union and became a government deeply mistrustful of the United States. To be sure, the Sandinistas developed a nation-wide literacy campaign. It was their crowning achievement to date. Fidel Castro sent twelve hundred Cuban teachers to aid in the project. But a simple fact remained—the FSLN needed to do more for the average Nicaraguan.

"The CIA," Raoul said, "is shit. They're as stupid as they

come. They force their way of organization upon us, a way that cannot succeed. They insist on an archaic command structure because it gives them better control. It's like a pyramid with the commander at the top. It fits with their American view of unity but we all know it doesn't work here in the jungle. We should divide our force into smaller, semi-autonomous components or cells. It's what Che did in Cuba. If we use the American's scheme, the defeat or annihilation of any one element will result in the defeat of the overall movement. We need to be like the many-headed hydra of ancient mythology: When one head is lopped off, two more emerge in its place. Then our movement can recover from defeat as long as one cell is able to survive."

Maria sneered through ruby lips. Her smile disappeared. "Those bastard Americans are trying to tell us how to fight our war. I say to hell with them."

"They are usurping our revolution," Raoul agreed. "They demand to train and arm us, direct our operations besides conducting independent military actions of their own. I'm getting tired of their aerial bombing raids as if we were mere puppets. They never communicate anything to us. What we did at Ocotal this morning—" Raoul paused as Armando strode onto the porch and asked if anyone wanted another beer. When no one spoke, he went back inside the café. "The place will be crawling with the army. It's getting late and we need to get back over the border before nightfall. Shall we go?"

"What about Carlos," Maria asked. "Do we try to get him out?"

"It would be difficult, Maria, if not impossible. The place is guarded for blocks around as well as the underground catacomb of cells. I have heard that from the entrance to the prisoners themselves, there are multiple checkpoints and guards. It would take much planning. And lots of luck."

The group stood. Maria took Raoul by the arm and pulled him aside.

"I'm going to Managua tonight," she said. "Armando's going to take me. I'll meet you back here tomorrow afternoon. Okay?"

"Getting more information, eh? Please, Maria, be careful. You know the man you see is extremely dangerous, he kills for the sheer thrill of it. I would hate to find your body in the garbage dump of a Managuan slum."

They stood at the end of the porch and watched the others. Raoul continued. "Maybe you could entice your friend to help, eh, Maria? The man is very powerful and if he issued the order, Carlos would be free tomorrow."

Maria stood on her toes, kissed Raoul's cheek, and squeezed his arm. "I'll see. Maybe I can persuade him to help Carlos. I would have to do it in such a way as to not arouse suspicion. And don't worry, Raoul, I know what I'm doing. I haven't disappointed you yet, have I?"

As Raoul and the ragtag band of brothers tramped into the jungle, he turned and watched Maria wave from the porch of the Café Central.

CHAPTER 4

A man sporting aviator sunglasses, a dark suit, and a crew cut dropped his bag onto the lobby floor of the Intercontinental Hotel in Managua and rang the service bell. After completing the registration form, he found his room on the second floor and tossed his leather suitcase onto the bed. Rain, which had begun as he boarded his flight in San Jose, Costa Rica, had followed him into the Nicaraguan capital. He removed his tie, opened the French doors leading to a small balcony, and breathed the fragrant, humid air. In spite of the rain, Managuan traffic was heavy and noisy. His taxi had taken him south from the airport through open country where the parched and dusty fields were getting a much-needed soaking.

Years after the devastating 1972 earthquake, Managua was still reeling from the tragedy. The central part of the capital remained a mountain of rubble and on the way to the hotel, he noticed that even the Roman Catholic cathedral had not been rebuilt. His taxi driver warned him not to venture alone into the suburbs, for the surrounding areas still had no street names and the slums were especially dangerous after dark. Most houses in the newly built sections had no street numbers. Addresses were given, the driver explained, by points of reference, if one did not know forty or fifty basic ones, navigation was impossible. People gave directions to their homes or businesses from a familiar restaurant, government office, or statue because most of the landmarks no longer existed. The Pepsi-Cola plant, for example, had collapsed in the earthquake and its remains had long since been bulldozed away, a fact that did not deter people from saying they lived near the plant. Getting lost in Managua was easy to do.

The pyramid-shaped Intercontinental Hotel once housed the infamous underground bunkers used by Somoza and his family, while to the east and behind the hotel was El Chipote, a subterranean prison buried in the hillside. Built by Somoza and used to torture his enemies, the prison was still used by the Sandinistas. Suspected counter-revolutionaries and other enemies of the government were thrown into tiny, dark cells and subjected to repetitive interrogations for hours on end and told that they were about to be executed. The Sandinistas used El Chipote principally as a detention and interrogation center rather than a long-term prison; all the detainees were political and only a few were held longer than a month or two. The man in the hotel room knew that inside El Chipote, a counter-revolutionary leader wondered what the future held. It was that man he came to liberate.

After a few minutes of observing the traffic below his balcony scurry through the rain, the man returned to the living room, opened his suitcase, and found the secret compartment that contained a short-wave radio. He carried the unit to a table near the balcony doors and extended its antenna. He sat in a steel-framed chair and keyed the microphone.

"Mother, this is Cobra," he said. "Mother, this is Cobra. Do you read?"

The radio squawked with static. The man listened and adjusted the frequency dial.

"Cobra, this is Mother. Go ahead."

"Near heart of dragon, repeat, near heart of the dragon. No activity. Will call later. Give regards to Wolf Man. Out."

Satisfied with the check-in, the man named Cobra returned the radio to the hidden compartment. He changed into blue jeans and a faded black shirt, stowed his aviator sunglasses in the dresser, and retrieved a pair of horned-rimmed ones. With his deeply tanned arms and a canvas cap that hid his short haircut, Cobra blended well with most of the Latinos in Managua. He took a quick look around the room, closed the door, and headed downstairs to the hotel café.

☙❧

Colonel Perez knocked on the door of the apartment he rented for Maria when she was in Managua. The rain had stopped and the stars were beginning to shine in the clearing sky. He had bathed, splashed on Maria's favorite cologne, and held a bouquet of red roses. Flowers were hard to come by, and he hoped they would put her in a festive mood. Lately, she seemed preoccupied and remote, a fact that unsettled him.

Maria answered the door, dressed in a red floor-length dress with a low bodice that accentuated her round, full breasts. She didn't smile as Perez admired her.

"Ah, you look lovely, my dear," he said. He handed the roses to her. She returned his smile and allowed him to brush past her.

"You're early," she said in a matter-of-fact tone. "I'm not quite ready so fix yourself a drink. You know where it is."

She disappeared into her bedroom and Perez poured himself a glass of his favorite Napoleon brandy. He kept the liquor for his personal enjoyment, as Maria did not like the taste of alcohol. He sipped and looked around. The apartment was part of his relationship with Maria. He knew that she lived somewhere in San Pudra, a slum neighborhood where street fighting often occurred. It never occurred to him to attempt to locate her house, for she was always available when he wanted her. The apartment's rent was paid from money he took from his discretionary *commandante's* account. Usually, he and Maria dined at the fashionable Managua Country Club, danced for an hour or two, then returned to her apartment where he spent what remained of the night.

She entered the room and Perez stood, reveling in her stunning beauty. She had pulled her long, dark hair into a tight bun and wore the diamond necklace he had given her on the first anniversary of their meeting.

"You look even more ravishing than the last time, if that's possible," Perez said. "Is that a new dress?"

Maria twirled around for his inspection and placed her pug-shaped nose on his cheek.

"Don't you remember, you fool? You bought this dress only last month. Honestly, Ramon, your mind is starting to go." She turned her back to him. "See how low the back is? It was what intrigued you about the dress in the first place."

Perez placed his brandy on the marble coffee table and took Maria into his arms. He kissed her neck and looked into her round eyes.

"You shouldn't tease me about something that may be true," he said. "Now, where do we dine tonight? The usual?"

"Please, Ramon, no more of the country club set. Enough is enough. Let's go somewhere…how would you say?…risqué. A tad bit bawdy, perhaps?"

"Yes, my sweet, of course. The food at the country club has been heavy on my stomach of late. I've been somewhat bilious." Perez patted his stomach. "I know just the place, a dark, little café near the Plaza Espana. It is around the corner from the Minister of Interior's office and we may have to wade through the goats and chickens. You would like such a place?"

Maria adjusted her hair in the mirror that stood next to the door. The plunging neckline of the red dress was having the desired effect. He would take her anywhere.

"Oh, yes, my darling," she answered. "But how do you know of this place? "

"Captain Salazar," Perez said. "He frequents the place. The music is loud, the drinks potent, and the dancing energetic."

Maria stroked his cheek and winked. "You know how to make me happy. And later tonight it will be my turn to please you."

Perez nearly had an orgasm when she opened the door and brushed past him and one of her breasts brushed his arm. They scrambled into Perez's Mercedes and sped down the pot-holed street into the darkness.

৩৩৩

Cobra sat in the dark hotel café and sipped his beer. Managua had put him in an ill-tempered mood, for the city was not what he remembered. The beer was Nicaraguan piss and the steak he tried to swallow was most likely from a freshly killed goat. Not only was there no beef, but the locals needed written permission from the government before they could even slaughter a cow. Imported beer was difficult to find and the local brew tasted as bad as the water at his hotel. In addition, the cinemas, once favorite gathering places, had become filthy and unpleasant.

Television, operated solely by the government, ran never-ending Soviet and Eastern-bloc propaganda films. The National Theater had ceased operation because its air-conditioning no longer worked and parts were unavailable. The National Symphony, one of Cobra's personal favorites during his last visit to Managua, had been disbanded. The capital was in turmoil—Managua was the epicenter of the revolution where explosions, street fighting, and assassinations were common, and innocent civilians were the usual victims. The advantage of all this chaos, he reasoned, was that it would be easy for him to get around without being noticed. Back in Washington, Wolf Man was intolerant of blown covers and failure. Cobra tried to console himself by pretending he was eating prime rib back in the States.

Tired of fighting the steak, he left the hotel and found a small café located near the Plaza Espana. It was filled with boisterous laborers, black marketers, and prostitutes. Everyone drank the local beer and, across the smoke-filled room, Cobra observed a pool game in progress. A radio played Cuban music and most of the café's patrons accompanied the words with loud, raucous singing.

Once seated in the rear of the bar, Cobra noticed a well-dressed Nicaraguan enter and escort his lady to an empty table in the far corner. The table had obviously been reserved for them and a waiter promptly stood nearby, pad and pen at the ready. Ordering drinks, Cobra surmised as the waiter nodded and left the pair alone. The man most likely was an aristocrat, for only people with money in Nicaragua could afford silk suits. He was large in stature and, as he talked, he ran his thick fingers over a balding head.

Cobra took a sip of his beer and studied the woman. She was dressed in a revealing red dress but looked fatigued by the man's conversation. Her elegant long fingers played with the drink before she brought the glass to her lips. Red lips, the kind men might lust over. Cobra admired the large diamond that hung around her slender neck. Probably worth a fortune, he figured. He smiled knowing what the overweight official would have as his after-dinner repast. At least not all women in this god-forsaken country were peasants in greasy clothing. Who was she? An actress? No, the theater was closed. A model? Possibly. She was too young to be the fat man's wife. After a few moments of reflection, Cobra settled on the fact that she was the man's personal mistress—it was the way things were done in Central America.

Cobra ordered another beer and, after it came, made his way to the pool table. He sipped and watched as money changed hands among the crowd. Two men chalked their cues amidst a throng of people yelling encouragement. Scanning the café, he noticed the small room near the back. Long strands of beads hung from the room's doorway obstructing a clear view of its interior. Picking his way through the crowd, he positioned himself for a better look. Dense smoke filled the café but, through the haze, he noticed six men playing cards. A short man wearing a white apron and carrying a tray of empty glasses exited the room.

"No, no," the waiter said. "Not to come back here, *senor*. Please, up front."

The waiter blocked Cobra's view of the room and, using his stomach like a battering ram, tried to push him back to the main part of the café.

"*Americano?*" the waiter called over his shoulder.

"No," Cobra said. "Puerto Rican."

He returned to his table only to find it occupied by three young men who were immersed in a heated conversation. He glanced toward the woman's table. The couple was gone. Too bad, the woman was stunning. But enough of such thoughts—

back to business. First, liberate a contra rebel from El Chipote prison. Then, he could entertain thoughts of the woman.

e∕ɔe∕ɔ

At Maria's apartment, Perez turned into a sex-obsessed animal. She hated this part of their relationship and vowed never to subject herself to such an indignity once it was over. As Perez pawed and floundered over her body like a beached whale, she ignored his slobbering and tried to think of her friends in the mountains. Usually, after one of these trysts, she had important information to relay to them, for Perez, drunk and sex-starved, would talk incessantly. She had told Carlos, on more than one occasion, that she didn't know how much longer she could continue, that her dedication to their cause had a certain limit beyond which no one in their right mind would ask another to venture. The sight of Perez sickened her to the point of nausea and she fought the impulse to spit in his face. Her only recourse tonight was to pleasure the man as quickly as possible.

Perez had his clothes off and he was sweating profusely. He pulled her onto him and forced her head into his groin. When Maria didn't pull away, he lay back on the satin pillow and allowed her to do her work. *What she did for her country!* How ironic that this man, the man who supplied her with information about the government's plans, was preparing a search for her friends. She thought about biting Perez's member off but quelled the impulse. She would never see the light of day inside an El Chipote cell. Her actions now were automatic and she distanced herself from Perez's corpulent body with thoughts of Carlos. How terrible it must be for him. Her heart ached for the suffering she knew he must have been enduring. It would be a formidable task to get Perez's assistance, but she had her ways.

Perez arched his back and exhaled a loud, gurgled cry of ecstasy. After heaving his ample body around in the bed, he lay satisfied, and soon was snoring. Maria got up, straightened her dress, went into the bathroom, and brushed her teeth. Re-

turning to his side, she ran her hand along his thigh. Perez
looked at her through a drunken stupor.

"My darling, you know the El Chipote prison?"

Perez nodded, eyes glazed and fixed.

"You can order a man's release, my love?"

Perez nodded and stared at Maria through the erotic haze.

"My cousin," Maria said. "He is there for no reason. There
have been no charges against him and he misses his girlfriend.
Could you not help him, my precious pet?"

Perez moaned an acknowledgement and turned on his side
to face the wall. Maria sat in a rolled-leather chair, lit a cigarette, and watched Perez snore loudly from across the room. *I
wonder if your wife knows where you are tonight. You filthy,
murdering, Sandinista pig. Do you know how easy it would be
for me to slit your slimy throat right here and now? Or use the
pistol I have hidden in my purse? One day, senor, it will happen and I pray you see it coming.*

CHAPTER 5

A week after the explosion in Ocotal, Slater drove to Managua to do his monthly grocery shopping. The sun was high overhead and punished the lush countryside with a ferocity known only in the tropics. The week had been filled with three funerals in Ocotal, presided over by the local padre, followed by burials on a hillside overlooking the small village. Ileana, dressed in her finest skirt and blouse, wailed without shame each time the padre mentioned her dead cousin's name.

The week had also been filled with personal turmoil for Slater. Dreams of limbless soldiers, dying in Hue, woke him from fitful sleep each night while guilt of wanting to remain neutral in Nicaragua's civil war troubled him during the day. The truth was he simply had seen so much conflict that he had not recovered emotionally. It wasn't that he was a pacifist, he just was sick of bloodshed. Visions of his close friend having been blown apart by snipers near the Citadel in Hue continued to haunt him, though it had been years since the battle. He knew of the contras, of course, but he thought he could do his job in San Rafael and remain aloof from all the fighting and bickering. Still, the thought troubled him that he might cower in the face of the present conflict. But another truth was that he had come to care deeply for the people of San Rafael. However, he hated bloodshed of *any* kind, hated confrontations. To illustrate the point, hadn't he run instead of dealing with the problems in his marriage? Hadn't he run instead of facing life in the big city? No, it wasn't those things at all. He was simply afraid, but of what he wasn't sure. Afraid that becoming embroiled in the country's politics and war would lead to his collapse as a man. The horror of Vietnam was responsible for what he was today.

He was a green recruit, a member of Marine Task Force X-Ray, which had little or no urban combat experience. When his unit entered the city, enemy snipers opened fire inflicting heavy casualties. The gold-starred, blue-and-red National Liberation Front banner was flying atop the historic 120-foot-high Citadel flag tower. In the days leading up to the Tet holiday, hundreds of Viet Cong had already infiltrated the city by mingling with the throngs of pilgrims pouring into Hue for the celebration. They easily moved their weapons and ammunition into the bustling city, concealed in the vehicles, wagons and trucks carrying the influx of goods, food, and wares intended for the days-long festivities. Like clockwork, in the dark, quiet morning hours on the last day of January, the stealth soldiers unpacked their weapons, donned their uniforms and headed to their designated positions across Hue, in preparation for linking up with crack People's Army of Vietnam and VC assault troops closing in on the city. Infiltrators assembled at the Citadel gates, ready to lead their comrades to strike key targets.

As they wormed their way through Hue, Slater and his company saw many men cut down. Most cried out for their wives or mothers before they died. After several weeks of fighting, Slater and his friend, Bill Andrews, neared the Citadel, the walled fortress that housed the Imperial City. The fighting intensified. Slater and his friend came under attack by machine-guns and rockets. Andrews darted for a partially-demolished wall and was cut down in a hail of gunfire. Slater could not reach him for hours and endured the man's cries for help until finally, they ceased. Medics later pulled his body to safety and Slater saw where a rocket explosion had ripped away an arm. And each February for fifteen years Slater had said a silent prayer and cried for his friend whom he met one hot afternoon on Parris Island.

Now, driving south through the Great Rift Valley and its fertile lowland plains, he watched the farms roll by. The country had three major climatic zones—the drier, fertile Pacific region held a line of volcanoes from the Gulf of Fonseca to Lake Nicaragua; the wetter, cooler Central Highlands where San Rafael was located; and the hot, humid Mosquito Coast on the Caribbean Sea. The soil of the Rift Valley, enriched with volcanic ash, yielded some of the country's best crops in the well-cultivated and densely populated part of Nicaragua. A few large estates occupied the valley, which were lined by dozens of small farms. Corn, beans, and sugarcane were grown in immaculately groomed fields. Volcanoes were active. The country was subject to earthquakes and volcanic eruptions, and hundreds of shocks occurred each year. The capital city, Managua, was virtually destroyed in 1931, and again in 1972. He drove through the province of Leon and was dismayed to see the devastation that had occurred since his last drive to the capitol. The contras and Sandinista army had been at each other again. A rice and bean farm that once supported many workers now stood empty, its fields scorched and dotted with bomb craters. A vast expanse of army barracks and numerous helicopters had replaced the once-productive crops. Slater steered his way around two women with mules loaded with corn and watched a Soviet-style helicopter buzz down a tree-lined runway and land on a cracked, concrete tarmac. He chuckled to himself. The Sandinistas moved fast when they wanted to.

He turned southeast around the southern end of Lake Managua and entered the city on Cuesta de los Martires Boulevard that took him directly to the Plaza de la Revolucion. He drove into the Mercado Oriental, the capital's largest market and parked his truck on a street within walking distance of the market's entrance. The Oriental no longer contained many of the essentials most Nicaraguans needed, which made it difficult for Slater to find his necessary soap, bottled water, and food. Usually, on each visit, he strolled the aisles, listened to the vendors tell stories of the market when Somoza was President. Then the shelves were filled with goods of all kinds.

Soap and toilet paper were never in short supply, even though the cost might have been prohibitive. The two things Slater craved the most, meat and vegetables, were never in abundance at the Oriental.

He walked down the aisles pondering the edibles and now and then put an item into his wicker basket. He hated canned milk but was forced to buy a dozen cans for the powdered variety was gone. As he absentmindedly went about his shopping—the funerals in Ocotal were still on his mind.

Ileana's cousin, the deceased Eduardo, was laid to rest in his favorite baseball cap and jacket. The jacket Slater gave him after the man showed up on his doorstep shivering, having fallen into the river that raced through the nearby gorge. The padre was a man Slater knew as a quiet but devout anti-Sandinistan and he read softly from a bible. When Eduardo's stiff body was lowered into the shallow grave, Ileana broke down again and sobbed. Slater had held her thin body in his arms as everyone sang a Nicaraguan hymn.

He locked his groceries in his truck and crossed a busy street to his favorite bar, the Maya, located down the block from the Mercado Oriental. Out of the sun, the temperature was a good ten degrees cooler. He took a seat and looked around. It was the middle of the afternoon and the Maya was beginning to fill with the usual crowd of unemployed and disgruntled men, most in their teens and twenties. He paid for the beer, leaned back on his barstool, and listened to the wheezing of the overtaxed air-conditioner. The bartender ducked out the back door when a group of men and a woman dressed in dark pants and combat boots entered. No one greeted them. The young woman glanced around the darkened bar finally fixing her gaze on Slater. She strode across the room and touched his arm.

"*Americano?*" she said.

He shrugged.

"Please, sir, follow me and you won't get hurt. This way."

"What?" Slater said.

The woman's stern order caught him unawares and he balked. She grabbed his arm and pulled him off his barstool.

"This way. Now."

"What's going on?" Slater said, annoyed with the woman.

She pushed him out the rear door of the bar earlier used by the bartender who had not returned. When Slater turned, to say something to the woman, a deafening explosion threw the pair to the ground and they were engulfed in thick, black smoke. Gunshots rang out amidst a cacophony of screams. The bar's patrons—panic-stricken and bloodied—fought their way out the door, hurtling themselves over Slater and the woman. Some collapsed in the alleyway. Flames shot through the roof and, in the distance, a siren wailed.

"This way," the woman ordered, pulling Slater to his feet.

They ran into the San Padua slum, crossed the street in front of a house with a high, wrought iron gate, and continued down a narrow, back street lined with wooden shacks littered with garbage. Slater glanced over his shoulder and saw an army tank and jeep heading toward them. The woman shoved him along.

"Quickly," she shouted as they tripped over the rubble that lay scattered about.

The woman jerked Slater around a corner and he was lost in a maze of alleys and wooden shanties. Men and women peered at them from around doors and through windows. At the end of a crooked street, she pushed Slater into a ramshackle house.

Slater collapsed on the floor, chest heaving. The woman pulled him to his feet and dragged him into the back room.

"Stay here." Her stern, dark eyes flashed and her long hair was matted against her face. Slater struggled to breathe.

"How did you know?"

The woman put her finger to her lips.

"Quiet, *senor*. This is a safe house but please do not leave. The security police will be searching the neighborhood any minute now. You must remain quiet or they will find you. It would mean your arrest."

"What for?" Slater was in no mood to be hiding from the Sandinistas. He had done nothing wrong.

"Just stay calm and wait for me. I will return later and

guide you out of San Pudra. But, please, stay here and don't make any noise. You understand?"

"Who are you? What the hell is going on? What is your name?"

"Maria. That was a well-known government watering hole. Low-eshcelon officials mingle with the common folk and try to convince them the government cares about peasants. We tried to get our friends out of there but I didn't expect to find an American. Unfortunately, I fear two of our members were killed in the blast. It is so sad."

With those words, Maria left Slater to himself in the strange, unoccupied house. He had no idea where he was and no idea who Maria was, except it was obvious that she was involved with the contras. He propped himself against a wall and noticed hammocks hanging from the stucco walls and a small table in the room's center. On a low shelf next to a tiny, propane stove, he found a bottle of water. He dragged himself to where he could reach it and downed its entire contents in one long gulp. Intense pain shot through his ankle when he tried to stand and he crumpled back to the floor. My god, he thought, a woman contra. The thought had never occurred to him that women fought in the resistance. When he'd glanced into her large, brown eyes all he saw was a beautiful woman. He had not expected to see a warrior. Where did they get all their firepower? Who was their leader? Where was the Sandinista army? These questions swirled around his overtaxed brain and intensified the pain in his ankle. As sirens wailed in the distance and darkness descended upon San Pudra, he lay quiet and waited for the woman's return.

⁊⳺⁊⳺

Colonel Perez briefed Captain Juan Salazar about the upcoming maneuvers into the Central Highlands along the Honduran border. They would begin the convoy in the morning.

"So soon?" asked Captain Salazar. "My wife was hoping I would take her dancing tonight."

Irritated by the man's reluctance to get moving, Perez blew

the smoke from his lighted cigarette into Salazar's face. "You will spend tonight making ready," he ordered. "We will move out at 5 a.m. and head directly to Ocotal. Our first order of business is to interrogate the farmers up there. We will bivouac in the jungle and decide our next move, depending on the information gained after forcing the peasants to talk."

Salazar looked out the window of Perez's office and drummed his fingers on the colonel's desk. "I understand. Will we fight, sir? I mean, will we engage the enemy?"

"Of course, you imbecile. We will drive them out of the jungle and then exterminate them. My dear Captain, have you lost your stomach for such encounters?"

"I am older now, Colonel, and wiser. If the National Directorate would allow a few compromises with the contras, this whole affair would die a natural death. There would be no need for all this bloodshed. With all due respect, sir, these people are our brothers."

"I am in no mood for philosophical prattle. These contra jackals, Captain, wish to topple our government, one we fought for and died to protect. We cannot allow them the satisfaction of returning this country to the old ways. I am surprised that you cannot see it. Most of these contra bastards are former members of Somoza's *Guardia*, or do you forget so soon?"

"But, Colonel, the *La Prensa* prints stories of Sandinista cruelty each week. Surely, they can't all be fabrications. I have known many of these men and women most of my life but still we kill them with amazing proficiency. The government you and I helped to create hasn't been responsive to the poor. It—"

"Poppycock!" Perez interjected. "We will have no more of this treasonous talk. If Secretary Rivas heard you talking this way, you would be spending your days in El Chipote, instead of enjoying your grandchildren. Now listen up—we will take three vehicles, a half-track and two jeeps. The ones with those .50 caliber machine-guns. Make sure your men have plenty of sidearms and ammunition. And take the 75 mm recoilless rifle. Plenty of food. We may be in the field for several weeks."

At the mention of the word *weeks*, Salazar hung his head in acquiescence then stood and saluted Perez. As the captain left the office, Perez chuckled to himself. Dancing indeed. These young officers weren't cut of the same cloth as himself when he fought daily battles against Somoza. The fighting instilled a certain barbarity, a hardness of the heart toward death and dying. He prayed that, when the going got tough, he could count on Captain Salazar.

დდდ

Slater awoke with a start. It was dark and still Maria had not returned to the safe house. The pain in his ankle had subsided for the moment. He shifted his weight, rubbed his eyes, and attempted to focus on the table beside him. He was thirsty, like his mouth was full of salted popcorn. In the darkness, he fumbled through the dishes looking for another bottle of water. Finding none, he stood motionless and peered through the small window above the sink. Had Maria been arrested? What if she was in jail? What if she wouldn't return? Just as he was about to venture into the street, she burst through the door and closed it behind her.

"Good, you're still here. I worried that you might have gotten scared and left. Are you all right?"

"Yes, thanks to you. I want to thank you for what you did this afternoon. You saved my life."

"It is nothing. I happened to notice you as we entered to clear the bar and just acted instinctively. What is your name?"

"Slater. Jim Slater. And your last name?"

"Martinez. This used to be my grandmother's house. Now my family uses it for storage. As you can see, there's not much to store in Nicaragua these days."

"This is where you live, then?"

"I grew up in this neighborhood. But now I fight. Freedom for my people. Do you have a vehicle near the bar or something?"

"Yes," Slater said. "My truck is parked down the street from it. I had been grocery shopping and—"

"Come, then. I will take you back there."

In the moonlight, Maria led Slater back through the maze of streets while he quizzed her about the explosion. They kept to the shadows as they talked.

"You are a contra, then, Maria?" he asked trying to keep up with her quick pace.

She nodded.

"But you just blew up a bar and killed several innocent people. You said so yourself. I don't understand, what the point was. What was so damned important that it necessitated all the killing?"

"Like I said earlier, Jim. It was a hangout of government officials. I think we took out a few."

"You think?" Slater said. "You blew up a building and you just think you killed the right people? How does killing justify your cause? Dammit, but I've seen all this before in Vietnam."

"How long have been in Nicaragua, Jim?" Maria's voice took on a sharper edge.

"A little more than a year," Slater answered, not sure where her question was leading.

"And you think you know what is best for us? You weren't raised here. You weren't subjected to the pain and suffering, first under Somoza then the brutal Sandinistas, were you? Of course not. Isn't the height of hubris to know what is best for a people without ever having lived among them? We didn't make the rules, Jim, the Sandinistas did. But we sure as hell are going to play by the ones they made."

Maria's eyes shot quick glances over her shoulder as they continued on their way back to Slater's truck.

Slater was taken aback by the woman's fierce strength of mind. His knowledge of women in the military was limited to secretaries and clerks, never a woman fighter. Her beauty combined with the grit and calm determination she displayed made her strangely alluring. He changed the subject and told her of his work in Pueblo Salto and the school he had built. She seemed touched by his concern for the children.

"I know what it means to not be able to read," she said. She directed him into another twisting, deserted alleyway. "I could not read until I joined the contras two years ago. My good friend, Carlos, taught me. Now I read Plato, Mark Twain, and Carl Jung. You know of Mark Twain, Jim? The great American writer?"

"Of course. Everyone in America has grown up with those stories of his. You like them, Maria?"

She smiled and grabbed Slater's arm and pushed him in a new direction.

"Oh, that Tom Sawyer. He was a character. We have children like that in Nicaragua—do you know? Very resourceful, our Tom Sawyers. Mr. Twain would have liked it down here, no?"

Slater laughed. Maria's perfume hung on the cool, night air. She was different now. While gone she must have bathed, changed clothes, and combed her hair.

"I grew up in Las Manos," Maria continued. "It is a remote village along the Rio Coco River. When I was sixteen, a Sandinista rocket hit our house and it killed my parents. I was playing baseball in a field nearby and when I heard the explosion, I ran to our house. Flames were everywhere. I hardly recognized the burned bodies of my mother and father. And the smell I never forgot. That day I vowed someday I would settle with the Sandinistas and make them pay for what they did."

Maria had an easy manner and Slater was mesmerized by it. Only hours earlier, she had been in a bloody fight and running for her life. Now she was going on about Tom Sawyer and her parents as if nothing had happened. Her round breasts bounced freely and Slater couldn't help but notice her nipples as they protruded through her shirt. Her slender body maneuvered the twisted streets with ease and her eyes sparkled as she talked. Soon, they were back at Slater's truck.

"Good-bye, Jim," she said. "I'm sorry about this afternoon but am glad you weren't hurt."

She turned to leave but this time Slater took her arm.

"Maria?"

"Yes?" She turned to face him while he fumbled for the right words.

"Can I see you again? I mean you saved my life. The least

you could do is allow me to thank you properly. Possibly over dinner? Soon?"

"I can't. I'm sorry, I just can't. I can't become involved with anyone at the moment. If there wasn't this stupid war, then maybe. But it's simply impossible."

"But—" Slater tried to protest but Maria stopped him.

She kissed him on the cheek and pulled away. "Please, no. I am happy you are safe. Let's remember that. There is nothing else."

Maria disappeared into the night. Driving home, the dangers of driving through the countryside after dark did not matter for his thoughts danced around the young woman contra fighter, who earlier had killed then talked about it calmly as if it were a walk in the park. Maria, in a matter of a few short hours, managed to turn his thoughts away from his school, his work. In a single afternoon, she transformed his preoccupied life into a longing to know more. Was she drawing him to her perilous life as a jungle warrior? She seemed so matter of fact about what had happened earlier in the day. He remembered the villagers of Vietnam and how their simple life, amidst a war and hardships, tugged at his heart. Was it happening again? Could he afford to let it? Had he not decided to remain emotionally aloof from the politics of this country? He had no idea where in Managua Maria lived. He struggled to put the chance meeting out of his mind and concentrated on the drive home. But still the thought nagged at him—would he see her again?

CHAPTER 6

Cobra rose early, showered, and dressed. It was two hours before dawn and he wanted to arrive at El Chipote before the morning's activity began. He wore a light-colored, linen suit that hung loosely on his muscular frame. His dark complexion aided his disguise as a Sandinista official and, as a final touch, he added a fresh cut flower to his lapel from the hotel's complimentary bouquet. Cobra rummaged through his suitcase and from a leather valet removed a handful of identification cards. Among those he searched was his own CIA identification card, which bore his real identity, Allan Casey. He searched the cards until he found the two he wanted—one identifying him as a member of the staff of Minister of Defense Fernando Rivas. The picture on the front bore the Minister's engraved seal. The other card was a national identity card that assured all viewers he was a natural-born Nicaraguan and Sandinista. The order to release the prisoner was typed on official letterhead and signed by Rivas himself. It was a masterful forgery. To complete the illusion, Casey found his Nicaraguan passport and placed the three items in the breast pocket of his suit. A wide-brimmed, Panama-style, straw hat completed his wardrobe. After a final, quick look in the mirror, he shut the door behind him, went downstairs, and hailed a taxi.

Casey had been a field agent for the Company for ten years and had been stationed in Costa Rica when his orders for the

El Chipote mission landed on his desk. Agents had a free run in Costa Rica because the country provided a safe haven for their covert operations in surrounding Central America. His prior assignment, arranging arms transfers to the contras in El Salvador, was put on hold until after he managed to get the contra leader out of prison.

In a shoulder holster under his jacket, Casey carried his Baretta 9 mm pistol with silencer and full clip. If his plan succeeded, he would not have to use it, but he was comfortable in the knowledge that he would kill anyone who got in his way. Carlos Mendoza was to be freed at all costs.

Casey's plan was simple enough. Impersonate a high-ranking Sandinista official and demand Carlos's release. If the deception did not work, he was prepared to shoot their way out of El Chipote. If the sleight of hand was successful, he hoped to get Carlos onto the street where they stood a reasonable chance of getting out of Managua ahead of the security police. The trick was going to be coaxing the suspicious guards to open his cell door.

The State Security Police ran El Chipote, and their reputation for ruthless and degrading treatment was known throughout the country. The name itself had tremendous psychological impact on those who heard it. With the beginning of Sandinista rule, Secretary Rivas had decreed an end to the old-style forms of torture that had been used in Latin America for generations. In its place, he implanted a much less bloody, though arguably more effective, system of coercive pressures. Rather than have his prisoners kicked and beaten, tortured with electric prods, or burned with cigarette butts, he had them sealed in poorly ventilated dark closets where the heat was intense and the inmates lost their sense of time and place. Confinement was interrupted at odd intervals, with the inmates subjected to hours of draining interrogation, ending with the usual threats against their family. The disoriented and sleep-deprived prisoners freely gave up information when threatened with the death of a parent, wife, or child.

The prison complex itself was a vast structure buried in a rocky hillside behind the Intercontinental Hotel and across from Tiscapa Lagoon and the Mirador Restaurant. It had been built by Somoza and used by his *Guardia* to interrogate and torture anti-Somozan revolutionaries. The only part of the prison that was visible from the street was the decaying guardhouse in front of a black iron gate. The road beyond the gate disappeared into a grove of trees, which hid the entrance to the complex from view.

At the guardhouse, a courteous soldier attired in a starched khaki uniform stopped him. From his belt hung a 45-caliber pistol and the man saluted smartly when Casey approached.

"*Buenos dias,*" Casey said in polite Spanish.

The soldier nodded.

"*Identificacion?*" The guard held out his hand and Casey noticed his immaculately groomed fingernails.

Casey produced the cards and gave them to the man. He took a deep breath to control the pounding in his chest while the guard inspected them. It had always been this way, the unbridled flight or fight response at the beginning of a mission. Over the years, he had learned to control, even modify, these emotions and use them to his advantage. His pounding heart kept him focused, ready for the slightest hint of trouble—for the earlier it came, the bigger the advantage over his opponent. He concentrated on his breathing and waited while the guard inspected the forged documents. The Company employed the best forgers in the business and their work was universally praised as superior quality. Except once in Angola, but Casey pushed that thought from his mind.

The guard looked at Casey, handed his identification cards back to him, then without a word, waved him into the compound. As Casey proceeded to the gate, the man stepped inside the guardhouse and pushed a button, which activated the heavy iron doors. It creaked loudly as it swung open to allow Casey's entrance.

Once inside, he followed a predetermined plan. He had memorized the layout of the complex from smuggled documents the Company had procured. Around the curve and to the right of the gate the administration building stood as a low, whitewashed, stucco building. Only the portico and entrance were visible, the rest of the building extending underground. Casey clipped his identification card to his lapel and once inside made his way toward the waiting room. Three ranking Sandinista army officers stood at the far end of the room engaged in a private conversation. As Casey approached, they gave him a peculiar look but kept chatting among themselves.

He strolled through the small waiting room, passed the soldiers, and turned down a dimly lit hallway. No one else gave him more than a fleeting glance.

At the end of the hallway, a rotund sergeant sat perched on a stool behind a high window and eyed Casey with a frown. Casey handed the document ordering Carlos's release to the sergeant, who took it with a greasy hand and adjusted his bent eyeglasses. He then handed the man his Minister of Defense card and stood motionless while the man scrutinized it. He had a large, round face with bushy eyebrows and he clicked his tongue repeatedly while he studied the documents. Casey shot a quick glance at the name on the sergeant's uniform: Jose Ruiz. His pulse quickened while he waited on Ruiz to complete his inspection. If the man wavered, Casey would kill with a shot to the head and hope he could find Carlos in the labyrinth of cells. Behind him were two army officers with sidearms and he felt their gaze on his neck.

"This man—" Sergeant Ruiz said.

"Carlos Mendoza," Casey interrupted.

The guard held up a hand to silence Casey.

"Yes, *Senor* Mendoza. He is to be freed? He is to be placed in your custody?"

"Yes. By the order of Secretary Rivas. You are to hand him over to me and I am to take him to the Minister's office. Important business."

The guard sneered at Casey through the dirty spectacles. "What business could be so important?"

"I don't know what it is about. I was just told to get the man and bring him to the palace as soon as possible. More interrogation, probably. Why don't you call the Secretary, I am sure he would be happy to explain his reasons. But I assure you, sergeant, it will be your head if I am late."

Casey's pulse pounded as he concentrated on the obese man in front of him. One false step here and he was dead. A group of uniformed guards armed with AK-47s and automatic pistols entered the room, stood behind Casey, and waited their turn with the sergeant. They talked in broken Spanish, which made it difficult for Casey to understand all they were saying. On the desk lay a large pistol that Casey surmised belonged to the sergeant. Ruiz looked up from the documents and pointed to a chair.

"Please sit," he said, "while I verify this order. You can use the chairs over there next to the window."

Casey had not expected this delay. He turned and sat while Sergeant Ruiz picked up the telephone. If the sergeant did indeed call Rivas, the game was over, Casey would have to resort to gunplay, and the odds of success would be much less. He thought of his mother back in the States and wondered if he would see her again. Shooting his way out would most definitely, blow his cover, a fact that would irritate his superiors, no doubt. Shifting his weight, he felt for the pistol underneath his coat and waited.

☙❧

Standing in his jeep, Colonel Perez motioned Captain Salazar to start the convoy rolling. As the three vehicles crossed the newly constructed compound, he admired the new Soviet-made helicopters, the morning sun glinting off their rotors. There were four of the larger and faster Mi-8s with 57 and 80-millimeter rockets, 500 kilogram bombs, with twin 23-millimeter machine guns mounted on the front. Their twin turbines could maneuver two dozen fully armed soldiers at 250 kilometers per hour. In addition, six of the smaller Mi-2s armed with 57-millimeter rockets sat in a line on the tarmac next to the steel-framed hanger. Able to carry up to eight passengers, they would come in handy if, and when, he found the contras. There was nothing like a low flying chopper with a courageous pilot to flush well-hidden guerrillas from their hideouts in the jungle.

The base was located on the western shores of Lake Managua on the road to Leon. The sun had just cleared the mountains when Perez led the convoy through the fields of the Sebaco Valley, the fields owned by a wealthy landowner who managed to adjust to the changing fortunes of Nicaragua and live with the Sandinistas. Beyond the valley northward, the air turned cooler and the highway climbed through coffee plantations until the pavement ended seventy miles south of the Honduran border. After the convoy crossed the Rio Pueblo River, gunfire sounded in the distance. Perez halted the convoy to confer with Salazar.

"How much farther to Ocotal, Captain?" he said.

"We turn onto the dirt road up ahead," Salazar said. He pointed to a narrow lane leading into dense foliage. "It's about a two hour drive through the jungle. Beyond Ocotal the mountains become more rugged and difficult."

"You heard the gunfire?"

"Yes, Colonel. Colonel Antonio may have his forces up that way. Maybe they encountered the revolutionaries."

"Or maybe, the *contra-revolucionarios* are holding their own maneuvers," Perez said, eyeing his captain.

"That is certainly possible, Colonel."

"And we go through Pueblo Norte on the way? Your hometown?"

"*Si*. There is a small gasoline storage facility at Pueblo Norte and we can refuel there."

Colonel Perez nodded, climbed back into his jeep, and motioned the convoy toward the dirt path. The jeep pitched from side to side, as its wheels sunk into the myriad potholes that were unavoidable, while the remaining vehicles crept along behind. A remote world enveloped them with hardwood trees and pines, making the jungle nearly impenetrable, while the screams of howler monkeys and the calls of toucans beckoned them forward. Orchids, of all colors, and mosses covered the jungle floor, providing a perfume pungent to the senses. Up until now, they had been traveling through open fields where it was easy to spot the enemy. As the verdant vegetation grew denser and began to engulf them, Perez realized that they were at the mercy of the contras. Here, the thick jungle created superior hiding places where a small band or squad of guerrillas could be waiting in ambush.

Another burst of artillery fire and explosions sounded in the distance. Perez wondered if his friend, Antonio, an army *commandante* who had been sent to this area a month ago, was under attack. He shot a glance at the vehicles behind him and motioned Salazar to widen the gap between them. Salazar nodded and soon his jeep was fifty meters behind Perez's rear bumper. They inched along the rutted trail, periodically stopping to get their bearings, as the vegetation closed around them. Overhead, the jungle's canopy blocked the sun's heat but sealed the humidity around the convoy. Noticing how much harder it was to breathe in the dense air, Perez couldn't fathom how the peasants lived in this environment. The sticky air clung to his shirt and the sweet, peaty odor of decaying foliage tickled his nostrils. The people who lived here somehow managed to adjust to this trying climate but Perez knew it took its toll, for most of them didn't live beyond their sixties. The deeper they plunged into the jungle the darker it became and the temperature dropped precipitously. As they gained altitude, he stopped perspiring.

After more than an hour of slow going, the convoy arrived at Pueblo Norte and stopped for fuel. The underground gasoline storage tank had been placed in the small farming community for use by the coffee plantation nearby. At the end of the harvest season, a long line of farmers filled their loaded trucks with gasoline before commencing the long drive to Managua. A dilapidated building stood next the tanks and Salazar sauntered inside to sign the receipt. Slowly, each vehicle took on fuel and when finished, Perez told Salazar to break for lunch. The pair leaned on a jeep and studied a map. The men told jokes to each other and ate their lunches. The road twisted northwest out of Pueblo Norte and led further into the mountains, where it eventually dead-ended at Ocotal. Since leaving the capital, they had not seen a single contra or encountered any shelling. Except for the distant gunfire, the day had been uneventful.

Pedro, Perez's driver, ran up to the colonel and pointed to the north.

"Colonel, there's movement up on the ridge line. A small squad of men wearing camouflage."

Perez looked in the direction Pedro was pointing. "Are you sure? I can't see fifty meters in this infernal jungle."

"I climbed a tree to get a better look. I saw them up there."

Pedro pointed again to the ridge that separated the convoy from Ocotal. Perez nodded and slapped Salazar on the back.

"Let's go, Captain. You may yet see action before the day is done. *Vamanos!*"

❧❧❧

Hand near his weapon, Casey constructed an alternate plan in the event the current one failed. With all the armed soldiers roaming the prison, he doubted he could shoot his way out. Was there a way to get to Carlos if the forged orders were discovered? Probably not. He might be able to kill the three guards in the anteroom, and possibly the sergeant behind the desk, but then what? As Casey was weighing the options, Sergeant Ruiz cleared his throat and waved to him.

"*Senor,* there is no one at the Ministry of Defense at the moment. I'm afraid I cannot authorize this man's release without an official verification. Maybe later."

Casey's mind was in a whirl. He brought his frame to an erect posture and narrowed his eyes. "Sergeant, I'm much too busy to put up with the problems of the government's communication lines. If you do not produce this man in one minute I will have you before a court-martial so fast you will be in one of those cells yourself. Do you understand?"

The sergeant's eyes bulged. He removed a handkerchief and blotted his forehead. His puffy cheeks turned red as he attempted to speak. "But, sir," he said. "I'm just trying to do my job. It's—"

"Bullshit! You have the official order before you and if you don't produce the prisoner this instant, there will be hell to pay. Do I need to say this a third time?"

"No, sir."

Dejected and beaten into submission, Sergeant Ruiz left and Casey watched him through the bars of the locked door as he ambled down the hallway toward the cells. He was gone less than five minutes and returned leading a man who shielded his eyes from the glare of light. Carlos was dressed in filthy pajamas and his face and hands were covered with dark, purple blotches. Ruiz led him by a rope tether that bound his arms and, with each jerk, Carlos stumbled forward.

"Open," the sergeant said.

A young corporal sprang from his chair and unlocked the barred door. The sergeant pushed Carlos through the opening ahead of him.

"There," he said. "Take him and be gone. I trust my cooperation with the Secretary's assistant will not go unnoticed. Or unrewarded. Have a good day, sir."

Casey met Ruiz's gaze for a long time until the sergeant looked away.

"Sergeant, I give the orders here. And you can rest assured that a detailed report of your attitude will be filed with the Secretary."

The sergeant locked the door behind the man and returned to his desk. Eyes wide he removed a bandana from his pocket and wiped his perspiring brow. Casey jerked Carlos across the room and out the door. While Carlos struggled with his rope restraints, the pair scurried toward the prison entrance. At the guardhouse, Casey heard a telephone ring. The guard stuck his head out the guardhouse, phone in an ear, and stared at them. Casey instinctively reached for his 9 mm and, when the guard held up a hand, aimed the weapon. The guard dropped to one knee and drew his pistol, but not before Casey fired two shots into his chest.

The man pitched sideways into the dense underbrush alongside the gate, but he was still breathing when Casey and Carlos reached him. While Carlos worked on opening the gate, Casey pumped another round into the guard, silencing his gurgling moans.

"Who the hell are you, man?" Carlos said, looking dazed

and dumbfounded by the killing and his sudden escape. "What in god's name is going on?"

"No time for answers now," Casey blurted, pushing Carlos forward.

Sirens wailed behind them amidst a loud commotion from the administration building.

"This way," he screamed at Carlos.

The two men dashed through the gate and down a serpentine alley that ended at the rear of the Intercontinental Hotel. A delivery truck was parked next to the rear service entrance and they moved past it into the hotel. Unnoticed, they jolted through the deserted lobby with Casey still pulling the dazed and stumbling Carlos behind him. Once inside his hotel room, Casey freed Carlos's hands and tossed the man a bottle of water.

"My names Casey, Allan Casey," he said.

Carlos drank greedily from the bottle.

"CIA. I'm here to get you back into the jungle. How bad are you hurt? Can you travel?"

"Yes, thank you," Carlos said. He panted a few times before taking another drink. "I've been beaten but I'll survive. But how did you know where I was?"

Casey smiled. "We knew. Now, we need to get you out of this hotel before the place is crawling with Sandinistas."

Casey grabbed his leather valet with identity papers and another pistol from his suitcase. He tossed the gun to Carlos. "You may need this," he said. "Let's go."

Carlos was still wheezing when Casey checked the hallway. No one in the halls. The pair descended the stairway at the end of the hall to the lobby and scurried out the rear door. On the street, sirens pierced the afternoon air and a speeding jeep almost ran them over. They crouched behind the delivery truck until the street was empty then made a dash to Casey's car.

CHAPTER 7

Maria's squad of contras relaxed in their primitive camp in the remote Honduran jungle near the Nicaraguan border. Oblivious to the rain that fell in sheets outside their command tent, they huddled beside an outdated stove that crackled away the afternoon chill. Alberto had laid a crumpled map on a rickety card table and, while they studied it, they talked in hushed tones. The lantern hanging on the tent's center pole caused Alberto's shadow to dance against the walls of the tent.

"I say we should blow this bridge here," he said, pointing to a location on the map. "It connects two government farms with the main road through the north-central corridor. A lot of potatoes and beans move over it."

Maria shook her head.

"No good. Like you said the other day, Alberto, if it hurts the people, then we should avoid it. Let's find something else."

The others nodded in agreement and Luis, still sensitive over the Ocotal bombing, pointed to another location.

"I know this area here," he said. "The government uses this power station while on maneuvers. It's off-limits to the farmers, so it will be deserted. It's perfect."

"That's the ticket," Maria said. She leaned over the table to get a better look.

"If I'm correct," Luis said, "this substation provides electricity for the province of Nueva Segovia. If we blow it, we can dismantle the power to all government offices around there. I vote we do it."

Julio and Raoul nodded in agreement.

Maria was having second thoughts. Her pensive look brought the others up short.

"I ask the same question, again. Won't we force a lot of innocent people out of electricity?"

"Most of these farmers don't have electricity anyway, Maria," Luis said. "They use kerosene lamps for lighting. Better to be without electricity than involved in a gunfight."

"Or food," she said. "All right, I vote yes."

"It's settled then," Alberto said. "Let's move tonight."

"We'll take old Thumper, there," Maria said, pointing to the M79 grenade launcher. It had earned its nickname from American soldiers in Vietnam due to its distinctive report. "And our M224 mortar. They should do the trick, especially if we use a point-detonating fuse. Can you get us there, Luis?"

"Of course. It's rough terrain but it shouldn't take long. It's not far across the border about forty kilometers. No problem."

"Let's not get too cocky, fellas," Maria said. "Look what happened to Carlos."

"Carlos was careless," Raoul said. The others nodded. "When we spotted that patrol we should have left immediately. Instead, Carlos wanted a shot at the chopper and got himself captured. If he had listened to me, he would be here right now."

"We shouldn't hold that against him," Maria said. "You can't blame the man for wanting those guys. If his gun hadn't jammed, he stood a good chance of bringing those bastards and that helicopter down."

Julio and Raoul snickered. Maria generally did not talk with such emotion. She knew it betrayed a deeper feeling for Carlos and threw a pencil at Julio.

"Okay, gang." Raoul folded the map and placed it in a knapsack at his side. "We're outta here at midnight. We'll take the jeep and Luis will drive. Let's get over there and back before dawn so try and get a few hours shuteye before then."

The group dispersed to their own tents. Maria found hers, ducked out of the rain, and crawled into her sleeping bag. Relaxing was impossible, as a myriad of thoughts prevented her from sleeping. Where was Carlos? Was he being tortured? Did the dead farmers in Ocotal have decent burials? What about Perez? She heard he was mounting a patrol into the mountains and knew that soon he would be scouring the jungle. From now on, they would have to be on constant alert. Outside, the rain continued to pelt the tent with loud splats. She zipped the sleeping bag to her chin to prevent crawlers from finding their way inside her clothes. In addition to the beautiful butterflies, whose large larvae lived among the thick vines, there was the *pica-caballo*, a giant spider that ate birds. Then there were the slithering, foot-long centipedes, hideous scorpions, the infamous fer-de-lance snake, and deadly coral snakes who presented real dangers to those who weren't careful. Adding to her anxiety, were tales of the mammoth anaconda and how, once it coiled around a person, could choke the life out of you. She snuggled deeper into the bag and focused her thoughts on the events in the bar and the *Americano*. It wasn't his blond hair and strong chin but was his eyes that Maria remembered, steel blue that sparkled like turquoise. She lingered on the vision of him driving off into Managua's darkness.

Her regular trysts with Perez left her feeling dirty and violated. Several times, she had thought of telling Carlos she could no longer go through with the charade, but since the affair began months ago, they had demolished a dozen Sandinista targets, even ambushed a column of soldiers. Maria jumped when she heard Raoul's voice outside her tent. She wiped her eyes with the back of her hand and crawled outside.

It was dark and the rain had stopped. The lantern from the big tent was now on the hood of the jeep and cast a yellow glow through their camp. The chirps of crickets and squeals of tree frogs pierced the cool night. In the distance, something screeched and the noise sent a shiver down Maria's back. Probably a jaguar looking for a mate. Julio and Luis were loading the jeep with the grenade launcher and Alberto was checking his M-16. She slung her rifle over her shoulder and grabbed the bag of mortar shells. Once everything was ready, Luis silently climbed in behind the wheel and started its engine.

Maria, Alberto, Julio, and Raoul jumped into the vehicle and Luis threw it into gear. When the jeep lurched forward, its motor almost died.

"Easy, Luis," Raoul said. "Don't kill us before we get there."

They laughed and clung to the seats as Luis got the jeep underway.

They rode in silence until they had crossed the border into Nicaragua, then Maria tapped Luis on the shoulder. She shot a glance toward the rear of the jeep where the three men appeared to be dozing.

"How much farther?" she said.

"Three kilometers to the substation," Luis said. "Another fifteen or twenty minutes. Hang on, the road is bad here because no one uses it except during the coffee harvest."

"My father tried to work for the coffee cooperative," Alberto said, yawning. "He rarely got paid and they made him sign a loyalty oath. Besides that, the government would come by every month and question him. He finally got tired of it all and found another job."

They continued on, allowing the night sounds of the jungle to engulf them. Luis maneuvered the jeep along a narrow road that followed the spine of the mountain. In reality, it was more like a trail than a road and Luis struggled to dodge the many tangled roots that grew across it. Potholes in the road caused the jeep to lurch sideways, forcing Maria to say a silent prayer for their safety. As they wormed their way deeper into the jungle, she was aware of the glowing eyes that peered at them from the darkness. She lost track of all the twists and turns and hoped that Luis would be able to find his way back. The jungle was now quiet, the insects no longer chirping, the larger animals no longer on their nightly prowls. The only sound was the whine of their jeep when Luis stepped on the gas or braked to avoid an obstacle. The canopy above blocked any view of the sky and Maria could not tell if the moon was up or if clouds obscured the stars. The rain had left a coolness in its wake and she shivered. The air was sweet, pungent.

Luis brought the jeep to a halt in a small clearing. In the distance loomed the electric substation, surrounded by a tall, barbed wire fence, its gray, steel superstructure barely visible against the black, velvet sky. It looked like a giant spider waiting for its prey. In the dark, Maria could barely make out a huge sign that read *No Trespassing* and another read *Danger! High Voltage!* Seeing the substation caused her heart to pound, as bile rose in her throat.

Alberto and Julio jumped from the jeep and began scouting the area, M-16s at the ready. Their boots sank into the soft, muddy ground, making soft sucking noises as they approached the fence. Satisfied they were alone, Alberto retrieved the mortars from the jeep and aimed it at the station.

"Millions of volts pass through this station from the power generator on the Rio Coco," Luis said in a low voice. "From here, the network spreads out through the province."

Maria watched as Alberto and Julio positioned the mortar and calibrated the weapon's azimuth to the target. Beyond the fence, a towering grid of transformers produced the recognizable hum of harnessed electricity.

"The thing might explode," Raoul said, "so watch out."

Alberto and Julio fired four mortar rounds in quick succession and the superstructure burst into flames. The explosions, along with the roar from the flames, rocked the clearing, and made hearing difficult. Maria ran to their jeep while the rest watched the raging inferno.

"Let's go!" she shouted above the crackling of the generators. "It's going to blow!"

No sooner had she yelled the warning than the substation exploded with a horrific *bang*, throwing steel beams a hundred feet into the air. One of the beams, launched as a missile, struck Julio in the chest. The force of the impact knocked him off his feet and he landed, crumpled, near the jeep. Raoul ran to his side and picked up his friend's head. Julio's eyes were wide and his mouth was filled with a dark ooze.

"Julio, Julio," he said.

Blood pumped from Julio's chest as he gasped for air. Raoul tore open his friend's shirt and gaped at the enormous wound through which part of Julio's lung protruded.

"Shit," Raoul said. "Alberto! Get over here. And bring the flashlight."

Alberto stumbled as he raced to Raoul and inspected Julio's wound. "Goddammit," he said, his eyes suddenly wide when the light shown on the man's wound.

Julio grabbed Alberto's arm and pulled him close. "H— how b—bad?" he stammered. He struggled to breathe but the air would not come.

"I can't lie, my friend. It's bad. I'm sorry."

Julio coughed and spit a large blood clot onto the ground. His wheezing grew louder and his face turned ashen. He closed his eyes and his body went limp. In the dim light of the flashlight, Maria realized that the wound was a fatal one. She choked down the bile in her mouth, the knot in her stomach gripped hard. She forced herself not to vomit. Julio opened his eyes and peered at Maria through small slits. His lips were near black and a bloody foam oozed from his mouth. She fought the panic rising inside, her pulse lashing her brain. Unable to control the convulsions in her stomach any longer she stepped into the darkness and vomited.

Julio tried to raise his head but it fell back into the mud. "It's all right. Our luck was bound to run out sooner, or later. It just happened to be me, that's all. Raoul—"

Raoul took Julio's hand and kissed his comrade on the cheek. Speaking only in a whisper, Julio continued. The words formed through the bloody foam and were interrupted with spells of coughing. "Please, Raoul—Don't leave me here— Take me back to camp—Don't leave me for the snakes."

"You're not going to die, Julio," Maria said, coming near, crying. Her tears fell on Julio's bloodstained shirt. "You're going to make it. We'll get you to a doctor."

"It's okay. I love you guys. Tell my wife that all I wanted was a better life for our children. Tell her—that I love—her."

Julio grabbed Maria's arm and continued in a stammering voice.

"You'll—do—it—Maria? Promise me."

"Of course, Julio," she said. "You're going to make it, you'll see."

The group scrambled to get Julio's limp body into the jeep and, with the fire still raging behind them, began the difficult journey back to camp. The rain had turned the ruts into a slimy quagmire. Luis gunned the motor forcing the jeep to slide and swerve northward toward Honduras while the group fought to keep Julio's body from being thrown overboard. It was nearly impossible to see, the jeep's headlights pitched beams of light left and right, up and down. No one spoke. The only sounds Maria heard were Julio's gasping breaths.

Somewhere inside Honduras, his breathing stopped.

Maria placed her head on Raoul's shoulders and sobbed. The clouds reappeared and it started to rain again.

At camp, Raoul and Luis dug a shallow grave and Maria helped the pair lower Julio's blood-and-rain-drenched body into the ground. While the men worked to cover Julio's grave with rocks, she found a piece of wood from the command tent, fashioned a crude marker, and pushed it into the damp earth.

"Too bad we can't take him back to his wife but it would bring the army. She would want to say goodbye. Maybe someday, when this stupid war is over, we can give him a proper burial back in his village. One of us should say some words over him," Maria said when they had finished. All were soaked from the work and the rain. "What should we say?"

"I can't," Luis said. "Maria, you say something."

Maria started but the words would not come. A large lump formed in her throat and she wept. Visions of Julio swirled before her—his smile, his laughter, his wife. She fought for control. Electric waves of nausea shot through her body.

"We will never forget you, Julio," she said in a voice barely audible over the rain. "We will never forget."

∽∾∽

When Perez arrived in Ocotal late in the afternoon, the sun was still high. The entire village turned out to watch the Sandinistas rumble to a stop. Captain Salazar found the four village elders and marched them to the colonel.

Nervous and frightened, they stood gathered around Perez, their eyes darting furtively among the soldiers. Perez took a deep breath, approached the oldest of the four men until his face nearly touched the farmer's, and began his questioning. "We are here to investigate the explosion the other day. It killed two CDS officials. What do you know about it?"

Before the man could answer, a dark-eyed young man spoke. "Don't forget, Colonel," he said, "but two farmers were killed, as well. We buried the men not long ago."

Perez ignored the interruption and continued to stare at the older man. He felt the man's resolve weaken under his menacing stare. He rubbed his disfigured ear.

"I'm waiting for an answer," Perez continued in a soft monotone.

The man gawked at the ground. "Nothing, sir."

Perez slapped the man's face with the back of his hand, producing a trickle of blood. The farmer stood with his head bowed, staring at the ground. After a long silence, he raised his head and returned Perez's glare. He spat onto the colonel's face.

"You shit!" Perez said. His scream could be heard throughout the village. He brought the butt of his AK-47 down hard on the man's skull and the farmer collapsed, blood poured from his head. Perez approached another man who began talking while his fallen comrade writhed in pain.

"That's better," Perez said.

The man sputtered clipped phrases and pointed into the jungle above Ocotal. Perez called for Salazar.

"This man says the contras hide in that direction, probably in Honduras. Is it possible, though, that they could still be in Nicaragua?"

"I doubt it, Colonel, but it would be worth the search. The road ends here, so we will have to proceed on foot. But there is always the possibility that they have not crossed the border. If they haven't and we can locate them, we could make them pay."

After the two officers returned to their jeep, the young farmer knelt beside the old man and covered his blood-spattered head with a bandana.

"Army whores," he said.

Perez turned to stare at the kneeling peasant for a moment then strapped on a backpack.

☙❧

Casey jammed the accelerator pedal of his rental car to the floor, while Carlos slumped in the back seat underneath a tarp, and hoped aloud that they might make it to the mountains. *Sweet Jesus* was all he could manage, *sweet Jesus.* The sun was on its downward arc toward the horizon and Casey believed he could make Pueblo Salto before dark.

They hurried past the squat buildings of the army base then sped through the Sebaco Valley. If they were spotted and stopped, Casey still had the pistol. He laid it on the seat beside him. The two men conversed little, but once Carlos broke the silence and tapped Casey on the shoulder.

"You CIA guys still helping us contras?" Carlos said.

Casey nodded. "Why do you ask?"

"Because we have heard that the American Congress does not vote any more money to help our cause."

"Those liberal assholes don't know what the shit is going on," Casey said, finding himself angered by the topic. "They would rather destroy a chance for freedom rather than get involved. Spineless politicians are what they are."

"If it is true, *senor,* our fight is over. There is no way our meager forces can match the weapons the National Directorate gets from the Russians. I pray to god that he hears my humble prayer and grants the Americans a clear vision to what is happening. I pray every day."

Finished with his outburst, Carlos again covered himself with the tarp. When they were on the final leg to Pueblo Salto, a thought struck Casey. An important element missing from the contra effort was their ability to conduct operations in secret. That singular fact nagged at him during the remainder of the drive northward. Secrecy was essential to every aspect of an insurgency's tactical goals, ranging from the creation of mystique, to the success of assaults on targets, and the protection of their underground. Even more serious was the absence of a working intelligence network and counter-intelligence system within the contra structure. For them, effective intelligence spelled the difference between life and death and the development of a full-fledged intelligence network should be one of the contra's highest priorities. These peasant fighters could learn much from the Americans. He realized that some of them resented his presence but he would try to get them to see things his way.

They drove into Pueblo Salto as the sun dipped behind the trees, giving Carlos a chance to orient Casey. Located at the edge of the rainforest and on the ridge of a rugged mountain, it was similar to other villages scattered throughout Nicaragua—small shacks lining the rock-covered dirt road.

"This is where we relax when we're not on maneuvers," Carlos said. "It has the area's only cafe."

Casey stopped the car, exited the vehicle, and leaned on its hood while waiting for Carlos. The CIA agent removed his sunglasses and squinted down the road. Pueblo Salto was quiet, with only a dog making its way toward them.

"Can we get a beer at the cafe?"

"The Café Central, senor, has the only beer in these parts. Armando serves imported beer when he can get it."

Carlos pointed down the street to the last wooden shack.

"There it is. And look, my comrades are sitting on the porch. Will they be surprised when they see me. This morning I was in that stink hole El Chipote and tonight I am with friends. Look, sir, they are laughing. Good, good. Come, I will introduce you."

It was what Casey had hoped for after rescuing Carlos. This would be his opportunity to meet with one of the most feared squad of contras patrolling the northern Nicaraguan jungle. Carlos's fame was known throughout the country and the group he led had killed many Sandinistas and destroyed many military installations. On one hand, they had been extremely successful—on the other, there was a lot they could improve. Maybe they would be receptive to his ideas. When the group on the café's porch recognized Carlos, they stood and cheered. Carlos, in turn, waved. When he reached the porch, Carlos joyously hugged each of them.

"Where's Julio?" he said after they were seated at the table.

Raoul took Carlos by the arm and pulled him close but Casey managed to overhear.

"Julio was killed last night. It was bad, Carlos. When we blew the electric substation in Nueva Segovia, he was hit in the chest by a steel beam. He died before we could get him back to base camp. We buried him there."

Casey saw the tears form in Carlos's eyes and he put an arm on the man's shoulder. Carlos shook his head and the group returned to their chairs. He turned to Casey and smiled through misty eyes.

"He was a good, decent *hombre,* and a damned good contra. I will miss him. Come, *senor,* and meet my friends and comrades."

Small puffs of dust flittered from Casey's boots as he ascended the few steps onto the porch. His eyes were riveted on the woman.

"Name is Maria," she said, extending a hand. "Welcome to our country club."

Together they sat in the shade of the porch while Casey briefed them on Carlos's escape. When he mentioned the much-needed intelligence system, he noticed the frowns on the group's faces. He encouraged them to think it over. It might make all the difference to their cause.

CHAPTER 8

The day following his brush with death and narrow escape from Managua, Slater dismissed school early and retired to his living room while contemplating events of the past week. He was aware the Sandinistas mistrusted Americans but allowed him to remain in the country because of his work in San Rafael. The National Directorate released a steady flow of anti-American propaganda over Radio Nicaragua, and it seemed to Slater that only a handful of contras and peasant farmers harbored warm feelings toward the United States. It seemed odd that the Sandinistas would berate the United States and, at the same time, welcome its professionals to their country. He was not the only teacher in Nicaragua, and he knew of doctors and nurses working in mission hospitals as well. During the previous month, he had weighed the pros and cons of remaining. At times, the situation seemed desperate, but only for Nicaraguans—he felt relatively safe. As a non-combatant, he provided a much-needed service to the peasants of the surrounding villages, but he realized that, if he wanted to continue with his school, he would have to find a way to remain neutral and not become embroiled in the insurgent uprising or the government's efforts to squash it. The smiles and thanks of the parents made it all worthwhile. However, the National Directorate could revoke his visa at any time.

Since his arrival a year earlier, he had seen firsthand the numerous failings of the Sandinistas, the centralized power of the government, the closing of private businesses, price controls, and production norms that stifled incentives. The Sandinistas, in the first few months of their sovereignty, ignored the first and most important of their principles—political democracy. They immediately set up a ruling junta, the National Directorate, made up of twelve top Sandinista officials. The Sandinistas promised political pluralism and free elections. But what had happened? Even the Sandinistas' call for international nonalignment was violated in the first years of the junta, who allied with the Soviet Union and Cuba, receiving heavy financial and military aid from these countries. They grew more and more distant from the United States and other capitalist nations, creating international alignments—contrary to what they had promised. Meat production was at an all-time low because only three government slaughterhouses were still operational. In addition, shortages of food and goods as well as a declining national earning power were fueling the insurgent movement. Most damaging to the Sandinista regime was the fact that middle-class numbers were on a rapid decline. In their effort to remove all vestiges of American imperialism, they put a lid on dissent, censored the news media, and forbade the publication of US baseball scores. When they placed a Roman Catholic cardinal to serve as Foreign Minister, the National Directorate sent a message that they were not anti-Catholic, only anti-capitalists.

Slater was aware that most Americans felt that the Sandinistas were Communists and he wondered if some of the government's failings could be traced to his country's politics.

The compelling vigor of the Sandinista movement came from a new breed of Nicaraguan students who, unlike their parents, were sympathetic to Marxism. They believed that Soviet Communism had vanquished poverty and social injustice and the success of Castro's revolution in Cuba reaffirmed their Marxist faith. Once in power, in order to build a popular base, they, by necessity, obscured their true nature and dressed the radical message in native clothing.

In 1979, television correspondent, Bill Flanagan, was gunned downed by Somoza's *Guardia* in Riguero. The incident energized the revolution throughout Nicaragua because, in part, the murder was caught on video by Flanagan's cameraman. The newsman and his crew were riding in a van marked as a press vehicle that had white flags on the bumper. When they stopped at a checkpoint manned by Somoza's National Guard, the lieutenant ordered Flanagan out of the van. After showing the lieutenant his press credentials, Flanagan was ordered to lie face down. With the camera rolling, the lieutenant shot Flanagan in the back of his head with his M-16. His Nicaraguan interpreter was also murdered. The world watched the event in horror as the video was aired on news channels. The Sandinistas marched into Managua with relative ease after his death.

Slater sat in his wicker rocker and attempted to concentrate on the current issue of *La Prensa* but found it impossible. Visual images of the victims in Ocotal caromed about his brain agitating him to the point of restlessness. He went to the kitchen and opened the refrigerator—no beer left. It had taken him six months to acclimate to the hot, humid climate, but now he was sweating and uncomfortable. Returning to his rocker, he closed his eyes.

He was back in Vietnam, the city of Hue, during the big battle. The US Marines, not being well trained in urban combat, found it a harrowing house-to-house, booby-trap-infested ordeal as they swept through every inch of the city. Armor and airstrikes were very limited, to keep casualties down. Allied forces were ordered not to bomb or shell the city, for fear of destroying the historic structures. Also, since it was monsoon season, it was virtually impossible for the US forces to use air support. The communist forces were constantly using snipers, hidden inside buildings or in small holes, and preparing makeshift machine gun bunkers.

His platoon had situated itself near the Citadel and was taking heavy incoming fire from the North Vietnamese Army. In less than an hour, all but two men were dead, he and a sergeant who, though wounded himself, managed to pull Slater to safety. Dead GIs littered the streets and their blood ran in thick pools everywhere.

Now, Slater decided to drive to the Café Central for a beer. He drove the ten kilometers to Pueblo Salto, parked his pickup in front of the café, and noticed a group of men and a woman sitting on the porch. When he approached, they stopped their discussion and stared at him. He scanned the group and held up a hand in acknowledgement.

"*Buenos dias, compadres,*" he said. "How's the beer?"

The men eyed Slater without smiling while he approached. A young man stood, smiled, and spoke.

"The beer is all right, my friend, if you like horse piss."

The group on the porch chuckled and continued to stare at Slater.

"My name is Slater, Jim Slater. I built the school down at San Rafael."

The man who spoke extended his hand. "We have heard of you, Senor Slater. You do good work for the children there. My name is Carlos and these ragged good-for-nothings are my friends."

At the introduction, the group on the porch relaxed and held up a hand as if to signal hello.

Slater took the chair Carlos offered and the woman stood, removing her sunglasses.

"Hi there," she said. "Remember me?"

Startled by the familiar voice, Slater jerked his head toward the questioner. "Maria! What are you doing here?"

Maria gave Slater a hug and returned to her seat. Slater ordered a beer from Armando and sipped it as Maria brushed her hair.

"Like I told you, Jim. This is what I do. I fight for freedom."

"But—"

"It's good to see that you made it out of Managua. I worried about you after you drove off. I've known about you and your work here but I hadn't placed the man with a face until now."

"But how come I haven't seen you before?" Slater was glad to see Maria again but was puzzled by her presence in Pueblo Salto.

"You don't come here much. We use this café as a place to unwind. Our base camp is over the—"

Casey interrupted Maria's comments by clearing his throat. She stopped in mid-sentence then changed the subject.

"I'm sorry," she said. "Jim, this is Allan Casey. Mr. Casey, this is the man I told you about, Jim Slater."

Casey removed his sunglasses and shook Slater's hand.

A strong grip, Slater noticed. "What brings you to Nicaragua, Mr. Casey?"

"Business," Casey said after a moment's hesitation.

"Any special kind of business?"

Casey finished his beer and stood to pay. A half-smile crossed his lips. "Just business."

Armando returned with more beer and Casey patted Carlos on the back. "Tomorrow," he said. "At the usual time and place."

Carlos nodded and Casey got into his truck and drove away.

"Who was that guy?" Slater said.

"Nobody in particular. Just an American friend."

"The only Americans who come to Nicaragua," Slater said, "are missionaries and the CIA. Which one is he?"

Carlos chuckled and nodded. "Let us just say he is a friend who helps our cause, from time to time. He got me out of prison."

"CIA, then."

Carlos snubbed out his cigarette and blew the smoke away from the group. "You are perceptive, Senor Slater. Armando told us you are a man with the peasant's welfare at heart. So can we count on your discretion in this matter?"

"I really don't wish to become involved," Slater said. "Your war is not my affair. There have been injustices on both sides."

At his suggestion that both sides of the war had committed crimes, he noticed Carlos put a hand on the handle of a knife hanging from his belt.

"But," he continued, "you have my word I will not divulge what I have learned today or your identities to anyone."

CRCRC

Colonel Perez was pinned down near the border by machine-gun fire coming from a group of contras. The convoy had surprised a small band of guerrillas and engaged them in a firefight, but he found himself and his men outnumbered. He ordered Captain Salazar to radio for reinforcements and waited impatiently for the helicopters to arrive and put an end to the battle. Near the rear of their entrenchment, a barefooted farmer sat on the ground, his hands tied behind his back.

Crouching low to avoid getting hit by gunfire, Perez made his way from the forward line of fighting back to the prisoner. The man's face was wrinkled and dirty, eyes wide, darting.

When Perez reached him, the prisoner begged for mercy. "Please, sir. I'm nobody important. I know nothing. I have a wife and children. Please let me go. My family needs me and my wife, she is not well."

Perez slapped the man with the back of his hand sending the man toppling to his side. He lay on the ground and continued to beg for his life. Perez spit his words out with scorn, saliva shot from his lips. "Shut up."

The man obeyed but he continued to weep.

"Where is your camp?" he said.

The farmer looked at Perez through tear-filled eyes and trembled, arms and legs moving in fitful spasms. "Please, sir. I am not a revolutionary. I am a farmer. I work on the coffee plantation. I know nothing."

Perez knew different. Knowing the man was hiding information, the colonel was determined to beat it out of him. He withdrew his pistol and punched the farmer in the stomach with it. The man doubled over and sobbed.

"You are far from anywhere, you imbecile. Where do you live?"

The farmer squirmed, still reeling from the blow to his stomach. "Ocotal," he blurted.

"I want answers. If I don't get them, you and your family will die. For the last time, where is your camp? Across the border? Where? I will not ask another time."

Again, the man pleaded. Tears rolled down his sunburned cheeks and he rolled on the ground. He strained against the ropes that bound his arms and chattered in bursts. Small puffs of dust circled around Perez's legs.

"Please. I said I know nothing. My family knows nothing. My children need their father. I beg you, *senor,* have mercy! I am but a poor farmer. Let me go."

Perez pulled the man to his knees and pushed the barrel of the pistol against his temple. The farmer babbled incoherent words, still pleading. A vision of Perez's grandmother shot through his mind and it drove him over the edge. "I have no time for such nonsense."

Perez stood, moved the barrel of his pistol against the back of the man's head, and squeezed the trigger. The farmer's brains splattered onto the ground and, after a few convulsions, he lay unmoving in a pool of blood. Perez dusted himself off. He detested these interruptions with the mission. When would these poor bastards learn that the army was in control and no one could escape its wrath? He returned to the fighting and found Salazar gathering ammunition.

"I want you to find that contra's family and bring them to me after the choppers arrive and put an end to this skirmish. I want his wife and children here, do you understand? I will teach these bastards a lesson they won't soon forget."

Over the sporadic gunfire, the helicopters could be heard, the humming of their rotors getting louder by the second. Salazar pulled the pin on a smoke grenade and threw it in the direction of the contras. As orange smoke billowed skyward, three helicopters made a diving arc and filled the area with rocket-fire. After a brief, sixty-second volley, it was over, the helicopters banked and headed south back to their airbase. After thanking the pilots over the radio, Salazar charged forward to search for bodies while Perez relaxed and smoked a cigarette. Before finishing it, Salazar returned pushing a woman and two small children if front of him.

The woman saw the dead man lying on the ground with half his head missing and rushed to him. She fell to her knees, sobbing.

"We found them not far from here. The man's wife and children," Salazar said to the colonel. He turned his back on his commanding officer as if he could not bear to witness what was about to happen.

Perez shot each one in the head but not before they begged for mercy. The woman and two children fell next to the dead man. Perez calmly reloaded his weapon and finished his cigarette.

"String them up from that tree over there," he said to Salazar. "Then be ready to move out. We're returning to Ocotal. I will radio a report to Secretary Rivas from there."

Perez left Salazar white-faced and retching.

ოჳ

Slater could not believe his good fortune in seeing Maria again. Since the explosion in Managua, he had thought of nothing else but her. The other contras took Casey's lead and left the two of them on the porch of the café. He and Maria talked for a while, exchanging pleasantries until Maria turned the conversation to a more serious tone.

"I grew up in the slums near where I hid you. When I was a child, I heard stories of Somoza, the dictator and butcher. My parents feared that one day the *Guardia* would come and arrest them, or worse, torture them for no reason. The United States supported Somoza and we hated the Americans for this. Somoza wanted to be king and pass his power to his son. I overheard my parents talk of how Somoza dropped the bodies of his enemies into the volcanoes on the outskirts of Managua. Each day there were rumors of clashes between the revolutionaries who called themselves *Sandinistas* and the *Guardia*. The Sandinista National Liberation Front named themselves after Augusto Sandino, a patriot who fought the Somoza government. My father was fond of saying: 'The problem is one man, Somoza, and that man has to go.'

"When I was older, I talked to people who had actually lived in the United States. I learned of the great contradictions of life there. I learned of the luxury that only a few countries enjoyed. Our newspapers were filled with stories of wonderful America where everyone had lots of money and enjoyed themselves. Some families even had two automobiles. Imagine that. Two. Everyone went to college and got a good-paying job. But we lived in stark contrast among misery and suffering. We had no jobs, no money, no television, and no movies. Our water made us sick while the fat cats like Somoza guzzled champagne with their meals."

Maria toyed with her hands, appearing embarrassed by her spirited monologue. The sun was setting and bathed her in an amber glow.

"It became apparent, after the Triumph of the Revolution, that the promises of the Sandinistas were not going to materialize. The assurances of a pluralistic political system, a mixed economy, and a foreign policy of nonalignment were made only for the purpose of gathering strength for the revolution's Marxist leaders. But that pales in comparison to what was done to the Miskito Indians.

"The Sandinistas largely ignored the Atlantic Coast Indians when they put together a strategy for revolution with absolutely no reference to the Miskito Indians. What conclusion can one draw? There was only one way that the Atlantic Coast Indians could become authentic revolutionaries. They had to take part in the Sandinista struggle on the same terms as everyone else. Their struggle as Indians did not matter.

"After the Sandinistas took power, Miskitos demands came to their attention in a most forceful manner. The Sandinistas were ill-prepared to respond in the proper fashion. Their ethnocentrism prevented this from happening. More importantly, there were important gaps in Marxist theory that prevented them from understanding the special oppression of Indian people. Dogmatic Marxism tends to view Indians as a relic of pre-capitalist society. For the sake of progress, they had to enter the working-class as rapidly as possible. Assimilation was the only worthwhile goal.

"All this is rather a long-winded way of saying that the Miskitos did not fit into the Sandinista schema of a society composed of capitalists and workers. The clear implication was that Miskitos were some sort of dinosaur-like relic that modernization—either of a capitalist or socialist nature—and would be swept away, sooner or later. And the sooner the better.

"At first, they supported the Sandinistas against Somoza. But after the Sandinistas took power and attempted to indoctrinate the Miskitos in Marxist dogma, the Indians resisted. The new government tried to put their own people in as leaders of the Indian community and, again, the Indians resisted. So they began to arrest Indian leaders. Some were murdered, most tortured. Our new Secretary of Defense, Rivas, was quoted as saying he would eliminate every single Miskito Indian. Probably fifty thousand Indians have been incarcerated in relocation camps. Most of them are at Tasba Pri Relocation Camp. *Tasba Pri* means free land. Ha."

Armando locked the door to the café, and Slater waved to the man as he left for home.

"When I was in Vietnam, I saw much the same thing," Slater said. "People starving because of war, my friends killed for no good reason. I decided, then and there, that war was no good. Nothing was ever accomplished by it and only suffering was left in its wake. But I guess people never change anywhere in the world. Someone always wants to rule. Dictators spring up all over the place."

The stars were out and the moon rose over the jungle, bathing the porch in a soft light. Maria sighed. "We are fighting for the right to be ourselves, to make our own mistakes, to raise our children the way we choose, nothing more. The Sandinistas do not want a free people.

"When my parents were killed I knew the National Directorate didn't seek to better my life, it only sought to control it. That is why I became a contra, Jim, to fight for the right to choose my own path. I want to build a good society, a place where, someday, my children can live and work in peace without fear or oppression. The greatest historical crime of the Sandinistas has not been their larceny or their centralization of power but their absolute refusal to develop the country they rule."

Maria's passionate explanation left Slater reticent. They sat on the café's porch lost in their own thoughts. She was beautiful, he thought, extraordinarily beautiful. And she was articulate—so very articulate. She spoke so intelligently that he realized this was no uneducated peasant woman sitting opposite him.

"You're incredible." He leaned across the table, stroked her wind-blown hair, and drew her closer to him. She didn't pull away. Her perfume engulfed his senses and he stared at her full, red lips, then kissed her gently. His heart pounded. Instead of pushing him away, she put her arms on his shoulders, lips meeting. Slater tasted the delicate sweetness of her tongue while a fire erupted inside him. When Maria pulled away, he caught his breath.

"I—I—" he stammered. "When can I see you again?"

"Shh." Maria pressed a finger to his lips. "I don't know. My duty is here. I told you I have no time for romances, Jim. I have other priorities and can't betray my friends."

"We won't betray anyone. Just see each other. Surely there can be no harm in that."

Slater noticed a tear on her cheek and he dabbed it with a finger.

"Damn," she said.

"You would prefer to not see me again?"

Maria kissed him again and this time pressed her bosom into Slater's chest. "God, forgive me. Tomorrow, I will come to San Rafael."

CHAPTER 9

Slater cleaned his small living room in preparation for Maria's arrival. Years of being single had removed all vestiges of civilization from his personal habits—clothes, books, and papers were strewn all about. He washed his breakfast dishes and swept the house. As a symbol of his spartan philosophy, the house was devoid of any decoration, except for a picture of his mother, and contained only a light-colored sofa along with his rocking chair. He stacked a few issues of *La Prensa* on a small, rectangular coffee table and, satisfied with his efforts, took a hurried shower. He donned a clean shirt and splashed himself with cologne.

He had thought of nothing but Maria since the fortuitous meeting the previous afternoon. Her kiss at the Café Central left him unable to concentrate on anything else. Now that school was over for the day, he could be left to his personal reveries. It was difficult to believe a woman like Maria existed here in the jungle. Beautiful and witty, she had the brains and grit to be a contra—brains and cunning. Slater found himself drawn to her, captivated by her beauty and vitality. She was so unlike his ex-wife, who spent most of her day complaining that they did not have enough money, in spite of him working night and day. He remembered when he came home exhausted and announced that he had quit his job at the agency. She launched into a wild, hysterical diatribe, accusing him of abandoning his responsibilities and threatening legal action if he didn't change his mind. She thought the world owed her a living while she played tennis or went shopping.

Maria was the opposite, possessing a self-confidence and sensuousness that excited him. The thought of her lips pressed against his lingered and heightened his expectation of her arrival. He was searching for the bourbon when there was a knock at the door. "Maria," he said.

She stood in the doorway and the two of them looked at each other until Slater pulled her inside. He held her close and kissed her, his head spinning. When she didn't pull away, he pulled her closer. When Slater thought he could bear it no longer, Maria backed away and took a deep breath.

"I can't believe I came here," she said. "It's so dangerous."

"It's dangerous for you to come and see me? Why?"

"No so much for myself but dangerous for you, possibly. If you are seen with me, it could spell trouble for you."

"I wanted, no, I needed, to see you again. Since yesterday, I have been unable to think of anything else. I'm afraid I didn't give my best at school today."

"It was the same with me. Last night was the longest night of my life. I lay awake, thinking of you. But I know I shouldn't be here."

When she looked into his eyes, Slater felt his knees turn to jelly.

They kissed again and he pointed to the sofa. "Can I fix you a drink? I have some American bourbon I brought from Costa Rica."

"That would be nice."

Maria smiled while Slater found two small glasses then poured the liquor. When he returned from the kitchen, she was looking at a copy of *La Prensa*.

"Any word about our raid in Ocotal?" she said. "I see in this issue that the butcher, Colonel Perez, has already exacted his punishment. Several people were executed and another guerrilla squad gunned down by army helicopters. Maybe it's time we listen to our American friend and become bolder in our fighting. Casey says we need to strike again soon, for our support in the United States is dwindling."

"So the man at Pueblo Salto was CIA? It's easy to spot those guys."

"Well," said Maria after a pause, "like I said—"

"Don't worry, Maria. I have listened to the Voice of America broadcasts the past month and I feel you're right about your support back home. Congress thinks you are nothing more than former Somoza guardsmen who want to wrench power away from the Sandinistas and reinstate the old ways."

Slater handed Maria a glass and sat in his wicker rocker. She took a sip before replying.

"That was true in the beginning," she said. "Most of the revolutionaries were members of the *Guardia* but, over time, the insurgency gathered momentum and was able to enlist freedom fighters from all parts of the country. But it is a simple fact of life, Jim. We cannot continue without the aid of your country—money and arms. Not when the government gets shiploads of weapons and helicopters from Cuba and Russia. Our weapons are meager and few. Even our camouflaged uniforms must last many months. Casey hopes for another C-47 to drop supplies sometime this week."

Slater was finding it difficult to follow Maria's remark, for he was focused on her lips. She had put on dark, red lipstick, and the color was a sensuous contrast to her olive skin.

"What?" Maria said.

"I beg your pardon?"

"I said we were hoping for another C-47 drop and you said something." Maria took another sip of her bourbon.

"I'm sorry," Slater said. "I was thinking of our embrace a moment ago. Forgive me."

Maria laughed and the sweet melody of her voice filled the small living room. He forced himself back to reality.

"The Americans are worried because they don't want to find themselves backing another dictator like Somoza. If Congress doesn't appropriate the money, maybe it can be found elsewhere."

"Where?" Maria returned the newspaper to the coffee table. "If I die, I want to go down fighting. We will carry this fight to the Sandinistas until there is not one of us left, this I can promise you and the American people. If you don't help us, we will continue the fight without American aid."

Slater moved to the sofa next to Maria, took her drink, and set it on the coffee table. He gazed into her round eyes.

"Enough of this talk," he said.

He took her into her arms and they kissed until out of breath and Maria pulled away.

"Please," she said, breathing hard. "I must go. Carlos will be worried. I didn't tell him I was coming here. I don't want him to know."

"You and Carlos, you—"

Maria put a finger to Slater's lips. "Shh," she said. "Nothing like that. Carlos is a dear friend and our leader, that's all. For now, it's better to keep this from him. I will tell him when the time is right. I really must go." She stood and straightened her clothes.

Slater escorted her to the door. Pausing before opening it, they embraced again and when they parted, he noticed a tear in Maria's eye.

"I miss you already," he said.

"I know. I won't be able to sleep again tonight. Casey has scheduled a meeting with Carlos and the rest of us tomorrow. Come to Pueblo Salto and I will take you to our camp. Carlos wants to show you something."

Slater nodded and watched her walk down the road until she disappeared and the jungle closed behind her. Returning to his rocker, he spent the rest of the evening replaying the events of the previous two days in his mind.

❧❧❧

Casey sat in front of a small campfire located within the Honduran rainforest and studied the group. He had not shaved since his arrival and the stubble on his face accentuated the shadows caused by the firelight. They were a smart and aggressive lot, but they needed strong leadership on how to wage a war. A dense fog hung over the forested mountain, preventing visibility much beyond the campfire. Luis stood guard at the edge of the small clearing, and the group listened while Casey outlined their needs as he saw them. In the background, tree frogs and monkeys squealed above the crackling fire.

The CIA agent spoke in measured tones. "First of all, Carlos, you need to begin following traditional guerrilla warfare operating modes. That means that you shift your training locations for the urban underground away from these camps along the border to ones that are even more remote and secure. Anyone assigned the task of training a new member must first thoroughly investigate and observe the new member for a while, to help weed out any Sandinistas that may have infiltrated your organization. Notice I didn't say *if* your group was infiltrated by the Sandinistas. Take it for granted that someone, anyone, may not be exactly whom you think them to be. You have to be ever vigilant when allowing outsiders in until they have proven themselves.

"Also, you must guard the identities of each other from the first day of training and do it with your lives. It has been far too easy for the National Directorate to locate your fellow soldiers and assassinate them.

"Finally, and this goes to my first point, you must exercise great care in whom you recruit. The Sandinistas have an effective counter-intelligence program and have found it all too easy to place agents inside your organization."

Carlos squirmed and lit a cigarette. He seemed ill at ease with Casey's analysis of their problems. "Traditional guerrilla tactics, you say? Sorry, they won't work here. We need more US help," he said.

Maria nodded in agreement.

"That's part of your problem," Casey said. "The greatest damage to your mystique has been the perception that you really haven't planned to win this war yourselves, but instead have been hoping that the United States would someday mount a Grenada-style invasion, and produce a quick victory. You need to realize that this war is going to take years and resolve to fight that long, if necessary. Otherwise, your counter-revolution will die."

Maria stood and brushed the dirt from her fatigues. She

ambled quietly around the campfire until she stood next to Casey. "What do we need to do in addition to what you have suggested?" she said.

Casey pulled a black notepad from his shirt pocket, opened it, thumbed through several pages, then looked at the group. "I hesitate to say," he said, "for I sense that we are not in complete agreement. I am here in an advisory position only. If you want, I can leave tomorrow."

Maria sat beside Casey and smiled. She glanced at Carlos when she spoke. "It's fine. Carlos is very independent with the way he views our path to victory. US strategy and organization has not always worked here in the jungle. Guerrilla warfare is new to you Americans, except for Vietnam. It has been a fact of life here for a hundred years. Right, Carlos?"

Casey nodded, answering for Carlos. "He will always be your leader. I do not come to usurp his position, but if you want my country's help and advice, then I am here for you. That's all."

"Go on," Carlos said. "I will hear you out."

Casey reviewed his notes, began summarizing what he had observed, and gave ways to correct the current situation. "Please don't be offended by this, but you need to develop an insurgent mentality. You think you have it, right? But, in particular, you must give higher priority to the social, political, and economic infrastructure for guerrilla warfare. As I mentioned earlier, you need to change the locations of your safe areas in Honduras to ones within Nicaragua and maintain strict security concerning them. To lessen your dependence on US support, you must develop a self-supporting supply system for food, weapons, and fuel.

"Most of your essentials will come not from the US taxpayers, but from ambushed enemy troops. So you need to start planning a supply chain and a couple of storage facilities. Mostly you need to strike deep within the Sandinista regime. That means Managua. It means assassinating someone like Colonel Perez or Minister of Defense Fernando Rivas. A strike on the National Palace, for example, would echo a similar Sandinista act back in 1978. Remember? You could win much popular support by striking at the heart of the enemy."

Carlos finished his cigarette and threw the butt into the campfire. The group remained silent a long while until Alberto broke the silence.

"What you are advising," he said, "sounds terribly difficult and complicated. How can we do all that you suggest? We are only a small group of freedom fighters."

Casey smiled. "Maybe it's time for you to meet with your brothers-in-arms and begin the process of organizing yourselves into a larger, more integrated unit. Your greatest asset is the fact that popular and world support for the Sandinistas is waning. People, whether they are doctors, students, farmers, or peasants, are waking up to the fact that the current Nicaraguan government has failed. Your propaganda efforts along these lines need to be expanded. You need to print your own newspaper in addition to *La Prensa*. The good news is that this is all possible and victory is within your grasp. It is not as hopeless as it sounds."

"What we really could use are some Stinger missiles," Maria said. Heads nodded in agreement around her.

"Nothing like those shoulder-fired missiles to bring down low-flying aircraft," Carlos said. "Those damn helicopters are our worst nightmare. A bunch of Stingers could tilt the playing field a whole lot in our favor. How about it?"

Casey chuckled. He wrote in a notebook then answered Carlos' question. "No doubt about it. I'll see what I can do for the next supply drop."

The group broke up and each member went to their sleeping bags. Casey felt relieved that they had not rejected his advice outright but appeared to give his words serious thought. He lay on the ground near the fire and looked up at the inky sky. The fog had lifted and he thought he could make out a few stars. Tomorrow, he would give the group a detailed plan for murdering Colonel Perez.

ᕷᕫᕷ

Maria couldn't sleep. She tossed and turned in her sleeping

bag until she was sore. Casey's words disturbed her but she knew he was right. To do what he suggested, however, would mean losing some autonomy over their war efforts. She suspected it would be an American fight, but what could they do? They needed US support but didn't want their war usurped by them.

She tried to calm the clatter in her head by thinking of Jim. Some invisible, unexplainable force drew her to him and its power over her judgement left her trembling. His quiet calm in the midst of the explosion intrigued her and she wanted to know more about this American. She sensed that her feelings were mutual on his part but could she trust him? Like the CIA agent had said, trust no one until they proved they could be trusted. He worked at the government's pleasure, so did that fact mean he harbored government sentiments? Surely not. Hopefully, being an American meant he felt as she did about their fight. She knew that, before their relationship could develop, he would have to prove himself to her and the group. The only thing left was to decide how.

CHAPTER 10

Colonel Perez sat erect in the elegant anteroom to Secretary Fernando Rivas's office. The burgundy velvet chair was a welcome relief after several weeks in the field. Across the room, Rivas's secretary was busy at a typewriter and Perez noticed that the page bore the official seal of the Minister of Defense. While waiting for Rivas to see him, he thought of his rendezvous with Maria later that evening. It would be good to feel her in his arms. Maybe they would dine at the Managua Country Club, although it was not one of her favorites, but he felt the need to be seen by the influential social set.

The door to Rivas's private office opened and the defense minister beckoned Perez to enter. When in the large, opulent office that overlooked the Plaza de la Revolucion, Rivas patted his colonel's shoulder.

"Good to see you, Ramon," Rivas said. "Please excuse the delay. I was on the phone with the president and he wished me to convey his pleasure with your efforts. He has heard the rumors that the US Congress will cut off all aid to the contras and, hopefully, American support for them is waning. Please, sit here."

Rivas indicated a sturdy, leather chair opposite his massive oak desk. He removed a cigar from a cut-crystal ashtray and made a show of lighting it and exhaling in satisfaction. After puffing away for a moment, he looked at Perez and smiled.

"Colonel. Please tell me. How did you find the perpetrators of the Ocotal incident? Our reports from the airbase commander indicate that you called for a helicopter strike on the insurgents. Is this true?"

Perez swelled with pride as he related the details of the campaign. Another contra group annihilated. "It was easy, Mr. Secretary. Just a matter of seizing a few peasants and making them talk. After that, finding them didn't take long. You say the president is pleased?"

He knew this story was only a half-truth for, in fact, they had responded to gunfire heard while moving northward.

Rivas fingered his cigar and shuffled through a pile of papers on his desk. "The president is always pleased when things go well. I myself do not condone the senseless execution of innocent peasants, however, though your mission was a small one in an ever-enlarging war, I wish to relay the president's regards and congratulations."

Perez sensed that Rivas wanted to discuss something besides the mission, so he waited for the secretary to broach the topic. For the time being, the man was content to praise him.

"As I said, your work in the field has not gone unnoticed, Colonel," Rivas said. "The president hopes you can be trusted implicitly. Is that true?"

"I hope my allegiance to Nicaragua is unquestioned, Mr. Secretary." Perez felt beads of perspiration form on the back of his neck. Something was brewing and the defense minister's speech had abruptly slowed to a measured rhythm, his tone more somber. "My loyalty to the president and the National Directorate is unwavering. I hope that fact is readily appreciated by you and our president."

"Of course. I just wanted to begin by impressing upon you the importance of your next assignment."

Rivas puffed on his cigar and fumbled with a stack of manila folders scattered on his desk until he found the one he wanted. Opening the file, he passed it to Perez, who opened it and studied the contents. The first page contained a photograph of a man. "You have heard of the contra commander, Carlos Mendoza?" Rivas said.

Perez nodded. "He has been a thorn in our side for a long time, Mr. Secretary. I understand he sits in El Chipote these days. Has he talked?"

"Hardly. He is no longer in the prison. He escaped while you were in the mountains. A man, whose identity is presently unknown, but probably CIA, walked into El Chipote with forged papers and identification and managed to get him released. He had faked papers from my own office. The insolence! Of course, the imbecile sergeant who allowed this catastrophe now sits in the cell Mendoza once occupied. This man, Carlos, is back in the jungles, most likely planning a diabolical plot to blow up the president's personal residence or some such nonsense. He must be eliminated, Colonel. That is your next assignment."

"You think they would have the *cajones* to try and kill the president?"

"You have been in the sun too long, Ramon, if you believe that they would not make such an attempt," Rivas said. "But it was just a figure of speech. The president doesn't want to take any unnecessary chances with this peckerhead."

Perez thumbed through the file and handed it back to Rivas. He was troubled, not with the assignment for he could handle it, but it would mean another month or more away from Maria. Weeks without air-conditioning. He was getting far too old to be running around the jungles looking for guerrillas and, at times such as this, he longed for the days when he was a mere corporal without the responsibilities or pressures of command.

"Do you have an idea where I should start looking?"

"He is known to frequent the village of Pueblo Salto, so you will be familiar with the area since it is close to your latest victory. In all likelihood, he has a camp in Honduras that he thinks provides him and his guerrillas a degree of safety. I cannot order you into Honduras, Colonel, but you may use your own discretion in pursuing him. Just don't report that you ventured across the border. I don't want to know. But wherever he is killed it will be in Nicaragua, is that clear? Good. Inquire at the Café Central and go from there. He shouldn't be too hard to find. Be careful my good friend, the man has known CIA contacts."

"How did we come by this information?"

Rivas scratched the scar on his cheek and stroked his mustache, as if trying to decide whether to take Perez fully into his confidence. After a moment, he spoke.

"We have an agent in the area, a person who has kept us posted at every turn. We know the CIA is aiding the contras and the man who freed this Mendoza jackal must be one of their operatives. We also know this particular group is planning something big. What it is, we do not know, at present. We presume it will be attempted here in Managua, so they must be stopped at all costs. Your promotion to general may depend upon your success."

"I will do my best, Mr. Secretary. That is all I *can* do."

"And remember, secrecy is our most important ally. Other than your Captain Salazar, trust no one, not even your men. Tell them only what is necessary and watch them closely. The contras could have learned a lesson or two in counter-intelligence methods themselves."

Rivas stood and Perez followed suit. He saluted the secretary then the two men shook hands.

"Good luck and good hunting," Rivas said.

He closed the door and Perez hurried to his waiting Mercedes.

"Home," he said to the driver.

He would relax and enjoy a hot bath before meeting Maria later in the evening.

᭐᭐᭐

Slater paused to wipe the sweat from his forehead. He had hiked up a long ridge-line and now found himself in a ravine somewhere near Honduras. Alberto had brought word to Slater that Maria wanted him to come to their base camp. He didn't know why, just come as soon as he could. After Slater released his students from class, Alberto handed him a map with directions, apologizing for not being able to guide Slater because he needed to visit his family in Managua. Keep his going secret, Alberto said, and leave his identification behind.

Slater was up early and on the way before sunrise. The village was empty and quiet. The single streetlamp at the corner cast a soft, hazy light, but other than the occasional dog or pig roaming the street, San Rafael was dark and deserted.

Struggling to read the map in the muted dawn, his mind was a jumble of disquieting thoughts. Why had Maria summoned him? Why couldn't she have met him at the café? Were she and her friends in some kind of trouble? The thought struck him that this contra business was a deadly affair and here he was, alone, in known guerrilla territory. If government forces or another contra group confronted him, without his identification, he could be in serious trouble. His pulse quickened.

The trail meandered through dense underbrush and Slater had to hack his way through with his machete. Mahogany trees, rubber trees, acacia, and balsams pushed their crooked arms toward him, while vines and roots from myrtles and begonias snared his feet. Ravines, steep inclines and descents, and stretches of rough ground interspersed with banks of thick mud. Late in the morning, he stumbled upon a shack and caught a glimpse of a fire burning on the ground. No electricity up here. He crouched behind a felled tree and waited, searching for signs of life at the shack.

Was he in Honduras or not? Too bad Alberto had not been able to guide him. The shack was in a small clearing and had walls of deteriorated lumber and a roof of rusted tin. One small window was beside a closed door. There was no sign of life in or around the shack. The small fire had burned to a mound of white coals and a dented coffee pot sat nestled in the ashes. Overhead, birds called to each other and the occasional monkey screeched a warning. Slater's pulse quickened, hoping no one knew of his presence. He waited behind the tree for a long while, intending to spot a farmer or soldier, but saw no one. Satisfied that he was alone, Slater continued up the narrow path.

Through the foliage, he saw a half-moon hanging low in

the sky and noticed the dark clouds forming around it. The way was difficult to follow in the dim light so he retrieved his flashlight. It cast an eerie beam through the jungle. The many twists and turns of the trail made knowing directions impossible while the roots and vines of the jungle floor made walking hazardous. It seemed to him he was on some sort of animal trail and wondered what he would do if he stumbled onto a jaguar. How in the hell did these contras find their way? The answer belied him. He knew they patrolled this area. If anyone stopped him, would they believe he was simply a schoolteacher? He uttered a silent prayer and pushed on.

The ill-defined trail forked. Slater stopped to rest and consulted the map. The rising sun began to push through the clouds and the temperature on the jungle's floor rose, the dew forming a vapor, causing droplets to collect on the large leaves of unidentified plants. It was going to be another hot day. He folded the map and returned it to his shirt pocket.

He stopped short.

A noise in the distance.

Somewhere in the jungle, something or someone was moving about. He jumped behind a palm tree, heart in his throat, breathing difficult.

The rustling of vegetation grew louder. *What a place to get caught by Sandinistas*, he thought and tightened his grip on his machete. A myriad of thoughts swirled through his mind. Why had he come here in the first place? Why couldn't Maria have come to San Rafael? If only he had a pistol. His dry mouth made swallowing impossible. He remembered tales of the jungle jaguar, the animal most feared by the farmers. They said the animal was so cunning he could be upon an unsuspecting person before he had a chance to defend himself. Slater nestled himself deep into the undergrowth as the sound came nearer.

Straining to hear, he noticed the rustling didn't sound human, just a low, scuffling noise.

What the hell was he doing in this impassable brush? The thought of his stupidity irritated him while he knelt, waiting.

Waiting.

Then he saw it. A pig! A goddamned pig, for Christ's sake. Slater stood, legs trembling, laughed, then cursed the animal when it crossed his path and continued to graze, seemingly oblivious to his presence. *I almost killed a pig with my machete.* He took a deep breath. Everywhere he looked, the jungle appeared the same. *Shit, have I missed a turn? There's brush to my sides, brush to my rear, brush all around. Where the hell am I?*

In his fear, he had lost the path. A new fear arose in his gut, the fear of being totally lost. He unfolded the map and studied the landmarks scribbled in Alberto's scrawl. Nothing made sense. He ought to be near a small clearing and, in the distance, he saw an area devoid of trees. Relaxing somewhat, he hacked his way to the clearing and, as he was about done, stepped into a deep mud hole.

"Shit!" His cry echoed through the jungle and sent a family of monkeys into a screeching frenzy. They disappeared, leaving him in silence.

His leg was deep in the mud up to his groin and, in a frantic attempt to free himself, he twisted his other foot at an odd angle. A bolt of pain shot to his waist—large beads of sweat formed on his face. While he struggled to free himself, insects buzzed his head, landing and biting. Pushing the pain away, Slater shoved both hands deep into the mud, grabbed his foot, and managed to work it free. The suction effect from the mud hampered his progress, but after ten minutes of grueling work, he freed his leg. He sat at the edge of the mud hole gulping air and drank most of the water in his canteen. A large, black and green snake crawled toward him and he chopped it in half with his machete. He hated those bastards—he hated snakes, especially the dreaded *quatro naris*. He didn't know what kind of snake it was, probably a pit viper of some kind with four *pits*. He had seen a farmer who was bitten by one and, in minutes, the man was bleeding from his nose and mouth. Only prompt treatment with anti-venom saved the man's life. Those damned pests were the main reason Slater never ventured far into the jungle.

His bloody hands felt as if they were on fire. His clothes

were drenched in stinking mud and sweat while his arms and shoulders ached from the effort to get as far as he had. Slater stood and hobbled to the clearing where he again consulted the map. Focusing through the pain that racked his body, he noticed a small stream that ran northward and he found it without difficulty. Satisfied he was no longer lost, he sat and rested. He drank what was left of his water while studying the surrounding terrain. It all looked depressingly similar. The jungle's canopy blocked most of the sunlight and what little there was caused deep shadows in the underbrush.

It was strange, being alone in this area. If the contra camp was nearby, he couldn't imagine living in a place such as this. There were no buildings anywhere and no smoke from a fire. His heart sank at the thought of making the journey back to San Rafael.

The sky darkened and it started to rain. He took shelter under a large, burned-out tree trunk, but it afforded little protection and soon he was soaked to the skin. The only good thing was that the rain washed the mud from his clothes. He turned his baseball cap around so the water ran over the bill and down the back of his shirt collar. He dug a shallow pit, piled leaves around his body to ward off the chill. The sun had disappeared completely and, with it, the afternoon light faded fast. He tried to read the map but it was useless, in spite of the small light from his flashlight. His thoughts were a blur and it was difficult to concentrate. He realized he could not make it to Maria's camp—he couldn't find the way. He knew he had to start back soon but decided to wait and see if the rain would end. He settled back against the tree and dozed.

He and Maria were in his bed. Her slender, brown body was on top of his and her erect nipples danced in his face. After the love making, he held her in the crook of his arm and studied her taut muscles. Asleep, she seemed at peace. Her soft facial features were in stark contrast to the rippled muscles of her arms and back. Her mouth, curled at the ends, together with her tousled hair, imparted an impish look. What was to become of them? It was no longer a choice for him whether he wanted to be with her, his world had been turned

on its ear since he met her. Her beauty, coupled with her passion for the contra cause, made her irresistible.

He awoke with a start.

Another noise.

This time he recognized the sound of someone walking. He
rolled onto his stomach and peered through the undergrowth.
The rain had stopped and the fog was lifting. In the distance,
he could make out three men in camouflaged uniforms and
two of them had automatic machine-guns slung over their
shoulders. A third marched ahead, using a machete to clear the
way.

Slater pressed his body deeper into the jungle floor and
watched the trio tramp closer. He fought the stinging in his
eyes for a clearer look. They walked with a steady gait as if
they knew where they were going. One of them was a woman.
He gripped his machete and eased it out of its sheath. The trio
kept coming, conversing in hushed tones. Were they contras or
Sandinistas? When they were within a few meters, he recognized the woman.

"Maria!" Slater jumped to his feet in full view of them.
"Maria, what the hell?"

Maria waved and when they were nearer, Slater recognized
Carlos and Luis. They waved and laughed.

"The sight of you," Maria said. "Just look at you. What in
the world have you been doing? Digging a foxhole?"

Slater shook Carlos's hand and Luis offered him a cigarette.

"Son-of-a-bitch," Slater said. "Where the hell am I? And
what are the three of you doing here?"

"Hold on, Jim," Carlos said, holding up a hand. "This is
going to piss you off so you better hear it sitting down. We—"

Slater wiped the mud off the blade of his machete. "Hear
what?"

"Jim," Maria said, "this you're not going to like, but we
had to know for sure."

"Know what for sure?" Slater said, staring at the three of
them.

Maria sighed and ran a hand through her tousled hair.

"This was a test to see if we could trust you. We had to know if you would lead the Sandinistas here. I'm sorry but we had to find out for sure. We didn't know. So Carlos and Luis devised this little test. You passed with it flying colors. I needed to know for myself as well. I hope you understand."

Slater felt as if the wind had been knocked out of his lungs. "You mean to tell me that I have been slogging around this goddamned jungle all day just to satisfy your morbid curiosity? Maria, you know my views on this war."

For a moment, the four of them stood there in the fading, afternoon light without saying anything further. Then Slater laughed and soon the others joined him. He hugged Maria and kissed her.

"I presume that since I passed the test I can kiss you in front of Carlos?" Slater said.

"Hey, *amigo*," he said. "I have brought you a nice beer for your troubles."

Carlos reached into his backpack, pulled out four bottles of beer, and passed them around. "Let us drink then head to our headquarters," he said.

CHAPTER 11

Deep within the Las Vegas salient, a peninsula of Honduras that juts into Nicaragua near the village of Jalapa, the three contras led Slater to a jeep that was parked on a deserted, dirt road. The border, Carlos explained, was only a few kilometers to the southeast. They followed a crooked trail to an abandoned bean field where a cluster of huts stood at its edge. A muddy mist began again and it splattered the jeep with large drops.

"I can feel their presence," Carlos said over the whine of the jeep's motor. He glanced about, concentrating.

"Who?" Slater said.

"Sandinistas. They prowl this area looking for easy targets, people like us."

"Aren't we in Honduras?" Slater said.

Carlos was intent on avoiding two deep ruts in the road and seemed not to hear.

Luis answered. "We are, but it doesn't stop the Nicaraguan Army. If they drag us back to Nicaragua, who is to say we were captured in Honduras? They would throw us in El Chipote and no one would hear our story. They hunt us down like dogs and when they catch us—" Luis stopped short and shot a glance at Maria.

"When they catch you they put you in prison. For how long?" Slater prompted.

Carlos raised a hand just as Luis opened his mouth. "The

cells at El Chipote are no bigger than a phone booth. One has to stand continuously, as there is no room to sit or lie down. Then, after a few days, they torture us, usually by castration. Sometimes then, they kill us. Sometimes they send our heads to our families."

"I thought they disavowed the old Somoza tactics," Slater said.

"Only publicly," Carlos retorted. "Poor peasants don't stand much of a chance with them."

Slater gulped and stared into the mist. The four of them traveled in silence for a while, bouncing and bobbing in the jeep.

"Be prepared," Maria told Slater. "If we see any, we'll kill them."

Carlos steered around a mud hole and they continued toward the camp. They drove past another row of wooden shacks then turned onto a convoluted path that wound through a pig pasture and ended at a tall, barbed-wire fence. A lone sentry stood in front of the gate. Carlos waved and the man opened the gate to allow them entry. "No one knows of this place," he said as the guard closed the gate behind them. "We have sentries posted every fifty meters."

They drove beyond what looked like the camp's munitions depot and Slater caught a glimpse of their weapons. Outside a rustic hut, there was a shoulder-high stack of rusty AK-47s. Captured, most likely. There were wooden cases stacked in rows and he was able to make out the stenciled label. American-made M79 grenade launcher, shells for the M2 or M224 mortar, and boxes of fragmentation grenades.

The mist brought with it an afternoon chill, causing Slater to wish he had his sweater from home.

After Carlos parked the jeep in front of a dilapidated shack, he led the group through a screen door and waved at Alberto and Raoul who were cooking in a makeshift kitchen. Slater noticed that Casey reclined in a hammock and appeared to be sleeping. From the kitchen, Raoul looked up and greeted them.

"Supper," he said. "One of Alberto's favorites, wild turkey and *gallo pinto*."

"Fantastic," Maria said and pushed Slater to a small, round table in the center of the room. "All we have to drink up here is *chicha*. I hope that is satisfactory, Jim?"

Slater nodded and Alberto placed large pieces of the bird on the table as the group gathered around in primitive chairs. Casey awoke, joined them, and nodded to Slater.

"Sorry about the deception," Raoul said. "But we had to know if you were shooting straight with us." He grabbed a turkey leg, bit into it, and wiped the grease from his lips with a dirty shirtsleeve.

"No problem, now that Maria explained the reasons," Slater said. "However, I was beginning to feel like I never would never make it back to San Rafael. It was getting darker and I somehow got turned around, lost. I was sure glad to see you guys come strolling through the jungle. But I admit I was pissed at first."

"We could have been Sandinistas," Maria said. "Your American goose would have been cooked then, for sure."

Everyone laughed. The thought of his rear end ending up like the turkey made for a humorous picture. Slater chewed the tough bird for a while then laughed again.

"Hopefully, the government knows that I am no threat to them and will leave me alone. I teach a school for them, remember? Besides, I'm non-political. I must admit I am inclined of late to hope for the contra cause." He glanced at Maria. "What do the Sandinistas care about a *gringo* like me?"

"Up here in the jungle, no one would believe you," Carlos said between mouthfuls. He sipped his glass of *chicha*. "Here, all *gringos* are CIA spies, Jim. Don't ever forget that."

"The important thing is that you passed our little test and we can now proceed with more important matters," Raoul said.

"Like I said," Slater repeated, "for a while I was mad as hell, but I guess I really can't blame you. We've only known each other a few weeks. By the way, does the Honduran government know you're here?"

"Well," Carlos said, smiled, and shrugged. "Most likely not. We don't talk with them directly but we've never hidden the fact that we're here, either. They have never come looking for us. As you can see, this is a pretty remote area."

"I'll say," Slater said.

The group finished their meal and Alberto tossed the turkey's carcass out the back door where two noisy pigs attacked it. Carlos and Luis lit cigarettes while Maria cleared the table of the dishes. They settled back into their chairs and hammocks and Slater waited until all had assembled in the small hut, then stood.

"I want all of you know that I want to be your friend. Basically, I'm here because of Maria, but you all probably know that. I'm not a contra and I wish to remain neutral. I'm not sure if I even want to know what your plans are. That way I won't have to lie to anyone who might ask. For now, though, please understand that I'm just a guy who likes a woman who happens to be a contra."

He noticed Maria smiling and nodding. Even in her camouflaged fatigues, she was beautiful.

"We know, Jim," she said. "Each of us hoped we could trust you and each of us understands your desire to stay out of the war. Your work at the San Rafael school is extremely important and your dedication has touched us deeply. The farmers of the area have accepted you and have entrusted their children to your care. It is such an honor for you but even more, it is an honor for each of us to know you. Even though you are not a contra, Jim, you are a fine *gringo*."

The group nodded in agreement when Maria finished and sat, face flushing from her speech.

"Casey and I have devised a plan to strike a serious blow to the National Directorate," Carlos said. "It was his idea and I agree that we should attempt it." He motioned to Casey who sat upright in his hammock while Carlos continued. "It will be dangerous and we will need luck on our side, but if we succeed it will plunge a dagger into the heart of the government."

Carlos sat back in his chair and waited for Casey to discuss his plan. He poured himself another *chicha* and sipped it methodically as Casey began.

"The plot is simple. Kill Colonel Ramon Perez."

"Shit, you're kidding!" Maria said. "Are you crazy? How?" Casey silenced her outburst with a raised hand.

"Hear me out, first. It shouldn't be that hard to accomplish. And you, Maria, are in a perfect position to do it."

"Me?" Her voice sounded tentative and nervous to Slater. Just moments earlier, her eyes sparkled, now they were squinting and sober.

"Yes," Casey said. "You've been spying on the man for months now. You have provided Carlos and the others much-needed information about the government's plans. The man calls upon you at your Managua apartment so you can handle this job easily. You're the logical candidate."

Slater sat up straight and focused his attention on what Casey was saying, not believing what he heard. Maria and Perez? He felt the blood drain from his head. What was this about an apartment where he visited her? His mind spun as he tried to put it together. Was Maria sleeping with Perez? Was that it? A hot anger welled from deep inside as he contemplated the possibility.

If that was the case, it was getting stickier—for they were talking of putting Maria's life in jeopardy, a lot more so than the dangers of walking through the jungle with Sandinistas lurking about. Surely she wouldn't accept this absurd task, whatever it is, especially now that their relationship was beginning to blossom. He glanced at her and she quickly directed her gaze at the floor.

Casey lit a cigarette and allowed the gist of his plan to settle. "You're the logical candidate because you have the access," he said. "All you will have to do is slip him a poisoned drink and walk out the door. He will be dead before you reach the street."

"What kind of poison," Alberto said.

"Just poison," Casey said, his mouth turned into a wry grin. "A special CIA concoction."

"Cyanide and rat poison?" Alberto pressed.

"Just poison, Alberto. I have the stuff with me. Maria, what kind of liquor does Perez prefer?"

Maria looked up from her boots and ran a hand through her

hair. She shot a quick glance at Slater who didn't return the look.

"Napoleon brandy," she said. "He can't get it very often. He loves the stuff. It's very expensive. When Minister of Defense Francisco Rivas travels outside the country, Perez has him bring back a bottle or two. That's all he has talked about for the past weeks."

"Gentlemen," Casey said, "if we can obtain a bottle of Napoleon brandy I'll put my poison it. Maria, here, can take it to her apartment and give it to Perez the next time he visits. Once he has ingested the brandy she can leave the apartment and we'll pick her up. The colonel will be dead before we leave Managua."

"There will be a celebration, to be sure," Luis said. "The man is a butcher. It will be good that he is gone."

Carlos spoke.

"How about it, Maria? What do you think? Can you do it?"

Slater sat dumbfounded. Was he going to sit quietly by and allow Maria to carry out this insane plot? He did not know what to say or how to object and, by the look Maria was giving everyone, she was certainly thinking about doing it.

"I don't know. The man is extremely dangerous and suspicious. If he thought for one instant that I was double-crossing him, he would kill me without hesitation." She snapped her fingers to indicate how quick she would die.

"You're our only hope," Casey said. "If you don't, there is no one else. The best we could hope for is a sniper shot and that's not near as reliable as poisoning. If you don't want to do this, everyone here will understand and not hold it against you. It is dangerous, that is for sure. I understand your reluctance, but how about it?"

"Any other options?" Carlos asked the group. "Say a car bomb?"

"A car bomb might be a good choice," Casey said, "but rigging his car would pose problems. His chauffeur never leaves the vehicle alone and the man is heavily armed."

Slater wanted to burst into the conversation and denounce the whole affair as ridiculous. His thoughts were still reeling from the first mention of Maria and Perez together. Did he hear correctly? Had she pried secrets from him in exchange for sex? He didn't want to believe it.

Maria thought for a long moment then stood and paced the hut. Slater's heart sank as she pondered her response, for he knew what she would say. Slater thought about interjecting something but decided against it, knowing it had to be Maria's decision. God, now he was witnessing a plan to assassinate a government leader, and at an enormous risk to Maria. So much for his resolve to remain neutral.

"All right," Maria said and she looked at Slater. Her eyes pleaded for understanding. Slater thought he could see a tear on her cheek. "When can you get the brandy? Perez probably is at my apartment this very minute and angry because I'm not there. I'll see him tomorrow night. Is that too soon? The sooner the better."

"As difficult as it might be, I think I can get a bottle in Managua," Casey said. "I can do that tomorrow and give it to you in the afternoon. I will already have injected the poison into it, so be sure, and I repeat, be sure that you do not drink it yourself. Stall, make up some excuse, but get Perez to drink alone. A few sips are all that is required. We can meet at my hotel room and I'll give you the bottle there. Sound acceptable?"

"Yes," Maria said. "Now I'm tired and want to sleep. Goodnight all."

She motioned for Slater to follow her outside and, in the dark shadow of the hut, put her arms around him. The mist had stopped and the air smelled of fresh earth, loamy and pungent.

After she kissed him, Slater cupped her chin in his hand.

"Please, Jim. No sermons. This is something I must do. What I did before I met you, well, what can I say? But things are different now—we have each other. Once this thing with Perez is done I will be free of him forever."

"I'm not sure I can understand, but I will worry about you. The jealous part of me can't understand why you would let Perez even touch you, let alone anything else. Aren't you carrying this contra stuff a little too far? Like I said earlier, I wish

I didn't know what was going down. Maria, if something happens to you—I don't—Promise me—"

"Don't, Jim, please. I was spying on Perez long before I met you. We both knew that it was a crazy idea to get involved with each other. Now we must be adult enough to carry on."

"You aren't spying, you're sleeping with the bastard. Maria, how could you?"

Maria had tears in her eyes. "It's part of the fight, Jim."

"But I don't want to be a part of any fight," Slater said. "I just want you. Without this crazy war, if possible."

"You should know that's impossible right now. I'm in this whether I want to be or not. I've come too far to abandon my friends or what I believe in. Maybe, in some small way I can pay the Sandinistas back for what they did to my parents."

"I don't want to lose you, Maria. I've had all the bloodshed I can handle."

"I know. It's difficult. If you can't accept my life as it is at the present, then maybe we should end our relationship now, before it goes any further."

The matter-of-factness in her voice startled Slater. He couldn't bear to face the future without her. Anger at himself, the war, the improbability of their relationship thriving, and at Maria's past life with Perez gnawed at his gut, pumping bile into his throat.

They walked together until Maria stopped in front of a square, wooden hut. She turned and took Slater in her arms. "This is where I sleep. Promise me that when the morning comes, you will forgive me for putting the insurgency ahead of our relationship. Right now, I cannot do otherwise."

"Let me sleep with you tonight, Maria. To know you at least once before something dreadful happens. I love you."

"Shh. Don't say that. Not yet, anyway. And no, you cannot stay with me. I'm afraid I would lose my resolve and drop out of the contra effort altogether. Please don't ask it of me, Jim. If you do, I will give in, and I wouldn't be able to live with myself."

With a brief kiss on his cheek, she disappeared into the hut, leaving Slater alone in the darkness pondering her words. His body ached every time she was near. He prayed that Maria would still be alive at the end of the week.

ళఠళ

Colonel Perez rapped on Maria's apartment door and waited but no one answered. He knocked again, this time louder than before and, still, the door did not open. He paced the hallway, pondering what to do next. Should he go inside and wait for her? He knew she would be angry and indignant at such a confrontation. Instead, he would just take a few minutes to look around the apartment. What if she had been unfaithful to him?

He found his key, unlocked the door, and let himself into the darkened living room. Perez switched on a light that sat on a bamboo table at the end of a brocaded sofa, ambled about the room, and inspected the contents of the drawers of her desk, which sat along the far wall of the apartment. A bright, Oriental rug woven with a flower design covered the wooden floor and muffled his steps. He entered Maria's bedroom and searched through the clothes in her closet. He didn't know what he was looking for and hoped he would find nothing.

He drew a much-needed strength from Maria, which enabled him to carry out the duties of his command. She was correct in her assertions that the insurgents were fundamentally like him, Nicaraguans who had long suffered at the hands of dictators. He could have easily become a contra, had it not been for his friendship with Deputy Rivas. In his quiet moments alone, he knew the peasants had legitimate concerns but if they were afforded victory, he would lose everything—his house, his title, his pension. Maria never discussed her loyalties, no matter how he tried to pry them out of her, but it did not matter, as long as she continued to see him and pleasure him.

He rummaged through her dresser and found only the silk and satin nightgowns he had purchased. The room smelled of lavender perfume and for a moment he was transported back to the last time he was in her bed. Too bad she wasn't here now, waiting for him to arrive. Tomorrow night would be different.

He returned to the living room, picked up the phone, and dialed a number. Salazar's clerk answered.

"Tell Captain Salazar that Colonel Perez wishes to speak with him," Perez said in his most formal tone. He waited for Salazar to come to the line.

"Captain," Perez said after listening to Salazar's salutation, "please have the men ready tomorrow at midnight. We move against the contras to find that dog, Mendoza. I will eat dinner at the club tomorrow evening, then change clothes and report to the compound. We will move north promptly at twelve. Understand?"

After hanging up, Perez took one final look around the apartment and left. Tomorrow, tomorrow. Now he had to make some excuse to his wife for returning home so early. Maybe she would believe that the president had been especially short-winded.

CHAPTER 12

The following day, Casey strolled through the garden of the Intercontinental Hotel past the bougainvillea-lined hourglass swimming pool and into the lobby. The attendant behind the registration desk waved to him.

"Mr. Smith," the mustached man said with a wave.

"Yes," Casey said. He eased his large elbows onto the black, marble counter and waited.

"*Senor,* while you were out, two men asked for you. They said they were in Nicaragua on business and were working a deal with you. I gave them your room number and they went upstairs. That was yesterday. I haven't seen them since and they did not leave a message."

Casey's senses were now on full alert. "Were they Nicaraguan?"

"I don't think so, *senor.* They could have been but I think they were Honduran or Mexican, although I could be mistaken."

Casey was annoyed with the attendant's seeming lack of discretion. "Did you allow them into my room?"

"Oh no, sir, I would never do such a thing. I would be fired immediately."

Casey bolted up the stairs to his room and stood outside the door studying it. He listened for movement inside but heard nothing. He gripped the door handle and turned it. Relieved at finding the door still locked, he opened it with his key wide enough to peer inside. The room was empty but a horrible mess greeted him. The room was in shambles—torn apart with the contents of his dresser strewn on the floor. His suitcases were open and his clothes scattered everywhere. He picked his way around the clutter and found the bedroom in the same condition. The bed had been torn apart and there were deep gashes in the mattress, its stuffing on the floor.

Casey followed basic Company procedures formulated over decades of covert operations around the world. Surely, the two men wouldn't think him as careless as to leave anything incriminating lying around. He checked the radio and found it was safe where he had hidden it. Good. It had been a stroke of genius fashioning the small compartment under the bar. He had cut a rectangular hole in the wall, placed the radio in the cavity, and taped the piece back into place. Crude, but the intruders had overlooked it. He sat on the bed and tried to figure the *why* and *who* of it. Was his cover blown—or was this a simple burglary? He doubted the latter and, to his knowledge, no one knew he was in the country. In fact, his double was in Costa Rica at this very moment, continuing the façade. So who were the intruders? Did they know who he was and, if so, how had they found out? How had they managed to get into his room? Had the Sandinistas been able to trace him from El Chipote back to the hotel? The link was the prison but he couldn't figure out how they managed to trace him here. It was possible that someone had seen him and Carlos duck in the back entrance—seen the two of them together. It was the only way his cover could have been blown. Someone must have recognized Carlos and seen them together. If they knew who he was, he didn't have much time. Thoughts ricocheted in his head while he struggled for options. The poison, had they found it? He jumped up from the bed and ran into the bathroom where he unscrewed the sink trap. He found the thin wire and pulled an amber, glass bottle from the drain. Holding the bottle up to the light, he inspected its contents. Good, it had not been discovered.

Casey rang the front desk and told them about the room. The desk clerk offered to move him to a different floor so Casey agreed. He told the clerk that he had to go out and would leave his suitcase inside the door and they could move him at any time. He would be out until late.

He put on his horn-rimmed sunglasses, checked his pistol, and ventured onto Managua's streets in search of the Napoleon brandy. Time was now of the essence and he felt the pressure to buy Perez's liquor and get it to Maria. Casey inquired at the local grocers and markets around the hotel if they carried the liquor but was unsuccessful. He passed the broken remains of Managua's Roman Catholic Cathedral and noticed the shrubbery that grew through cracks in the floor. Most of what remained of the cathedral was without its roof and marble columns stood as solitary reminders of a past glory. Sagging roof beams cast eerie shadows into the few remaining rooms and acacia tentacles enveloped the shattered altar. Statues of saints were headless and armless. While he gazed at the church, he glimpsed a naked child run through the rubble and disappear. There must be families of squatters who had set up crude living quarters here.

Managua was a devastated city. Between the earthquake years earlier and the revolution, it was as if it had suffered a firestorm. Heaps of debris marked the locations of what was once a hardware store, a hotel, or a restaurant. He wiped the sweat from his brow and continued his search for the brandy.

He passed the San Judas slum, a combative neighborhood in central Managua. Numerous people gathered on the streets and were chanting slogans.

"Revolution or death!"

"Imperialism will never turn us back!"

"Traitors!"

The group appeared to be university students and they held signs with red letters, demanding food and justice. While men held clenched fists into the heavy air and continued their chants, Casey ducked down a narrow street to avoid being seen. The rumble of heavy trucks and a siren pierced the air. A convoy of military vehicles careened down the street and came to a halt in front of the crowd.

He peered from around the corner as uniformed soldiers

poured out of the trucks and beat the demonstrators with heavy sticks. Women and children were knocked to the ground by well-aimed blows to their heads and shoulders. Their screams echoed throughout the *barrio* but they did not deter the soldiers, who continued to flail away. When a demonstrator fell to the street, the soldiers dragged him or her to the rear of a canvas-covered truck and threw them into it. The scene was surreal, an unwarranted attack on unsuspecting citizens.

Several of the demonstrators managed to escape the soldier's fury but by the time order had been restored most of the mob were shackled and secured in government trucks. Before leaving the *barrio*, the soldiers placed barricades across the street and stationed guards at each corner. Probably going to stop anyone who tried to enter.

After much walking and searching, Casey found the bottle of brandy and returned to the Intercontinental. He was surprised to see Alberto waiting for him in the lobby.

"What are you doing here, Alberto?" Casey grabbed the contra's arm and led him around a corner where they had privacy. "I thought I wasn't going to see you yet. Is everything all right?"

"Cobra is not to worry," Alberto said, a wry smile on his lips. "I am in town to see my family, that is all."

"It is not good for me to be seen with you. You should know better."

"I just wanted to make sure you found the brandy. Carlos sent me ahead to check."

The explanation didn't sound like Carlos but Casey decided not to press the issue. Not in the hotel lobby, anyway. He watched Alberto leave and disappear around a corner. It was odd, his curiosity about the brandy.

ⲉⲟⲉⲟ

Maria took a long bath and allowed the hot water to soothe her aching muscles. Worry over the night's mission had produced a tight knot in her neck and back but now the heat of her bath eased the tension in her throbbing shoulders. She poured a handful of bath oil into the water and rubbed it into her skin. It smelled like lavender, Perez's favorite.

Late in the afternoon, she had contacted Casey at the Intercontinental and returned to her apartment with the poisoned brandy. The agent again warned her against drinking any of it. "Don't even put a drop in your mouth or on your lips," he had cautioned.

Whatever he had used for a poison, she hoped it was good enough to kill Perez for she was tired of playing the charade with him, pretending to like his clumsy lovemaking and forcing herself to act as though she enjoyed his bourgeois ranting.

She reclined in the tub and allowed her thoughts to turn to Jim. How she missed him already. Fate was playing a cruel joke to have brought them together only to cast them into an impossible situation where there could be no victory, only heartache. It seemed they were destined for sorrow, no matter how the war ended. Long ago, she had given up her life for dead, not looking beyond the next contra mission, realizing she would never live to see either success or failure. Then Jim Slater waltzed into her life and everything changed. Feelings of hope and a desire to live returned. Because of him, she found herself looking toward the future, one she had not believed possible until a few weeks ago. She thought she had buried hope deep enough, that it would never surface, but here in such a short period of time, she found herself entertaining possibilities of a new day.

She allowed the warm water to take her away from the stress and bloodshed to a vision of a possible future. The war was over. She and Slater were in the United States. They drove along a beautiful, tree-lined country lane, heading into rural New England to meet his mother. A warm, summer day engulfed them while they laughed and remembered the faraway war in Nicaragua. The counter-revolution no longer mattered—her dreams were a reality. She had forgotten the stench of the jungle and her filthy clothes, forgotten the fear of dying. Julio sat behind them telling a joke, as was his custom. He was very much alive. Slater put an arm around her and they listened to Latin music on the radio. The day was perfect—she was content.

The light in her apartment was fading when Maria awoke in the bathtub. She dried herself with a Turkish towel then sat at her bedroom table to fix her hair. She toweled it dry and brushed it until it shined. After applying makeup, she wound her hair into a small bun, fixed it with a diamond clasp, then slipped into her floor-length, emerald dress. With her thoughts still on Jim, she went into the living room.

The bottle of Napoleon brandy sat on the bar where she had placed it. She took it in her hand and inspected it. It looked like any other bottle of brandy Perez had consumed many times before. She could not tell it had been tampered with but fear, mingled with worry, clouded her thoughts, nonetheless. Could she go through with it? She was aware how Carlos and the others were counting on her, and the responsibility of the night weighed heavy on her mind, as she returned the bottle to the bar. She took a soft towel and polished the two snifters to remove any blemish that might detract from their elegance or arouse Perez's suspicion.

How quickly would the poison work, she wondered? Would he die before she could get out of the apartment? Hopefully, he would. She had to make sure he was dead before leaving. Would it be ugly? She had killed before but from a distance. Tonight would be different. She had never watched someone die up close. Would he struggle? Would he scream or rave?

Maria broke the seal on the bottle of brandy, careful not to get any of the liquid on her fingers. She stared at the lethal bottle and tried to imagine Perez's excitement when she showed it to him. He would laugh and praise her for her ingenuity then she would give him a glass and toast his successes in the jungle.

She was standing before the mirror in her bedroom when she heard a soft knock at the door. She walked into the living room, took a deep breath, and opened it.

Colonel Perez stood silent for a moment, a broad smile on his thick lips.

"Good evening, my dear. You look absolutely ravishing. What that dress does to my aging bones."

Maria stepped back and listened while Perez informed her they would be dining at the Managua Country Club before returning for an after-dinner drink. She picked up her mink stole, took Perez's arm, and followed him outside.

CHAPTER 13

E nsconced in his new hotel room, Casey had given the bottle of brandy to Maria and, after she left, showered and changed. He returned to the café near the Plaza Espana and noticed that it was open for business. Apparently, the explosion had not done extensive damage so he ate what the menu called steak and washed it down with a beer. Loud music filtered through the café and the crowd gathered around the pool table was the same as the other night. Through the smoky haze, he studied the room in the rear and noticed another card game in progress. He paid for his dinner, took a short walk to stretch his legs, and returned to his room to await word from Maria. Alberto was to rush her to the camp then Carlos would drive back to the Intercontinental. Casey sat for a while, thinking, then pulled the transmitter from under the bar. He keyed the microphone.

"Mother, this is Cobra. Mother, this is Cobra. Do you read?"

The radio was silent for a minute then crackled.

"This is Mother. Go ahead."

"Nearing touchdown. Quarterback will score tonight. Repeat, touchdown tonight."

"Affirmative, Cobra. Good luck. Contact your mother when game is over. Out."

The transmission completed, Casey returned the radio to its hiding place and poured himself three fingers of the scotch he purchased along with the brandy. He hoped Maria would carry out her assignment with professional shrewdness. She seemed to possess a positive attitude and boldness of action, but anything could happen. One thing he had learned from years of teaching Company recruits was that more often than not, a bold and brash position put the enemy off guard and resulted in an easy kill. But there could always be complications, something could go wrong and leave Maria dead in her apartment. After she was safely out of Managua, he would arrange for a C-47 airdrop of supplies. Since their last inventory of supplies, Carlos discovered they were dangerously low on ammunition so the plane was ready to leave Costa Rica when Casey gave the word.

The thought struck him that the demonstrators he had seen during the day were now in El Chipote prison cells being interrogated by their captors. The reports he had seen detailed the fact that the prison held over two thousand inmates, who were confined to small cells and deprived of food and water, in addition to being tortured. However, the arrest of fifty people didn't appear to slow the insurgency's resolve—for, on his way back to the hotel, another crowd gathered in front of the prison. There were more signs and more chanting. Day by day, the Sandinistas were slowly losing control of their country. He sipped the scotch and opened the balcony doors allowing the delicate, tropical breeze to carry the sounds from the street into his room.

 හිහිහි

Dinner at the Managua Country Club was a blur for Maria. She didn't remember ordering food or drink and spent most of the meal preoccupied with her upcoming task. Perez ordered an elaborate repast and washed it down with an imported white wine. His large girth did not hamper his ability to tango as he pushed her around the dance floor with the nimbleness of an athlete. She feigned enjoyment and allowed the music to push concerns from her mind. Beads of sweat, she noticed, dotted Perez' balding head. At the end of two tangos, he was breathless and begged to sit and rest. She could probably kill him by dancing until his heart gave out. It would make for a grand headline: *Woman jailed in tango death of army colonel.* So far, Perez was not suspicious. Her stomach churned.

Perez finished the wine and signaled their waiter for the check. Maria watched in silence while he handed the man a generous tip. At the Country Club's door, she glanced over her shoulder at all the people dressed in black tie and furs. Furs, for Christ's sake. Even hers was laughable. The goddamned bastards turned the air-conditioning down as low as possible so they could dine formally. After tonight she wouldn't be eating here again, which was disappointing, for the food was really good. The drive to Maria's apartment seemed interminable, as if Perez wanted his driver to wander through Managua's streets before arriving at her apartment. After ordering the driver to pick him up at eleven, he escorted her upstairs and seemed impatient as Maria fumbled with her key. Perez followed her in.

"What would you like a drink, my precious?" she said.

She crossed the room and opened a window that faced the street. Perez pulled off his tie, undid the top two buttons of his shirt, and relaxed on the sofa. Maria retrieved a bucket of ice from the refrigerator.

"Whatever you have, my darling," Perez said.

He seemed preoccupied but she opened the bottle of Napoleon brandy, filled two snifters, and handed one to Perez. Her heart pounded as he sniffed his drink.

"It's a special surprise, sweetheart. Napoleon brandy, your favorite. Tell me what you think of it."

"For me, my pet? How considerate you are to go to all this trouble. But where did you find it?"

"A small shop not far from here, my pet. I was lucky."

Perez fingered the glass and admired its color through the crystal. He stared at Maria through a crooked smile.

Does he know? How could he? Why doesn't he just drink the damn stuff and be done with it?

"I have noticed that you do not seem quite yourself tonight, Maria. Are you feeling ill?"

Maria shook her head and sat with her brandy next to Perez.

"You have been quiet for a long time, I have noticed." Perez moved closer on the sofa and put his hand on her thigh. "What is the trouble?"

"Nothing, my dear. Maybe the food didn't agree with me this evening. I'm fine, really."

Dammit, just drink the brandy. And be quick about it.

Maria pulled away as he inched his hand up her leg.

"See, you pull away. Have I done something to offend you, my precious?"

"No, Ramon, I'm fine. But, tell me. What do you think of the brandy? Is it worth a day's searching to please you?"

Perez sniffed the brandy again and raised the glass to his lips.

"But," he said, lowering the glass, "aren't you going to drink with me? I propose a toast. To us and our future together. May we always be as happy as we are at this moment."

At the exact moment, the crystal glass touched his lips there was a loud pounding on the door. Shouts came from the hallway. She jerked a look toward the door and saw it rattle on its hinges.

"What the hell?" Perez jumped up to answer the door and in the process spilled his brandy on her dress.

Maria watched as Perez threw open the door and stared into the scowling faces of a dozen army soldiers. She saw someone in the group and sank back into the sofa, fighting to control her reeling brain.

Alberto!

What was he doing here? Darkness closed around her, she felt herself go faint. Alberto. Why were the soldiers here? Alberto and the Sandinista Army? Her contra friend entered the room and faced Maria.

"Colonel, I'm sorry for this abrupt intrusion," Alberto said.

"Who the hell are you and what do you mean barging in here like this?" Perez said in a loud voice. "Just what is the meaning of this?"

Alberto pushed his way past the colonel, entered the

apartment, and stood in front of Maria. "I am sorry, Colonel," he said. "I am with State Security. We have uncovered a plot against your life. This whore intended to murder you. You have not drunk the brandy, I trust?"

Perez shook his head. His eyes were wide, and he was sweating.

"Where is it?" Alberto said. He stooped, grabbed Maria by an arm, and pulled her to her feet. When he twisted it, she felt a shock wave shoot into her neck. Her heart raced, and she weakened.

"Where's what?" Her knees buckling, she fought the darkness closing about her.

"The brandy, stupid," Alberto said. He turned to Perez who stood by the sofa with his hands on his broad hips.

"What do you mean?" Perez said. "What's this all about?"

"Tell him, Maria," Alberto said.

Perez looked at Maria with wide eyes and she knew he had no idea what was happening or why Alberto was there.

"Tell me what?" Perez said. He was red-faced and agitated by the sudden intrusion. He looked around the room at the soldiers still in the hallway.

Alberto pushed Maria into Perez's face and he delivered the news.

"Like I said, she was going to kill you, Colonel. The Napoleon brandy you were about to drink has been poisoned. If we had arrived five minutes later, we would be placing your corpse into a bag."

Perez's face contorted into a scowl, his lower jaw dropped. He stared at Maria who met his gaze with flashing eyes, her heart pounded.

"Maria, is this true?" Perez appeared stunned and Maria thought he might believe a lie. She knew he *wanted* to believe her.

She had to think and think fast if she was going to survive. Her only option was to deny Alberto's accusations. After all, he had no proof.

"This is the most absurd thing I have ever heard of," she said, her voice almost shouting. She turned to Alberto who was examining the contents of the bar. "And you, how dare you insult me in this manner? What proof do you have of these allegations, what proof?"

Perez put his arm around Maria and pulled her close to him. Alberto picked up the brandy bottle and held it out to the colonel.

"This is all the proof I need, Colonel. This is the poisoned bottle. I know, because I was part of the plan to assassinate you."

"You—you were? Who are you?" Perez demanded.

"Sir, I am a loyal servant of our president. As a member of State Security, I infiltrated this group of contras six months ago and have been reporting to Defense Minister Rivas. I assure you, Colonel, this woman is deadly. They set you up. The only reason this woman encouraged you was so she could get information from you. Tonight she planned to kill you. Her friends have CIA contacts and their leader is the dog, Carlos Mendoza."

"Mendoza!" Perez said. He turned to Maria. "Is this true? You are one of them?"

Maria's head spun while she fought for control of the situation. It was a gamble but it was her only chance of surviving this turn of events. *Alberto. How could you?* Maybe if she continued to take the offensive, Perez would come to her rescue. It was her only chance.

"Don't be silly, honey," Maria said. "This man is either insane or stupid. Who the hell does he think he is, breaking into my apartment like this? Accusing me of such crimes? Do you believe this of me, Ramon? I have never seen this man before in my life. Do something about it, now. For all you know this man is a contra, here to kill you."

Perez approached Alberto and put a hand on the man's arm. "Just a minute, senor. Before you go any further, let me see some identification. Better yet, wait a moment while I telephone Secretary Rivas to confirm all this."

Maria could see Alberto was not going to be denied. Her throat tightened, she was running out of options. Two men with Alberto were ransacking her bedroom and she noticed her dresses and nightgowns scattered on the floor. Alberto poured another glass of the brandy and approached her. He smiled and held the glass in front of her.

"Colonel, there is one way of determining the truth. Let this woman drink the brandy. We shall see who is telling the truth."

Alberto held the snifter out to Maria. Perez nodded his head.

"Go ahead, my dear, don't be frightened. Drink the brandy and all will be forgotten."

Maria looked at Perez whose eyes implored her to drink. She turned to Alberto still holding the glass in his hand. He smiled and winked. So Alberto was a traitor. How she trusted him, how Carlos trusted him. His trips to Managua to see his family had been an excuse to meet with Rivas. She had fallen prey to the oldest trick in the book, trust a colleague. Casey had warned them of this very thing. He had preached trusting only a handful of friends. But Alberto had been a friend for months. She, no Carlos and the others, thought they knew him. Carlos and Alberto had been childhood friends. She remembered Alberto going on and on about the government's treachery and how it oppressed the people. And now he stood before her, a traitor to each of them and all they had fought so hard to accomplish.

Maria brought her hand down sharply on Alberto's wrist and the snifter flew across the room, crashing onto the marble entryway.

"You bastard! How dare you?"

"I rest my case, Colonel," Alberto said. "You're lucky. You narrowly escaped an extremely painful death."

Alberto signaled the soldiers and four armed men saluted Perez. He retrieved the Napoleon brandy from the bar, handed it to one of the soldiers, then took Perez aside.

"These men will escort the woman to El Chipote. To be sure, she will tell us what we want to know. She will betray her comrade, Carlos. I know the location of their camp. The peasants living near the border, all they talk about is Carlos. That's all you hear, Carlos, Carlos. You would think the man is a god or something. When we are finished with this woman, Carlos will be no more."

Alberto nodded to the soldiers. "Take her," he said. "Bind her hands and take her."

Perez moved aside and watched the soldiers place Maria in handcuffs. She felt the cold steel close around her wrists but held her head high. They pushed her toward the door where she brushed against Perez. He stared at her.

"How, Maria? How could you do this? I gave you everything?"

"You gave me nothing." Anger welled in her chest until it overflowed as spewed venom. She couldn't hold it back any longer. "You are a pig and a bastard. Do you think I enjoyed your lovemaking, your clumsy attempts? You pleased only yourself. You are a disgrace to all freedom-loving Nicaraguans. Wait until I tell everyone at El Chipote how small your manhood is. They will laugh at you, you pig."

Spent, she spat in Perez's face and tossed her head backward in a final, defiant gesture. When Perez slapped her, she tasted blood as it oozed into her mouth.

"Get the bitch out of here," he said to Alberto. "Do with her what you will."

Alberto shoved Maria into the hallway. He kicked her and the blow drove her into the street where she fell in a rumpled heap. Two soldiers pulled her to her feet and shoved her into a government car.

CHAPTER 14

The night hung like thick velvet over El Chipote while lights over its entrance cast eerie beams through the dark haze. A guard stationed at the gate waved the staff car onto the grounds and it sped to the single-story administration building. A brusque, bearded soldier pulled Maria from the car and forced her down a narrow hallway into a dank, unlighted room, devoid of furniture. She smacked her parched lips and looked about. The concrete floor was wet with urine and stank of excrement. She sat in the only dry corner with her legs under her chin and her arms pulled tight around her knees. Shivering in the cold, Maria cursed Alberto and tried to focus her thoughts on what she was facing—torture, rape, possibly death. Thoughts of Alberto precluded her planning her response to the coming interrogation and she found rational thinking impossible. The sonofabitch. Now Perez knew the identities of everyone and even worse, Carlos's whereabouts, putting the whole northern insurgency in peril. She prayed Carlos might somehow hear of her capture and move the camp. Casey was right—one didn't know whom one could trust.

Maria flinched as a rat scurried across the floor and jumped when it brushed against her leg. She kicked at the rodent, sending it squealing into the darkness at the room's far edge.

Her heart rate, out of control earlier, had slowed and she tried to focus on her predicament. She figured the evil rumors about the prison were true and worried she faced hours of grueling interrogation or torture by some sadistic pugilist who got his kicks by inflicting pain on people. In vain, she attempted to organize her thoughts into a coherent story that would make sense. But no one was going to believe her. She needed an argument that would satisfy her interrogators, in spite of the fact that the brandy had been poisoned. Taking a deep breath, she tried to clear her thoughts, but it was difficult. They were in a jumble spiraling into a lurid quagmire. Her worst nightmare was now a reality. Someone unlocked the door to her cell and a beam of yellow light flooded the corner, throwing the shadow of a tall man across the floor and upon the wall behind her.

"Get up," the man said. "Follow me."

With her hands still locked in handcuffs, Maria struggled to her feet. The guard shoved her into a dimly lit hall whose walls and floor were constructed of moss-covered stones. The smell of moist earth greeted her nostrils as she stumbled forward. The dim illumination provided by crudegas lanterns did not provide enough light for her to see what lay ahead. At the end of the long hall, the guard kicked her into a room containing a timeworn desk and straight-backed chair. A light bulb hung by two wires from the ceiling. Once inside, the guard left and locked the door.

Alone in the cold room, Maria struggled to concoct a story that would satisfy her captors. Should she throw herself at Perez's feet and beg for mercy? It seemed the logical choice but she didn't think she had the stomach for it. Before she could organize her thoughts, the door opened. An army general entered and took a seat at the desk. Maria stood, silent. While the general picked his yellow teeth with a toothpick, he stared at her through squinted eyes.

"You have interrupted a most enjoyable meal," the general said. "I do not like to leave my dinner table in such a hurry. It is bad for the digestion."

The man slumped over the desk, his uniform decorated with medals. He motioned to a guard. "Please, remove the cuffs and leave us alone," he said. When the guard had complied with the order, the general continued. "You are in deep trouble, my dear. It will be much easier on you if you just tell me everything. Cooperation is your only ticket out of El Chipote."

He pulled a paper from his breast pocket and began to write on it. After writing a paragraph, he paused, looked at Maria. "Your name is Maria Martinez?"

Maria nodded.

"You have been charged with the attempted murder of Colonel Ramon Perez. Is that charge accurate?"

Maria hesitated for a moment then chuckled in a voice the general could not help but overhear. "So you say," she said. She noticed that the shoulder straps of her dress had been torn in the scuffle to bring her to the prison and that the general was staring at her bare shoulders. She instinctively pulled her arms up in front of her, covering the tops of her breasts.

"Come, come, young lady. I am giving you an opportunity to explain yourself before we begin."

"Begin what?" Maria managed to spit out the words in spite of her swollen tongue and bruised nose.

"The interrogation. Now, for the last time, what happened and who are your friends? More importantly, where are they?"

Maria stood silent before the general and stared into his dark, penetrating eyes as he stroked his thick mustache. Her interrogator stood and removed a nightstick from his belt, then strolled to her side. She looked straight ahead to avoid his gaze, heard him toy with the stick, slapping it into his hand. He walked around her and, with each circling, paused, face-to-face before her. She closed her eyes and waited.

She felt the crack of the nightstick against her cheek and sank to her knees. A thousand sparkles of light flashed before her and the pain plunged deep like a hot poker. Unable to hold back the tears she begged for mercy.

Another blow.

This time to the back of her head. Its force drove her facedown onto the concrete floor. She felt warm liquid flow down the back of her neck. Her stomach pitched yellow bile from her mouth while she fought the darkness that was closing in. She attempted to push herself to her knees but the general kicked her down. Through a swollen eye, she saw the nightstick come down again and again, as he rained blow after blow to her back and legs. She begged him to stop but the beating continued. Her resolve evaporated and she knew she would tell the man everything. When she raised her battered head to beg for mercy, the general struck her face with the end of the nightstick, propelling her backward and she lapsed into a black abyss where time and place no longer existed.

 භ෴ භ෴ භ෴

It was 2 a.m. and Casey still had no word from Carlos or Maria. He rose from the bed where he had been resting, found his 9 mm, and ventured downstairs. The lobby was deserted, the desk manager nowhere to be seen. Casey walked to the front door of the hotel and peered into the street. In the darkness, he saw that it was empty, a fact that allowed him to stand, unnoticed, at the curb. What in the hell had happened? Where was Carlos? Was Perez dead? Where was everyone?

He stepped into the shadows of the portico and waited as an army truck and jeep sped past. The Sandinistas patrolled the city throughout the night. He looked at his watch—two-thirty and still no sign of them. If Maria had succeeded, Perez should be dead by now. Another convoy of government vehicles turned the corner and rumbled by, forcing him to duck behind a bush next to the hotel entrance. In one of the three cars, he recognized a passenger. In the back seat of the lead vehicle sat Alberto, smiling. *Alberto.*

A bolt of unfamiliar fear shot through the CIA agent. Years of covert experience and training told him that something had gone wrong. He ran across the street and, using the hedge along the sidewalk as cover, walked to a place where he could see the entrance to El Chipote. The place was lit up like a Christmas tree and there was a long convoy of military vehicles parked along the road outside the gate. Something was happening—that was for sure.

Casey searched his pockets for the keys to his rental car.

Finding them, he drove through Managua's twisted streets, needing to get to either Pueblo Salto or the base camp before he was stopped and questioned or before the two men returned to his hotel room. He shoved the accelerator to the floor and sped around the western edge of Managua toward the mountains.

By the time he reached San Rafael, it was five o'clock and daylight was just beginning to illuminate the dirt road. He turned northwest and continued to Pueblo Salto. Silhouetted against the lights from the wooden shacks, farmers marched in silence to start their work in the fields. What was he doing here, anyway? He had no idea where Carlos was, if he was in Managua or the countryside. Casey sensed something had gone wrong. It was a gut feeling and one that he had trusted for many years.

In Pueblo Salto, the sun was up, the haze lifting. Casey pulled his car to a stop in front of the Café Central and killed the motor. A few farmers were on the road, walking to the coffee plantation and they stared at him. He got out, lit a cigarette, and paced around the café's empty porch. Should he proceed on to the base camp? He glanced at the sky and knew the absence of clouds meant the heat would be stifling. Going to the base camp would be foolish, an amateur's decision. In the distance, he heard the rumbling of a jeep motoring toward the village. Hurrying to the side of the café, Casey pulled his automatic pistol from his belt and checked to be sure it had a full clip. Satisfied, he focused his vision on the approaching jeep. It wasn't until the jeep was in front of the café that he recognized Carlos. Luis waved when Casey approached the vehicle.

"Carlos," Casey said. "What has happened?"

"I don't know," Carlos said, obvious concern in his voice. "Maria wasn't where she was supposed to be last night. We haven't seen her. Have you?"

"No, not at all. There was a long convoy parked at El Chipote and the place was crawling with military. Maybe she's been arrested."

"I told Carlos that something went wrong," Luis said. He

shook Casey's hand and the three of them sat on the café's porch.

"Where's Raoul?"

"He's at camp, preparing for the plane drop later this week. Shit, you really think Maria's been arrested?"

"Listen, Carlos," Casey said. "I saw Alberto in Managua yesterday. Would you happen to know why? He told me he was visiting his family."

Carlos shook his head, deep furrows on his face. "He told me was going to search the mountains for a place to move our operations." He strummed his fingers on the round table. "You say he was in Managua?"

"Yes. After I spoke with him, I never saw him again until a few hours ago. And here's the bombshell, Carlos. Alberto was riding in a Sandinista staff car and it was headed toward El Chipote."

"El Chipote?"

"Yes."

Carlos slammed his fist down hard on the table. "Damn! The son-of-a-bitch."

"Traitor," Luis said. "My mother told me that someday Alberto would do something stupid."

Casey was puzzled. "How so?" he said.

"My mother, she knew us when we were younger, remember Carlos? She met him when you brought him to our house for dinner right after we decided to fight the Sandinistas," Luis said. "We laughed and talked that night and Alberto was proud of the way he stole bread from the bakery the week before. Mother didn't like his being a thief and told me so later. Alberto. I can't believe it."

"Well, that settles it," Carlos said. "She's in prison and is probably being tortured at this very moment. What can we do?"

Casey stood, stretched his legs, and thought about the problem. The sun was high and he wiped beads of perspiration from his upper lip.

"I heard talk while I was in Managua about you," Casey said and pointed to Carlos. "There is a price on your head. Perez has orders to hunt you down like a dog and kill you. You—we—must be very careful."

"What about Maria?" Luis said. He was cleaning his hunting knife and shot a questioning look at Casey.

"By now, Perez knows who you all are and can recognize each one of you on sight from photos he has seen. Maybe I can convince Slater to lend a hand. I know my way around the prison since I pulled Carlos out. Maybe, with Slater's help, we might be able to pull it off again."

"Blow the place?" Luis said.

"Get her out of there," Casey said.

"There will be extra security now that they know we're involved," Carlos said. "It would be extremely dangerous."

"I don't think anyone could get in the place now," Luis said. "The whole army will be there."

Casey smiled. "Once Slater finds that Maria is being held there, he will be more than glad to help. The two of them are in love, or didn't you know that?"

Luis laughed and Carlos threw up his hands. "We know," he said. "That's all we have heard about for the past two weeks. Jim Slater. Jim this and Jim that."

"Okay, here's the deal," Casey said. He pointed to the jungle beyond the end of the road. "Find another location for your camp. Just abandon the present one and move the weapons to another location. I'll talk with Slater. He seems to be a man that we can count on. Doesn't say much, just capable. Once we have developed a plan, we'll contact you by radio. Is yours still working?"

"Yes," Luis said.

"Good. Now, I'm off to San Rafael. Be careful, gentlemen. Perez is likely to be headed this way, and he'll be a madman now that Maria has betrayed him."

Casey jumped into his car and headed south toward San Rafael. In his rear-view mirror he watched Luis and Carlos push into the jungle.

CHAPTER 15

Perez pushed his column of men and machines all morning. When they stopped alongside the road for a brief rest and lunch, Captain Salazar approached him, smiling. His gate was brisk and he saluted the colonel.

"Sir, we have a radio report of a large encampment just beyond the border, north of Pueblo Salto. Shall I radio for reinforcements?"

"Contras?"

The captain nodded.

Perez finished his cigarette and ambled to his jeep at the head of the column. "No," he said. "No reinforcements. This shall be our victory. Let's move, Captain."

Salazar gave the orders and soon the convoy was rolling toward the village. Perez considered this campaign to be his appointment with destiny, and he was proud to bear the mantle of mythological Mars taking the sword of devastation to the insurgents. The capture of Carlos Mendoza would shatter, once and for all, the fantasy of the man's omnipotence and would bring Perez the recognition he deserved. Hanging the renegade's corpse in the town square, for all to see, would be a lifeless reminder that mounting a force against the Sandinistas was to court disaster.

The previous night he had labored to expand his military convoy. It meant an early phone call to Rivas for additional men and vehicles but was successful, making reinforcements now unnecessary. His force stood at fifty men armed with AK-47s; two Soviet T-55A tanks with their Petrov D-10 100 mm guns; six Russian-made NSV .50 caliber, heavy machine guns that could fire thirteen rounds per second; and plenty of ammunition. When they encountered the enemy, they would blow them off the face of the map.

Although he was confident in the absolute certainty of the outcome of his mission, Perez was saddened by the events of the previous evening and Maria's arrest. He was thankful, of course, for Alberto's timely arrival, but his heart ached for her. It was impossible to believe she betrayed him in the way she had. To pry state secrets from him while he was in the throes of rapture was one thing—to attempt his murder was something else. How foolish he must appear to her because he never had the slightest suspicion of her motives. Possibly, he was much too mesmerized by her beauty and the sex to take a serious look at their relationship. Maybe she was telling the truth but, why then, didn't she drink the brandy? Of course, she knew it was poisoned. It sounded childish and stupid but he wondered if it might be possible to recapture what they had if she survived El Chipote. He had never known a woman like her.

Late in the afternoon, the convoy arrived at Pueblo Salto. The tanks ground to a halt across the road from the Café Central and after ordering his men to bivouac and post sentries along their perimeter, he sauntered to his jeep and picked up the radio. He wanted to update Rivas on their location. They would begin the hunt for contras in the morning.

ℰ৲ℰ৲৩

Slater closed the school early, went home, took a shower, and changed his clothes. Carlos and Maria would arrive at any minute and he longed to see her again. He hoped that she would have dinner with him and then talk until the sun faded into the trees behind his house.

He heard a car and looked out the window. It was Casey but Maria and Carlos weren't with him. He stood on the porch while Casey emerged from the vehicle. "Where's Maria," Slater said.

Casey's thick eyebrows narrowed and he squinted against the sun. "Something's gone wrong, Jim."

Slater stepped off the porch and the two men shook hands. "What do you mean?"

"We think Maria's in El Chipote. Alberto betrayed her."

"No," Slater said. "What happened?"

"We don't know. This is all conjecture but we think Alberto turned her over to the Sandinistas and they took her to the prison. He told Carlos he was going to the camp but I saw him in Managua. He told me he was going to see his family but he probably betrayed Maria. One of our sources mentioned a heavy military convoy was being sortied from the base north of Managua. I suspect Perez is mounting a counterstrike against us and time is running short. Carlos, Luis, and Raoul are in the process moving the camp to a new location. They are going to radio me when they have found a suitable site. You still have your short-wave radio?"

Slater ignored the question about the radio. "What about Maria?"

"Most likely she's being interrogated by professionals. God help her."

Slater could not swallow and he wiped droplets of sweat form the back of his neck. Maria was right. The consequences of their romance were beginning to plague them. He no longer felt like an innocent bystander.

"Will they kill her?"

"No. But after they have finished with her, they will know everything and will not rest until we are all dead. The bourgeois Sandinistas will not tolerate an attack on one of their own. I came up here because I knew you would want to know."

"Yes, thanks, Casey. What can I do to help?"

"You once told Carlos that you wanted no part of this war, remember? That you wished to remain neutral. Do you still feel that way?"

"I dunno. I once felt that I had seen all the blood and gore I ever wanted to see. I witnessed peasants fighting each other while in Vietnam. What did it all prove? Nothing, absolutely nothing. Christ, now that Maria's been arrested, I don't know what to think. I'm not sure I can stay out of the fight any longer."

"It's hard to remain neutral when you see the suffering up close, isn't it," Casey said. "You're in love with her aren't you? She's changed the way you think."

"Of course. I cannot imagine a life anymore without her. If it means involving me in their fight, I guess I'm in. But do you think we can get her out of there? Bribe the guards maybe?"

"Good, I hoped you would feel that way. I have thought about a bribe, but it would be risky. Besides, the fund to support our movement grows smaller by the day and there's not much money left, I'm afraid. We will have to find another way."

After a short pause in the conversation, Slater put his hands on his hips. "By 'we' do you mean you and me? I will do whatever needs doing, of course."

Casey patted Slater on the shoulder and they walked inside. Slater poured two glasses of bourbon and they continued their discussion.

"I've been in El Chipote before so I sort of know my way around. Getting in will be difficult and once inside it will be trial and error finding Maria for I have no idea where exactly she would be."

"Wait a minute," Slater interrupted. "Are you talking about a rescue attempt? You and me going in there and pulling her out? Christ, man, have you gone outta your mind? It can't be done."

"It will be risky, no doubt about it. But really, Jim, when you think about it, there's no other way. Do you want to just wait and see what happens to her? If they don't kill her, they will send her to a relocation camp and use her as slave labor. Is that what you want?"

Slater downed the rest of his bourbon and shook his head. "There is nothing else, then?" he said.

"Listen. Anything we try will put her life at risk, that's the point. In fact, her life is already at risk. There is no help from the States and my boys will not even think of more involvement. So you and I must think this one out ourselves. And yes, it will be risky for us. For me, however, it comes with the job. You, on the other hand, need to think seriously about helping. Carlos, Luis, and Raoul are out because their photos are now hanging in every military commander's office. So I ask you again, Jim. Are you up to helping me?"

Slater stood and strode around the room. After a few moments, he broke the silence. "Of course I will. What's the plan?"

Casey handed his empty glass to Slater who refilled it with another shot of bourbon. "The cells are arranged in a maze of underground passageways and portals and are heavily guarded by well-armed soldiers who will not hesitate to shoot us on sight. Right now, I have no idea how we're going to get her out so may I stay here with you until we work something out? Is that acceptable?"

"Of course. What if Perez shows up here?" The thought occurred to Slater that if Perez discovered him in Casey's company the colonel would never believe his protests of being an innocent bystander.

"Is there someplace I can hide if he comes?

"There's a small, underground root cellar out back. It's big enough for one person," Slater said.

"Officially, you are neutral and are here to run the school. I don't think even Perez would attempt to provoke an incident with the United States. Most likely, he would leave you alone."

"Damn," Slater said. "How in the hell did we get into this mess?"

Casey did not respond to the question but, instead, drank the rest of his bourbon.

"Oh, well. Listen," Slater continued. "I was hoping to fix dinner for Maria and me. I have a pig in the oven. Shall we eat?"

"Fine, Jim, fine. We can bounce a few ideas around and see if they float."

"You mean run them up the Yankee flagpole and see if they fly?"

They chuckled. Slater brought out the pig and set it on the table. Casey helped himself to more of the bourbon and dug into supper.

∾∾∾

Maria's head felt as if it would explode. She ran her fingers over her pulpy face to determine if anything was broken. Blood, dried to a thick crust, left a dreadful taste in her mouth and caused convulsions in her stomach. She had not had any water and she was parched, her tongue thick, swollen twice its normal size. In addition, she was weak and disoriented. How long had she been here? Where was she? What had happened?

She used the cold, concrete floor of the prison cell as an icepack on her face. The odor of the room no longer made her , and she opened an eye, only to look into the face of a large rat sitting on his hind legs staring at her. He squealed and ran to the nearest corner when Maria pushed herself upright. Every sinew and muscle cried out. She tried to stand but couldn't muster the strength.

Footsteps.

A metal cup appeared through a hole at the bottom of the door. She drank the cool water then fell onto her back, exhausted by the effort. For a few moments, she thought she was drinking the clear, mountain stream near where she played as a child.

Bang! The door swung open, a guard entered. He grabbed her by the hair and pulled her to her feet. Pain shot through her and she screamed.

"Follow me," he said, seemingly oblivious to her condition.

The guard pushed her into the small office where she was tortured. She wept when she found herself again in front of the general. The light bulb flickered and merged the man's shadow with hers on the floor.

"I'm quite surprised by your courage," he said. "Your

bravery has not gone unnoticed. I shall not strike you again."

Maria said nothing, concentrating instead on controlling her emotions. The general rose and handed her a handkerchief and when she blew her nose, blood and mucous issued forth in a sticky ooze. Finished, she riveted her attention on the man through her swollen eyes. He was slight of build and walked with a decided limp. Long, slender fingers held the nightstick, the one he had used on her. In a blinding flash, the image of him standing over her, hitting her, returned and she cried out.

"There, there," the general said. "Please do not cry. Your courage has earned you a small gratuity. My name is General Cabezas, the warden here. But forgive me, you do look terrible."

Cabezas poured a glass of water from a pitcher and handed it to Maria.

"Here you are, my dear. Drink this, it will help."

Maria drank the water, and it cooled her throat. She handed the glass back to the general.

"That's better," he said. "Please sit in the chair. We have a problem here, uh...I'm sorry I forgot your name."

She stumbled into the chair, grateful to off her feet. "M—Maria."

"Yes, Maria. Our problem—really it is your problem but your silence has made it mine—is that you need to come clean. Tell me what you know."

Maria tried to focus her attention on Cabezas, but the room spun, and she said nothing.

"As I said a moment ago, you shall not be beaten again. You must know, however, that you will never leave this place until you have told me what I want to know. Do you understand? I will place you in a cell in the deepest regions of the prison, a place we reserve for our political prisoners. If you think it is dark in your present cell, wait until you have experienced your new one. Now for the last time, where is Carlos Mendoza? And who is his American contact?"

Maria stood before the general, silent. She tossed his handkerchief onto the desk, raised her head until she could see him through her swollen eyes, and laughed. "You low-life bastard," she said in a low tone. "Kill me now and be done with it."

The general stood, pulled a bandana from his coat, and wiped his face. He paced in small circles while he swatted his palm with the nightstick.

"Guard," he said.

A uniformed soldier entered the office and saluted.

"Take this whore back to her cell."

The guard snapped to attention and grabbed Maria's arm. Cabezas picked up his gloves, doffed his nightstick at her, and strode to the door.

"Good night, my dear," he said and left her alone with the guard.

ᛒᣠᛒᣠ

Their dinner finished, Casey and Slater sat outside the house and the CIA agent lit a foul-smelling cigar.

"One of the troubles with Nicaragua," Casey said, "is the absence of good cigars. The Sandinistas get all the Cubans for themselves and leave these infernal things for the rest of us. Once, when on assignment in Cuba, I purchased a whole case of Cubans and brought them home. My father and I enjoyed the hell out of them."

Slater smiled. "I never thought of you as having a family, Allan. You were close to your father?"

"We had our moments," Casey said. "But when I joined the Company his attitude toward me changed, softened a bit. I guess he was somewhat pleased I was serving my country. He fought the Japanese in the Second World War, even earned a Purple Heart. He was a mail carrier after coming home. Not much money each month but a nice pension in the end. I haven't talked with him in a while."

"You enjoy your work, don't you?" Slater said.

Casey flicked ashes from the cigar. "It's a living, as they say. But frankly, I could not imagine doing anything else. I just hope we can make a difference down here."

He puffed several times to ensure the cigar was lit then settled back in his chair.

"I imagine it's an exciting life," Slater said. "Exciting but dangerous."

"It does have its moments," Casey said. "Because of that I never had a wife or children. Couldn't see leaving a passel of kids at home, wondering if I would ever come back. In addition, I don't really like children all that much. So it's best I don't have a family of my own, I guess."

"Normally, I would tell someone that viewpoint is a sad one but, in your case, it makes good sense."

Casey dashed his cigar ashes onto the ground. "Now, to business," he said. "I managed to scrape together five thousand in cash and can use the money to bribe a number of people. Down here, it should go a long way. I figure we bribe the guard and the sergeant at the prison desk. I've met him before and he's a case, believe me. The security should be at its weakest around three in the morning and, hopefully, we can get to the cellblocks. From what I saw the last time I was in there, each door has a square window about chest-high and a small opening at the floor where they push the food in. Each block has a jailer with the keys. He's the one we must get to. It's my guess that finding the right cell is going to have to be done by trial and error. Follow so far, Jim?"

"No problem. Once we find her, will we have to shoot our way out?"

"I dunno. If the guards we bribed are cooperative, hopefully not. If they choose to sound an alarm, then yes, we'll shoot until we run out of ammunition. It's risky but it is the only chance we have."

Slater whistled and rolled his eyes. "I can't leave Maria in there and do nothing. I've fallen in love with her."

Casey flicked more ashes from his cigar and watched the breeze blow them past the road. "Everyone knows that already. Don't worry, Carlos approves. He sends his regards, by the way."

Slater was numb with disbelief, he couldn't help it. "How funny it all seems," he said.

"How's that?" Casey continued to puff on the cigar.

"Here I am, a peaceful schoolteacher, about to engage the

Sandinistas in a covert action, planned by the CIA, which, in all likelihood, will get me killed. What would Mother say?"

Casey snubbed the cigar out and looked at Slater. "What would she say?"

"My mother, bless her soul, has a knack for cutting to the chase—"

"Blunt, eh?"

"Oh yeah and how. 'My boy,' she would say, 'I thought you were a pacifist. I thought Vietnam gave you enough trouble to last a lifetime.' That's what she would say."

"Quite a sense of humor, it seems."

Slater saw the irony also—he was no longer neutral.

CHAPTER 16

Colonel Perez studied the map that Captain Salazar spread out on the hood of his jeep. It was just after dawn and the spider monkeys and Amazon parrots chattered overhead in the steam produced by the idling tanks. With a dirty finger, Salazar pointed to an area on the map.

"Right here, Colonel. Their camp is right over the border and near this river, that parallels the primitive road. It shouldn't be too difficult to find."

"What does intelligence say about contra patrols in the area?"

Salazar buckled his pistol belt and adjusted his helmet. He waited until a soldier walked past before explaining. "The camp is located in a compound surrounded by a tall fence patrolled by heavily-armed sentries. According to our reports of the last few days, they usually send out one patrol each morning and another in the afternoon. The rest of the men usually remain in the compound unless they have a specific mission to perform. Mostly the bulk of their force operates after dark so today we should find them lounging in the compound. How do you suggest we proceed Colonel?"

"We'll surprise them with a swift, double-pronged attack. I will take the majority of our forces through the main gate while you and your men will support my left flank. You will enter the compound here from the west." Perez noted an area on the map and continued. "See, there is a road that winds its way northward and the compound's perimeter should be just to the east of it."

Salazar looked where Perez was pointing for a moment, then nodded. "They won't know what hit them, Colonel. What about chopper support?"

"Not today, my friend," Perez answered. "It will be our victory, our victory alone. Get the men loaded."

Salazar saluted and returned to the convoy of trucks and tanks that had sat idling while the two men talked. He hollered at a sergeant and pumped a closed fist for emphasis. With a deafening roar, the drivers brought the huge monsters to life. Diesel smoke belched into the clear sky as the column awaited the signal to move out.

Perez stood in the back of his jeep and looked over his shoulder. Salazar gave the ready sign, from the rear of the column and jumped into his jeep. Perez, enjoying the moment, thrust his arm forward and led his convoy northeast into the jungle. The canopy grew thicker and Perez's palms were moist at the thought of engaging the enemy, nerves on the raw edge, anticipating the moment of battle. He was always like this right before combat—focused, intense. His eyes darted about the forest for any sign of movement. The bastards were experts at camouflage. It was funny, but when he was in the field, it seemed so natural, as if he was born to be a *commandante*. But when he was at home in Managua with Maria, he didn't care if he ever saw action again. He wondered if all women had the same effect on their men. Sadly, there would no longer be a Maria, not now or possibly ever. If she survived her ordeal at the prison, would she ever forgive him for sending her there?

The narrow trail, which served as a road, became more difficult to negotiate, slowing the convoy's pace to a slow crawl over ground turned to rock and punctuated by deep mud holes. Earlier in the morning, a tank became mired so its tracks would not turn. Salazar hooked two trucks up to it and managed, with great effort, to pull the tank out of the hole. With a loud, sucking sound, it popped free from the mud's grasp and the convoy was again on its way.

Perez could handle the mud holes. He could handle the monkeys who stole food from their bivouac at night. He couldn't, however, handle the snakes that prowled the jungle floor and slithered through the trees. His fear originated in childhood when he had been careless and was bitten on the hand. Although he survived, the skin on his hand turned black and fell off. The experience taught him an invaluable lesson of jungle survival—keep an ever-watchful eye out for the bastards and a machete close. He looked down at the ground and tried to see through the carpet of vines, leaves, and vegetation. Somewhere, crawling under all that stuff was a goddamn snake waiting for him to step out of his jeep. He lit a cigarette and pushed away his fear.

Salazar honked his horn from the rear of the convoy, and Perez ordered his driver to stop. When the captain caught up with his colonel, he was out of breath, his face red.

"The border is right over this next hill, Colonel. Surely you don't plan to cross. Are you sure you want to proceed?"

"You think I'm afraid of the Honduran government, Captain? If so, you are mistaken. They won't know we were here, I assure you. If, and when, they find out, we will be long gone—couldn't prove it was us. No, my dear Salazar, the border will pose no barrier to our forces."

"Yes, sir. Once inside Honduras," Salazar said. "the road turns east and we will be at the tip of the Las Vegas Salient. The contra camp is located just beyond. Another hour, I would say."

"Fine, Captain. Give the men a rest and have them check their weapons. I don't want to be surprised by a band of wandering renegades."

☙☙☙

With Maria in prison and Casey and Slater in San Rafael, it fell to Carlos, Luis, and Raoul to move the camp. Each drove a vehicle loaded with food, clothes, weapons, and ammunition through the Las Vegas Salient until they were back across the border in Nicaragua.

Now and then, Luis jumped out of the truck and carved a way through the dense vegetation. Consulting his map, Carlos thought the ideal location would be near a small river that ran along the base of the mountain on the eastern boundary of the coffee plantation. That side of the mountain was scarcely populated, for most of the farmers lived in Pueblo Salto or San Rafael. It would be an excellent location, secluded from passing traffic since the roads were to the south of the river. A nearby clearing the size of a soccer field would serve as a drop zone when the C-47s arrived.

The heat became more oppressive and the jungle denser as the day wore on, but the three men persisted in their trek. Late in the day, they stopped, consulted the map one last time, and set about erecting tents and organizing their gear. With dinner cooking, Luis, who had taken a walk to reconnoiter the area, returned with a concerned look on his face.

"What's the matter," Carlos said.

Luis pointed with his finger. "That way, there is a bridge over the river. Let's look at your map."

The men studied Carlos's map and he shook his head. "It's not supposed to be there. Are you sure, we are in the right position? Where we want to be?"

"Of course," Luis said. "We are right here." He pointed to a spot on the map. "And the bridge is here. It's not on the map, that's all."

"How deep is the river there?"

"Deep. Probably ten feet or so. Why?"

"Too deep for vehicles to cross, eh? Maybe we'll just blow the damn thing up."

"One more thing, Carlos," Luis said. "I saw smoke beyond the river."

"Smoke?" Carlos said.

"What kind of smoke?" Raoul said. His face twitched when he looked in the bridge's direction.

"Campfire, most likely. Fires mean people, usually."

"Or diesel smoke? Sandinistas?" Carlos said.

"I couldn't tell who it was or how many. Maybe just a farmer and his family."

"Or the enemy," Carlos said. "We'll find out soon enough."

❧❧

A sliver of a moon illuminated the road along which Carlos, Luis, and Raoul slinked, single file, toward the bridge. Marching through the jungle's dense foliage, the threesome carried two mortars and a grenade launcher and, upon reaching the bridge, took a position on the near side of it, behind a rock outcropping. Carlos motioned to Luis and Raoul, who worked to set up the mortars with a well-practiced rhythm. Observing the bivouac beyond the bridge with his binoculars, Carlos studied the gathering of men and vehicles. He could barely make out the silhouettes of a few military trucks and soldiers walking back and forth in front of them. He scanned the encampment, searching for signs of Sandinistas but in the darkness, it was difficult to tell.

Juan's squad of contra guerrillas was not expected to be this far south. He was more likely to be in Honduras for the next few days. Carlos strained to identify the markings on each vehicle but could not identify them. It was possible that they were Juan's, but they could just as well belong to the government. He was following the line of trucks with the binoculars when he spotted a large, black object at the rear of the convoy.

He focused the binoculars, straining to make it out. It was more than a shadow; it was something big—a new kind of vehicle, perhaps. Then it dawned upon him what he was seeing. It was a tank, for god's sake. A damned, Soviet T-55A tank. And behind it was parked one similar. Where did they come from?

He waved to Luis and Raoul. They each took a turn looking through the binoculars. Raoul let out a long, low whistle.

"I can't believe it," he said. He turned to Luis. "Do you see them?"

"No shit," Luis said. "Colonel Perez?"

"Most likely," Carlos said. "Either that or a scouting party.

Those tanks indicate that in all likelihood it's the main column, looking for us, no doubt."

"We can't blow the bridge now, can we?" Luis crawled back to the mortars. "Once we did they'd crush us in an instant."

The trio crawled fifty meters back into a dense, thicket of roots, vines, and tall grass.

"No way can we do anything by ourselves," Carlos said. "I'll get on the radio and find out where Juan is located. Maybe he's close and can help. I'd sure like to blow those bastards into thin air. Those soldiers will be patrolling this area so we're going to have to move our camp even farther back. We need to do it now, while it's still dark."

The three men made their way back to their tents in silence then began striking camp.

"How did we get so lucky?" Raoul said.

"Lucky how?" Luis said.

"To pick a spot for base camp right next to those Sandinista butchers."

"It's your suave and debonair personality, my friend. It attracts Sandinistas like moths to a lantern."

"And your mother should have drowned you, Luis. It's too bad she had to birth the likes of you."

Carlos listened with humor to the two men's bantering. It was just like them, trading insults this way. Ever since meeting up, they argued and insulted each other's family heritage. He picked up the mortars and loaded them into the jeep then looked around. It was quiet, except for the sounds of crickets and tree frogs. The cool, mountain air energized their work and they soon were on their way.

∞∞∞

When Slater returned home from the school, Casey busied himself by drawing a map of what he remembered of El Chipote. He wore blue jeans, a black, short-sleeved shirt, and sported a pair of hiking boots. An ashtray full of cigarette butts was evidence that Casey had been hard at work for several hours. The two men sat on the small porch while Casey explained to Slater.

"This is what I remember from the time I was there," he said pointing to the drawing. "Here's the main gate which is right next to the Intercontinental Hotel. The road through the gate curves around to the administration building. This part of the prison—" He pointed to the side of a round hill directly behind the administration building, "—is all underground and extends a quarter-mile back into this mound here."

"You've decided against bribery, then," Slater said. "I thought you were going to try and bribe some of the guards to get her out."

"I've thought it over and it just won't work, Jim," Casey said, shaking his head. "With guards all over the place it isn't practical, there's too many of them. It's going to be difficult but we are going to have to go in and get her. I don't see any other option that's workable."

Slater looked at the map and nodded as Casey explained the details.

"Now, somewhere up here on the hill, there are ventilation shafts or sewage portals. Rather than going in the front, it seems to be a better plan to get in through one of them. From there, if we can make it to the main hallway, which I think is located here, we should stand a chance of success."

"How do we find Maria?" Slater said, disturbed that they had no idea in which cellblock she was held and that they seemed to have no chance of finding out before going in.

"I've been racking my brain to recall whether or not the main hallway in the administration building branched or not. I seem to remember that it divided into two, smaller passageways about fifty feet from the desk. If we could get into those hallways, we could each search one and save time."

"Once we get her out of her cell, how do we get beyond the locked entry in the main office? You said bribery was out of the question."

"Grenades." Casey let the word sink in before continuing. "Blow the door off its hinges. It's the simplest, most reliable method of extrication I know of. Hopefully, the shock of the explosion will cause enough confusion that we can get past the guards. But we may have to kill a few. Once outside, we make our way over the hill and run to the fence next to the hotel. Cut our way through the fence and we will be back in my room in fifteen minutes. What do you think?"

"I would prefer to bribe some of the guards rather than use force. It seems too risky."

"No chance. Like I said, there's too many to begin with and the process would take too much time. No, we need to get in and out quickly. The grenades will cause a tremendous amount of confusion so, hopefully, no one will be paying any attention to us. If they do, they're dead. There's no way we can get her out without risk of getting ourselves shot in the process. Are you having second thoughts?"

"I think it's insane," Slater said. He looked at Casey's boyish grin accenting his straight teeth. Slater sighed. "It's just the sort of thing that *will* get us killed. I am not afraid but the last time I shot at someone was in Vietnam. I hope I have the stomach for it."

"The more I thought about it, Jim, this plan seemed better than bribery. We couldn't possibly bribe everyone in there, there's too many of them. Besides, as I said, the explosions will hopefully work to our advantage by creating enough panic so we can get out."

"I don't know," Slater said. He couldn't believe he was about to embark on a covert mission along with the CIA.

"Give me a better plan."

"The trouble is I don't have one. You're the expert. Maybe it's just insane enough to work." The two men were silent while Slater mulled the options. "Okay, I'm with you," he said after a few minutes. "Let's do it."

"I need to inform my station chief of our plans. I'm going back to Managua and my hotel. See you later."

After Casey left, Slater sat and thought of Maria, hoped beyond hope that she was still alive and that they could find her. If they succeeded, he was never going to let her out of his sight again. He thought of his mother and wondered what she would say when he brought Maria home. He wasn't sure she would approve, but it didn't matter, for he was determined to spend his life with the woman.

CHAPTER 17

The sun was bright and overhead when Perez and his convoy thundered to a stop in front of the tall fence surrounding the contra base. No sentries were posted at the makeshift gate so Perez ordered a tank to push through and the convoy followed. Several wooden huts were inside facing a circular clearing. When Perez motioned to the rest of the convoy, the remaining tanks belched diesel smoke into the clear sky and followed. Captain Salazar gathered a few men and began a systematic search of the houses. Perez followed behind, his .45 at the ready, while he and Salazar did their reconnaissance. Finding nothing, he returned to the clearing and explored the camp's perimeter. Finished, he stood, lit a cigar, and waited on Salazar, who returned clutching a paper.

"This was their camp, Colonel," he said. "They left this behind."

Perez grabbed the paper and studied the document. It was filled with dates and numbers.

"What do you make of this, Juan," Perez said.

"Dates and radio frequencies. They left nothing else behind, no codebooks, no maps, nothing. You've got to give them credit, when they decide to move, they do a thorough job of it. I've got four men searching their garbage dump so maybe we can learn something from there."

"We're close, Juan, extremely close. I can smell them. My gut tells me that they left this place within the past few days.

Our problem is we don't know in which direction they went or if this is Mendoza's group. It doesn't matter but, just once, I'd like the opportunity to get my hands on that dog and take his corpse back to Managua. I would love to see Secretary Rivas's eyes when I throw the man's head at his feet."

Before Salazar could respond a sergeant ran up to them, saluted, and turned toward the captain.

"We found their garbage, Captain. This way."

The man turned and led Perez and Salazar to a row of huts at the edge of the clearing behind which three soldiers stood next to a deep hole full of burned refuse. Salazar fell to his hands and knees and began fumbling through the trash. While his captain searched, Perez puffed on his cigar until a foul, decaying odor wafted upward and forced him to move up wind. Salazar, along with several of his soldiers, continued his digging and searching, holding an occasional can or bottle up to inspect it.

Perez paced around the hole, nervous, waiting. After a half an hour, Salazar produced an empty, cellophane cigarette pack, held it up, and Perez walked over to where Salazar was stooped and took the crumpled paper from him.

"Cigarettes, Colonel. American cigarettes. It proves that this is where Carlos has been hiding."

"Good work, Captain," Peres said. "American cigarettes, eh? It means that they have American advisors here. The CIA. Very good, Captain. Tell the men that they have done a commendable job, let them have lunch, then we will be on our way."

"The CIA, sir? Do you think when we find them the Americans will be with them? Could we ask for better luck?"

"American or Americans," Perez said. "I don't know. If we can kill or capture an American agent, it will prove to the world that the United States is supporting the contra bastards. Rivas has told me how the president is tiring of the Americans' continual denials of the help they provide. This might be a way to humiliate them, who knows? Their left-wing Congress may be forced to investigate."

Salazar nodded and left Perez to finish his cigar. The colonel watched his captain give the order for lunch and, during the meal, strolled the camp and chatted with his men.

҂ᴐ҂

Just inside Nicaragua from the Las Vegas Salient, Carlos, Luis, and Raoul stumbled upon a Sandinista fuel depot. The depot consisted of three, large, portable tanks—each supported by four legs, each standing twenty feet off the ground, and casting long shadows in the late afternoon sun. They were guarded by two government soldiers who lounged in the doorway of a small tent nearby. Remaining in the trees, Carlos motioned them out of the jeep and onto the ground. He was surprised the guards had not heard them coming. The warm earth was pungent and crackled as he crawled to a fallen tree, its huge trunk shielding him from the sentries. It was quiet, except for the soft sounds made by the soldiers talking. They appeared oblivious to the contras' arrival. He crawled back to where Luis and Raoul were lying.

"Can you believe our luck?" Carlos said. "They're just waiting there like sitting ducks."

"How many fuel tanks?" Raoul said.

"Three," Carlos said. "Each holds twenty thousand gallons. It's going to make one hell of an explosion when they go."

"Why are they this far north?" Luis said. "Usually the government doesn't like to venture this close to Honduras. If they are caught across the border, it makes for a sticky political mess."

"Casey told me his intelligence warned of fuel depots up here. Their locations are a closely guarded secret and even he had no idea where they were. The Sandinistas have patrol squads roaming these mountains but where they hide is anyone's guess," Carlos said. "Luis, you take the grenade launcher and we'll fan out from here. Once we get within firing distance, we'll take out the two guards and use the grenades on the tanks. Raoul, head west and I'll crawl straight ahead. Luis, circle around to your left and approach on my flank. Let's do it."

Luis grabbed the grenade launcher and pulled on the vest which contained the grenades. The three men crawled toward the hut like large snakes slithering through the undergrowth until, near the tent, Carlos stopped and glanced around a tree stump. The three of them found a slight depression in the ground, huddled together, and kept their weapons close.

Sitting in front of the camouflaged tent, the guards continued their animated discussion when one of the soldiers pointed beyond the fuel tanks. Carlos figured he needed about twenty more meters before he would have an accurate shot. Fearful that there could be a Sandinista patrol in the area, he knew that their attack would have to be swift, exact. Continuing on, he saw Luis worm his way through the brush, his M-16 slung over a shoulder. On his right, Raoul was close enough to strike when he gave the signal.

One of the soldiers looked directly at Carlos but turned into the doorway of the tent and laughed with his fellow sentry. Crawling closer, Carlos could hear them discussing their girlfriends and wondering when they would see them again. One man was planning on being married soon and wanted his wedding to be in Managua.

Carlos crept closer.

Too bad, he thought, it won't happen.

He raised his hand and Luis and Raoul shouldered their automatic rifles. Carlos lowered his fist, and the three of them riddled the soldiers with a barrage of bullets. The pair fell, motionless, onto the ground. Carlos scrambled to his feet, ran to the building, and pumped a round into each dead soldier for good measure. Lying in front of the doorway, legs askew, eyes open, the sentries' faces were covered with blood. While Luis shoved a grenade into the launcher and aimed it at one of the fuel tanks, Luis and Raoul followed. With a loud *pop,* it shot a grenade onto the platform that circled the tank. A giant fireball erupted, followed simultaneously by a thunderous explosion that knocked Carlos to the ground. Luis reloaded the launcher and fired again.

Another fireball and explosion followed, louder than the first. The resulting firestorm produced a deafening whirlwind, its heat intense. When Luis tried to load the grenade launcher the third time, it jammed.

"Hurry!" Carlos yelled over the roar of billowing flames.

Luis worked to free the jammed grenade from its launcher. The clearing was a raging inferno with the fire approaching the remaining tank. He cursed the grenade, until it popped out of the launcher, shoved another grenade into the barrel, and pulled the trigger. This time the grenade arched' through the torrid air and landed on the remaining tank. It must have been completely full of fuel—for when the tank exploded, the concussion slammed the trio into the soft ground. They watched the rising flames devour everything in their path, the roar deafening. Thick black smoke billowed skyward, engulfing them. Carlos's lungs burned with each breath. He shouted a command. They ran to the jeep and stood, breathless, their eyes riveted on the raging inferno.

"Shit!" Luis said.

"Hallelujah," Raoul said.

"Biggest bang I've seen in a long time," Carlos said. "And like Maria wanted, no civilian casualties. Let's get a beer, I'm parched."

"I have a bottle of whiskey back at camp," Luis said, smiling.

"Then let's get out the hell of here before someone finds us. Good work Luis,"

Safely ensconced back in camp, each man drank a toast from Luis's bottle.

෧෩෧

Slater and Casey trudged through the Intercontinental lobby unnoticed and sat in Casey's room, watching the colors of sunset dissolve into dark purple. Casey pulled a pouch from his shirt pocket, removed a wad of tobacco, and shoved it into his cheek. He poured two glasses of bourbon and, with darkness descending, along with Slater, put the final touches on their plan to liberate Maria.

The new hotel room was a simple one, not at all like the

one Casey had before the break-in. The creeps who had ransacked his room had not returned, so far as he was able to determine. Slater sat on the faded, brown sofa while he opted for a tufted, worn chair. After checking to make sure there was no one lurking outside, Casey closed the gold balcony door curtains. Relaxing with a drink, he reviewed their plan.

"Earlier, I scouted the area behind the hotel and found a path that leads up the hill behind the prison. There's a fence at the prison's boundary and ten meters inside are two ventilation shafts. The fence doesn't appear to be electrified like I thought it might be so don't worry, you won't die that way."

Slater smiled and sipped his bourbon. "I had hoped that you would be able to prevent my death, Mister CIA expert. Isn't that what you guys train for?"

"Listen, fella," Casey said, "don't put that kind of responsibility on me. You're responsible for keeping your own ass out of trouble. This is going to be risky, no matter how you cut it."

"I wasn't worried earlier but now I am. I've never done anything so foolish in my entire life. Without your specialized training, my goose is cooked. I'm a goddamned schoolteacher, not some trained counterintelligence agent. I'm in as promised, but I'm in over my head."

Casey laughed but noted the seriousness of Slater's remarks, for the man's forehead was wrinkled and his eyes were narrowed slits.

"Not being neutral worrying you, eh? Natural enough, I suppose. The truth is, either one of us could get ourselves killed, but you need to put that thought out of your mind. Consider this a suicide mission, and you'll be fine. Once we're inside, I'll take the far hallway and you take the other one. Speed will be essential and we cannot loiter. If you encounter a guard, don't ask questions—shoot to kill." He noticed an amused look on Slater's face and waved a finger in the air. "It's imperative that we locate her quickly. If you manage to find her first, blow the door with a grenade and yank her out. Sing out and we'll meet back at the intersection of the prison blocks. I'll lead us out of the administration building. When we get to the front door, we'll either shoot or blow our way free then head for the cover of the trees. Stay away from the main gate. Once in the trees, we'll return the way we came, down the backside of the hill to the rear door of the hotel. We should be safe if we can make it back to this room without anyone seeing us. Sound plausible?"

"We can't help but be discovered by the guards. You know we will have to shoot our way out."

"I know it sounds impossible but we don't have any other options. Except maybe to leave her there."

"Leaving her there isn't an option for me. It sounds irrational and psychotic, but, you're right, there's no other choice. I admit I'm scared, really scared. It's only that I hadn't planned to die at such a young age in such a faraway place as Managua. Will they take my body back to the States when this is all done?" He didn't wait for Casey to answer but kept talking. "Mother's going to be upset, which is the understatement of the century. If I don't make it, I at least hope Maria will get out."

"You're halfway there, Jim. Once you decide that you are already dead, the rest is easier. Just concentrate on the task at hand and pray for the best."

"That's easy for you to say, Casey, you do this for a living. I came here as a teacher and now look at me. I guess I have only myself to blame."

"Blame for what?"

"Falling in love with Maria was the last thing I expected. I was so engrossed in getting the school up and running that it left little time for anything else, let alone romance. I never even looked at a woman until Maria happened to pull me out of that bar. She warned me not to involve myself with her and her life, her cause. She said over and over that only heartache could come out of it. Initially, she didn't want to become involved with a *gringo* but I kinda kept at her until she acquiesced. So you see? It's actually my own fault."

"Gave in to your manly charms, eh?" Casey said and chuckled. "You're hung up on her, I can say that."

"It's taken me years to work through all the shit I went

through in Nam. I don't know, maybe I came down here to put the demons to rest once and for all. For a long time, I feared my inability to cope with the horror was the result of some flaw I had inherited from my father. He owned a garment factory in New Jersey and every night drank himself into a stupor. He'd play country music, cry in his whiskey, then pass out in his chair."

"What's he doing now?"

"He's dead. I watched him bleed to death in his bed. Ulcers." Slater took a long drink of his bourbon and stroked his forehead. "He died before the ambulance got there. I hated the man for the way he treated my mother and me and I never forgot the sight of him lying dead on those bloodstained sheets. For the longest time, I worried that I was just like him."

Casey stood, stretching his legs. "Your mother raised you, then?"

"Yeah. She did the best she could. At least he had some life insurance. It helped put groceries on the table until I was old enough to work."

Casey returned to his chair. "Why did you fear you were just like him? You don't seem like that sort to me."

"When my marriage turned sour, my ex convinced me it was my fault, that somehow I hadn't measured up. In the end, she wanted—no, demanded—something I couldn't provide."

"Like what?" Casey said.

"I dunno. Maybe security. It seemed to be what she craved most. And for the longest time I thought my inability to provide whatever she needed was an indication of my own inadequacy. I was the one that failed in the marriage."

"There is no such thing as true security, Jim. The world is full of tragedy, most of it just around the corner."

"Waiting to pounce on an unsuspecting, innocent schoolteacher, eh?"

"There are evil people out there and they make for evil circumstances. Good men, men of conscience, have to make a stand somewhere along the way."

Slater nodded and Casey continued. "The rebel's victory was widely hailed as a triumph over what was seen as one of the worst violators of human rights in the Americas. Ironically and tragically for the close to three million Nicaraguans, the Sandinistas have proved that they surpass their predecessors in abusing the basic rights of their own people. In Nicaragua, there is an all-out war on the human rights of all those who oppose the regime. The victims number in the thousands and include journalists, businessmen, politicians, Catholics, Moravians, the Miskito Indian tribes, and even Nicaragua's entire Jewish community. Today's human rights violations affect all aspects of Nicaraguan life. There are restrictions on free movement, with torture; denial of due process; lack of freedom of thought, conscience, and religion; as well as denial of the right of association and unions."

Shadows filled the room and the two men continued to talk until time for supper. Moved by Slater's openness about his marriage, Casey related his own story. "I grew up in a small, Midwestern town," he said. "When I graduated from high school, I didn't know what I wanted to do. My parents, of course, wanted me to attend the state college but I wasn't sure. So I joined the army, became a member of the military police, and was stationed at our embassy in Laos. While I was there, I went to jungle warfare school in Thailand and, before I knew it, was teaching the intelligence and counter-intelligence course at the School of Americas in Panama.

"When my time in the army was up, I went home and tried to find a job. What a laugh. I missed the intrigue and the remote locales I left behind, so I called a former MP buddy who worked for the Company. He arranged an interview and soon I was on the payroll. My first assignment was in Angola where I helped UNITA fight against the Soviet-backed MPLA. It was a civil war and thousands of Cuban soldiers fought with the MPLA. I left when they came to power. From there, I went to Afghanistan to train the Muslim mountain fighters, then was transferred to Costa Rica eighteen months ago."

"You're not afraid of dying?"

"That possibility goes with the territory—you learn to live with it. Most of my assignments have been more hazardous than this one. I'm basically an advisor down here. But the counter-revolution needs Carlos and I can't let Maria rot in El Chipote. It's my fault she's there—it was my idea to assassinate Perez. The one thing you learn is to clean up your own messes. But enough of me."

"I didn't think our government or the CIA condoned assassinations," Slater said.

"Get real, Jim." The corners of Casey's mouth curled in a smirk. "You should know different. Wherever American interests are at stake, the Company uses every tactic at its disposal to ensure success. Neutralization is just one of our many weapons.

"Take counter-intelligence, for example. It is my main purpose in Nicaragua. Effective counter-intelligence enhances security and helps achieve surprise. Any effort that is designed to prevent the enemy from obtaining data helps reduce the losses the command suffers. My greatest frustration is in getting the contra forces to understand that each individual combatant is an agent of counter-intelligence since he can provide information on the activities of the enemy. Much of this depends on the individual soldier. But enough of that, please continue with your story. You were talking of your failed marriage."

Slater stood and pulled the curtain back from the window and looked out into the night. Stars twinkled above. The streets were busy with traffic. "I guess I was running away when I came here. I had tried to play the Wall Street game and worked for an advertising firm, but didn't have the stomach for it. My wife craved the parties and excitement of life on the merry-go-round but eventually I had to get off. I was overweight, drinking too much, and hating myself in the process. I was sour on life and desperate for something to rejuvenate my sagging spirit. Mother suggested the Peace Corps and I taught English and water purification in Costa Rica for a few years. When the Sandinistas took control here, they established this literary program, so I came to teach along with several thousand Cubans. That small school behind my home? I built it myself with the aid of a few villagers. It's been a slow process, and a lot of hard work, but I've grown to love these people. For the first time, I feel I'm doing something important. Something for which I'm suited. I've been able to sleep at night, something that hasn't come easy for a long time. The nightmares are a thing of the past."

"And Maria?"

"Maria was so unexpected I can't explain it. The day we met was like a dream. I can tell you that no other woman in my life was ever worth risking everything, that's for sure. Any love in your life, Allan?"

"No. Not that there haven't been a few narrow escapes. This work doesn't allow for much romance. Usually just one night stands. I admit it would be nice to get home for a few months and catch up with the women."

The men sat and drank until Casey noticed Slater dozing on the sofa. His hope for a family had disappeared long ago, the day he joined the Company. Slater was lucky. Finding a woman like Maria was asking too much of random fortune. It had to be fate, kismet, which brought the two together. He hoped all would proceed well. Tomorrow night, they either had a date for Maria's liberation or an opportunity to meet in the hereafter.

CHAPTER 18

Perez paced the narrow, rutted roadway, watching his column of vehicles warm their engines. Captain Salazar and two sergeants arrived for the commander's meeting and saluted. The day began as a routine one in the field with a breakfast of jerky, orange juice, and coffee. Finished eating, Perez put on a clean uniform and scraped the mud from his boots before summoning Salazar and the sergeants. A hot sun blazed down onto the circular clearing, forcing him to don sunglasses retrieved from a shirt pocket. He enjoyed commanding troops in the field and the mirrored glasses helped maintain a proper distance between himself and his men. The chasm between officers and enlisted men was the hallmark of every known army since Napoleon and Perez enforced it rigorously.

After Salazar's salutation, Perez began the meeting.

"What is your best estimate, Captain, of the direction of the contra forces from here? Do you believe they're still in Honduras?"

"South, I would think, Colonel. Something tells me that they are back in Nicaragua." Salazar conferred with his two sergeants then continued. "Sergeant Mena has seen some tracks several kilometers in that direction." He pointed to the south side of the compound and the sergeants nodded in agreement. "If those tracks belong to them, then they have crossed back over the border and cannot be too far from here.

They may be only a few kilometers from where we are standing at this moment."

Perez stiffened at the thought. "Our fuel dump is that direction?"

"Yes, it is. We can fill up there and not waste much time."

At that precise moment, a deafening explosion echoed through the jungle. Seconds later, the concussion hit the convoy and rattled the trucks and tanks. The ground beneath Perez's feet trembled and he steadied himself on the windshield of his jeep. To the south, he saw a column of black smoke billow skyward and watched flames dance among the treetops. He stared for a moment in disbelief.

"What the hell was that?" he said. "My binoculars, Sergeant."

Perez joined the group of men who were running to the south side of the vacant compound and were staring at the smoke cloud that hovered over the jungle's canopy.

"Our fuel," Salazar said. "Our fuel dump is in that direction, sir."

Perez realized that Salazar was right. He cursed. "Those good-for-nothing bastards," he said. "Captain, send a patrol of four men to investigate. I want to know what happened. Report back as soon as you know the status of our fuel. Go now."

Salazar left to form the patrol while Perez continued his ranting. "By God, I'll have their balls. And I'll hang their heads from the fence posts in Pueblo Salto. They shall not humiliate Colonel Perez. By God, I will have their heads."

He watched four men scramble into a jeep and race toward the smoke. Then he eased his large frame into his jeep and waited for word from the patrol.

⊆⊆⊆

Slater and Casey spent the evening organizing equipment and packing it into two knapsacks. They stuffed nylon climbing ropes, rappelling gear, a flashlight, wire cutters, and a hacksaw into each pack then turned their attention to the weapons. Casey handed Slater a 45-caliber semi-automatic pistol and an M-16 with two clips. After a run-through on how to load and lock a magazine, he handed Slater a set of black fatigues and face-black.

"Put these on," he said. "They will help. Lucky for us there's no moon tonight. I've noticed the clouds forming in the southwest. We may even get some rain."

"What about security cameras?" Slater said. "How do we get past them?"

"I don't remember seeing any," Casey said. "This is an old prison and State Security hasn't bothered to update it that I know of."

"But you don't know for sure?"

"Like I said, I don't remember seeing any. The National Palace is a different story. It's all high tech there."

Slater checked his gear and weapons again in silence. He was preoccupied with thoughts of Maria, had she been mistreated or tortured? He silently repeated Casey's earlier mantra. "You're already dead. Convince yourself of that fact and things go smoother."

Casey looked out the balcony window onto the street below. "The streets have been quiet the last few days," he said to Slater. "Not many demonstrations."

"Not after the government rounded up the perpetrators of the last one and threw them in jail. It seems every time there is a gathering of people friendly to the contra cause, the army shows up and arrests them, exactly like Somoza. Suppressing free expression."

"Most definitely," Casey said. "But our contra friends have not been entirely free of culpability themselves. The fundamental difference between democratic insurgents and their communist counterparts is the avoidance of military operations that lead to civilian casualties. Military targets are the objects of insurgent strategy. Kill civilians and you are simply a terrorist. We must develop in the hearts of these contras a high regard for human rights or the result will be the same as with the Sandinistas. Some of the contra leadership is already realizing this and things are starting to change but, until recently, the contra commanders have not provided the affirmative leadership that insisted on proper conduct. As a result, a number of events occurred in the field that damaged the contras' reputation, both in Nicaragua and abroad. They simply cannot abuse their own people. Carlos has finally realized that popular support is impossible if they do not change their tactics. Incidental collateral civilian loss is one thing but to actually target civilians is unacceptable. The US wants democracy here for very good reasons. Democracy has its own moral imperatives, as you well know, but it also has advantages that are profoundly practical. Democratic states do not attack their neighbors and destabilize regions. Democratic states do not find it easy to declare and carry out war. They have built-in controls against aggression and genocide. These freedom fighters must learn these lessons of history if they are to survive the long haul."

Slater closed his pack and buckled it. He stood beside Casey who was still watching the street.

"There are no good answers, are there?" he said.

"Unfortunately not. My job is to develop a certain unity and organization within the contra command. The truth is that there are about one thousand contras in the north and they have been living among the people and have inflicted substantial damage on the military. What is unique about Carlos's squad and a few others is that they have been operating outside the regular contra command structure. Because of that, there is no overall plan of action or strategy. Chaos. So the answer is not as simple as it appears on the surface."

Slater looked at his watch. It was eleven thirty. Casey wanted to start toward the prison around 1 a.m. so he had a few moments in which to relax. Relax, the very thought was a joke. The waiting bothered him. It was beginning to wear on his nerves. He would just as soon go now and face whatever there was to face but recognized Casey's experience in these matters. He would do the best he could. Like his father used to say: '*Son, do your best, it's all a mule can do.*' His father. He had not thought of his father for such a long time. Charles Winchester Slater had died before his only son had graduated from high school but not before he had profoundly influenced

Slater's life. For the worse, he might add. As a business owner, he was never around when the family needed him. Business, that was all Slater ever heard from the man. Business, it
was as if it was the only important thing on the planet. Business and alcohol. What about a boy needing time with his father? Having someone to talk to about growing up? Someone
to take him fishing and hunting? Someone to talk to about the
meaning of life. His father had been in an alcoholic haze until
that fateful day he puked up blood until the life was out of
him. No, Slater never missed his father.

He stretched out on the bed, closed his eyes, and tried to
sleep, but it would not come. He thought of Maria but it was
no use. His mouth was as dry as dirt and tasted just as bad. He
tried thinking of the school but sleep was far away. His stomach rolled, pushing foul-tasting bile into his throat. He felt
sluggish and was worried—worried that he would not make it
back from the prison. What then? Dammit, how did he get
himself in this mess in the first place? Was it Maria's fault?
No, of course not. Not directly, anyway. He had vowed to
never again find himself in a position of trying to justify killing, but here he was, doing just that. He prayed that all would
go well during the next few hours.

He awoke to a tug on his arm and looked at his watch. It
was 1 a.m. and Casey was donning his pack. Slater rose,
splashed water over his face, shouldered his pack, and picked
up his M-16. His muscles ached. Casey opened the balcony
door and went over the edge of the railing, climbing down the
drainpipe that emptied into the hotel's courtyard. Slater peered
over the edge and Casey signaled for him to follow.

The iron railing was cold to his touch when Slater hoisted
himself over it and reached for the drainpipe. The patio and
swimming pool area was deserted and quiet. On his way
down, a hotel worker passed below him. He hesitated till the
man was gone then jumped the remaining five feet to the soft
ground. Casey led the way to the rear of the tiled patio and
crouched behind a hedge. Slater noticed Casey's eyes darting
over the grounds then watched the man's backside while the
agent crawled past the wrought-iron gate. He stopped behind

an unoccupied delivery truck and signaled an all clear. Crouching low, Slater sprinted to Casey's side and, together, they proceeded to the hill behind El Chipote.

They crossed the grassy field with ease, neither of them looking back at the hotel. Casey had been right, there was no moon, only black velvet clouds, no stars. Moving quickly and silently, they made their way up a gentle slope until Casey stopped short.

A ten-foot fence greeted them, looming large in the darkness. Casey removed wire cutters from his pack and with four sharp snips opened a hole in the fence. No alarm sounded. Slater breathed a sigh of relief and followed Casey.

The hill that housed the prison was more like a knoll in the middle of the city and El Chipote's security force kept it mowed. In the 1960s, Somoza built the prison and it was to be moved after a state-of-the-art facility was completed. Only Somoza understood his reason for building the prison next to the Intercontinental Hotel but Slater learned that his personal bunker used to be located in the hotel's basement.

Short, scrubby vegetation covered the rocky mound and offered no resistance to their hiking. Crouching low, the pair made their way up the mound, M-16s at the ready. The night air was cool with a soft breeze blowing up the hill. The place was quiet—no sentries on patrol. Slater followed Casey behind a large rock where he paused behind a sparse tree to scan the prison's perimeter. Casey raised a hand and pointed. Slater instinctively knew the signal—they were no longer alone.

Something was out there in the darkness.

Slater peered into the dark but could not make out what had gotten Casey's attention. But then he heard it. A low rumbling noise. It stopped then started again. Whatever it was, it was getting closer. Then Slater recognized the sound—a jeep. Casey motioned and the two men ran to a shallow ravine where they fell onto their stomachs. Slater's pulse quickened as the jeep advanced nearer. When it reached a distance of a few meters from them, Slater could make out the silhouettes of two soldiers, one driving, the other manning a mounted machine gun in the rear seat.

Slater buried his face deeper into the grass while the jeep rambled past. The pounding in his chest moved to his throat and he gripped his M-16 tighter. He could hear the men singing. Pausing only meters away, they directed a searchlight into the trees, its bright light illuminating the forest's edge. Continuing their patrol, the jeep disappeared into the darkness. Slater realized he had been holding his breath and breathed a long sigh of relief.

Both men scrambled to their feet and Slater followed Casey to a flat area where, protruding from the ground like short obelisks, were two, metal ventilation flues ten meters apart. Slater stooped to touch one when Casey stopped him.

"Wait," he said in a low voice. He put an ear over the duct and listened for a moment. Satisfied, he slapped Slater on the back. "This is it. Good luck. I'll take the one down there. Use the hacksaw to cut the top off these things. Remember, holler if you find Maria and we'll meet at the intersection of the two hallways."

With that admonition, Casey scrambled to the next ventilation shaft and left Slater rummaging in his pack for the hacksaw. It was now or never. Time to suck it up and do the job.

ᏋᏬᏋᏬ

Perez was low on fuel. He paced around the destroyed fuel tanks, spewing venom. The flames were all but gone but the pungent smell of burning gasoline and smoke irritated his throat. Captain Salazar worked the men with shovels to put out the few flames that remained. The smell reminded him of Managua during the final days of the revolution when he rode through its streets and up to the National Palace. Combined with the 1972 earthquake that leveled the capital, the war that raged in Managua left the city buried in burned rubble. He wondered if his beloved city would ever recover. If only the fighting would cease, the country could heal its wounds, rebuild, and look toward a brighter future. But he knew that Nicaraguans killing each other only deepened the scars, making it impossible to forget the atrocities the other side had committed. Brother killing brother was not a path to reconciliation. At heart, he was a soldier. He loved donning the uniform. Nevertheless, with the passing of each day, he realized what the uniform was beginning to stand for—killing and oppression. He worried that the government was losing its moral imperative.

Perez tramped down the line of convoy vehicles. Without fuel, he was dead in the water. He could bivouac nearby but it would take two days for fuel from Managua to reach him. He was screwed and he knew it. In all probability, Carlos was nowhere near the area and was tossing back beers in some *cantina.*

He had no choice but to wait for the fuel supplies to arrive. Earlier, he told Salazar to make the request top priority so it would go directly to Rivas. It had taken most of the day, but now the captain reported the motor pool division in Managua was loading his fuel onto trucks. When the dense clouds of smoke lifted, Perez retrieved a bottle of Napoleon brandy from his duffel and took a long pull. The liquid burned and he smacked his lips. The liquor brought to mind thoughts of Maria and the poisoned brandy she had offered him. What was happening to her at this moment? When he got back to Managua, she was going to pay. To hell with hoping for a reconciliation.

CHAPTER 19

A gush of cool air filtered upward through the ventilation shaft, drying the sweat on Slater's forehead. It had been tough work sawing the protective metal cover off with a hacksaw. Thankful that his work had gone undetected, he buckled his climbing harness around his waist and clipped the rope to the shaft using a metal eyelet inside. Maneuvering his large frame into the shaft, he pulled against the rope testing it, then dangled his legs into the darkness below. He began lowering himself an inch at a time using the rappelling technique Casey showed him at the hotel. It took several attempts but, once he got the hang of it, he descended without incident. Hanging in the black abyss, it took a few minutes for his eyes to accommodate but, after several minutes, he was still unable to make out the bottom of the shaft. The backpack dug into his shoulders while his M-16 hung at an awkward angle over his back.

Downward, he continued, sliding along the rope and stopping every few feet to check his bearings. *God grant me a strong rope.* The darkness of the shaft caressed his face like black velvet. After descending what he calculated was ten meters, he noticed a faint glow of light filtering up from the bottom of the shaft. He placed his feet against the side of the shaft to steady himself and continued his descent until he hung a mere five meters above the opening into the main hallway. His senses were on full alert, straining to hear voices below. But there were none. All was quiet except for the pounding in his head. Then muffled sounds percolated from the hallway into the ventilation shaft and hung there like a country ham in a smokehouse. Slater reached for his M-16 but was unable to get the weapon off his back. He knew he was a sitting duck hanging from the end of the climbing rope. Placing his feet against the sidewall of the shaft, he braced himself and watched as the shadows of two men passed beneath him. When he was certain they were gone, he lowered himself to the wire screen that covered the opening into the cellblock hallway. He pushed against it. Nothing. It didn't budge. He wondered how Casey was making out. Had he lowered himself into the hallway?

Slater pushed harder and the screen moved an inch. Working his finger through the opening, he managed to pry the screen up enough for his body to fit through. With each tug on the screen, it creaked softly. He grabbed the side of the opening, turned himself upside down on the climbing rope, and peered through the opening. Dim light from a couple of lanterns lit the narrow hallway. No guards. Righting himself, he contemplated his next move. Without making noise, and careful not to drop anything onto the floor below, he disconnected the climbing rope, wiggled through the hole, then fell to the floor.

∽∾∽

Casey was in trouble. Halfway down the shaft, his rope became tangled with a carabiner and the resulting knot halted his progress. He tried several times but could not free the rope. He could cut himself loose and fall the rest of the way, but suspended as he was in darkness, it was impossible to make out how far he was above the hallway or even if he could land without injuring himself. Damn, he thought. The rope appeared to be twisted around the metal figure-eight rappelling device used to slow his downward momentum. With the darkness impeding his progress, he worked by feel trying to solve the dilemma caused by the nasty tangle of rope. After a quick scan of his situation, he figured his weight had caused the knot of rope to tighten, making it impossible to unravel. His fingers ached from the work. He was wasting precious time and the longer he stayed in the shaft the more likely was the chance of his discovery. The darkness of the shaft made it difficult to discern the cause of the entanglement but it seemed the figure-eight had turned at an awkward ninety-degree angle on the rope itself. He tried forcing it back to its proper position but it would not budge. Precious minutes were ticking away.

He grabbed the climbing rope above him, pulled with all the strength he could muster, and was able to raise himself enough for the figure-eight to pop free, allowing the tangled rope to fall free below him. Breathing easier, he continued his descent toward the shaft's opening.

ୡୢୡୢ

Standing motionless, Slater peered down a long, dark passageway illuminated only by dim lanterns spaced unevenly along the stone wall. The cobblestone floor reeked of human excrement and moist earth. The air, which hung like a heavy shroud in the underground catacomb, made for difficult breathing. Along each wall was a series of oaken doors each bearing a number and a small opening. There were no sounds or movement. He checked his .45, brought the M-16 to his waist, and began walking down the hallway. At any moment, he knew he could encounter a guard or group of soldiers. He moved the safety lever on the M-16 to the *Fire* position and continued. He paused at the first doorway, peered through its window, and noticed a black form huddled in a dark corner. The prisoner's back faced the door, making it impossible to tell if it was a male or female. Could it be Maria? It didn't appear to be her. After a quick deliberation, he continued down the hallway.

He remembered Casey's advice and screwed the silencer onto the .45's barrel. An eruption of gunfire now would spell disaster.

Methodically, he crept down the hallway, pausing to peer into each cell. Halfway, he stopped short at a window, a woman was sprawled on the floor, her body illuminated by a beam of dim light that shone into the cell. Slater looked up and down the passageway, still alone. He rapped on the door with the butt of his rifle.

"Hey," he said. His voice was low, not more than a whisper.

The body didn't move. He called again.

"Hey, woman. Look here."

The woman turned on her side and looked at Slater. He was stunned at what he saw. Her face was covered with dark, foul bruises and her eyes were mere slits. It wasn't Maria. The woman said nothing, put her head back onto the concrete floor, and moaned.

Slater saw that he was close to the intersecting hallway where Casey said they would rendezvous. He glanced over his shoulder then continued his search. At the moment he approached the next cell, two soldiers turned the corner, stopped, and stared at him. One reached for his pistol and the other ran back the way he came. In an instant, Slater brought the M-16 to his shoulder and fired a fuselage of bullets into the soldier, which pitched him onto the concrete floor, his uniform splattered with blood.

Slater moved forward, straddled the dead body, and aimed his rifle at the back of the fleeing soldier. He hesitated, calculating his next move. The man shrieked an alarm. Too late— the place would be crawling with guards in a matter of seconds. He could hesitate no longer. He pulled the trigger, the short burst from his M-16 hit the man in the back, sending him reeling into the stone wall then crashing onto the cobblestone. A red ooze formed beneath the guard's body.

Panicked, Slater resumed looking into the remaining cells in the hallway, nerves frayed and on edge. No longer concerned about being discovered, at each window he called Maria's name. Seconds mattered. He would be overwhelmed very soon. Four doors to go. His mouth was dry, his head throbbed but somehow he managed the strength to look into the next cell.

"Maria," he said. "Are you in here?"

There was an imperceptible moan from the far corner.

"Maria, is that you? Please, whoever you are, show your face."

A slumped form emerged from the darkness and crawled toward the door. Slater jumped. It was Maria. She was only a remnant, a skeleton, of what he remembered—hair matted with dried blood, one side of her face contorted with an ugly swelling. He noticed the fluid ooze from her nose when she pulled herself to the window.

"Stand back, Maria. It's Jim. Casey and I are here to get you out. Stand back, I'm gonna blow this door."

Maria staggered into the cell's dim recesses while Slater fumbled to find a grenade. Hands trembling, he pulled the pin and tossed the grenade against the door. A thunderous *boom* knocked the door off its hinges and billowed black smoke toward the ceiling. But the hole caused by the grenade wasn't very large, too small for Maria. He pulled another grenade from his pack and was about to pull its pin when Casey appeared at the end of the hallway.

"Find her?" he shouted through the smoke that surged down the passageway and engulfed him.

"Right here! This ought to do the trick."

Slater threw the second grenade and it blew the splintered door into the cell. Slater leaped through the smoke into the room, seized Maria by an arm, then pulled her into the hallway.

Casey grabbed his arm. "This way." He ran to the intersection of hallways pointing his M-16 down each passageway.

Slater hauled Maria after him, steadying her each time her legs buckled beneath her bruised body. At the intersection of hallways, she collapsed in Slater's arms.

Casey turned right and was met by a band of soldiers, their rifles at the ready. Without giving them a chance to shoulder their weapons, Casey opened fire and continued firing as he ran toward them. Slater followed. They leaped over the dead bodies and ran through a steel door to the administration building.

Maria seemed more alert.

"Jim, is it really you? I never thought I would see you again. I can't believe it."

"Just hang on," Slater said. "We'll talk later."

Another wave of guards appeared. This time they fired first and the bullets ricocheted past Slater's head, causing bits of the stone wall to pelt his face.

Casey spun and grabbed Slater by the shoulder. The hallway erupted in pandemonium, with gunfire sounding up and down the hallway. Two guards appeared in front of them and Slater emptied his clip into them sending a shower of blood over the cobblestone floor. He caught up with Casey who had a blood stain on his shirt.

"I'm all right," he said. "Just a shoulder wound. Let's go."

The piercing wail of an alarm screeched through the prison as Slater and Maria followed Casey to their last obstacle, the iron gate at the entrance to the administration building. The gate was affixed to a low wall and beyond was the front door. Past that was fresh air and freedom.

Slater leaped into the on-duty sergeant's office and shot him dead with his .45. The man's eyes widened in horror when the three bullets tore into his rotund body.

Meanwhile, Casey strapped two grenades onto the gate. Slater looked behind them and realized more soldiers were scrambling after them. Shouted commands could be heard over the wailing of the alarm. A dozen soldiers fell to their stomachs and began firing their weapons. Bullets zinged past, a few of them bouncing off the gate with loud *pings*. Casey and Slater pushed Maria behind the wall just as the grenades went off. The resulting blast blew the gate into a mass a twisted metal. Slater shoved another clip into his automatic rifle as more soldiers bolted into the room. In a fusillade of rifle fire, Casey's and Slater's bullets ripped them apart, sending bodies flying in different directions. One soldier careened through a window and out onto the lawn.

The trio bolted through the door into the moist, night air as the siren continued to howl from the depths of prison. More soldiers raced toward the administration building.

Casey darted along a narrow sidewalk until he reached a

rustic walkway where he stopped. He beckoned Slater and
Maria to follow. Ten meters down the walkway, he ducked
into a clump of trees then made his way over the hill until
Slater recognized the lights of the hotel. The muffled sounds
behind them worried him. The soldiers were close.

Casey pointed toward the swimming pool and the hotel's
rear entrance. "The back door!"

The trio burst into the hotel's empty lobby. Only the night
manager was on duty and he was asleep behind the desk. They
jogged up the stairs to Casey's room and, after locking the
door behind them, Maria and Slater collapsed on the floor.
Casey crossed the room, closed the curtains to the balcony
door.

Slater held Maria's bloody head in his arms and looked into her bloodshot eyes. She looked a mess, a swollen, broken
face protruding from a bloodstained prison tunic. She was
limp, bruised, and incoherent. She smacked her lips and tried
to open her eyes.

"Water," she said.

Casey filled a glass from the tap and brought it to Slater
who held it to her lips. She tried to drink but only managed a
few sips before falling onto Slater's chest, sobbing.

"There, there," he said. "You're safe now, sweetheart,
you're safe. No one's going to hurt you."

Casey went to the balcony and peered through the curtains
onto the street below. It was apparent he was having difficulty
with Maria's emotional outburst. "It's not over yet, Jim," he
said. "One of us needs to watch from up here until we're sure
they're looking elsewhere."

The room was dark. Slater and Maria lay on the floor while
Casey stood watch. Slater covered Maria's shivering body
with a blanket and tried to get her to drink the water. Once,
Casey brought him a moist towel and Slater gently worked on
Maria's bloodied face, removing most of the dried blood. He
held her close and she responded to his touch by nestling her
head into his shoulder.

"What about the night manager?" Slater asked Casey. "He
could have seen us."

"I dunno. Let's hope he's a contra at heart or else was really asleep as he seemed."

"You think they know we're here?"

"Probably not. They must think we would be trying to get out of the city. Hopefully, we can hole up here until we know for sure what they're doing. I need to clean my shoulder."

Slater turned his attention back to Maria. She cried until the early morning sunlight began to filter through the curtains.

CHAPTER 20

Without fuel to move his convoy, Colonel Perez knew he was a sitting duck, for he was stranded, unable to continue the pursuit. It had been twenty-four hours since he had informed the National Directorate of his predicament and he was still waiting for the motor-pool tank trucks to arrive. If they were attacked, he wouldn't be able to mount much of an offensive—there was only his infantry and the tank-mounted machine guns. That fact meant that an attack by the contras would be difficult to repel. He was at a decided disadvantage.

Captain Salazar posted sentries around the convoy and sent out reconnaissance patrols in order to receive a timely warning if the contras were indeed nearby. A mess tent stood in the center of the circle of jeeps and half-tracks and the men took turns eating and patrolling the perimeter of their bivouac. A corporal set a large plate of jerky, bananas, and a cup of luke-warm coffee on the wooden desk in Perez's tent. He returned the soldier's salute and devoured his lunch. While munching the tough jerky, he scrutinized their position and his men. He was proud of the well-seasoned troops, trained and schooled in modern tactics of jungle warfare. While fighting the dictator Somoza, the Sandinistas' advantage stemmed from their Cuban advisors and Castro's experience in leading an insurgency. Besides Cuba, Venezuela and Panama became major suppliers to the Sandinista movement.

Now, as if repaying the debt, Nicaragua was helping the Marxists in El Salvador.

Perez was a captain when the fighting escalated in early 1979. Somoza had rejected a mediator's final proposal for free elections, which left the United States with no options for dealing with the crisis. In protest, the American administration withdrew its military mission from Nicaragua, sent back to Nicaragua the last members of the National Guard who were being trained in the United States, cut the size of its embassy staff in Managua, and canceled several aid projects. Perez felt contempt for America who, he reasoned, had abandoned his country even though he had detested Somoza. When American interests were threatened, they pulled out, leaving his people to fend for themselves.

Salazar brought his plate of food to Perez's tent and the two men ate and talked.

Perez was in a reflective mood. "You know, Juan, back when we were fighting Somoza, most of us believed in the revolution and its ideals. But I remember how bitterly some complained when the fighting accelerated the deterioration of the country's economy."

"I too, remember," Salazar said. "The cotton crop wasn't planted, cattle were dying, and Nicaragua was on the brink of collapse."

"The devaluation of the cordoba only served to make matters worse."

"You fought in Leon, didn't you, sir?"

"Yeah. We took control of the city and began a systematic extermination of the *Guardia*. They were a tough lot. I remember that."

"Remember when the OAS met in emergency session and demanded that Somoza step down?"

"June, 1979," Perez said. "The US couldn't decide whether to continue backing him or not. After the owner of *La Prensa* was assassinated, America could not be seen as supporting the bastard, so they pulled out. Somoza found himself isolated internationally and had no place to procure the weapons he needed."

"It didn't take long after that. Somoza left for Miami in July."

"His leaving was more than we could have hoped for. Unfortunately, we inherited a nation dismantled by the civil war and crippled by forty years of one-family rule."

"But the bastard finally got his in the end. We took care of him in Paraguay, didn't we?"

The colonel didn't acknowledge this last remark by Salazar. Somoza's assassination had been accomplished by Rivas's secret police in an astonishing display of intelligence and retribution. While riding in an unarmored Mercedes along the streets of Asuncion, Somoza was attacked by a Sandinista assassination team who fired an RPG-7 anti-tank shell from close range. The warhead tore open and incinerated the Mercedes, killing the former dictator instantly. Perez had heard from inside sources that Fidel Castro had planned the operation and armed the assassination team. Afterward, Perez had girded himself for the long process of nation building and took a personal vow that he would not allow the intoxication of triumph to overrule his sense of justice. But the contras proved to be another matter. If they were bent on destroying what had taken years to accomplish, he would defend the National Directorate to the end, if necessary.

౭ఎ౭ఎ

Carlos, Luis, and Raoul were literally stuck in a difficult situation. The jeep in which they were riding had plunged into a mud hole and was mired to its front axle. Carlos paced around the vehicle several times then kicked the front fender.

"Damn," he said. "What the hell else is going to happen? We need to be moving. I'm sure the army isn't far behind us. This is ambush territory."

Luis, who had been driving at the time, offered a suggestion. "Carlos, you and Raoul push from the front while I put this thing in reverse. Let's see if we can't rock this baby out of the hole."

Carlos and Raoul complied. The pair began pushing on the

jeep's front fender while Luis spun its four wheels flinging mud in all directions. But the jeep didn't budge. Its rear tires were on solid ground but offered no help in propelling the vehicle out of the mud.

"Get some logs," Carlos said. "Let's see if we can't get them under the tires for better traction."

Luis jumped out of the jeep and helped Carlos and Raoul slide the tree limbs under the tires. It was difficult, heavy work and soon the trio was covered in the foul-smelling mud. Luis cranked the engine and tried to back out of the hole. Once, he almost succeeded but a limb snapped and the jeep lunged back into the hole. They leaned against the jeep, resting.

"It's too far to walk back to camp," Carlos said, after each of them lit a cigarette. "We're going to have to free this damned thing ourselves, and quick."

At that moment, the Sandinista Army emerged from the forest and surrounded them. In their vain attempts to free the jeep, Carlos had not heard them approach. He shot a glance into the back of the jeep and winced at the sight of their weapons just beyond reach. To make a grab for them was suicide. Luis and Raoul jumped to their feet and raised their hands. Heavily armed soldiers, led by a sergeant, approached Carlos and brandished an AK-47 under his chin.

"So, *amigo*," the sergeant said. "I see that you and your friends are stuck. And now you are prisoners, you contra pigs."

Carlos said nothing, opting instead to observe Luis and Raoul stand with raised hands.

"Please stand, *amigo*," the sergeant said.

"I'm not your *amigo*," Carlos said. His voiced hissed with venom.

"It does not matter, senor. But it is a shame that you should find yourselves the victims of such an unfortunate incident as this. You and your friends will most surely hang. *Vamanos*."

The sergeant motioned with his rifle, prodding Carlos ahead. They tramped through a maze of undergrowth three abreast, surrounded by the government soldiers. Carlos knew better than to hope for a miraculous rescue in such an isolated

place as this. Their hands bound behind their backs, they
trudged with difficulty through the mud. Where had the soldiers come from? He hadn't even heard them. Anger flushed
his cheeks. He should have known better. He could still make
a run for it. Better to be shot down trying to escape than face
the end of a rope.

They wallowed up a shallow ravine after crossing a small
footbridge that hung over a fast-flowing stream. The sergeant
directed the column south along a narrow trail until the jungle
once again engulfed them. Once, the sergeant stopped for water and signaled to keep quiet. Carlos thought of yelling, hoping it would get someone's attention but, feeling the barrel of
an AK-47 at his head, reasoned against it.

Carlos's eyes met Luis's and he nodded. Luis bumped into
Raoul who looked at Carlos. When the patrol rounded a
mound of tall brush, Carlos let out a yell and started running.
Luis and Raoul each ran in different directions and, for a moment, it appeared that their captors were caught by surprise,
dumbfounded by the confusion. Pursued by two soldiers, Carlos dashed through the jungle, tripping over vines and hidden
branches. He scrambled down a steep ravine and splashed
through a shallow stream. When the soldiers stopped at the
stream, Carlos managed to widen the gap between them.

Gunshots rang out behind him, tearing up bits of ground
around him. He struggled to remain on his feet as the bullets
slammed into trees, barely missing him. One lucky shot and it
would be all over. His boot caught a stump, throwing him into
a dense pile of leaves and branches. With his hands still bound
behind him, he fell on his shoulder and a bolt of pain ricochet
through his body. Frantic, he wormed his way deeper into the
thicket. Peering through the vegetation, he watched the soldiers race along the edge of the ravine. Finally, their voices
vanished in the distance.

He lay submerged in the foliage, until dusk settled on the
mountain, then worked himself free of his bindings. Pulling
himself to his feet, he looked around. It was quiet, the usual
chatter of monkeys and parrots replaced by an eerie stillness,
which was disconcerting. The only sound was his own heavy

breathing, and it took a great effort to get air into his lungs. He had a general idea of the direction to Pueblo Salto and started walking.

എൻ

The gunfire at the head of the convoy caused Perez to take a quick gulp of his coffee then run to investigate. He could see a group of his soldiers at the edge of the jungle pushing two, ragged men ahead of them. The prisoners wore mud-covered fatigues and one of them cradled a bloodied arm. Salazar met the column and, when the captives halted their progress, he forced them onto the ground, their hands bound behind them. The sergeant saluted Perez.

"We found these two north of here, sir. Another man got away."

Perez put a hand on his pistol and hissed, "Get up, you contra bastards."

The sergeant pulled the two men to their feet and pushed them toward the colonel.

"Names?"

The prisoners stared at the ground. The sergeant chuckled then cracked the ribs of one prisoner with the butt of his rifle. The man groaned and doubled over.

"Luis," he said, between gasps.

Perez looked at the other man and held up a finger.

"Raoul," the man said.

"You are the perpetrators who blew up our fuel tanks yesterday, yes?" Perez said. He noted their hostile gaze and stuck his face close to the one called Luis. "I'm asking. You are responsible for that?"

The man remained silent, his glare fixed on Perez. Perez turned on his heels to direct his questions to Raoul.

"And you? You were part of the attack on our fuel?"

The prisoner remained silent, staring at the ground. Now impatient, Perez turned and issued a command to Salazar. "Blindfold them," he said. "Then bring them to my tent."

Perez ambled to his tent while Salazar searched for a bandana to comply with the order. Inside the tent, Perez sat on his cot and took a stiff drink of his brandy, followed by two more large gulps before Salazar pushed the prisoners into the tent and removed their blindfolds.

"If you do not cooperate," Perez said, "I will have no choice but to hang you both. However, if you choose to help us find your companions, I might have compassion and spare your lives. You have a friend, yes? The one who escaped?"

Luis and Raoul said nothing. Perez saw no remorse on their faces nor did they beg for mercy.

"You must be thirsty. Sergeant, bring these men some water."

The sergeant left, returned with two large bottles of water, and offered it to the prisoners. Both shook their heads.

"Come, come, gentlemen," Perez said. "Maybe I was too harsh earlier. Did we not all fight that dictator Somoza and desire the same thing from the revolution? Did we not want freedom from oppression and equality? You have not given the president enough time to make improvements in Nicaragua. He wishes that I extend his understanding and willingness to put these unfortunate misunderstandings behind us. It'll give you a chance to turn over a new leaf, so to speak. What do you say?"

The prisoners remained silent. Their eyes, however, were riveted on Perez.

After a long pause, he rose from the cot. "Very well. Have it your way."

Luis stepped forward and spat upon the colonel. "You," he said, "are a butcher. We fight for our freedom. May God have mercy on you."

Perez took a bandana and wiped the spittle from his jacket then motioned to Salazar. The captain led the prisoners into the clearing, pushed them onto the ground in front of the sergeant. Back in Perez's tent, he pleaded with Perez. "Please, sir, do not hang them," he said.

Perez took another drink and chuckled. "What do you suggest we do with them, Captain? Spank their bottoms and send them home to mother?"

"No, sir."

Perez noted the agitation in Salazar's voice and toyed with his watch.

"I think we should take them back to the barracks and lock them up," Salazar continued.

"Then what?" Perez said. His patience was growing thin.

"They should be forced to stand trial, Colonel. If we kill them, it will only strengthen their cause. They will become martyrs."

Perez exploded. He felt the vein in the middle of his forehead throb as he ranted at Salazar. "Their cause? I don't give a goddamn about their cause. The sooner we kill these bastards, the sooner we won't have to worry about their cause. Are you suggesting, Captain, that I don't follow moral constraints in war? If so, please say so. You are dangerously close to insubordination."

Salazar locked eyes with Perez for a long, silent moment then stepped back into the door of Perez's tent. "No, sir, I'm implying no such thing. But I believe that if you kill these contras, the world will call it murder and there will be hell to pay. We will not be able to escape the wrath that follows. These prisoners are our own countrymen, for Christ's sake. The Geneva Convention states—"

"The Geneva Convention be damned! These men are not part of a national army. They are the enemy, Captain, terrorists. Don't ever forget it. They are shit and don't deserve to live. I knew you had no stomach for this sort of thing. It's too bad that the dengue fever that killed your wife didn't take you as well. This meeting is terminated. That is all, Captain."

Salazar reddened, withdrew, and Perez followed, holding the brandy bottle in a firm grip. He had a headache along with the burning in his stomach. Luis and Raoul were pushed into the rear of a truck and forced to stand while two ropes were thrown over a thick tree limb. A thin soldier fastened a noose around their necks. At the same time, another soldier secured the other end to a tree. Perez walked to the side of the truck and looked at the prisoners. For a moment, their eyes were locked on each other. Perez wished they would beg for mercy but neither man did so. He took another drink of the brandy and raised his hand. A private scrambled into the truck and started its engine.

"See you in hell," he said and brought his hand down to his side.

The truck lurched forward leaving the prisoners swinging in the air. Their bodies jerked a few times then dangled motionless at an awkward angle. Their bulging eyes continued to stare at Perez. He drew his pistol and shot each one in the head. The men stared at the swinging bodies. Captain Salazar ducked his head and walked away.

"Leave them be," Perez said. "It will be a lesson to whoever finds them."

He returned to his cot and finished off the brandy. Mission accomplished, or at least most of it. Now to find the dog, Carlos. He knew Secretary Rivas would approve of today's action but he would have to watch his captain. The man was growing soft and weary of war and might easily betray him. Maybe it was time to have him reassigned to another unit. Perez lay back on his cot, closed his eyes, and allowed the effects of the brandy to carry him away from the field of battle.

ல௸ல

Maria felt better although her face was still a dark purple from the torture she endured at El Chipote. She lounged in Casey's hotel room, recovering, with Slater and Casey for two days. Only then did Casey deem it safe to travel. They took Slater's truck to San Rafael and were now ensconced in his house. Along the way, they kept a sharp eye out for Sandinistas but never saw any. Casey had proceeded on to Pueblo Salto to look for Carlos, Luis, and Raoul. The group needed to reassemble to assess their current situation. Maria lay on Slater's sofa, eyeing the coffee he held out for her.

"Thanks," she said and sipped the hot liquid. "Are you all right?"

"Never better. Now, anyway. For a few moments back there, I didn't think I'd ever see you again. I've never shot anyone at close range before. I was really shook up for a while."

"I thought I was done for and would spend the rest of my life in that hellhole but you delivered me. I never, for one moment, ever thought you would actually come. I prayed and hoped, of course. Fortunately, my prayers were answered. You must know I love you."

Slater went to the kitchen and returned with a damp cloth. He sat beside Maria, dabbed her face with the cloth, and stared into her large, brown eyes.

"You have the most beautiful face," he said. "No wonder I'm in love with you."

Maria tried to hide the swelling and smiled.

She touched her face and winced. "How can you say that with me looking like this?"

Slater lowered his voice to a whisper. "I'm in love with you, Maria. If it's the last thing I do, I'm going to find a way out so we can leave this insanity behind. I want to take you home, introduce you to mother. I know she'll be happy."

Maria's eyes filled with tears and she placed a hand on Slater's shoulder. "I love you. I want you to know that. I love you more than I've ever loved anyone in my life. But we need to locate our friends and find out what has happened to them. Only when I am assured my comrades are safe, can we talk about a future together. Can you understand?"

Slater nodded and kissed her softly on the cheek. She responded by pressing her aching body against him and felt his warmth envelope her. They kissed until Slater picked her up and carried her to bed then crawled in beside her. She turned and faced him, tears streaming down her swollen cheeks.

"Please," she said. "I'm not ready yet. I—I just can't."

Slater kissed her again on the cheek and she felt him curl beside her. She was soon asleep.

CHAPTER 21

Carlos stumbled into Pueblo Salto, weak and out of breath. He collapsed into a chair at the Café Central and wiped his head with a bandana. Armando stuck his head through the door and waved at him.

"Something to drink, Carlos? The beer it tastes good on such a hot day."

"No, Armando. Bring me water, please. I'm very thirsty."

Armando brought a bottle of water, set it on the table in front of his friend, and watched Carlos gulp it down. Finished, he wiped his mouth with the back of a dirty hand.

"Thanks," he said.

"*Senor,* where have you been? You have been gone many days and you look terrible. Where are Maria and the rest of your friends?"

"Armando, there's been a disaster. I have been—"

"No," Armando said, "on second thought, I don't want to know. It will be better if it remains a secret with you."

Carlos nodded and finished his water. Armando left and returned with another bottle. Carlos tried to calm his nerves as he drank.

"Maria is in prison," he said between gulps. "And Alberto turned out to be a Sandinista agent and double-crossed her. I don't know where Luis and Raoul are. Have they passed through the village here?"

Armando ignored the question and pressed Carlos for more

details. In spite of his earlier pleadings to remain ignorant, he seemed to care for the group. "Maria. In prison? Where?"

"El Chipote."

"Shit, oh dear," Armando said, shaking. "No, Luis and Raoul have not been through here in many days. The last time I saw them they were with you. But please, Carlos, do not tell me anything more. I don't want to have to face the army when they come. And I feel they will come very soon. How long can you go around blowing up things?"

"I'm dead already, Armando. It's just a matter of when I will be buried."

With that explanation, Armando disappeared into the café and left Carlos alone. He would hike to San Rafael and wait for Slater and the others to show up. Maybe they would have news of Maria. He remembered that Casey and Slater were going to try to bust her out and he hoped they were all sitting in Slater's house toasting each other. He drank the last of the water, waved at Armando through the café's open window, and began the walk to San Rafael.

☙☙☙

Slater was changing the tire on his truck when he heard Carlos yell from the edge of the jungle. He looked up and from a distance saw the contra leader running toward him. At the truck, they embraced.

"Where have the hell have you been, man?" Slater said. He slapped Carlos on his back and watched the dust erupt from his jacket. "You, Luis, and Raoul were supposed to have relocated your camp. Did you?"

"No," he said, shaking his head. "Our jeep got stuck in the mud and we were ambushed by a government patrol. I lost Luis and Raoul in the jungle, we all ran in different directions. I hope they were able to get away."

The sun was high and fierce and Slater squinted at Carlos. "Let's go into the house. Maria's here. She'll want to see you."

"She is?" Carlos let out a whoop and ran ahead of Slater.

Maria jumped to her feet and greeted him with a long embrace.

"So you two did it?" Carlos said to Slater who had followed him. "How on earth did you pull it off?"

Slater went to his refrigerator, brought beers for each of them, and they sat, Maria between them, on the sofa. Carlos held up his beer.

"To Maria," he said.

They toasted Maria's escape then Slater told Carlos the details.

"Alberto," Maria said, "the sonofabitch is a traitor. He put me in that infernal snake pit and if I ever see him again, I will slit his throat."

"And Casey, where's he?"

"He is on his way to Pueblo Salto," Maria said.

"I just came from there and didn't pass him. You don't think he's disappeared do you?"

"I'm sure Casey can take care of himself," Slater said. "Tell us about your encounter with the army. What happened?"

Carlos took another gulp of the beer and rubbed his legs. Maria took his hand in hers and held it while he talked. His capture was a solemn, somber story that brought her to tears. He told them everything, beginning with the blowing of the fuel tanks to their capture by the soldiers. His voice cracked when he got to the part where they had managed to get away.

"I remember glancing over my shoulder," he said, "and seeing the soldiers chasing Luis and Raoul into the trees. It was the last time I saw them. I heard gunshots. I dunno—I hope they got away."

Carlos's words brought more quiet sobs from Maria. Slater said nothing, all he could think of was to hold Maria close.

∽∾∽

Casey found a crowd of angry people when he arrived in Pueblo Salto. In the middle of the dirt road, a group of farmers were standing in a circle, cursing, and several of the women wept while the men paced around them. He approached and pushed his way through the gathering to where he could see what was happening. He recognized the contorted bodies that lay on the ground amidst the villagers.

Luis and Raoul.

There were black rope burns around their necks and their swollen heads were at odd angles to their bodies. Each had a bullet wound to their head and their throats had been slashed. Their open eyes possessed a pained look as if they had watched their captors hang them. Luis's tongue, swollen and dark, protruded from his mouth.

Casey stooped and examined the bodies. Aware that the villagers were watching his every move, he systematically rummaged through the dead men's pockets but found nothing. After the inspection, four men carried the corpses out of the sun and onto the porch of the café.

One of the men signaled Casey. "Do you know these men, senor?"

Casey nodded. "Yes, I do. They were friends of mine."

"Pardon me for prying," the man said, "but are you are American?"

Casey nodded again, wondering why the stranger had asked the question.

"We know that Americans are helping the guerrillas fight the Sandinistas. These men are contras?" the man asked.

"I don't know," Casey said. "I thought they worked at the coffee plantation."

"Not that I ever saw. Maybe the Americans have sent you to spy on us."

Knowing the man could be an informer, Casey diverted the discussion to another topic. Too bad Slater wasn't here, for the people trusted him.

"No. I'm a friend of Jim Slater's in San Rafael. You know, the American school teacher?" Several of the men, who had gathered around Casey, nodded and he continued. "Will these men get proper burials?"

The farmer stepped forward and looked at Casey as if trying to size him up. "Yes. We will see to it. Someone will noti-

fy their families. Senor, more of my people die each month.
This war cannot last forever. Do all soldiers think us poor
farmers are stupid? Do they think we have no feelings? Tell
them, senor. Tell them to stop the killing."

Casey left the bodies on the porch and began his walk back
to San Rafael. He took his time for he wasn't in any mood to
give Maria and Slater the sad news.

લ૭લ૭

When Casey told Maria, Slater, and Carlos about Luis and
Raoul, Maria fainted onto Slater's sofa. Slater fanned her
while Casey tried to bring her around by massaging the backs
of her hands. Revived, she sipped on a bottle of water.

"How can this be happening?" she said, crying. "First,
Julio, now Luis and Raoul. Alberto is a traitor. I'm not sure I
can take much more."

She put out her hand. Slater took it and kissed it.

"I know," Carlos said. "Hanged like dogs. I can't believe it.
But this is war." He turned to Casey who sat with a puzzled
look on his face. "Who did it? Or might I guess? The only bastard who has been roaming around up here is the butcher Perez. How about it, do we know it was him?"

Casey returned from what appeared to be a deep preoccu-
pation and gave his opinion. "It was Perez, I'm sure of it. Carlos is right, the man has had the run of these mountains in re-
cent months. You need to come up with a plan that will deal a
significant blow to the Sandinistas, kill the bastard if you can.
We may be too small a group to do something devastating but
we can still make their lives miserable, maybe even reduce
their numbers a bit."

"We tried murder. It didn't work. Sometimes, I've known
small guerrilla groups that could actually do more damage
than a whole battalion," Carlos said.

"Like what?" Maria said, sitting up, looking better.

"I don't know, yet." Casey stood. "But after a good night's
sleep, I'm sure we will be able to think of something. I'm
bushed so I think I'll turn in. Can I sleep on the porch, Jim?"

"Of course. I have a few spare blankets if you and Carlos want one."

Casey motioned to Carlos.

"Come on. Let's leave these two guys to themselves. I'm sure they would like a little privacy."

Casey and Carlos carried the blankets onto the porch and closed the door behind them. Slater hugged Maria then kissed her. He tried to concentrate on the feel of her warmth, and the touch of her skin, but his mind was spinning from the news of Luis and Raoul.

"It's all so sad," she said. She pulled back and ran her fingers through Slater's hair. "I mean Luis and Raoul. They were so young and eager. All they wanted was freedom and a home for their children and families."

Slater looked into Maria's eyes, noticed that the swelling had diminished. "They died for what they believed. No man can ask for more than that. Their cause will live on and give strength to their memory. Freedom, Maria, doesn't come easy or cheap. The history of my own country shows that."

"I know, Jim. It's just that it doesn't seem fair, that's all. To give that last full measure."

"Maria, I think it's time for us to discuss our future, you and me. I want to take you home, marry you."

Maria shifted her weight on the couch and stiffened. "I want it too. But it would be like deserting my fallen comrades, especially now. Deserting Carlos. He's given so much, I can't bear to leave."

Slater took Maria by the arms and looked her straight in the eye. He felt her tremble under his touch. "If we want the same thing," he said, "then why not go home? I'm afraid that if you continue in this insane war, that one day you won't come back. Then it will be your body, they bury in Pueblo Salto. Don't you love me enough to leave this madness behind?"

Maria cried and her crying made him feel ashamed. He wished he could take back the callous question.

She looked at him, eyes red. "You're asking me to choose? How can you do that? Do you think I have no honor?"

"I'm asking because I love you, dammit. Or doesn't that

make any sense to you? Why do you make it a question of honor? Are you so wrapped up in this insane war that you have no time or place in your heart for love? Are you saying that you have been able to suppress the feelings you have for me? Is fighting the only thing that makes you feel alive anymore? That makes sense to you?"

Slater was on the verge of losing his temper with her and he realized it. He rubbed his eyes. "I'm sorry," he said. "I didn't mean to berate you."

Maria stood and used her hands for emphasis. Her face was red and she was noticeably upset. Her brown eyes darted across the room. "My darling, how can you think that of me? You must know that I love you. But I was a part of the insurgency before we met, and it's something that I have to complete before I can allow myself the pleasure of a future. Why is it so difficult for you to understand? Why do you think I haven't allowed myself to make love to you? It's because if I did, I know that I could never stay in Nicaragua. I would turn my back on my country and leave with you, never looking back, and I couldn't live with myself if I did. Please don't force me to choose between you and what I see as my duty. If you make me choose, I would gladly leave duty and honor behind but would end up hating myself in the end."

"But you must know that you have no chance of winning," Slater said. "The tide is against you and if the States quit sending arms and advisors, you will surely die a horrible death at the hands of the Sandinistas. As God is my witness, I believe with all my heart that the cause is hopeless."

Maria went into the bedroom and closed the door. Slater sauntered out onto the porch where Carlos was already snoring. Casey propped himself on an elbow and whistled.

"She's some woman—that she is. You're a lucky *hombre*, Slater."

"Yeah, I know."

Slater sat on the steps, looked up at the stars, and tried to count his blessings. Difficult as it was, he would not pressure Maria again.

If a future together was to be, then it would happen without further meddling on his part. He would not ask her to betray her comrades.

"We need that air drop," Casey said. "How about three days from now? I can radio Costa Rica in the morning?"

"Fine," Slater said. "Just fine."

He continued to gaze into the velvet heavens until Casey's breathing was slow and regular. Overhead, a meteor blazed across the sky and the thought struck him that it was a metaphor on his life at present. Before Maria, he was happy in his noble neutrality, staying above the fray. Now, he had successfully overcome his deepest fears about violence and bloodshed, worked through all that stuff, but was he any closer to winning Maria over to his desire to get the hell out of Nicaragua? Obviously, by her last remarks, it was not to be. Not in the near future, at least. Was there an honorable and happy ending to his predicament? Or was he destined to burn out like the meteor? He lay on the porch, closed his eyes, and wondered.

CHAPTER 22

Colonel Perez was near exhaustion. He sat in Minister of Defense Rivas's opulent office and listened to the secretary's harangue that lasted the better part of an hour. The thick, black cigar that Rivas lit at the beginning of their meeting was now only a smoldering stub. Rivas continued to hammer him with the same repetitious questions.

"Are you telling me, Colonel, that you almost had Mendoza in your grasp and managed to let him slip away?"

"I told you this before, Mr. Secretary. If the contras had not blown up our fuel depot, the man would be in El Chipote right now. We were close, so close. He just slipped between our fingers, that's all."

"Such an unfortunate consequence," Rivas said. He poured himself a glass of water from a chrome tumbler and drank it down.

"These contras know that area like the back of their hand," Perez said, not waiting for Rivas to finish his lecture. "We missed hanging all of them by a matter of only a few minutes. If we had refueled the convoy before the explosion, they would not have gotten far. I did everything I could."

"Colonel." Rivas put up a hand and smiled at Perez. "The simple fact is that you have had two excursions into the mountains, with minimal results, and nearly got yourself killed by a woman whom you or your staff did not thoroughly check out." His tone turned vulgar and a dour expression formed on his face. "The president, although initially impressed with your handling of this situation, is now losing patience with your ineptness and your excuses. The time has come for more positive results."

Perez looked out the window with a certain sense of pride, in spite of the secretary's scolding. The sun was beginning to cast late afternoon shadows over the distant mountains and a cool breeze filtered through the window. He knew Rivas was right. On the other hand, his intelligence had been accurate enough to locate Mendoza's band of contras. It was his misfortune that the contra leader had escaped his grasp. The contras must have found the fuel tanks by accident, and it was Perez's bad luck that had sent their tanks skyward, leaving his convoy out of gas.

"Mr. Secretary, I am as concerned about these matters as you, but—"

"Enough!" Rivas said. "You have two weeks to produce this scoundrel. If you're not successful, I will find someone who will be. Do I make myself clear, Colonel?"

Beads of sweat popped out on the back of Perez's neck and he thought about interjecting an opinion but decided against it. Rivas was on the edge. Perez didn't want to push the man further.

"In addition," Rivas said, "you will avail yourself of the latest intelligence reports concerning contra movement in the mountains. You will brief me when you have devised a plan of action. Is that clear?"

Perez thought he was going to pop a cork. The blood rushed to his temples and banged away, in rhythm with his heart. How dare the man? The minister knew that he was perfectly capable of engineering a plan of his own design to bring Mendoza to justice. This was Rivas's ultimate affront, to challenge his ability to command and have him ask permission, like a little schoolboy before going into battle. Perez massaged the sides of his head and tried to remain calm. Smiling, he nodded his understanding.

"That is all, Colonel," Rivas said.

Perez rose, clicked his heels together, and saluted the Minister of Defense. He turned toward the door guarded by two uniformed soldiers.

"One last detail," Rivas said. "The story of your tryst with this contra woman is all over town. There was even an article in *La Prensa*, making a spectacle of your foolishness. My wife called your wife and chatted at length with her—now she's accusing me of the same thing. She may have even hired a detective, for all I know, so the risk is not worth it, anymore. Your parading this woman throughout all our social circles, Colonel, has left many of us having to dump our lady friends. You have a lot of damage to atone for. I wish you luck. Good day."

Perez hurried down the marble stairway and out the front door to his Mercedes. He ordered the driver to take him to Maria's apartment where he could be alone and not have to face his wife. Not now, if what Rivas had said was true. The Mercedes stopped at the front of the apartment and Rivas ordered the driver to wait for his return.

Inside Maria's living room, he removed his jacket and foraged through the cabinets in the living room and kitchen. He found a half-full bottle of his favorite brandy and poured himself a large glass. He grimaced and fought to keep from gagging on the liquid while he sat in the brocaded chair, lit a cigarette, and studied the apartment. The security police had taken all of Maria's clothes and personal items so the place was vacant except for the furniture. It was not supposed to turn out this way. He pondered the first few times he and Maria had been together and struggled to figure out what behavior might have given her away.

His wife was another matter. He figured she suspected his philandering but she never mentioned her suspicions. If what Rivas said was true, regarding the newspaper article, his wife would smear his name to all her friends and the name *Perez* would not be worth anything. He poured another full glass of the brandy and noticed it went down much easier.

His thoughts vaulted back to Maria. She had been smart, he concluded, for he was unable to recall any indiscretions on her part. She was composed, courageous, and calculating. He had been so captivated by her charm and beauty that he allowed himself one fatal flaw—he trusted her—a relative stranger. In his eagerness to take her to bed, he had turned his back on common sense. He muttered a vow never to make that mistake again.

෴

A large crowd gathered under the grueling sun in Pueblo Salto. Slater, Maria, and Carlos were among the throng that stood at the edge of the tiny cemetery. Several women wept as the priest from San Rafael spoke from a tattered Bible.

Two wooden boxes containing the bodies of Luis and Raoul lay beside two fresh graves. The coffins were crude and fashioned by a man in the village who had been a carpenter under Somoza. Slater sweated in the hot sunshine as the priest finished his words and threw a handful of dirt into the graves. Four men lowered Luis into the ground and, without saying a word, picked up Raoul's coffin and lowered it into its grave. After a final word from the priest, the crowd began to dissipate leaving several men behind to fill the holes.

Slater tried to put the deaths of the two men into some sort of context but had difficulty doing so. War was hell, or so the saying went, but that didn't mitigate the loss of good men. It didn't in Vietnam and it didn't here. When good men died, even for the cause of freedom, something went with them. And here, Nicaraguans killing Nicaraguans, made their deaths that much more senseless. Somoza was bad, to be sure, but now the Sandinistas were perpetuating similar crimes against the population. With each generation, the insanity never seemed to end.

"I need a beer," Carlos said. The trio walked back to Slater's truck.

They found Armando at his café and the man brought each of them a cold beer. His eyes betrayed feelings of remorse.

"Did you know their families?" Maria asked him.

"No, *senorita,* I did not. I knew them because they were friends with you and Carlos, that's all. I figured all of you were contras but I didn't want to know anything more. How were Luis and Raoul killed?"

Carlos drank his bottle of beer in a long gulp before answering. He pulled his canvas hat down over his crooked nose and toyed with his copper bracelet. "The Sandinistas killed them," he said. "They had finished a mission when the army found them and hung them, the bastards."

"Casey says that if you don't get fresh supplies in the next few days, the government will gain the upper hand," Slater said.

"I thought you were neutral, Jim," Carlos said.

"Not after getting Maria out of El Chipote. Somehow, I have been thrust into the middle of this civil war, my friend, whether I like it or not. It's difficult to remain neutral in view of my feelings for Maria."

"Falling in love complicated things, didn't it?"

Carlos chuckled and Maria blushed.

Slater took her hand in his. "It's turned me into a confirmed contra supporter," he said. "But I don't want to see action. I still wish to remain out of the fighting. Let's say I have contra sympathies and let it go at that."

"It's hard, Carlos, for an American to fight in a war that was not of his making," Maria said, coming to Slater's defense. "Besides, I want him to stay alive."

Armando brought another round of drinks and Slater paid for them. The village of Pueblo Salto was empty and the road to San Rafael deserted.

Slater stood and stretched his legs. "My country keeps fueling the killing. I don't understand." He paced around the porch. "I wonder what's keeping Casey," he said. "Shouldn't he be here by now, Carlos?"

"Do not worry, *amigo*. He will show up sometime. He needed to use your radio to contact his station chief in Costa Rica to make sure the drop is on schedule."

"Who flies these missions?" Slater asked. "Surely not the CIA."

"No. It's a company on contract with them. I thought I heard Casey call them Corporate Air Services. They fly out of

Miami, land in San Jose, then fly over the mountains of southern Honduras and northern Nicaragua to a spot we call the Hammerhole."

"How do you all work it?"

"Simple. A C-47 comes in low over the prearranged drop zone, dumps their load, then returns to Costa Rica. Once we cut the crates loose from their parachutes, our men load them onto trucks."

"Aren't you worried about an RPG round taking them out? Flying low and slow, it seems, makes for an easy target."

"We worry about it all the time, of course. Hopefully, our sentries who scout the area would be able to notice if the army is around and we would call off the drop."

Casey arrived in a car he borrowed in San Rafael and joined them on the porch. Armando handed him a beer and they drank while Casey briefed them.

"It's all set," he said. "Tomorrow night. Same location as last time. Grid coordinates 268 and 411. Carlos, get your friends on Slater's radio and let them know. We will need their help."

Carlos nodded.

"What do you get on these air drops, Carlos?" Slater asked. He was interested in how the Americans had been aiding the contras.

"Medical supplies, weapons, ammunition, dynamite, and C-4 plastic explosive."

Slater let out a low whistle.

"It's been difficult," Casey said, "to get the larger weapons in by air drop so we're in the process of clearing a seven thousand-foot strip in the middle of the jungle. Mongoose, it's called, and it will be visible from the air to planes using the standard Pacific-side air corridor from San Jose's Aeropuerto Juan Santamaria. We will use L-100s which are civilianized C-130s. But for now the supplies come in by C-47s. Once the runway is completed, there will be a shipment of Stinger anti-aircraft missiles. I mention these things in strictest confidence, Jim. Down here in this heat it's easy for me to get carried away and shoot off my mouth."

"Don't worry, my friend." Slater laughed and smiled at Maria. "Your secret is safe with me."

"You can count on Jim," Maria said. She leaned over and patted his arm.

"I know," Casey said. "I had the pleasure of his company in El Chipote, remember? He's a good man to have around in a pinch."

"Enough about me," Slater said. "I want to know what you folks do for fun around here? Or is it all work and no play?"

Before anyone could answer, Casey slapped the table with his fist and stood. "By God!" he said. "You have hit the nail on the head, Jim. You'll be happy to know that next week Archbishop Quintero is having a reception at the diocese grounds on the shores of Lake Managua. It's a semi-secret affair with most of the influential anti-Sandinista elite invited. It should be great fun."

"What'll keep the army from bombing the place and killing everyone?" Maria asked.

"Public outcry, I suspect. It wouldn't do their cause one bit of good if they assassinated the whole of the insurgency in one night along with the archbishop. Then who would they have to fight?"

Evening was beginning to settle over Pueblo Salto and the fading light was turning a deep azure. Armando gathered their empty beer bottles, locked the café, and said goodnight to the group. When the sun sank below the jungle canopy, a gentle breeze stirred and Slater and Maria headed back to San Rafael with Casey and Carlos following behind. Slater glanced at Maria, her brown hair blowing in the breeze. Good grief, now he was going to an airdrop.

CHAPTER 23

Under a dark and starry sky, Slater, Maria, and Carlos ventured into the mountains above Pueblo Salto. No clouds were visible and the silver moon illuminated the path to the drop zone. Riding in Slater's truck, they kept their guns at the ready while Carlos sat next to the passenger door and gave directions to Slater.

The road was deserted. Winding through the jungle in the cool night air, Slater relaxed with the jostling of the truck as it bounced along. Ascending the mountain, they zigzagged around mud holes and ravines that were barely visible in the pale moonlight. Here he was, aiding and abetting the covert guerrilla actions of the damned Central Intelligence Agency. It was a long ways from his college days and Vietnam. However, no amount of rationalizing could overcome his sense of guilt and frustration with his relationship with Maria. He might as well face it, there was to be no relationship until she could free herself from the shackles of Nicaragua that bound her to Carlos and the contra cause. Pressing her to make a decision now, he knew, was hopeless and counterproductive. So, he had to give her the distance, freedom to go her own way. Only when she decided there could be time for them, would anything more be possible. Hard as it was, he had to resign himself to that idea. There was no alternative.

The road divided at a rustic, wooden hut that sat next to a plowed field. It was quiet and dark except for the moonlight that reflected off the hut's tin roof and into the truck. Carlos checked his map then signaled Slater to follow the path to the east. Past the farm, the clearing dissolved again into jungle and the narrow road became a serpentine trail.

Slater looked at the luminous dial on his watch. 12:30 a.m. According to Casey, the plane should be arriving any minute. Slater braked hard to avoid a wild dog that darted in front of them and watched the animal scurry into the underbrush. Maria put her head on his shoulder while Carlos whistled a lively tune. He glanced out the rear window and was relieved to see no one following them.

"Here," Carlos said. "Stop."

Slater stopped the truck at the edge of another clearing, indistinguishable from the one by the farmhouse. The clearing was the size of a football field and bordered by the jungle. In the weak light, the short grass glistened like jewels on a calm lake. A gentle breeze fluttered over the field and against Slater's face. Carlos pointed to the end of the clearing.

"Over there. Drive to there and park in the trees."

Slater did as he was told and soon he had stopped the truck in a clump of dense cedar and mahogany. The trio jumped out of the vehicle. Carlos grabbed two lanterns from the back of the truck. He gave one to Slater.

"Light this and put it over there," he said pointing to the middle of the clearing. "They'll use these as guides for the drop. Get back here after you get it into position. The plane will only be a few meters off the ground and I don't want you accidentally injured by one of the crates."

Slater found a match in his pocket, lit the lantern, set it on the ground in the center of the clearing, then ran back to the truck. He heard the drone of an approaching aircraft in the distance behind him. Meeting at the truck, Slater and Carlos searched the sky for the plane's silhouette. Maria stood beside him clutching his arm with a cold hand.

Slater thought he heard the whine of a motor and scanned their perimeter. Carlos pulled a flashlight from his field jacket and flashed the light in the direction of the sound. Two flashes. Slater made out the return signal, three short flashes of light. The noise grew louder until a large military half-track loomed out of the sticky darkness and rumbled up to the pickup. Four men jumped to the ground each one wearing camo fatigues. They waved at Carlos.

"*Buenos noches, amigos,*" Carlos called as they shook hands.

Slater noticed the men's stares and Carlos smiled.

"This is Jim Slater, an American. He is helping tonight."

"CIA?" one of the men asked.

"No," Carlos said. "*Amigo.*"

The men nodded and each shook hands with Slater. *So friendly and trusting*, he thought, not at all like the Sandinistas he had known.

Everyone stood at the edge of the clearing waiting the aircraft's arrival. The purring of its engines lowered in pitch, signaling that the plane was on final approach to the drop zone. Maria put her hand in Slater's and took a deep breath.

"I hate this part," she said. "They're always so low. A mistake could mean disaster."

At that moment, a large shadow with two powerful lights dropped out of the nothingness above and swooped over the field. The roar of the plane's engines was deafening and the squall created by its prop-wash rustled Slater's shirt. He shielded his eyes from the blowing dust. Then, as quickly as it dropped onto the clearing, the plane roared to life and climbed back into the velvet sky. When Slater looked back at the field, he saw two large crates sitting in its center. The four men hopped into the truck and raced to the payload.

"I thought you said they were going to use parachutes," Slater said to Carlos.

"Too much wind, I guess. It's their call. This is better for us actually 'cause we don't have to chase those infernal parachutes all over the damned jungle. Let's go help load."

Carlos led the way, with Maria and Slater struggling to keep up. Each wooden crate was four feet on each side, weighing, Slater guessed, around four hundred pounds apiece. There were rope handles on the sides of the crates making them easily lifted onto the half-track.

"What's in here?" Slater asked.

"Machine guns, ammunition, dynamite, and C-4 explosive. Should make a big bang, yes?" Carlos laughed as he mimicked an explosion with his hands.

"What's the C-4 for?"

"Two hundred pounds of C-4 goes a long ways down here," Carlos said. "We use it for bridges, buildings, that sort of thing."

The trio returned to Slater's truck and followed the half-track through the jungle. The new base camp, Slater noticed, was carved into the dense vegetation, which allowed the forest's canopy to shield it from the prying eyes of Sandinista helicopters. Without headlights, it was difficult to make out the main gate of the camp where a young man in his early teens walked guard duty. The gate was nothing more than a sawhorse placed across the trail.

He relaxed when he saw the trucks, sauntered to Slater's window, and shined his flashlight into the cab. Carlos smiled and waved at the man.

"Arm?" the man asked with what Slater surmised was a password of some sort.

"Chair," replied Carlos.

The man saluted and opened the gate to allow the two vehicles entry into the compound. Slater remembered that there had not been much time to build huts. The camp was dark and quiet. The half-track stopped in front of a long, olive drab tent and its four occupants jumped out and began unloading the two crates.

Once the crates were inside the tent, Carlos closed the flaps and switched on the crude light bulb. Everyone gathered around as he took a pry bar and began opening one of the boxes. With a loud *crack*, he popped the top off and they all peered inside. There were fifty M-16s, and cases of 7.6 millimeter ammunition. And the much-desired RPGs. Slater noticed the square, metal containers with the words *Danger— Explosive Material!* stenciled on them.

"Ah, the C-4," Carlos said picking up one of the metal cases.

Slater felt Maria against his arm and continued staring into the box.

"More bang for the pound than dynamite," Carlos said.

Slater wasn't listening, his mind somewhere else, anywhere than in a highly fortified contra camp deep in a Nicaraguan jungle. If he was caught here, he knew what it would mean. And after what happened to Luis and Julio, he was convinced he wouldn't be able to talk his way out of it.

"We're going to use this stuff in Managua," Carlos said, "and make those bastards pay for what they did to Luis and Julio. Right, Maria?"

Slater watched Maria nod in agreement and felt his heart sink to his abdomen. It dawned on him, once again, that she was going all the way with the revolution. But, of course, he was, too. He knew his words alone would not stop her so he decided against trying—they had been through it before. She was not going to abandon her loyalty to the contra effort it was that simple. His choice was plain—either give in to the insurgency or forget about Maria. He could not bring himself to do the latter.

Back in San Rafael, Slater fixed himself and Maria an egg sandwich and they ate as the first glimmers of morning got under way. Carlos stayed in Pueblo Salto, for he wanted to eat breakfast with Armando.

Slater sat beside Maria as they ate. "You're committed, aren't you?" he said.

Maria nodded while she chewed.

"I hate to keep pestering you with this but I want to ask you one last time to reconsider your decision. I know I said I would go along with whatever you decided but I need to know once, and for all. Do you think there will ever be a future for us?"

Maria kissed him and touched his lips with the tips of her fingers. "Of course. There is only one thing more important in my life than you, Jim. And that's the dog who butchered Luis and Julio. I have decided that once I have avenged their deaths, my conscience will be free to allow me to follow you wherever you want to go. I love you. I need you. I want to spend the rest of my life with you. I can't be any plainer or simpler than that."

"What if the worst happens and—"

"We can't think of that now. I'm having great difficulty keeping it out of my every thought. The thought of dying without the intimacy we both crave causes me great pain and anxiety. But, it's the way it must be, for now. I'm sorry but we've been through this before."

Slater finished his sandwich and took their plates to the kitchen. When he returned, he brought two cups of re-warmed coffee.

"I don't know if I should tell you this or not," Maria said, "but you are a big distraction. I hope telling you won't make your head any larger than it is already."

Slater laughed and Maria smiled.

"So, what's next on the contra agenda?" he said.

"Casey was going to get the details about the archbishop's reception and try to procure a few invitations for us. It would be a nice diversion for us after all we've been through, don't you think?"

Maria walked into Slater's bedroom and he followed. They lay on the bed with her curled up inside the crook of his arm and slept until there was a banging on the front door.

CHAPTER 24

The *barrio,* or neighborhood, of *La Palma* lay on the western outskirts of Managua where the lakeshore turned northward and the main highway continued on to the city of Leon. The official residence of Archbishop Marco Quintero and the diocese's offices of the Roman Catholic Church were nestled comfortably on the shores of Lake Managua, at the northern edge of *La Palma.* The complex was a grand affair made of alabaster marble and gold-inlaid, deep purple tile. The pink of the marble glistened and shimmered in the setting sun and the view from the archbishop's balcony was a stunning, panoramic scene of the unfathomed, somber waters of the lake.

The reception hall was crowded. A five-piece band played waltzes, while impeccably dressed waiters in starched white jackets mingled among the guests and served cocktails, along with hot and cold hors d'oeuvres. Most of the guests were adorned in their finest gowns and jewelry. The men wore tuxedoes. Archbishop Quintero, a tall, gangly man in his early fifties, made the rounds welcoming everyone to his home.

Slater wore his best slacks and an open-necked shirt while Carlos wore jeans and a plaid shirt. He felt noticeably out of place. Casey had rushed back to his hotel room and put on his only suit. Neither of them desired to risk arrest by returning to Maria's apartment for a dress so Slater had taken Maria by the Mercado Oriental and bought her one. They arrived in two

vehicles, Casey's rental car that carried the CIA agent and
Carlos, and Slater's truck in which he brought Maria. Slater
and Maria paced around a large, stone fountain and waited for
Casey and Carlos to arrive.

"The National Directorate won't shut this party down?"
Slater said.

"Carlos says no," Maria said.

"This amounts to an anti-Sandinista rally, Maria. I can't
believe the government would allow this sort of thing."

"Normally, they wouldn't, but this is a Church function.
The Sandinista regime still has a few supporters, among the
Catholic priests and bishops, although not as many as in years
past. The Church seems to be unified in their opposition to the
Sandinistas because they say the government is fostering god-
less communism. The Sandinistas, on the other hand, want to
foster amicable relations with the Church and have incorpo-
rated some church officials into prominent government posts.
The National Directorate is well aware of the international
ramifications that would ensue if they raided this place and
arrested everyone."

Casey and Carlos arrived and the group walked into the
spacious, arched entryway. Casey presented his invitation to a
husky priest who ushered them to the banquet hall.

Enormous crystal chandeliers hung from the hall's high
ceiling and they cast beams of reflected light upon the guests
below. Slater and Maria didn't recognize any of the guests,
most of whom sipped champagne and talked in small groups.
They found the long, ornate buffet table, at one end of the hall
and filled their plates with heaping portions of roast beef, venison, wild turkey, potatoes in a thick cream sauce, and slices
of thick, crusty bread. They stood together, enjoying the spectacle of Managua's finest, and listened to the band while they
ate. A woman engaged Slater in conversation. She was dressed
in a plain, black dress and carried a small fur on her shoulders.

"You look American," she said to Slater.

"Yes, ma'am," he said.

"Business or pleasure?"

"I beg your pardon?" Slater said.

"Are you in Nicaragua for business or pleasure?" the woman said.

"Oh, I'm sorry. I teach at a school in San Rafael. I came here as part of the literacy program. I've been there for over a year."

"You have Sandinista sympathies, then?" The woman put her empty glass on a silver tray as a waiter passed and picked up a new cocktail. She looked at Slater curiously.

"No, not at all. I'm here to teach, that is all. I stay out of politics. And you? What do you do?"

"My husband is the owner and publisher of *La Prensa.* You have heard of it? It's the only anti-Sandinista paper in Nicaragua. The government has shut us down numerous times, for what they call misinformation. My name is Estrella Digas. And yours?"

"Jim Slater. I have heard of your paper, of course. And I read it every week. I applaud your efforts."

"My husband, Rubio, works hard to combat the communist pigs. Our paper has already been emasculated, by heavy censorship and, when the government closes our doors, it sends a symbolic message to the world that the Sandinistas are prepared for battle and are willing to take whatever steps they believe necessary to assure victory. Only after one of Nicaragua's Roman Catholic bishops was expelled from the country and there was an international outcry, did they allow us to go back to press. But, alas, the poor bishop never returned."

While Mrs. Digas talked, Slater continued to eat. Maria and Carlos listened as the woman explained her views.

"My husband's father, who started the paper many years ago, was gunned down by Somoza's men in 1978. On January 10, while he was on his way to a meeting here in Managua, they forced his car to the side of the road then opened fire. You would think that my husband would favor the Sandinistas, no?" The woman watched as several heads nodded. "Well, the Sandinistas have succeeded in inflicting enormous damage on Nicaragua, just like their predecessors" she said. "They have imposed economic policies that have failed in every country on earth where they have been tried. Take the health care system, for example. Somoza had wiped out polio by 1983 and cut the infant mortality rate in half. Now, the health of our children is in crisis, once again. Schoolchildren have no books or pencils. Food is in short supply and inflation is at one thousand percent. Only the Catholic Church and most of its priests have been of support to us."

"I know," Slater said. "I see the results of their policies every day in San Rafael. It's a shame, really."

"But when the President of the United States imposed an economic embargo against Nicaragua, he pushed us to the brink of bankruptcy and economic collapse. In capitals throughout Europe and Latin America, United States diplomats encourage governments who are friendly to us not to send aid. They have advised private lenders that although Guatemala, El Salvador, and Honduras are good credit risks, Nicaragua is not. It has been this way for a long time now. While a law student, my husband began taking part in demonstrations against Somoza. Now he writes against these new policies."

"You are not for this new government?" Maria said.

"Not at all. In fact, the contras are our only source of hope. The Americans have decided to help them in their counter-revolution so there may be some good come from it, I don't know. As a mother, I deplore the violence and bloodshed, of course. The blood of many of my countrymen has stained our flag, *senor*. The question is whether it will have been shed in vain. However, when the World Bank refuses to loan my country money to buy tractors and livestock for our farm cooperatives, it is a sign that the world does not care what happens in Nicaragua.

"The Sandinista dictatorship has taken absolute control of the government and the armed forces. It is a communist dictatorship. It has done what communist regimes do, created a repressive state security and secret police. They have harassed, tortured, and expunged the political opposition and, in many cases, murdered them. Now, they are arresting the relatives of the political prisoners, forcing them to confess. Peasants tell my husband of entire villages, homes, stores, and churches being burnt to the ground by the army. They tell of animals slaughtered, crops burned, and villagers taken away at gunpoint in government trucks. My people are taken to secret prisons or relocated to camps and never seen again."

Slater could tell that Maria was infatuated with Mrs. Digas and watched the two of them. Mrs. Digas seemed a strong-willed and opinionated woman, much like Maria. They both possessed a charm that came from deep-seated confidence forged on the anvil of hard times. The more Slater got to know these outwardly simple people the more he realized he was the ignorant one.

"You are aware I'm sure, Mrs. Digas, that we Americans fought our own civil war. It nearly destroyed our country and it took half a century to mend the chasm that followed." Slater took another mouthful of food and waited for Mrs. Digas' response.

"It's too late to preach, Mr. Slater," she said. "That's like closing the barn door after the horse is out, as you Americans like to say. We are committed to this revolution and will not rest until the National Directorate is toppled. It's them or us."

Slater smiled and tried to sound as light-hearted as he could. "Pardon my ignorance, ma'am, but who is us?"

"All freedom-loving peoples in Nicaragua," Mrs. Digas said. "All people who want to enjoy the fruits of their labors and live in peace with their neighbors. Unfortunately, the current Sandinista government has abandoned its open vision committed to Christianity, replacing it with a mythic fundamentalist vision to win people over. But it's making an error—society's increasing secularization, a progressive vision of faith and a traditional vision that always keeps the religious aspect independent of the political one, all contribute to making people uncomfortable, when political leaders try to manipulate their religious sentiments. Only the sectors with the most backward vision of the world and society can possibly be in agreement with the current government's way of framing things.

"The Managua clergy is quite varied, but all are conservative and like to be close to power and to the most powerful economic and political sectors. A good many of our priests have been won over by the government's policy of economic support for works, religious events, and land donations and have thus sacrificed their freedom to assume critical or prophetic positions regarding the country's situation."

Casey arrived with a drink in his hand and Slater introduced him to Mrs. Digas. The woman smiled and looked about the reception.

"I must excuse myself," she said to Slater. "And be careful whom you talk to tonight. The National Directorate has ears everywhere."

After she was out of hearing distance, Casey wanted to know all about Mrs. Digas.

"Who was that?"

"Her husband is the owner and publisher of *La Prensa*," Maria said.

"She has very definite views on this war down here, Casey," Slater said. "I suspect she could run for office if this country ever held free elections. However, I was beginning to tire of her long-winded explanations. Thanks for rescuing us."

"She might win if the Sandinistas don't blow the paper to kingdom-come first," Casey replied.

"If I had a Yankee dollar for every peasant or farmer jailed for their criticism of the government, I'd be a rich man today, Senor Jim," Carlos said.

"Listen, folks," Casey said. His voice sounded impatient and he set his plate on a passing tray carried by a waiter who seemed lost in thought as he ambled among the crowd. "I've learned some important news. It's imperative that we discuss it later tonight. Maria, do you think you and Jim can find your way to my hotel room later? It's a risk, I know, but if you two can keep out of sight, it shouldn't be hard to avoid being seen by the government patrols."

Slater looked at Maria and they nodded their heads.

"Good," Casey said. "Carlos will stay with me and I'll fill him in on the details on the way back to the hotel. In the meantime, enjoy yourselves. It's a great party."

Slater and Maria watched Casey and Carlos disappear into

the throng of people. Later, he thought he caught a glimpse of Casey leaving the hall by a rear door.

ໆ৯ৎ৯

Casey and Carlos sat in Casey's darkened room at the Intercontinental Hotel and waited for Slater and Maria. Casey knew that the plan he had devised along with Carlos was dangerous, possibly suicidal. It would be a difficult sell now that Maria and Slater were a twosome, people in love didn't take risks. They didn't put their life on the line and that was what this new mission would require. He turned to Carlos. "Beer?"

"Ah yes, my friend. A beer would be nice. The cocktails at the party were satisfactory but nothing beats the taste of a cold beer."

Casey foraged in his small ice chest, grabbed two beers, and handed one to Carlos who sat in the overstuffed chair. Neither talked and soon there was a muffled knock at the door. It was Maria and Slater.

"Okay," Slater said. "What's the big deal?"

Casey tossed two beers to Slater who gave one to Maria. When they were sitting in a semi-circle around him, he began.

"There's going to be a huge reception at the National Palace next week. I guess to outdo the one tonight, I don't know. Anyway, everyone in the government will be there. I was thinking, what an ideal time to strike back at the Sandinistas. We could blow most of the government off the map. What do you two think?"

He turned to watch Slater and Maria's reaction to his plan. He continued in spite of their open-mouthed stares. "Carlos agrees with me. It's an opportunity we shouldn't pass up. If we blow the palace, it could mean the turning point and could very well put the bastards out of business."

Maria set her beer on the wooden table and looked at Casey. "How did you learn of this reception?" she said.

"At the party tonight. I overheard a conversation with that newspaper woman."

"Mrs. Digas?"

"Right. Her husband owns *La Prensa.*"

"How would we do this?"

"We've got enough explosive and dynamite to do the job," Carlos said, picking up the discussion. "If we can get it into the palace without being seen, we should be able to pull it off."

Slater did not appear convinced. "Have you guys gone totally off your rockers? You're going to walk in the palace and calmly blow the place up? It's insane. It's suicide."

"It's an ambitious plan, to be sure," Carlos said. "But if we can do it..."

His voice trailed off as Slater held up a hand.

"That's the big problem, right? How do you get the stuff into the palace? We have no information regarding locations of sentries or their schedules. We would need a blueprint, or some kind of drawing of the place, in order to move around once we are in. More than that, how do we get out without blowing ourselves up in the process?"

"Blueprints are easy to get," Carlos said. "The Ministry of Interior has a public works office that has that sort of stuff."

"Even for the palace?"

Carlos shrugged at the question.

"What about security? Surely, they have a sophisticated surveillance system, Casey. You said so yourself."

"The blueprints might have something about the security system," Carlos said.

"That's too risky," Maria said. "What if they report whoever goes asking questions about the National Palace? That's sure to turn some heads."

"I agree with Maria," Casey said. "Let me see if I can arrange for my station chief in Costa Rica to supply that information. The Company usually has access to all sorts of data. If they do, they can send it by courier."

"It'll have to be quick. You said the reception is next week, right?" Slater finished his beer and yawned. "You still haven't answered by question. How do we keep from killing ourselves in this insane mission?"

"Timed explosions, Jim. Simple enough to place timers on

the C-4 to give us the time to get out of the building. We would be long gone when the place goes up."

"And the timing?" Slater said, still probing for answers.

"Yes. We have the time, I believe, if we start tomorrow. What do you say? Is it a go?"

Three nodded in agreement while Slater shook his head in disbelief. They held their beer bottles outstretched until they clinked together.

"To the cause," Carlos said.

CHAPTER 25

Perez was mad as hell and he lashed out at Captain Salazar. After the dressing-down by Rivas, he had walked to the Ministry of Interior building to obtain the latest intelligence reports concerning contra activities and found nothing new. There had been no discernible troop or squad movement since their return to Managua. He was in no mood for Salazar's suggestions and, even though another foray into the northern jungle would be fruitless, Rivas wanted it done. Fueling his anger was the fact that if he were in the field, he would not be able to attend the National Palace reception, which he was determined to do. The palace would be crawling with beautiful, young women and he needed a replacement for Maria. His wife's constant harping to take her out was getting on his nerves. It would be nice to meet a young thing and get her into Maria's old apartment. The lure of power and sex was much too great a temptation and he was not going to be put off by some stupid order from Rivas.

To his pleasant surprise, Salazar gave him an alternative. Since the whereabouts of the contras was no longer known, why not use helicopters to search the mountains? They could sortie a half dozen choppers and spend the day patrolling the jungle, then return to Managua after dark. This way, Salazar said, they could cover five times the territory than on the ground and, if anything looked promising, they could set down and investigate. If they happened to engage the enemy, they would have a decided advantage from their gunships.

After spending most of the afternoon on the phone with Rivas arguing the benefits of using the helicopters, Perez secured approval for their use. He promptly requisitioned four aircraft from the base north of Managua and arranged to be in the air at morning's first light.

෬෩෬

Casey spent the morning talking to his station chief in Costa Rica. He needed a set of blueprints or drawings of the National Palace that the CIA had stored away somewhere. Apparently, the fax machine in San Jose was not working and they were having trouble communicating with Washington. A blueprint did exist, he was told, for ever since the Sandinistas took power in 1979, the agency had painstakingly gathered intelligence concerning government buildings and residences, as well as on the main players in the new regime. Nothing was going to happen, however, until he got his hands on the blueprints.

Casey knew that a contingent from the Sandinista Armed Forces and the security police shared the security of the palace. The security police took their orders from the Ministry of Interior while Secretary of Defense Rivas controlled the army. Under Rivas's authority, the security police resembled a military type staff organization, headed by a former FSLN brigade commander. Individual operating sections were responsible for traffic, public safety, prisons, communications, surveillance, legal processing, and embassy protection. Interestingly, women made up a substantial proportion of the force.

The Directorate of State Security had been immensely successful in a number of operations, including the unraveling of numerous assassination plots against the country's president. Modeled after its Cuban counterpart, its officials had been trained in Cuba and the office continued to have a large number of Cuban advisors.

The security police's popularity improved as they uncovered bands of ex-national guards and threw them into prisons throughout Nicaragua. The state security torture facilities and prisons, patterned after Soviet KGB methods, were designed from Cuban plans, which, in turn, originated in Moscow. Cubans, who had at least five years' experience of working in the Soviet Union, trained their interrogators. One of the early victims of this torture was a Miskito leader, now a leader of one of the groups fighting against the Sandinistas. Between the two forces guarding the palace, their presence provided a formidable barrier to sabotage. They were the country's elite who had spent intense, formative years in the prevention, arrest, and repression of the counterrevolutionaries. Not much was known about them, except that most of the peasants were deathly afraid of their black uniforms.

Earlier in the day, Maria had gone to see a cousin who lived nearby and left Slater to strategize with the group. Slater had said he was going to see Mrs. Digas and left after he finished his coffee.

Carlos napped in the bedroom while Casey sat near the balcony door, watching traffic on the street below, waiting for his call from Costa Rica.

Around lunchtime, a smiling Slater walked through the door and removed a piece of folded paper from his hip pocket. He laid the paper on the living room table and beckoned Casey.

"Eureka," he said. "Look what I got."

Casey peered at the paper and laughed. He unbuttoned his shirt and smacked his lips as he studied the document.

"Where did you get this?" he asked.

"I told you I was going to see Mrs. Digas today," Slater answered. "She remembered me from the other night and was very gracious and accommodating. So I asked if she attended many functions at the palace and could she draw a sketch of it from memory. I was right, she was happy to oblige."

"Wasn't that a little risky, Jim? You didn't clear that with me first. Besides, you told me you didn't want to involve yourself further."

"I guess I am, after all. At least as long as Maria is going to risk her life, I need to do whatever I can to help. I've been drawn into this fight whether I want to be or not. Besides, I've decided to get Maria outta here. When this is all over, we'll make a run for freedom."

"Does she suspect anything? Mrs. Digas, I mean?"

"I'm sure she suspects something. But given her paper's unceasing censorship of the Sandinista government, I doubt if she cares. My feeling is that, even if she knew what we were about, she would look the other way."

"Nonetheless, Jim, you need to clear these things in the future with me. Understand?"

Slater nodded and the two men bent over the paper.

"Now, what do we have?" Casey asked.

"Well, first, as you know the palace sets on the western edge of the Plaza del Revolucion and is next to the office building of the Ministry of Interior." Slater pointed to the document and continued. "The driveway circles around in front of the building which has a façade of windows. This, you all know. In addition to the arched front door, there are two other entrances, one on the south side of the building and another entrance here at the rear. This south door is the least guarded but is activated by an electronic sensor, you need a magnetic card to get through it. The front door is guarded by security and everyone entering the building must submit to a body search and pass through a metal detector. Mrs. Digas has never been to the palace late at night and doesn't know if the security is any less at that time but it stands to reason that it would be. I suppose we could pose as some sort of delivery or repair service but it begs the question of how are we going to get several pounds of C-4 into the building?"

Casey thought for a moment, uneasy at the gravity of Slater's question. It wasn't surprising that the Sandinistas had developed an elaborate a security system but it worried him. "That's too bad," he said. "This means we may have to kill a few people just to gain access to the palace which will compromise our time inside."

"But now for the good news," Slater said. "Mrs. Digas told me of an underground tunnel that leads from the basement of the Interior Ministry to the basement of the palace. And the ministry's building is a lot less secure." Slater paused a few moments to let the thought settle on Casey. "If we can gain access to that tunnel, then we would have a straight shot into the National Palace. Look, during the reception everyone will be in the main ballroom, here." He pointed to the hand-drawn map again. "If we placed the explosives directly above the reception hall, the blast would collapse the ceiling into the main ballroom. It would be mass panic. Who knows? You might even get lucky and get the president."

"Tell me more about this underground tunnel," Casey asked.

"Mrs. Digas didn't know anything more, other than its existence. Maybe Carlos and Maria could check it out on the sly and report what they find. Possibly the tunnel ends in the basement of the palace and we would then need to get up to the second floor. The main ballroom is on the first floor here." Slater again used a dirty finger to indicate the ballroom's location.

"What about security where the tunnel exits into the palace?" Casey asked.

"Don't know. We might have to overpower a handful of guards but there would have to be fewer than what would be at the main entrance during the reception."

"Or at either of the other's," Casey added. "It's worth a look, Jim. Good going, you do excellent work for a contra."

The two men laughed as Maria let herself in the hotel room and kissed Slater. She carried a large bag of groceries. Carlos appeared from the bedroom rubbing his eyes and straightening his tussled hair.

"What's new guys?" she asked.

"Jim has discovered an intriguing possibility for getting into the palace. Tell her."

Slater briefed Maria and Carlos on the information he had gleaned from Mrs. Digas. When he was through, Carlos slapped Slater on the shoulder.

"Good, my friend, good. Assuming that we can get into the building, how do we get from the basement to the second floor without being seen? There's going to be a lot of people in the

Palace that evening. Why couldn't we plant the stuff a day ahead of time and be out of there when it goes off?"

"I thought of that," said Casey, "but to leave the C-4 in there and hope it wouldn't be discovered is leaving too much to chance. It's getting to the second floor without being seen that's the hang-up."

"I've thought of that, too," Slater said. "Mrs. Digas said that there is a freight elevator somewhere in the building. It must open into the basement for that is where deliveries are made. No one will be using that elevator during the reception."

"What about video surveillance?" Maria said. "Security cameras?"

"Jim, you could scout that out, couldn't you? You could devise some excuse to see someone at the Nicaraguan Social Security office located in the palace. They are in charge of the country's literacy program and as a teacher you could talk to them about your school."

"Right. I've wanted to know when they were going to get our new readers, anyway. I could say that while I was in Managua I decided to stop and ask in person."

"And while you're there, you can make a mental note of where the security cameras are located, if any, and where that freight elevator is."

Moments ago, they had nothing but now Casey was beginning to visualize a promising plan. *It might just be possible*, he thought.

"Let me suggest that we use my room here as our base of operations. Jim, tomorrow you go to the palace and Maria and Carlos go to the Interior Ministry. Then tomorrow night we will meet back here to discuss what we found. Agreed?"

The three nodded and Casey folded the drawing of the National Palace and put it into a shirt pocket.

"Won't the desk manager get suspicious?" Slater said, "With all of us coming and going?"

"Not to worry, Jimbo," Carlos said. "I have learned that the night manager is a loyal anti-Sandinista. He will not see us, I assure you."

"Listen, people," Maria said. "I'm starved. I brought food, so what do you say we eat?"

The small group watched Maria empty the sack of groceries and together they made a platter of sandwiches and ate in silence.

⊱⊰

An hour before sunrise, Perez donned his flight suit in the briefing office at the helicopter hanger. The strong, pungent odor of AVTUR aircraft fuel filled the room. He pointed to the large map in front of Salazar, two army sergeants, and four helicopter pilots. The dawn was already heating up and was in stark contrast to a comfortable night spent under air-conditioning. His cool home, however, did not compensate for the boring dinner Perez had with his wife while listening to her ceaseless criticism. She had read the article in *La Prensa* and she knew all about Maria. In addition, she needed more money if she was going to wear a new dress to the reception. As a couple, they had not attended such a function in a long time and she wanted to impress her friends. Surely, she argued, in light of the newspaper article he didn't want her to be the laughing stock of the reception. While they ate, she chewed her food vigorously and talked between mouthfuls.

Peres watched her with detached amusement. Her bloated face exaggerated her crude features. Then there was her hair. My God, why couldn't she do something with her hair? It fell in straight strings over her cheeks giving her a mangy dog look. There was nothing about her that excited him. He was lonely now that Maria was gone and he made a mental note that he would soon begin looking for another playmate. This time he would thoroughly check her out before putting her up in the apartment. He could not afford another mistake as with Maria. And when he had finished with the contras, no one would care or dare say anything.

He listened for over an hour before telling her to buy whatever she wished. Anything to shut her up. She had the nagging habit of answering the questions she put to him without allowing him time to answer for himself. She was full of meaning-less gossip about everyone they knew and her ramblings annoyed him. Standing in front of the men in the briefing office, he took a deep breath and sighed. It was good to be out of the house.

"Men, here is our flying zone for today." He pointed with a metal pointer to the plastic-covered map next to him. "We will cover this area sector by sector, with each aircraft covering one sector each day. Radio frequency will be 156.22 and you will report any sightings to me, pronto. You will wait until I give order before engaging the enemy as I wish to participate. With our rockets, we ought to make quick work of these contras. Any questions?"

A pilot with jet-black hair and a pocked face raised his hand. "Are we to assume, Colonel, that any forces encountered in this area are hostiles?"

"That is why," Perez replied, "I want you to contact me before commencing your raid. The final decision is mine. To answer your question more directly, there are no known friendly forces in the four sectors we will patrol today. I have seen to it that they have all been repositioned. Anything else, gentlemen?"

There being no further questions, the group donned their flight helmets and walked to their waiting helicopters. The sun was peeking over the eastern shoreline of Lake Managua so Perez attached the sun visor, jumped into the copilot seat beside the pilot. One of the sergeants climbed into the rear of the cabin and manned the machine gun. The pilot started the aircraft and soon the rotor was whirling above them. Perez watched the pilot go through a brief checklist then activated the radio.

"This Able Leader," squawked Perez. "Air cav units, please report."

"Able Leader, chopper one ready," was a crackled reply.

"Chopper two, ready."

"Chopper three, ready to fly."

Perez gave a circling motion with an extended index finger and the pilot raised the collective on the helicopter. In unison, the four aircraft accelerated down the short runway then streaked skyward and banked for the northern mountains. As the countryside shrunk beneath them, Perez appreciated the lure of flying above the jungle canopy. It certainly beat pounding and hacking one's way through it on foot.

CHAPTER 26

After a breakfast of bananas, rolls, and coffee, Slater kissed Maria and watched as she and Carlos set out for the Ministry of Interior. When the door had closed behind them, he poured himself another cup of coffee. Casey sat at the small table by the balcony door and glanced through an old copy of *La Prensa*. The bright sun was low on the horizon and cast a long shadow from the hotel to the far side of the street.

"Casey, I want to talk to you about Maria," Slater said.

"Again, Jim? I thought we settled this yesterday?"

"I know, but the more I've thought about it, the more worried I am. When it comes time to break into the palace, I would like to leave her out of the mission. You, me, and Carlos ought to be able to handle it. I don't want the possibility of her getting hurt."

"It's out of the question, Jim. We are going to need her. Not only to carry a portion of the explosives, but to watch for guards. I appreciate your concern but if Maria knew you were pleading on her behalf, you know what she would say."

"She'd be madder than hell and tell me to mind my own business. I just don't want to see her get killed."

"If it happens, it happens. Remember what I said during her rescue attempt? You're planning too much into the future for both your sakes. I have a feeling that once this mission is over, you'll be able to convince her to leave Nicaragua."

"You don't think that if a victory is imminent, she would want to be a part of it?"

"Between you and me, Jim, this war is far from over. Maybe once Congress gets off its lazy ass and appropriates enough funds and we can get decent weapons down here, things might be different. But right now we're hampered by our people's apathy toward democracy in Latin America. They don't want to spend money on someone else's war, so the contras have had to get its funds and equipment on the sly. No, victory is a long way off and the tyranny and oppression will continue."

"I don't want to lose her, that's all."

"Like I said, put it out of your mind until this thing is done. Think of her not as a lover but a fighter, and then just do your job. She's not yours yet. She belongs to Nicaragua and her fellow fighters. Either that, or go back to San Rafael and teach school."

Slater was not prepared for Casey's bluntness but he knew he was right—it was the way it had to be. At present, Maria would not hear of anything else, and he didn't want his complaining to create a division within the group. He showered, put on fresh clothes, and brushed his teeth while Casey finished his coffee.

Back in the room with Casey, he continued. "I didn't mean to complain. You're right, maybe this thing I have for Maria is getting in the way. I admit that I'm no longer as objective as I was a few weeks ago."

Casey rose and stood next to Slater. Their eyes met and the CIA agent gave him a pat on the back. "Don't worry, my friend. It's tougher because we know and care about each other. You'll do fine. Remember El Chipote?"

Slater chuckled and turned to leave. "What are you going to do while we're away?" he asked.

"Try to get some information from San Jose," Casey said. "Any information has got to be better than none."

On the street, Slater hailed a taxi and instructed the driver to take him to the Plaza del Revolucion. He handed the driver a handful of cordobas and sat silent until they reached the Plaza. A mob of people walked along the sidewalk and the concrete plaza. The automobile traffic was heavy, cars honked at each other, and pedestrians hurried to their appointments.

The National Palace stood as a colonial masterpiece on the edge of the plaza. Ornately adorned with twelve, white columns and marble façade, it sparkled in the sunlight, and banners waved over large posters of Augusto Sandino, the patron saint of the Sandinistas, a guerrilla fighter who resisted the United States Marines in the twenties. The man was the Nicaraguan equivalent to Cuba's Che Guevara. Above the portico, the words, *Palacio National,* were inscribed in dark letters and, on the upper side of the cupola-like center, was engraved the country's coat-of-arms. Slater brushed his hair behind his ears and began the climb to the arched front doors.

A uniformed guard greeted him, asked his business, and directed him to a walk-through metal detector. Once inside, the guard frisked him and again inquired as to his business in the Palace.

After explaining that he was a teacher in San Rafael and wanted to discuss a few matters with the Nicaraguan Social Security office, the unsmiling guard directed Slater to the second floor then turned his attention to another visitor. Near the center stairway, Slater made a quick mental note of the interior of the palace. Mounted high on the wall were two cameras, each aimed opposite each other and pointed down the long hallway. When he reached the end of the main hall, he saw several men moving pieces of furniture out of an elevator. He watched for a moment then returned to the middle of the building. The tile was a black-and-white-checkerboard design and the footsteps of people walking echoed around him. He found the ballroom at the southern end of the palace on the main floor, just as Mrs. Digas remembered. It was a long, rectangular room, about a hundred feet in length and forty feet wide. It was home to five lavish chandeliers and ornate ceiling molding extended all around the ballroom. Heavy, scarlet curtains hung from tall, stately windows that filled the room with a delicate daylight. At the far end of the room was an elevated orchestra stage. There were four security cameras mounted near the ceiling in each corner and aimed toward the room's center. Studying the room, he felt a tap on his shoulder. It was a security guard.

"Sir, this room is off limits at the present," the man said. "Please move on. May I direct you somewhere?"

"No, thank you," Slater said and headed for the main stairway across from the front door. The guard's watchful gaze tickled the back of Slater's neck until he was on the second floor. He turned the corner and walked down the hallway in the direction of the freight elevator and again was noticed by the same delivery men. This time they were pushing two desks into the elevator. A bolt of fear shot through him. They know, he thought, they know why I'm here. The fat worker stared at him. Slater's pulse quickened while he walked the length of the hallway counting the steps until he figured he was directly over the center of the ballroom. Seventy-six steps. He fought the impulse to look back at the deliverymen. Were they still watching him? What if they reported him to security? He would have botched the mission. He tried to remain calm. He felt his pulse slow and drew a long, deep breath. On either side of the hall were two offices whose doors opened into the wide hall. Between the office doors was another small room. Slater opened the door and glanced inside. Mops, pails, and brooms filled the space and he quickly closed the door before anyone spotted him looking inside. The closet was a great place to set the explosives.

After constructing a mental map, Slater left the palace, hoping that the workmen hadn't suspected anything and wanting to get out of there before they did. He hailed a taxi and ordered the driver to the café on the Plaza Espana, where he drank a beer and ate a foul-tasting sandwich. Taking a paper and pencil from his pocket, he sketched the location of the video cameras and freight elevator along with the approximate distance to the janitor's closet above the center of the ballroom.

An ill-kempt man with a week's worth of beard and a tattered shirt stumbled over to Slater's table and sat opposite him. The man stared at him through blood-shot eyes and ran a dirty hand over his mouth. Slater thought him slightly drunk but said nothing. When he finished his beer and started to leave, the man caught his arm.

"You American?"

"No," Slater said, impulsively. "I'm British." He rose to leave. The last thing he needed was a confrontation with a drunken peasant.

"Don't give me that horse shit," said the man. "I can spot an American a block away." The unshaven man put a finger to his nose and sniffed. "The smell, that's how."

"I'm sorry," Slater said, trying to free himself from the man's grasp. "I must be going."

The man tightened his grip and pulled Slater close enough that he could smell the stale alcohol. He almost gagged.

"My wife is in prison, *senor*. They took her away last night. They said she was an anti-Sandinista, but, sir, I swear it on my mother's grave, my wife was never such a thing. All she ever wanted was to cook and raise our children. Now she is gone. Our children need her, *senor*. Please, help us."

The crescendo of the man's voice caused the few patrons in the café to stare at them. Slater tried to pull away but again the man protested, this time, even louder.

"Maybe you know someone in America, *senor,* who could take pity on my poor wife. Someone who could help her."

The man was blubbering and causing exactly what Slater had hoped to avoid, a scene. He grabbed the man's arm, jerked free of his grip, threw a few cordobas on the table, and hurried, while behind him the man continued his ranting. Slater took several side streets then hurried back to the hotel, hoping no one followed him.

ကာလက

In the basement of the Ministry of Interior building, Maria pulled Carlos around a corner and put a finger to his lips. Someone was following them. They had found the narrow stairway that led down into the dimly lit basement and were inching their way to the palace. The walkway was cluttered with boxes full of papers and files, office furniture stacked high along the walls. Every few yards, a small alcove adjoined the hall and held additional equipment. They stopped for a moment in a dark alcove and listened.

At regular intervals, footsteps approached in the direction of the Ministry building then faded in the distance. Carlos peered around the corner and shook his head.

"I don't see anyone," he said in a soft whisper. "Let's keep going."

He took Maria by the hand and led her into the main hallway. They continued toward the palace. Fifty yards farther the tunnel veered southward and the available light became dimmer. At a steel door at end of the hallway there were more footsteps. Maria glanced over her shoulder but saw no one. When a cat screeched and scampered in front of her, she jumped and pulled Carlos toward the door.

They scurried up a short stairway and pushed open the door leading into the palace basement. Inside, they found themselves in a long, well-lit room containing high shelves along its entire length. Numerous people were standing between the rows of shelves and it appeared that they were cataloguing and retrieving documents. Maria pointed to the elevator. Once inside, they rode it to the first floor without being noticed, ran down the tiled hall, and opened the door to the ballroom at the opposite end. The crowd of people in the main lobby seemed oblivious to their presence and the security guards at the main entrance paid them no attention. It all seemed part of a busy, normal day. They paused for a moment to get their bearings, then stumbled out into the bright sunlight.

"Shit," Maria said. "Who was that in the tunnel? Did you ever get a look at him?"

"No," Carlos said. "Maybe it was only a worker or janitor. Actually, I was surprised that there weren't more people down there going from the ministry to the palace."

Maria sidestepped a preoccupied man dressed smartly in a business suit who was reading a newspaper. She hooked an arm in Carlos's and walked back to the hotel.

"At least we know we can get from the Ministry of the Interior to the palace without being seen. If we are lucky. How will we gain access to the ministry after hours is the next question."

"I suggest we pack the explosives into suitcases or bags and carry them into the building before it closes then hide in the tunnel until after the reception gets underway. A big problem is going to be getting down that long hallway on the second floor, though. We will have to kill anyone we see."

"Let's see what Jim was able to find out about the palace. Ten pounds of C-4 plastic divided four ways isn't that much. What other equipment will we need?"

"I dunno. Maybe Casey has some ideas. Here we are, let's find out."

The pair entered the Intercontinental and bounded up the stairs to Casey's room. Maria knocked twice then once and Casey opened the door.

"Good," he said. "You're back. Jim just returned, also."

Maria kissed Slater on the cheek and the group sat in a semi-circle on the living room floor.

"All right, Carlos, what did you find?" Slater asked. His eyes narrowed and the wrinkles on his forehead deepened as he waited for Carlos' answer.

"Just as we expected. The tunnel leads directly to the basement of the palace, near the freight elevator. It presents a small problem because the elevator is at the opposite end of the building from the ballroom."

"I know," Slater said. "I was up there. But there are two small offices on the second floor directly over the ballroom with a janitor closet between them. We can set the explosives in that closet. Since they won't be cleaning until after the reception, they shouldn't be discovered. Unless, of course, a guard or watchman happens on to us."

"Then they're dead," Casey interjected. "Either that or we are. I found four duffel bags that we can use to haul the C-4 and other equipment. By the way, the party is the day after tomorrow and begins at eight o'clock. Promptly at midnight, there will be a toast to the president and everyone will watch as he waltzes alone with his wife. It's a Nicaraguan custom. At that moment, all of the palace will be in attendance, and even the security force's attention will be on the president. It should allow us time to set the explosives and get the heck out of there."

"Good," Slater said. "Let's pack the bags and inventory our supplies."

Casey stood and left the room. While he was gone, Maria kissed Slater again and put her arms around him. Carlos found a beer in the refrigerator and was opening it when Casey returned with an armload of gear.

"Here's the bags," he said, dropping the load onto the floor. Along with the duffels, there were two climbing ropes and a set of carabiners. When he turned to get more equipment, Slater stopped him.

"What are these climbing ropes for, *amigo?* I thought I had seen my last rope back in El Chipote."

"Just in case, Jim. One thing you learn during guerrilla warfare training is that there is no such thing as being overprepared. Carlos, what about the C-4 and the other weapons?"

Carlos took a gulp of his beer. "My men will deliver them tomorrow night. They will bring the grenades and the ammunition. We can load up then."

"What about silencers?" asked Slater. "One shot and the place will be crawling with guards."

Carlos shook his head. "None, I'm afraid, other than the one on your .45," he said. "We'll just have to hope for the best. But I do have my trusty Bowie knife." He held up a large-bladed knife and wiped its sharp edge with a long finger.

Slater shot a glance at Maria then Casey. "I know," he said. "Pretend that I'm already dead."

The group laughed at the remark and Casey nodded. "If we can bring the insurgency to the capital, it will help the cause immensely," Casey said. "It will be a big step in your march to freedom."

Maria wondered how Slater could be so cavalier and nonchalant about the mission. Her insides were churning and a bitter taste had risen to her mouth. Now, with the raid only a day away, her palms were cold and clammy and she fought to calm the raging inferno inside her.

CHAPTER 27

From the cockpit of his Soviet Mi-2 helicopter, Colonel Perez studied the jungle below as the mountainous terrain loomed ahead. He referred to the map he balanced on one knee and, with a gloved hand, pointed to the northeast. The pilot nodded and banked the aircraft. Perez watched as the trailing aircraft followed suit. The sun was high enough to shed a golden hue over the dense green canopy below and the humid air that had settled overnight was now rising as a thin white vapor upward through the trees.

Perez was not a man given to the appreciation of nature or objects of art, as was Maria. How the woman loved paintings and music. He could never match her love of the outdoors or the simplistic beauty of Nicaragua's remote regions. He considered himself a simple man of action, a man of the times. Bolstered by early victories during the revolution, he found he loved commanding troops and, at age twenty-seven, had become the youngest Sandinista *commandante*. This latest excursion against the contras, he pledged to himself, would put himself back in Rivas's good graces, maybe earning a medal from the president.

It was good to be away from the nagging of his wife, although he knew there was more in store once he returned home. It wasn't that she was a bad person, albeit possessing a gossiping nature. Like most Nicaraguan women, she liked jewelry and fine clothes and loved to show them off. But he needed what she couldn't give—intimacy and sex. The woman had long since decided that the bedroom was made for sleeping and nothing else. She had let herself go to the extent, that even if she wanted it, Perez knew he could no longer accommodate her. It was an excuse, of course, he used to lure other young women to his apartment but he had convinced himself it was all her fault.

He checked the grid coordinates on the map against the reading on the console panel of the helicopter. The sectors they were searching were lined up parallel to each other, west to east, in order to allow for quick support if surprised by ground troops.

"This is Abel Leader," Perez said into the microphone. "We're nearing our search areas. Are you birds ready?"

"Abel Leader, this is Chopper One. We're heading to our sector now. See you at the rendezvous point."

Perez recognized Salazar's voice as he watched the chopper turn east into the rising sun.

"Abel Leader, this is Chopper Two. We're following Chopper One to our sector. Good luck."

"Chopper Three. Our sector is just over this next rise. Good hunting, Colonel."

The three helicopters all banked eastward and Perez nodded his approval.

"This is Abel Leader. If you spot the enemy, you will not engage him until I am on the scene. Repeat. You will call for backup. I don't want anyone trying to be a hero. That is my prerogative."

The small, fast-flying helicopters zoomed low over the jungle and fanned out into their assigned sectors. Perez felt his stomach knot from the G-forces as they swooped down to begin the search. Up in these mountains, the dense jungle made viewing anything on the ground a difficult, time-consuming task. Occasionally, when they flew over a clearing, he got a good look, but the rest of the time, he had to strain to see through the thick vegetation. The ground was still in shadows but Perez hoped he would be able to make out movement if, and when, it happened.

The squadron's other helicopters were out of sight and Perez leaned forward while the pilot guided the aircraft down for a closer look. Speeding low over the treetops, their prop-wash caused the branches to sway beneath them. Perez concentrated his efforts first on studying the map for landmarks, then searching for signs of the contras, while they continued to zig zag across the sector. He thought if they could get lucky, those contra bastards wouldn't stand a chance.

Each time the pilot banked the chopper into a steep turn to begin another run over the jungle, Perez fought to keep his breakfast down. It had been a while since his last helicopter ride and he still had not adjusted to the G forces. The morning, he realized, was going to be spent enduring steep banks at high speeds and he braced himself against his nylon harness in anticipation of the next turn.

A voice crackled in his helmet and Perez turned to see the pilot smiling. "The one rule of the cockpit, Colonel," the pilot said, the morning sun glinting off the man's helmet. "You mess it up, you clean it up. There should be a bag under your seat, sir."

"Thanks," Perez said. "Do I look that bad?"

"Your green face matches your flight suit, sir. Don't worry, it happens to the best of us. Try to keep your eyes on the horizon—it helps."

Perez nodded, reached under his flight seat, and found the small sack referred to by the pilot. He opened the small window on his right shoulder and a rush of fresh air revived him. The sun had gained elevation on the jungle below and was hurling shafts of light through the trees improving visibility. They crisscrossed the sector in a west-to-east fashion, methodically working northward toward the Honduran border.

Captain Salazar's voice squawked in his ear.

"Able Leader, this is Chopper One. We have contact, repeat, we have contact. Do you read?"

"This is Able Leader. What is your position?"

Perez struggled to hear Salazar over the drone of the helicopter's engine. Salazar slowed his speech and gave him the coordinates.

"We're ten miles due north of the village of El Bocca. There is a large contingent of contras below. Follow the Rio Wana River and you can't miss them. Going down to engage."

Perez pointed eastward, the pilot pushed the cyclic to the right, and they sped toward El Bocca. Perez keyed the microphone. "This is Abel Leader. All birds converge on Chopper One's location. Be prepared to engage the enemy."

Perez's pilot pulled on the collective pitch beside his left knee and the chopper screamed skyward. Once at altitude, Perez was able to calm his reeling stomach and focus on his map. They were fifty miles from rendezvousing with Salazar— twenty minutes. Fifteen, if they were lucky. Now, as he had often done during past military actions, he crossed himself in the sign of the Church. His instinct told him that it was better to be lucky than good. He reached into the front pocket of his flight suit and fingered his rosary.

"This is Chopper One. Beginning our attack now."

Perez screamed into his microphone. "Dammit, Captain! I told you wait until my arrival! Do not engage, repeat, do not engage!"

Perez envisioned Salazar's helicopter swooping low over the treetops to make an initial pass over the enemy. He looked at his watch. Fifteen minutes to target. If the chopper could have flown faster with Perez getting out pushing it, he would have gladly done so. It was an eternity before he heard from Salazar's voice again.

"This is Chopper One. We have just made our first strafing run with our machine guns. Boy! Look at them run. We've got them, sir! We've surprised them, by god! Let's hit them again."

Since Perez's helicopter was the furthest to the west, the other gunships would arrive over the target before he would. He fumed in disbelief that he was going to miss the action. He would have Salazar's balls for this insubordination.

"Chopper One, here. These guys are running around like a bunch of headless chickens. We've destroyed most of their unit and are starting another strafing run. Shit! Wait a minute. They're shooting RPGs at us. Goddamn RPGs!"

Perez glanced at his watch and, when he looked up, he saw a plume of smoke sprouting upward in the distance. Three helicopters circled the target and over the loud roar of their rotors, he could make out the gunfire. There was a deafening explosion and Salazar's frenzied voice rang with panic over the radio.

"Shit! This is Chopper One. We're hit. A goddamn RPG! We're going down. No, wait a minute."

Perez listened helplessly has he heard Salazar scream to his pilot.

"No good! We're not flying. Hang on, we're going down."

Perez was now close enough to see the helicopter spin around its rotors in a classic auto-rotation fashion. Black smoke belched from the rear of the cabin as the gunship plummeted earthward. More gunfire erupted from the edge of a small clearing and he scanned the area for signs of the enemy. There. He pointed to the far edge of the clearing and continued to watch Salazar's helicopter spiral toward the ground.

"Colonel—"

Salazar's voice was panicked and pleading.

"Hang on, Juan!" Perez shouted into his radio. "Try to set it down easy and we'll pick you up."

At the exact moment that Perez lifted his finger from the microphone, the out-of-control helicopter augered into the jungle floor. Shock waves followed an enormous fireball and flung Perez's chopper around like a rag doll. His pilot fought for control of the aircraft at the edge of the rising flames. On the ground, the wreckage of Salazar's chopper was a burning heap, a raging inferno that no one could have survived.

"Take her down," Perez commanded the pilot. "We need to get those men out of there." His thoughts became one of helping his captain and crew, his earlier cursing vanished from memory.

Perez's pilot maneuvered the helicopter until its skids were just above the trees. Bullets rang past Perez, the occasional thud indicating that a one had hit the chopper's fuselage.

"This Able Leader." Perez fought to keep his voice from cracking. There was no sign of life from the charred gunship, no movement. "You birds shoot any contras on sight, do you hear? I'm going down to help."

With the order came a barrage of cannon fire from the aircraft above them. Perez's pilot coaxed their helicopter down to the clearing next to where Chopper One lay burning. The wreckage site was deserted but Perez knew the contras were close, waiting for the precise moment when he jumped out of the chopper. It was too damned risky, he knew, but Salazar would do the same for him if he were lying helpless in a burning helo. When the helicopter landed with a thump, he opened the door and scrambled from the cockpit.

He drew his Stechkin 9 mm pistol and ran toward the downed aircraft, the smell of smoke and jet fuel greeting him at the grisly scene. The helicopter was a crumpled, burning wreck. He climbed through the wreckage to Salazar's door and tried to open it. Stuck, the crumpled metal had jammed it shut. There was a gaping hole in the rear of the aircraft where the chopper's tail section once had been. The air was at once filled with a barrage of bullets. With his pistol at the ready, Perez made his way through the hole and crouched on the floor in what was once the aircraft's cargo bay. Salazar lay on his back, motionless, his flight suit burned into his body. Perez crawled to him, recognized the massive head wound with white brain matter oozing from it, and fought down the urge to vomit. Snaking his way into the cockpit, Perez found the pilot slumped over his controls. His right arm was missing, and the man was dead.

Back at Salazar's burned corpse, Perez fought to free the body from the wreckage. The aircraft's fuselage had collapsed inward pinning his captain against the bulkhead. The helicopter's windshield was a mass of broken glass and shards were stern throughout the wreckage. A small flame still flickered in the rear of what was left of the aircraft consuming the last of the aviation fuel. A heavy odor of cordite permeated the air. Wires and hoses lay scattered about.

After he had pulled Salazar's body out of the wreckage and onto the ground, gunshots erupted from the trees at the edge of the clearing. One bullet slammed into the side of the helicopter forcing him to take cover on the far side of the aircraft. He fired into the trees until the clip was empty. Listening, he wondered if it was safe to continue—whoever they were they were silent for the moment. *I hope I don't die here*, he thought. *I will miss the president's party.* Crawling back to Salazar's lifeless body, he grabbed the captain by the arms and dragged him free of the wreckage, hesitated, and looked around. No more gunfire, the only sounds were those of the flames beating skyward. Perez uttered a silent prayer and pulled Salazar toward the waiting chopper while his other aircraft patrolled the skies over the skirmish site. Close to his helicopter, more gunfire erupted but he managed to get Salazar aboard.

"I need to go back for the other man," he shouted to his pilot above the whirling rotors.

"Forget it! We need to get out of here. It's too hot. Let's go."

Perez shot a glance back to the crumpled chopper then returned his gaze toward his pilot. "Five more minutes," he called.

The pilot shook his head and yelled at Perez. "Dammit, sir! Get your butt in here or I'm leaving you behind. If they hit this bird, you'll never make it back. Now, move it!"

Shocked by the pilot's outburst, Perez hopped into the cargo bay. As he scrambled forward to the cockpit, a bullet struck him in the right leg and knocked him to the floor. He dragged himself toward the front of the aircraft but the intense pain made the task difficult. His stomach turned sour when the chopper rose into the smoke-filled air and headed south toward Managua.

Using an elbow for traction, he pulled himself into the cockpit where the pilot tossed him a first-aid bag. He ripped open his flight suit and studied the wound. The bleeding had stopped but the bullet had left a single, inch-sized hole that passed cleanly through his calf muscle. Dried blood had caked on his leg and the pain sent shock waves into his frazzled brain.

Perez took a strip of gauze from the first-aid bag and gently wrapped it around his leg. The pain began to wane and his head stopped spinning.

"Are you all right, Colonel?" the pilot asked when they were halfway back to the airbase.

Perez nodded and tried to smile. "You wouldn't have really left me back there, would you?"

"Academic now, sir. But my idea of a nice afternoon helicopter ride is not to get blown away by some stupid guerrilla fighters. We were lucky to get out of there when we did."

Perez settled back against the chopper's bulkhead and allowed its buffeting motion to calm his raw nerves. Knowing the contras had gotten the better of him, once again, left him discouraged and ashamed. He didn't know how he could keep his failure from Rivas and the man would surely report this latest mission to the president. But after taking stock of what had happened, he realized how lucky he was to be alive, even though Rivas and the president might consider it better if he had been killed in action. What had the secretary said? If Perez could not handle the job, he would get someone who could. Perez was sure there was another *commandante* eager to make his reputation with the National Directorate. He felt the rank of general slipping from his grasp.

CHAPTER 28

The afternoon turned nasty and the trucks carrying the plastic explosive were late getting into Managua. Rain came down in vertical sheets and formed serpentine rivulets up and down Avienda Bolivar in front of the Intercontinental Hotel. Casey, Maria, Carlos, and Slater sat in Casey's hotel room and waited, hoping that the rain would end soon. Carlos paced while Maria and Slater played cards on the floor near the balcony. Casey worked the radio and attempted to reach Costa Rica, but because of the storm he was unable to do so. The doors to the balcony were open and a gentle breeze blew the humid air into the blades of the ceiling fan that turned quietly in the living room. Carlos stopped his pacing, took a pillow from the sofa, and lay on the floor beside Maria and Slater.

"This is it, Maria," he said as he adjusted the pillow under one arm. "Our greatest mission yet. It may be the turning point of the insurgency."

Maria shuffled the cards, looked at Carlos, then smiled and patted him on an arm. "Maybe. We'll see. It's what we've been waiting for, isn't it? Are you worried, Carlos?"

"Always. I always feel like my arms and feet are made of lead at times like these. I remember similar feelings just before soccer games when I was a child. But somehow when the match began, the butterflies and lead disappeared. It's like Casey said, Maria. If we can show the Americans that we can deal a deathblow to the Sandinistas, then it might generate greater aid for our cause. We're dead in the water without US help."

Carlos noticed Slater looking at him and waited for the man to say something. Slater sat opposite Maria and returned his attention to the cards in his hand.

"What were you going to say, Jim?" Carlos asked. "I've come to know that look of yours. What is it?"

"Nothing," Slater replied. "It's just a thought. Why don't you all give up the cause, go live in the mountains? If this war wasn't going on, I doubt if the National Directorate would bother you up there. They could care less about the farmers and peasants. It's the fact that you're trying to squash the government that has them up in arms. You could probably live pretty well if the fighting stopped."

"You're playing...what do you Americans call it?...he devil...something."

"The Devil's Advocate," Maria interjected.

"*Si*," Carlos said. "That's it. If I did not know you better, Jim, I would think you have given up on our revolution."

"It's what Socrates did all the time, Carlos. Play the Devil's Advocate."

"Socrates?" Carlos said.

"Never mind. He was an ancient philosopher. Don't you ever feel that you are fighting for nothing? Look at the logic of the situation—you have no arms, no munitions, no organization, no national leader, and no plan for victory. My reason for wanting to remain neutral is because I don't want to get myself shot."

"Neutral?" Carlos asked. "You know that's impossible, you said so yourself. How can you be neutral after risking your life for Maria? By now, you most certainly have a price on your head. No, my friend, you're no longer neutral."

"He's just being a jerk," Maria said, playing a card. "He's about as neutral as a Yankee fan during the World Series."

"Just trying to protect my investment," Slater said. He reached across the pile of cards and pinched Maria on the cheek.

"It is a good investment, I might add," Carlos said. He watched Maria brush the cards away and jump on Slater. The two rolled on the floor until she had Slater pinned beneath her. "Come, come, children. Here's Casey, maybe he has some news."

The three of them looked up and saw the CIA agent standing next to the balcony, frowning.

"Still nothing," he said. "I can't raise Costa Rica and I have no idea when the truck will get here. Tonight's the reception and we need to be in the Ministry of Interior before it closes. The damned truck is probably stuck in the mud somewhere."

"Or they met with resistance from the army," Carlos said.

"What will we do if they don't show up?" Maria said.

Carlos shook his head and played with the copper bracelet on his wrist. He rubbed his crooked nose. "I don't know, Maria. Nothing, I guess. Plan something for later, maybe. I've waited for this moment for such a long time, the truck can't be late. It just can't."

"We've still got a few more hours," Casey said. "Let's try to stay calm and worry about that when the time comes."

Maria curled up alongside Slater and fell asleep. While Casey dozed in the chair next to the sofa, Carlos tried to think of alternate plans. Short of blowing up the president's personal residence, nothing that they could accomplish would be able to top what they were about to do. It would put them on the map and get everyone's attention. Since he was a child, he had felt the sting of government repression, first with Somoza, and now with the Sandinistas. It seemed to him that the fighting would go on forever. He heard people were fighting all over the world. Why couldn't those in power realize that simple people just wanted to live in peace—be allowed to farm and raise their children without interference. No, after tonight, no one would ever call them insurgents again. They would be heroes.

၁၁၁

Perez cussed as he stood in front of his bathroom mirror

and struggled with his tie. His leg hurt like hell and he was forced to use the crutches he had been given at the base hospital. From the bedroom, he could hear his wife, Aurielo, softly humming an old Nicaraguan folk tune. He had taken two pain pills and had downed three jiggers of Napoleon brandy, but the pain still shot up his leg and into his head. He labored with the tie, frustrated with his inability to make a knot.

His ordeal of the past twenty-four hours had left him nervous and irritable as if his courage had been stripped away. Salazar's death had shaken him to his core. He kept replaying the scene of the crash. The captain's eyes were open and his brains were all over the floor of the helicopter's cockpit. Perez told himself repeatedly that nothing could change what happened—the captain died a brave man. And when he told Salazar's young widow, she had not wept but stoically braved the news and thanked him for his kindness. Had he suffered? It was the only question she asked. After assuring the woman that her husband died a brave warrior, Perez had gone home and found the bottle of brandy.

"Damn this tie," he shouted from the bathroom.

Aurielo came running, helped him finish the knot, and folded down the collar of his starched shirt. She wore the new chiffon and silk dress she purchased while he had been away and it made her hips appear not quite so wide. She patted the tie and waddled back into the bedroom where she began applying her makeup.

Many years ago, his wife had been pretty enough. When he courted her, she had jet-black hair, penetrating eyes, and a svelte figure. But the ensuing years had not been kind to her, etching deep furrows into her face and adding sixty pounds to her frame. Her skin color was like the doughboy they saw on American television. Aurielo simply couldn't light his fire anymore. And now, he had been shot up and the damned pain made him miserable. He was tired of fighting, tired of killing, tired of these daily jaunts into the jungle. He should be a general now, wining and dining with the beautiful people of Nicaragua. He took another pull on the brandy and waited for Aurielo to finish making herself presentable.

He had been fighting all his life, from the times he had to defend his mother's honor in the slums. She had been burned when their house caught fire and the scars had disfigured her once-beautiful face. The taunts of the other children fueled within Perez a zeal and determination never to lose a fight. He learned street fighting by the time he was in school, fighting other boys who called his mother ugly, disfigured—a witch. But it didn't stop the jeers and laughter, and he just continued to fight. As a member of Somoza's *Guardia,* he received some direct training from US sources. It was not to prepare the *Guardia* to defend Nicaragua from foreign attacks. Instead, the *Guardia* was taught to defend Nicaragua from internal threats. The training also provided the *Guardia* with a more formal ideology—anti-communism. This became the doctrine to rationalize any and every act since all challenges to the Somoza regime were seen as subversive. These subversives were to be eliminated by any means necessary, consequently encouraging the use of torture.

The School of Americas offered a wide range of courses, which went from radio repair and auto mechanics, to counter-insurgency, jungle warfare, urban warfare, and military intelligence interrogation. Most of the courses, whatever their focus, had some class time devoted to discussing the threat of communism. Perez had taken the course entitled Intelligence and Security, which included the nature of the communist world threat and countering the insurgency threat. Thus whatever technical skills he had been taught, the SOA also included the repressive techniques he had learned so well.

But he couldn't stomach Somoza's atrocities so he left, joined the insurgency, and fought well. Now he was tired of the fighting. It was time to reap some reward for all he had been through since he joined the military. He poured himself another shot of brandy and knocked it back.

"I've been thinking, Ramon," his wife said, half watching him out of the corner of her eye. "You've been much too busy hunting these stupid contras. Why don't you ask Secretary Rivas for a vacation and we can go to San Salvador. You love the city and the change of scenery will do you good."

Aurielo powdered her nose and switched her attention to her eye shadow. God, how this woman irritated him and he longed to be in Maria's arms. His wife was an abject failure when it came to pleasing him and he had given up trying to teach her. After twenty, dismal years of marriage, she was simply a fixture in his life, like the furniture or his Mercedes. A vacation with Maria would have been exciting, even erotic, but with Aurielo, he couldn't bear to contemplate it.

"No, I can't," he said. "Not right now, anyway. Maybe next year."

He noticed his wife's frown and sat on the bed. Aurielo continued her prattle. "I spoke with Secretary Rivas's wife the other day," she said. "They have bought four more polo ponies to add to their stable, two mares and two geldings. One of the mares is a beautiful chestnut, Ramon. They might be willing to sell her to us. I was thinking that maybe we could buy her and begin raising ponies along with them. Mrs. Rivas is an expert on breeding and raising horses and it would be something that might help me pass the time."

"Where would we get the money? Those horses cost a small fortune. There's no way we could ever afford it." Perez's mind was still in the slums, his thoughts on his mother.

"Mrs. Rivas says they possibly could allow us to pay for the horse over time. Maybe even have the payments taken out of your salary. It would be good, don't you think, to have a diversion in our lives? We never had children." Her voice became low and critical. "Lord knows you are in need of diversions."

"What is that supposed to mean?" Perez asked, anger in his voice.

He stood and slipped his feet into his loafers and stood beside Aurielo. His only diversion was a traitor, but god, how he missed her.

"Just that it would take your mind off the troubles you've been having lately, that's all."

Perez felt the blood surge to his head and he fought the desire to slap Aurielo's face. Instead, he put on his dinner jacket and combed his hair.

"Out of the question," he said. "I'm surprised at you for even considering it. You've got enough to keep you busy with your garden club and luncheon group. All I need is some asinine horses running around and wreaking havoc."

"But, Ramon. I told Mrs. Rivas that I was sure you would be interested. Won't you reconsider?"

"Absolutely not. You can just tell the old bag that your husband has better sense than to invest in something that eats while he sleeps."

Aurielo finished her makeup and brushed her hair. Perez could tell her feelings were hurt but he didn't care. She put on her diamond necklace and disappeared into their bedroom closet.

"Hurry," he said. "I don't want to miss the reception line."

ℯↄℯↄ

Slater awoke to the sound of gentle rapping on the hotel's door. He opened it a crack and noticed a group of men standing outside. When he recognized one of them from the drop zone, he opened the door. They moved quietly into the room and dropped four large duffel bags on the floor. Carlos awoke and shook hands with the men then introduced them to Slater and Casey. The rain had stopped, but low, menacing clouds still hung over the capital city.

"Ah, the explosives," Casey said and he began to inspect the bags which were full of C-4 blocks. "Did you bring the detonators?"

The man familiar to Slater wore olive drab fatigues that had seen better days. They were mud-stained and his shirt was full of small tears. He nodded and retrieved a small bag from inside a large one after which he produced a handful of pencil-shaped detonators and a large coil of detonation cord.

Casey grinned. "Good work. And I see you brought the HotShot electronic detonators also. Great. Electronic detonation works the best, especially under these circumstances. Jim, you and Carlos start packing this stuff into our packs, but be careful. We don't want to end up in South America."

Everyone laughed at the joke and began the work in earnest. Maria woke and joined the group. They had one hour to get into the Interior Ministry before it closed and they needed to locate a hiding place in the tunnel after doing so.

After loading Casey's car with the explosives and other gear, the group said goodbye to their friends from the jungle and began the drive to the Plaza de la Revolucion. They headed north toward the southern shore of Lake Managua and the railway. At the busy intersection of Calle Julio Buitago they waited for the light to change then continued past the Mercado Oriental to the Plaza. In front of the National Palace, they could see numerous military and State Security Police guards patrolling the plaza and stationed on the palace steps. Casey parked the car on a deserted, narrow street to the west of the palace behind the Ministry of Interior. Duffels in hand, the group headed for the door on the north side of the building, shaded by a small grove of trees and out of sight from anyone who might be loitering at the rear of the palace.

Slater was astonished. In spite of all the security at the palace, the Interior Ministry was devoid of guards. It didn't make any real sense. The Sandinistas were so worried about their precious palace that it never occurred to them a threat might come from somewhere else. He threw the duffel over a shoulder and helped Maria with hers.

"This way," Carlos said.

He pointed to the grove of trees and they scurried behind a hedgerow that led to the corner of the building. They stopped while Carlos peered around the corner.

No one.

He ran to the door, pushed it open, and they scrambled down a set of concrete stairs into the ministry's basement.

"This way," Carlos whispered. "Be quiet. There may be a guard down here."

He led them into a darkened corridor that opened into the main tunnel. Carlos stopped and waited. Slater's heart pounded and his palms were moist which made gripping the heavy duffel difficult. It fell from his hand and hit the concrete floor with a loud thud.

"Shit," he said. Without looking, he knew three pairs of eyes were staring at him.

"It's a good thing that stuff won't go off," Casey said in a low tone when Slater picked up the duffel.

"Shh," Carlos said. "There may be guards in this tunnel. Let's go."

He led them down the dark tunnel toward the palace. There were water puddles everywhere and, as they approached, rats squealed in their pursuit of higher ground. The group sloshed through the ankle-deep water until Carlos found the small alcove, a few meters from the stairway, leading to the main floor. Ducking into the dark anteroom, they set their duffels on a wooden table and caught their breaths.

Casey looked at his watch. "Five p.m.," he said. "Just in time. Now to wait."

"The freight elevator is in the palace basement right up those stairs." Carlos looked at the drawing of the palace provided by Slater. "I think if we start around ten, it would give us plenty of time to wire the plastic, set the timers, and then get out before the explosion. What we need to do now is rest. And wait."

Great, thought Slater, *six hours standing in this cesspool. We're sitting ducks if anyone happens by*. He removed his M-16 from a duffel and shoved in a clip. He noticed Casey retrieve his S&W 459 and push a fourteen-round magazine into its handle. He smiled at Slater and nodded. Each of them leaned on the concrete walls for support. No one talked. Slater attempted to occupy his thoughts with what he and Maria would do after the explosion. Of course, he would try to convince her to return with him to the States. It was their only hope for a life together. Freedom. He had taken it for granted all these years but, here in this tiny country where tyranny and oppression was the rule of the day, freedom was not an abstract idea. These people risked everything for something they believed would make a profound difference in their lives and the lives of their children. He had once thought that he and Maria could continue in San Rafael but now knew it was impossible. Casey was right—Slater could see that—the war was a long way from being over. It would take years before freedom came to Nicaragua. He would just have to make Maria see that their love for each other was more important that the counterrevolution. At least, she had said as much.

His legs ached so he squatted and tried to rest by laying his head on his knees, but found it difficult. This mission was insane. Why had he gone along with it? Their success hinged on quickness and stealth, being able to get in and out of the palace without being seen.

Remember, he told himself—you are already dead.

CHAPTER 29

The enormous, elegant ballroom on the main floor of the National Palace was alive with excitement. Everyone who held an official position in the Sandinista government, from the president down to the lowest aide, was gowned and jeweled in their finest evening wear. Women wore lavish silk gowns and furs while their escorts strutted like peacocks in tuxedoes or uniforms adorned with campaign medals. At one end of the ballroom, a long table was piled high with foods of all kinds and stiff waiters mingled in the crowd, holding silver platters of finger foods and champagne. On an elevated stage behind the buffet, a string orchestra played medleys of waltzes, tangos, and an occasional rock and roll number. People ate, drank, and talked in groups. Ambassadors, cabinet ministers, army generals paraded through the crowd, smiling and bowing to bejeweled ladies who returned the attention with flirtatious smiles.

Secretary of Interior Fernando Rivas and his wife stood in the receiving line with the president and his cabinet as the National Directorate welcomed the guests to the palace. Rivas's wife was a tall, stately woman in her late thirties with jet-black hair pulled into a tight bun behind her head. She wore a pink chiffon evening dress and around her neck hung the diamond and emerald necklace that Rivas had given her on their tenth wedding anniversary.

The couple smiled and shook hands with the hundreds of

people who filed past to pay their respects and be greeted by the president.

Rivas wore his blue military uniform with the blue and white Nicaraguan sash draped across his chest. His many medals were lined in three rows over his left breast pocket and his sword of office hung from his left hip. Now and then, he would smile at his wife and feign boredom with the proceedings but the truth was he was having the time of his life.

At nine o'clock, the receiving line adjourned so the president could pass through the buffet. Rivas led his wife to the table and began filling his plate with caviar, roast pig, wild turkey, venison, and fried alligator. He passed on the raw fish he liked so well, for it had a tendency to upset his stomach. He didn't want anything to put a damper on the evening. His wife put a small portion of a few items on her plate and sauntered over to a group of women who were gathered next to a bank of windows along the far wall. As he shoveled large bites of food into his mouth, he felt a tug on his elbow.

"Good evening, Mr. Secretary," Colonel Perez said.

Rivas turned and nodded at the colonel.

"I believe you know my wife, Aurielo, Mr. Secretary."

Mrs. Perez held out her hand and Rivas took it, stiffened to attention, and kissed it. She blushed and stepped back behind Perez.

"It is good to see you, Colonel. I trust that you and your lovely wife are enjoying yourselves?"

"Most certainly, sir. It has been such a long time since I have seen most of Managua's finest gathered in one place. The rich and the powerful, they say."

"The rich get richer, Ramon, but I ask you, is it possible to be more powerful than we are at this moment? The country is ours and we can do with it as we want. Doesn't that possibility fill you with excitement?"

Perez nodded and took a glass of champagne from a passing waiter. "It is good to be living in the city, eating caviar instead of sitting in jungle trying to unseat that bastard Somoza."

Rivas nodded in agreement and shoveled in another mouthful. He continued to listen while Perez talked with an animated hand.

"Aurielo tells me that you have purchased four more magnificent polo ponies. Your stable of fine horses keeps getting larger, Mr. Secretary."

"One of the mares is out of Secretariat. She has a very good bloodline and should throw some fine colts."

"I appreciate your kind offer of a mare, sir, but under the present financial circumstances, I don't see how I could afford such a fine animal. My wife, she speaks without consulting me."

Rivas couldn't believe that Perez talked about his wife this way behind her back. It was another reason why the common fighting man should be isolated from the elite.

"By the way, Colonel. I would introduce you to the president but I'm afraid he isn't very happy with you at the moment. Your constant blunderings of late have put him in a sour mood and a meeting would only upset him more. I hope you understand?"

Perez walked a few steps away from his wife and waited for Rivas to follow. Rivas thought Aurielo looked helpless, alone, without her husband. Most men would not leave their wives standing the way Perez did. Another reason he didn't like the Colonel.

"I have been thinking, sir," Perez said, "that my moment of truth will come soon with that Carlos fellow. I can sense it. To be sure, we have had some bad luck of late. Those bastards have given us trouble but the tide will turn, Mr. Secretary. I will personally bring you the man's head in a basket."

Rivas hated discussions of such vulgarity at social functions while Perez made excuses for his blunderings, so he excused himself and left Perez alone with his wife.

∽∾∽

Slater glanced at his watch, ten o'clock. Carlos and Casey motioned for him and Maria to follow up the steps into the palace basement. He helped Maria shoulder her duffel and brought up the rear of their column. His legs ached from the long wait in the dank tunnel and he stretched his cramped muscles while he hurried to the doorway. Carlos cracked the door open and peered into the basement. He nodded and scurried into the large, underground expanse that served as the palace's storage facility. Rows upon rows of tall shelves housed everything from office furniture to files. Low-watt light fixtures that hung from the high ceiling provided the only available light and their feet made muffled squeaks on the concrete floor.

Signaling the group to follow him, Carlos hurried down an aisle between two rows of tall shelves. The basement was quiet and seemed deserted, only the creaking of water pipes punctuated the stillness. The freight elevator was located at the west end of the Palace basement and it was a long hike carrying the heavy duffels. Each time Carlos came to a break in the shelves he stopped, paused a moment, then continued toward the far end of the basement. After plodding what Slater thought was a good hundred yards, they arrived at the elevator. Its doors were closed.

"Here we are," Carlos said in a hushed tone. "One floor up is the main floor which is where the ballroom is located. It's down there." He pointed to the opposite end of the building. "We need to go up two floors and make it to the other end in order to find that janitor closet."

Casey dropped his duffel and pushed the elevator call button. Nothing happened. Slater looked around and prepared himself for a confrontation with a security guard. The corner of the basement was dark and from where he stood, the elevator door was housed in a black shadow.

Casey again pushed the call button and the group waited for the doors to open. Still nothing. From behind a row of shelves, Slater heard footsteps. Soft footsteps, like cushioned boots on the concrete floor. He motioned to Casey and pointed in the direction of the sounds, which became louder with each second. Casey nodded and pointed to Carlos who understood the situation and crouched closer to the wall. Slater's heart raced. His fingers felt icy and numb.

The footsteps drew nearer. A guard stepped into view. Slater and Carlos jumped him and wrestled the man to the ground. Slater tore the man's AK-47 from his hands while Carlos clamped a hand over his mouth. Casey, withdrew his S&W 459, and was about ready to bring it down on the man's face, when Carlos plunged his knife into the guard's neck. A muffled groan issued from the man and his eyes rolled backward. Slater's hands trembled. He was shocked by the quickness of Carlos's actions.

"To hell with tying him up," Carlos said. He pulled his knife from the guard and stepped over the corpse.

"Where's the damn elevator?" Casey hissed. "Why won't it open?"

"Maybe they have turned it off for security reasons because of the reception," Maria said.

She helped Slater drag the guard's body behind a row of shelves then stood staring at the closed door with the rest of the group.

"Of course," Carlos said. "We're going to have to pry it open."

"Why not just take the stairway?" Slater asked. He was beginning to get a funny feeling in the pit of his stomach.

"Too risky," Carlos added. "Too many guards.

"But if the elevator isn't running, what good is prying it open going to do?" Maria asked.

Casey reached into a duffel, pulled out a metal crowbar and held it up. "We'll have to climb up inside the elevator shaft," he said. "It's our only way."

He went to work with the crowbar. It took ten minutes of heavy prying but he was able to open the heavy, metal door enough so that Slater and Carlos could slip their hands around the edge.

Together, they pulled it open and stared into the pitch-black void of an empty elevator shaft.

Slater took the flashlight offered by Casey and pointed it up to the top of the shaft.

"What do you see?" asked Casey. He sounded impatient.

"Is there a floor above the second one?" Slater asked.

"There seems to be part of a floor above the second. Why?" Carlos asked.

"Good. The car is stopped at the level above the second floor. I thought the building only had two floors but there must be a small alcove up there just to park the elevator. If we can get up to the door on the second floor we can pry it open like we did this one."

"We're going to have to rope up and scale the inside of the shaft," Casey said. "Everybody, put on your climbing harnesses. Jim, you go first, then Maria and Carlos. I'll bring up the rear."

Slater studied the shaft with a flashlight to map the climb. The rays of light made an eerie scene as they bounced off the walls of the elevator shaft. "There's a small ledge next to the elevator door where we can stand once we get up there."

When everyone was in their harness, Slater took the end of the rope and tied himself in then clamped his duffel to it. He took a cluster of carabiners and began the perilous climb up the shaft. Don't look down, he reminded himself. He tucked the flashlight into his harness and worked in stages, struggling to ascend the steel structure of the elevator's tracking mechanism. When he had made it about twenty feet, he found a round, steel beam where he was able to fasten a climbing nut and, by attaching a carabiner to it, clip in the climbing rope. Typical climbing drill, he thought. The rope played out beneath him and soon he saw Maria begin her ascent. She grappled with her duffel and Slater realized its weight was pushing her off balance.

"Keep the duffel on your hip," he called to her. "You're letting it swing free. It's going to knock you off, if you're not careful."

"I can't," she cried. "I'm not strong enough."

"Yes you can, Maria. Just swing the bag around onto your hip. You can do it."

Maria was close to disaster. If she could not proceed any farther the entire mission could be compromised.

"You're going to have to, honey. You don't have any other choice. Close your eyes for a moment then try again."

Slater watched Maria attempt to force the duffel around onto her hip but each time the bag slipped and pulled her at an awkward angle. She dangled from her harness and he could do nothing to help. She finally got her body under control and slid the duffel onto her hip. He breathed a sigh of relief and returned to his climbing.

Slater scrambled to the door on the main floor and waited. The light from his flashlight cast dancing beams through the dusty shaft while Carlos and Casey began the climb upward. It was a slow, arduous process but Slater managed to reach the narrow ledge next to the elevator door on the second floor. Above him was the bottom of the elevator itself. He managed to get an arm around a beam to steady himself, pulled the crowbar from his belt, and prayed that no one used the elevator. If it started down, it would crush all four of them.

The cold numbness in his fingers disappeared and Slater's clothes were damp from the stifling heat in the elevator shaft. Standing on the ledge, he shoved the end of the crowbar into the crack between the doors and pulled with all his strength. The doors didn't move. He tried again and the doors creaked opened an inch. After a deep breath, Slater pulled again, and the doors moved another inch. Peeking through the narrow opening he noticed the hallway beyond was dark. No footsteps of security guards. He continued working and after much effort had the doors open wide enough to crawl through.

Slater wormed into the hallway, peered back into the dark shaft, and watched Maria inch her way to the doors.

"Give me your hand," he said, reaching over the edge. "And don't look down. It's a long way to the bottom."

He grabbed Maria's outstretched arm and pulled her into the hallway where she sat, gasping for air. Carlos followed at the doors, then Casey. Together, they huddled for a moment in the dark hallway.

"Shit," said Maria. "I opt for going home another way."

"Down is much easier than going up. I can attest to that," Slater said.

"Just jump, right?" Carlos said.

Casey chuckled. "We need to be back in the tunnel when

the blast occurs, so I'm afraid we're going to have to rappel back the way we came. We can't just walk out of here. Sorry."

Slater followed Carlos's lead and lugged his duffel down the hallway. They had encountered only one guard, a fact that surprised Slater. The long hallway was empty so, pulling their bags behind them, they jogged to the other end. Once they reached the last few meters of hallway, Carlos stopped and pointed to the janitor's closet between two office doors.

"Here's the room where we place the explosive," he said, throwing his duffel on the floor. "We'll put the C-4 in here, wire it up, and get the hell out. Fifty pounds of the stuff should do the trick."

Casey stood and slapped Maria on the back. She was still breathing hard and shot a disgusted look at him.

"Good going, Maria. You're a hell of a guerrilla. I'd be proud to have you in the Company. The detonators and timers are in your duffel."

Maria removed the items and handed them to Carlos who had already placed the plastic explosive on the floor next to a wall. It took ten minutes for the group to unpack the C-4 and wire it with detonators and HotShot timers. Slater looked at his watch. 11:30 P.M. Thirty minutes to the president's toast. They set the timers for midnight and stepped back into the hallway. Slater stopped dead in his tracks.

"There's someone at the far end of the hallway," he whispered.

"Guard?" Carlos asked.

Slater peered around the corner of the closet and allowed his vision to adjust to the darkness. He cocked his head to one side and listened.

"I can't tell, but I don't think so. It sounds like two people, a man and a woman."

The darkness made it difficult for Slater to tell for sure who was on the floor with them. The noise sounded like laughter—no, more like two people giggling. Then he saw them—a man and woman leaving an empty office. They stumbled toward the stairway. The man was dressed in a tuxedo and the woman wore a rumpled gown. When they reached the stairway, they embraced. The man's hands were all over the woman until she pushed him away, giggling. They descended the stairway and headed, Slater surmised, back to the reception. He looked at his watch. 11:43 p.m. They had seventeen minutes to reach the safety of the tunnel.

The group scrambled down the hallway and found the elevator door as they had left it. The man and woman had been so interested in their lovemaking that they had not recognized that its doors were ajar. One by one, they rappelled down the shaft to the palace basement and, to their relief, found the guard's dead body had not been discovered. Head pounding, Slater took Maria by the hand and ran back to the alcove in the tunnel. When Casey and Carlos caught up with them, Slater looked at his watch—11:57 p.m.

So far so good.

Only minutes left.

CHAPTER 30

A thunderous explosion rocked the palace's foundation and brought the walls of the ballroom crashing down upon Perez and his wife. The blast disintegrated the entire ceiling and shot tiny pieces of the crystal chandeliers through the air like shrapnel, ripping and tearing into the bodies of reception attendees. The explosion and the concussion from the shock wave traveling at over eight thousand meters per second sent bodies flying all over the place. A siren wailed an alarm and the ballroom filled with a thick cloud of dust and smoke. The guests, who moments earlier had been feasting on fine food and drink, now screamed in the darkness. Most of them were buried under a huge pile of rubble occupying the space that used to be the ballroom.

Perez was pinned under a massive wooden beam that had once supported the ceiling. He could not move, his head spun, and the ringing in his ears shot throbbing signals into his brain. He lay in pitch-black darkness while he struggled to collect himself but found it difficult. Pain in his wounded leg sent shocks throughout his body. He felt a warm ooze and, when he tried to move his arms, he realized that the front of his suit was soaked with blood. With his head reeling in pain and confusion, he tried to move the beam but it was no use— for a huge pile of rubble lay on top of the beam. It was going to take a miracle for anyone to find him.

Screams of trapped people echoed through the darkness

and again he attempted to move but the beam wouldn't budge.

"Aurielo," he called out. "Aurielo, are you all right?"

His wife did not answer. In the dark, he couldn't tell if she was nearby or had been thrown some distance by the blast. Screams of the guests, who somehow managed to survive, shot through the carnage like hysterical banshees of Irish folklore. Perez felt around him and his groping hand discovered a severed foot. Stunned, he threw the appendage down and vomited. Pinned and unable to move, Perez prayed—save Aurielo. Save Nicaragua's President. He shivered and realized he was going into shock. All he could muster besides the prayer was a repeated line—*Oh my god.*

In the dark distance, he heard the sirens of what he hoped were emergency vehicles. His legs were numb, he couldn't feel them. Or hold out much longer. He tried wiggling his toes but wasn't able to tell if they were moving or not.

It was ironic, wasn't it, that in his moment of despair, he prayed that his wife would be saved. Earlier in the evening, he had nothing but revulsion for her. He had looked forward to finding a new mistress, but in a split second, it all changed. His mind turned to Secretary Rivas and his wife and he wondered if they had survived. Was the president dead? If the National Directorate were all gone who would run the country? Perez was getting light-headed and figured his life was ebbing away.

A few lights flickered above him and, through his mental fog, Perez recognized that the emergency generator had been activated. Helpless in the eerie glimmer, he gasped when he saw the condition of his legs and the blood all over his chest. At what used to be the far end of the ballroom he could hear the shouts of people trying to gain entrance. He hoped it was rescuers and medical help. Perez raised his head and looked around again. *My god, the entire east wall of the ballroom is missing.* Nothing standing, only a gaping hole that opened onto the Plaza. Above he could make out the rafters of the palace. The blast had demolished the entire second floor.

Perez heard someone nearby and called out.

"Where are you?" the voice called back.

"Over here. I'm trapped under a beam and can't move."

"Who are you?"

"I'm Colonel Ramon Perez. Please help me. I can't feel my legs."

The sounds of the rescuers grew closer and the thought of being saved gave new life to Perez's struggle to survive. Two men, dressed in army uniforms and holding flashlights, appeared on top of the rubble pile. Perez saw one of the men turn and shout. Soon, two more men arrived and they labored to lift the heavy beam off him. It moved an inch but not enough for Perez to be pulled free.

"Please," he said. "My wife, where is my wife?"

"Calm down, Colonel. It's a mess in here. There's more help on the way."

It took a while until the four men managed to pull Perez from the rubble. When he tried to stand his legs buckled and he toppled onto a pile of bricks and mortar. His eyes darted over the rubble for his wife.

"Aurielo," he called, his voice cracking as he stumbled forward. "My wife, where are you?"

With help from one of the rescuers, Perez staggered through the debris, calling out for his wife and surveying the devastation. There was an enormous hole in the floor of the ballroom fifty feet in diameter and through the smoke, he could make out the bodies of countless dead at the bottom of it. The wailing had diminished somewhat, a fact Perez thought indicated people were dying, but he managed to stumble the length of the ballroom and get the attention of a security guard. "What happened?" he said to the man.

"Guerrillas," the guard replied. "Goddamned contras, I imagine. Who else?"

Perez reached out, grabbed the man's arm to steady himself, and heard him gasp.

"Sir," the guard said, "you're badly hurt. Let me get you to an ambulance."

"No, not now. I'm all right. Can I be of help?"

"No, sir. You wait right here. I'm going to find a medic. Please, don't move."

Perez sat on a pile of broken bricks and watched the guard and his rescuer disappear into the night. Dozens of emergency vehicles were parked outside their emergency lights flashing. It was apparent that the army had assumed control of the rescue. Waiting for the guard to return, Perez clutched his chest and tried to breathe. Where was his wife? Had she survived?

❧❧❧

Maria felt the tunnel lurch when the explosion tore through the palace. A water pipe nearby burst and spewed water down the corridor where the small group was assembled. The dim lights of the tunnel flickered twice then went out throwing them into total darkness.

Slater switched on his flashlight, took her by the arm, and followed Casey through the rising water toward the Ministry of Interior building. Upon reaching the door to the ministry's basement, Maria stopped and looked over her shoulder down the dark tunnel. They had done it. Damned if they hadn't done it. Now if they could just make it back to Pueblo Salto.

Water continued to spew from the broken pipes hanging overhead. Soaked, they raced through the basement of the ministry building and up a flight of stairs to the empty main floor. At the doorway to the outside, Carlos stopped and grabbed Maria's arm. He had the most bizarre look on his face.

"I'm going around to the front of the palace," he said. "I'll catch up with you in a few minutes."

"What?" Maria yelled. "Are you crazy or something?"

"I want to see it up close. Don't worry."

Casey was already running toward their car. Slater tugged on Maria's arm.

"Carlos, don't be stupid. Let's get outa here, while we still can."

Carlos pulled Maria away from Slater and kissed her on the forehead.

"I'll be all right and I've waited a long time. This shouldn't take long."

He was gone before she could protest further. She watched him sprint around the corner of the palace and disappear from view. Slater pushed her across the back lawn of the ministry and through the small grove of trees that had earlier hidden their approach to the building.

By the time they reached the car, Casey had the motor running. They scrambled into the rear seat and closed the door. Casey looked at them for a moment then turned his attention to the palace. "Where's Carlos?" he asked. He glanced back and forth between the rear seat and the street.

"He's an idiot," Slater said. "The dumb sonofabitch had to admire his work."

"He said it wouldn't take very long," Maria added.

"We can't wait," Casey said. "The place is crawling with police and military."

From the rear seat, Maria watched the jeeps and trucks race past them, heading in the direction of the palace. Only a few faint lights were visible from the inside of what was left of the building and the scent of smoke clung to the night air. A temporary morgue must have been set up on the plaza, for there were covered bodies lined in rows. But pandemonium still reigned throughout the rubble of the palace. Maria dug her fingernails into Slater's arm as she waited for Carlos's return.

"We can't stay here all night," Slater said. "Where is he?"

The question went unanswered. Maria's heart sank when Casey shoved the car into gear.

"That's it," he yelled. "If he can make it back to the hotel, great, but we can't wait any longer."

Without further explanation, Casey tore down a narrow street and, racing back to the hotel, passed a long convoy of trucks on Avienda Bolivar.

❧❦❧

Colonel Perez sat on a litter at the palace's entrance watching rescuers pull hordes of dead from the ballroom. The injured were taken to the plaza on the backside of the building to a makeshift aid station next to the temporary morgue. He stumbled outside into the night and grabbed a young soldier by the arm.

"Do you have a cigarette?" he asked.

He thanked the soldier as he lit up and inhaled the acrid smoke. His entire body was racked with pain. A bloody state security officer walked up to him and saluted.

"Are you all right, Colonel? You look a mess."

"I think it looks worse than it is," Perez replied. "I'll have it looked after in a minute."

The men stood and talked while the officer directed more rescue workers inside the building. The pungent smell of smoke and cordite penetrated Perez's nostrils and made breathing difficult. He hadn't seen his wife since the explosion and the realization that she would be found in the morgue weighed heavily on him. He didn't love her, he knew that. But she had been a faithful wife for many years and he had grown accustomed to her. Comfortable. She had made him a home, a refuge from the stress and strain of office, and now she could be gone forever. He felt ashamed that he had been so curt with her earlier in the evening. He wanted to go to the morgue and look for her but could not force himself to do so. Maybe later. The palace and plaza had become a nightmare, and he didn't know if the president survived. Come to think of it—he hadn't seen Rivas either.

Then, out of the corner of his eye, he saw a man walking, staring about. He didn't know why but something about him was familiar. He had seen his picture somewhere before but could not place it. The man approached the front of the palace and Perez noticed his torn shirt. He wasn't dressed in formal attire and Perez wondered why he was here. A curious on-looker? Perez watched the man casually stroll up the steps to the palace, stop on the concrete patio, and look up at the half-destroyed building. He wore a peculiar smile on his face, an almost laughing, haughty grin. It struck Perez like a lightning bolt—the face. He knew the face. He turned, took the police-man's AK-47 from his hand, and pointed at the man.

"Stay very still!" Perez yelled. "Now, come this way."

For an instant the man froze, the smile gone. His eyes widened as if he was contemplating his course of action, then he turned and ran.

"Halt!" commanded Perez.

The man kept running.

Perez fired a barrage of bullets and the man tumbled to the ground. He didn't move. With the security officer at his side, Perez limped to the corpse and turned it over. He noticed the copper bracelet, stooped, and wrenched it off the man's wrist.

"Senor Carlos," he said as he put a foot on Carlos's chest. "You contra bastard. I have you now. You cannot escape again." He turned to the officer who was examining Carlos's body. "This is one of the perpetrators of this horrible crime," Perez said. "And I can assure you he did not act alone. We must find his friends and make them pay for this holocaust."

The police officer rifled through Carlos's pockets but found nothing. Satisfied, he stood. "We are in the process of setting up roadblocks on all roads out of town," he said to Perez. "If his friends are still in Managua and try to leave, we'll find them, sir. I will report this immediately."

Perez felt a new burst of energy course through his body. He turned and began walking to the aid station. "Young man," he called over his shoulder, "I will find his traitor friends and all of the National Directorate will see, Ramon Perez is not a man to be trifled with."

CHAPTER 31

Back in Casey's room in the Intercontinental Hotel, Slater and Maria collapsed, exhausted, on the floor. Casey had parked behind the hotel to avoid detection by the countless police and military vehicles racing up and down Managua's streets. Breathing easier, Slater went to the bathroom, stuck his head under the faucet, and allowed cold water to run over his pounding head. Upon his return to the living room, Casey offered him and Maria a beer. He accepted it with a smile and drank it down in one, long gulp. Maria sipped hers and sat on the floor, her back to the balcony.

Carlos had not returned and Maria voiced her concern. "We should never have left without him," she said, her voice cracking.

"We had no choice," Casey said. "Time was running out."

"I hope he's all right," Slater said.

"I doubt it. He probably met up with the army and is under arrest at this very moment," Casey said.

Maria moaned.

"Or worse," Casey continued.

"God, I hope he wasn't killed," Maria said. Tears filled her eyes.

"We need to get you two out of here," Casey said as he took a drink of the beer. "Out of Managua."

"How?" Slater asked. "The streets are crawling with police and the army."

"They'll concentrate their forces at the airport and along the rift valley east of here," Casey replied. "The Pacific Ocean is closer to Managua than the Atlantic so they will be patrolling in that direction. The airport is out, obviously."

"What do you suggest?" Maria asked.

"The road that goes due east out of town eventually leads to Villa Domingo at the headwaters of the Rio Escondido. The river flows to the Atlantic Ocean at the fishing village of Cordoba, right on the coast. I can arrange for a seaplane to pick you up if you can get to the village and find a boat to take you past Isla Grande in the shallow water."

"How would you contact the plane?" Slater said.

"By radio. Remember I still have the one here in the room. My station chief in Costa Rica can arrange to pick you both up and fly you to San Jose. From there it would be an easy matter to return to the States."

Slater noticed the contorted look on Maria's face and took her into his arms. Her brown eyes starred into his. She hugged him.

"This is it, honey," he said. "Decision time. We need to get out of here, both of us. My work here is finished now, and there's nothing left for me to do. Eventually, the Sandinistas will find out that I was involved in the bombing and come looking for me. It's our only hope if we love each other. How about it? Will you come with me?"

Maria drew him closer and hugged him again. Slater kissed her and she pressed her lips hard against his.

"You know I love you so," she said. "I have dreaded this moment for such a long time but didn't think it would come so soon. My work here is unfinished, Jim. We have so much left to do—for Nicaragua—for all of our people. The good are giving their lives for freedom and I ought to be a part of it. If Carlos has sacrificed his life for the movement, can I do anything less?"

"I guess it's now or never. If we love each other, shouldn't we be together? It's quite possible that you could do more to help your friends from the States than here by raising money, that sort of thing. I love you and won't leave you behind."

Casey retreated to the bedroom, allowing Slater and Maria to continue their discussion in private.

"My mind is in a whirl. So much has happened so fast. I don't want to abandon my companions."

"You wouldn't be abandoning them. Most of them are gone, anyway. You would continue the fight from another battlefront, that's all." Slater could see that Maria was weakening so he continued. "So much has happened since we first met and I can't begin to imagine a life without you. But if you get yourself killed, what good will that do either of us? I would never be able to live with the fact that I did not take you with me."

Maria smiled. "I understand. You don't think I would be abandoning the cause if I left with you? My friends wouldn't call me a traitor? I need to know."

"Your friends are becoming fewer and fewer, Maria. Soon there will be only you. How do you plan to continue fighting all by yourself?"

"I dunno, but I would find a way."

Slater noticed the hesitation in Maria's voice. "Alive and in the States you could do so much more than here," he said. "Now, come on. You know your friends want you with me. You can't sit on the fence forever."

"You're right, honey," Maria said. "I'm with you. I hope your mother will like me."

Slater grinned, picked Maria up, and hugged her. Casey returned to the living room and smiled. "I'm glad. I know you made the right decision," he said to Maria.

"Yeah, if we don't get killed in the process," she replied.

"Okay," Slater called to Casey. "Call Costa Rica and tell them we're going to try it. What's next?"

He pulled out a map of Nicaragua and laid it on the table next to the balcony doors.

Casey returned and bent over the map. "Here's the road out of Managua," he said, pointing to the map. "And here's Villa Domingo at the end of the road. It's right on the river so you should be able to steal a *punta* and take it down river to Cordoba. It's about seventy-five to eighty miles from Villa Domingo to the fishing village. With the boat it should take you between five and six hours to reach the coast 'cause you'll be going with the current. Once at Cordoba, beg, borrow, or steal another boat to take you both to the seaplane. The water is shallow in this area so it will have to land some distance from shore."

"How far from here to Villa Domingo?" Slater asked.

"About a hundred miles. You shouldn't encounter any resistance. Like I said, I think most of the searching will be to the west of the city." Casey thought for a moment, took another drink of his beer, and smiled. "On the other hand," he said, "you might have to shoot your way through a roadblock."

"Thanks friend, for those encouraging words," Slater said. "And I thought I'd spend a few entertaining years teaching school in a third-world country. Soak up a little mysterious culture. What a turn of events."

"It'll take you approximately four hours to drive to Villa Domingo. If you leave in the next few hours, you can be there by dawn. Six hours on the river, eight at the outside, should get you to Cordoba around the middle of the afternoon. If I have the plane there by 4 p.m. you would still have several hours of daylight left in which to find it."

Slater and Maria studied the map for a few moments until Slater rubbed his eyes from the strain.

"That brings up the next question, Casey. The ocean's a big place. How do we find the seaplane in the middle of an ocean?"

"I've been thinking of that," Casey responded. "Look here. Right off the southern tip of the island, Isla Grande. It's directly offshore from Cordoba, at its southern end. The reef is particularly close to shore, which means deeper water beyond. That's where the plane will be waiting. With binoculars you shouldn't have much difficulty locating it."

"What if we're delayed or have trouble getting there?" Maria asked. She put an arm on Slater's shoulder and sighed. "What if we can't even get out of the city?"

"One thing at a time," Casey said. "You're going to get out of Managua if you have to shoot your way out. The plane can wait for a couple of hours for you to arrive. There's not much activity along the Mosquito Coast and the Nicaraguan Navy has most of its forces stationed on the Pacific side of the country. Let's say they'll hang around until 8 p.m. It should, as I said, give you plenty of time. But once we decide on a time and you both leave, I won't be able to change it. There'll be no way to communicate with each other after that, understand?"

"Wouldn't it be easier to hide in the mountains or get into Honduras?" Slater asked.

"The road to Leon will be patrolled the heaviest and the mountains will be the first place the army will look. No, it's better if you can make the Mosquito Coast. Be warned though, that this is some of the most sparsely populated, rugged, and untamed country you have ever seen. But if you stay on the river, you should make it okay."

Slater and Maria both took a deep breath. He looked at her and she shrugged her shoulders. "I'd rather die with you than in El Chipote, Jim," she said. "Let's go for it."

Slater sighed but nodded.

Casey stood, folded the map, and handed it to him. "Good, that's settled." He looked at his watch. "It's 12:45 right now. Why don't you two try to get a few hours rest and I'll wake you at four? You'll use my car, of course."

"Why don't you come with us?" Maria asked.

"I still have work to do here," Casey responded. "Who knows how many died tonight? By morning, the Sandinistas may have a new cabinet installed and I need to be here when that happens. You two, go into the bedroom and lie down, I'll wake you later."

Slater took Maria by the hand, led her into the bedroom, and closed the door. It seemed like forever since he last lay next to her and her warmth calmed his shaking body. As he tried to summon sleep, he couldn't help but allow the magnitude of the bombing steal into his thoughts.

"We killed an awful lot of innocent people tonight," Maria said, reading his mind. "I can't help but feel a tremendous amount of guilt over that. The wives of all those men—we weren't at war with them."

"I know," Slater said, pulling her closer to him. "But they were part of the Sandinista government too, in a way. They supported their husbands and the regime and, like it or not, they looked down on all the poor peasants and farmers. So they were not totally inculpable."

"Yeah, but they were human beings, just the same, and I feel sad they died at my hands."

Slater had no more words of comfort, for she was right. Innocent blood had been shed because of what they had done. He pulled her close and tried to asleep.

ഝഝ

Slater opened his eyes to Casey's gentle prodding, turned, and woke Maria, then stumbled into the bathroom. When he returned to the living room, Casey handed him the map and the flashlight.

"You'll want these," he said to Slater. "I've got an M-16 in the back seat of the car, along with another one fixed with a grenade launcher and several grenades. There are a dozen clips for the rifles as well. Keep them close and be prepared to use them along the way. I gave you a couple of flares in case you can't locate the seaplane. The orange smoke can be seen for miles. You still have the .45 I gave you?"

Slater nodded.

Maria pulled on a lightweight jacket and took the map and flashlight from Slater. He put on a sweater and looked at Casey.

"Casey," he said. "I...I..." he stammered, searching for the right words.

"Oh, stop it," Casey interrupted. "You two get outta here. Good luck."

Maria threw her arms around the agent's neck and held him for a while. After she kissed Casey on the cheek, Slater shook Casey's hand and gave him a hug as well. He noticed tears in Maria's eyes.

"Casey, you've been a good friend. I owe you my life. Always had a low opinion of you guys but you have restored my faith in the Company. At least here in Nicaragua. Thanks for your help."

"We're not all bad, you know," Casey said.

Slater realized the man was having difficulty saying good-bye and hugged him once more.

Casey smiled at Slater, his words slow in coming. "You two kids," he said. He wiped his eyes with the back of a dirty hand. "Now go. I hope you make your dreams come true."

With the admonition, he turned and went onto the balcony. Slater took the car keys off the table and Maria followed him to the rear of the hotel. The night was clear and balmy, the stars out in dazzling splendor. The pair jumped into the front seat and, with Slater behind the wheel, roared off into Managua's darkness.

"The road out of town is up this way," Maria said. "Turn right on the Calle de la Sierra and it is straight to Villa Domingo."

"My little navigator," Slater said and shot a quick smile at Maria.

He nodded, turned right at the street, and continued eastward through a quiet *barrio* toward Managua's city limits. The rental car coughed and sputtered through the neighborhood and Slater uttered a silent prayer that the car would hold out for four more hours. They were now on a flat stretch of road where the buildings and shops were few and far between. A brilliant moon shown through sparse clouds, providing good visibility.

"I will miss Carlos," Maria said.

"Too bad he couldn't have made it," Slater said.

"He should never have left but he was just that sort. His country and people meant more to him than anything. Freedom. Justice. That was what he lived for. Probably died for."

"It's possible he's on his way to the mountains," Slater said. "He may have managed to get out of town."

"No," Maria said, shaking her head. "He's dead, I can feel it. Even if he was captured, they have shot him by now. Do you think, Jim, that years from now, his people will understand why he paid the ultimate price for them?"

Slater glanced at Maria and smiled. "We both hope so, don't we? I believe his name will be revered and his exploits will be discussed for a very long time. He was a great man."

"That he was," Maria said and closed her eyes.

Slater let off on the accelerator and the car slowed.

"Look up ahead, honey," he said.

Flashing lights signaled the police and a military road-block. The vehicles themselves were shadows in the moon-light. Maria gasped and grabbed a rifle from the rear seat of the car.

"Roadblock," she said. "Casey was right. What'll we do now?"

Slater stopped the car several hundred meters from the convoy.

"You drive," he said to Maria. He scrambled to the passenger's side of the car.

Maria slid behind the steering wheel while Slater sat with the window down. He grabbed for the grenade launcher and shoved a grenade into its muzzle. In front of the roadblock he could see the silhouettes of men pacing back and forth in front of the line of vehicles. He stomach tightened, knowing they had been spotted and the police were ready to stop them.

"I want you to drive up there and stop a hundred feet or so in front of the roadblock," he said. "I'm going to lob two grenades at them and hopefully that's going to do it. Then you drive fast, as fast as this thing will go. When you get up there, jerk this baby off the road and speed around them. Head over there to your left so I can open fire with the M-16. Maybe I can get lucky with this thing. Can you do it?"

"I think so," Maria said. She smacked her lips, gunned the engine a few times, glanced at Slater, and smiled. "If for some reason we're killed, remember I love you. Now I regret never having made love with you. It was my foolishness, I guess."

"If this works, honey, there will be plenty of time for that later. I'm ready if you are."

The silhouettes moving around the roadblock loomed larger as they approached. Slater could see the men clearly. One was carrying what looked like a large machine gun while the other two looked at them through binoculars. One man put his binoculars in a pocket and talked into a radio. It looked to Slater that they were ready—just waiting for them.

Maria accelerated the car to within a short distance of the roadblock. Slater noticed more State Security Police cars and another military truck were parked across the road. The place was now crawling with armed men. He put the rifle on the seat between them, took the grenade launcher, and opened his door. With a loud boom the grenade went sailing into the night air and exploded next to a police car. Slater fired another grenade and it found its mark as well. The resulting fireball from the two grenades shot skyward.

"Go!" he screamed, scrambling back into the car.

Maria shoved the accelerator to the floor and the car lurched forward, speeding toward the inferno. Slater grabbed the M-16, stuck it out the window, and waited for Maria to make the jog around the roadblock. When she spun the steering wheel to the left, his body slammed against the door. It was like a dream or a movie when everything turns to slow motion. He saw two men silhouetted against the flames and pulled the trigger. With a loud burst, he cut the two men to the ground and braced himself for the shock when Maria cut back onto the road. When it came, he looked out their rear window and saw only a blazing mass of twisted metal. The men were gone. As they sped past the carnage, the heat was intense. Slater knew there were no survivors.

"Good job!" he called over the roar of the car's engine. "Now we're getting somewhere. They didn't know what hit them."

Maria didn't utter a word as they sped toward Villa Domingo. Slater knew she was preoccupied with her driving so he didn't say anything which might distract her. He put the grenade launcher in the rear seat and settled back to watch the trees alongside the road hurtle by them. Where in the hell did Maria learn to drive like that? Wherever it was, he was thankful that she had learned her lessons well.

Slater thought while Maria drove. In the past weeks, he had killed many men, many of whom were part of the Sandinista government. But tonight he worried that he had stepped over the line—he and Maria. Many innocent people had died in the Palace blast and that fact cast a heavy pall over his hopes for their future. Maybe he had been better off fighting the demons left over from Vietnam, rather than creating a host of new ones. Ones that he was sure would come later. He wasn't sure that their love could overcome their shared guilt over spilled innocent blood. He struggled to put the nagging thoughts out of his mind and concentrate on the task at hand—their immediate survival. Together, they would have to learn to live with what they had done in Nicaragua.

CHAPTER 32

Colonel Perez awoke in a hospital room with heavy bandages on his chest and legs and intravenous fluids flowing into his body. He was unaware of how he got to the hospital as the last thing he remembered was sitting in the makeshift aid station on the plaza waiting for the doctor to examine him. He tried to move but a sharp pain penetrated his chest and legs, stopping him short. He gazed out the window and noticed it was still dark, the clock on the wall read 5:30 a.m. Another hour and it would be daylight. He winced as he propped himself up on his pillows and rang for the nurse.

"Colonel, you can't be doing that," the nurse said when she entered the room and saw Perez sitting up in bed. "The doctor said you must have rest. You lost plenty of blood last night. We had to give you several transfusions."

"What's happened at the palace?" he asked. The movement left him feeling faint and he slumped back onto the bed.

"Oh, sir, it has been the most devastating nightmare. Over two hundred dead and a hundred more injured. You are one of the lucky ones. The doctor says a few days of rest and you'll be back on your feet again."

"In a few days the perpetrators of this demonic attack will be lost in the jungle. Nurse, call my headquarters and tell them to send my sergeant over right away. Quick."

"But, sir—" the nurse said.

"Do as I say! The future of the country is at stake."

The nurse threw up her hands in obvious disgust and turned toward the bedside phone.

"By the way," Perez said, "how is the president?"

"He escaped injury, Colonel. But the cabinet, they are all dead, *senor*."

"And my wife?"

"I do not know," the nurse said. She picked up the phone and dialed the airbase.

Damn, thought Perez. That meant Rivas was among those killed in the blast or possibly still missing. What had happened to Aurielo? Where was she? Well, he couldn't worry too much about her—he had more pressing matters to attend to. He needed to give chase to those perpetrators of the previous night's attack. He would grieve later for the death of Aurielo.

⁊❧⁊

Thirty minutes later, Sergeant Trujillo burst through Perez's hospital room door and stood at attention. Sweat poured off the sergeant's face and it was obvious he had not been to bed. The rumpled fatigues and deep lines etched in the man's face told Perez that it had been a rough six hours for this soldier. Before he could say anything, the soldier spoke.

"Sir. Earlier this morning we received word that one of our roadblocks east of town was destroyed. A car was spotted on the road heading east shortly after the attack."

Perez's eyes widened and he took a deep breath. *Those slimy bastards*, he thought. *They're heading for the Atlantic coast. Smart.* He would have bet anything that they would have opted for the Pacific Ocean west of Managua. It was certainly a shorter escape route going west.

"What's been done about it, sergeant?"

"We've spent the past few hours mobilizing our forces and getting ready to follow. When you say the word, Colonel—"

"Dammit!" Perez shouted loud enough to bring the nurse into the room. "Don't take a whole convoy. Get a dozen of our best men and take the jeeps mounted with the RPK machine guns and the recoilless rifles. Those 75 mm cannons ought to blow them off the map. Get going. I'm going to the airbase and will follow from the air. Have them get the Mi-8 ready and tell them I'll be along as soon as I can get dressed."

Perez waited for the sergeant to say something but the man just stood beside his bed as if dumbfounded by the instructions. Perez brought his hand down sharply on the bed. "Dammit, I said get going. And send a car for me."

The sergeant turned and fled the room. Perez fumbled with the handrails of the hospital bed and brought himself to a standing position.

"Get me my clothes," he said to the nurse.

"But, sir—"

"Goddammit," he cursed. "Does everyone have to argue with me? And get this damned IV out of my arm."

He must have scared the woman, for she busied herself with his clothes, including the bloodstained shirt. When they were laid out on the bed, she disappeared out the door. Perez's chest and legs ached. Each time he moved, a bolt of hot liquid shot through his body and he winced in agony. Barely able to hold his head up he prayed for strength to forge ahead. *The last battle,* he told himself. *This is to be the last battle. After these bastards are caught and hung, I can relax and enjoy the future. Who knows, with Rivas gone, a cabinet position might be mine, after all.*

The nurse returned with a bandage and pulled the intravenous catheter from his arm. After she dressed the site, he struggled with his clothes then stumbled down to the elevator, making his way into the small lobby. Outside, his driver was waiting in his Mercedes.

❧❧❧

The first rays of morning sunlight streamed across the lower portion of the central highlands and Maria kept the car's accelerator pushed as far to the floor as she could. They were running low on gas but Slater thought they had enough to make it to Villa Domingo.

The broad expanse of a high-mountain meadow made driving easy and. when they rounded a gentle curve, Slater spotted the bridge.

"Cross the bridge, then pull over," he said. "I'll blow the damn thing. It will slow down the posse."

"Posse?" Maria said. "I don't know that word."

"Just American slang, honey. Pull over there." He pointed to the far side of the bridge.

Maria did as he requested and stopped the car a quarter of a mile beyond the bridge. He took the grenade launcher and proceeded to fire two grenades into the structure. The explosion sent wood shards high into the air and left the bridge in tiny pieces. Back at the car, Maria marveled at the destruction.

"That should hold them for a while," she said. "I'm surprised we haven't seen any choppers yet."

"Me too," said Slater. "But rest assured, now that it's light, they'll be here. You can count on it. Blowing up that roadblock told them where we're heading."

On the move again, the road ahead was a serpentine ribbon, winding its way around rock covered hills and short tundralike grasses. Maria braked as they drove into the sleepy village of Villa Domingo. It was a typical Nicaraguan town with wood and metal houses and shops arranged in a straight line alongside the roadway. In the center of town was a rustic concrete square that housed a lone gazebo surrounded by a row of trees. Children ran about the square and there was a soccer game underway in an adjacent field. The sun was high but dark clouds formed in the west behind them, looking like rain. Good, Slater thought. Bad weather meant fewer aircraft out searching.

The route to Cordoba from the small inland river port of Villa Domingo had been one of the most strategic routes in all of Nicaragua, during the long years of war. From here, arms for the Sandinista Popular Army entered the country. Since the CIA and, by extension, the counterrevolutionaries, were able to obtain advance information about these shipments, they mounted an attack every time a boat carrying armaments arrived. But they had never been successful, for the Sandinistas had a good protection system.

Beyond the square, Slater noticed the tottering and weather-beaten wharf perched on stilts at river's edge. A lone man sat on a barrel, tending his fishing nets with sunburned hands. Sitting idly in the water, numerous empty *puntas* were tied up to the railing. The man continued with his net, oblivious to Maria and Slater's approach. Maria parked the car and they made their way to the wharf.

"*Buenos Dias, senor,*" Slater called.

The man looked up from his work and smiled. He stood and took Slater's outstretched hand, bowed slightly to Maria. His face was furrowed and most of his front teeth were missing. He pulled a tattered straw hat from his head.

"We are looking to rent a boat, *senor,*" Maria said. "We will be happy to pay a good price. We wish to get to Cordoba. Can you help us?"

The man studied Slater and Maria for a moment.

"It is my sister, *senor,*" she continued. "She is very ill and my mother cannot care for her by herself. This is my husband, *Americano.*"

The man looked at Slater then nodded. "How much?" he said. "I only have my little *panga* there." He pointed to a small, wide-bottomed boat with a small outboard motor that was moored to the wharf.

"*Mucho cordobas,*" Slater said. "We will leave the boat at Cordoba and you can pick it up whenever you wish."

Slater produced a fist full of Nicaraguan currency, more than the man had probably seen in a lifetime. The fisherman's eyes bulged and he pointed to a turquoise and white boat. He took the money from Slater and watched him retrieve the weapons from the car. Slater noticed his surprised look but the man put the money in his pocket and started the *panga's* motor, saying nothing about all the firepower.

Slater helped Maria into the boat, where she took a seat in its bow while he took a position alongside the motor. He grabbed the control handle, maneuvered the boat into the middle of the cappuccino-colored river, and headed downstream.

The man on the wharf waved until they rounded a bend in the river and he disappeared from view.

Going with the current made handling the boat easy and soon Slater had the craft settled on a smooth plane. The river was two hundred feet wide and the jungle shot past them on both sides. Running with the current, Slater hoped they could better Casey's estimate of five or six hours to Cordoba and make it in four. It would put them at the Caribbean coast around noon.

They put the Central Highlands behind them and entered the Caribbean Region, a flat plain that sloped toward the Caribbean Sea. Many of the rivers that began in the Central Highlands flowed through the plain. The Rio Escondido was one such river—called the hidden river because English pirates used to hide on it. The region's only good farmland lay alongside the riverbanks bordered by palm and pine forests.

Leaving Villa Domingo, Slater appreciated Casey's description of this region as wild and untamed. Speeding toward the Mosquito Coast, the rainforest became denser and more inhospitable. As they rounded a sharp bend, Maria pointed to an alligator patrolling the river. Once, Slater shuddered at the sight of a huge anaconda python slithering over a low-hanging tree branch. The river was the color of café au-lait, thick and slow moving. They motored past banks covered in bright green vegetation, and, in places, tall palm trees hung over the water, obscuring their view of the sky. Deeper into the rainforest, the jungle took on a misty, ethereal look with howls and screeches emanating from its deepest recesses. Slater knew they had better never have to venture into the rainforest because inexperienced men had disappeared, never to be seen by their families. The jungle was a foreboding place for Nicaraguans, full of wild beasts and mysterious spirits waiting to pounce on unsuspecting interlopers. Locals had a natural, understandable fear of the jungle, especially at night. Unseen snakes and roaming jaguars kept most farmers inside their huts until dawn. Once, a jaguar had prowled into San Rafael, terrorizing the residents until it was shot and killed by a group of farmers.

Slater studied the map given him by Casey, noted there was a series of rapids farther downstream, and prepared himself for a portage of the boat and weapons. Delving deeper in the rainforest, he was reminded why the area was called Costa de Mosquitos—for, in spite of the boat's speed, large black mosquitoes sucked blood from his hands and neck, causing large welts to form on his bare skin. In the bow of the boat, Maria swatted mechanically to keep the bugs away. In San Rafael, he had heard of the much-feared river blindness carried by these infernal insects.

The filarial disease infected humans when the mosquitoes bit and the infective larvae were injected into the skin. Worse yet, there was no drug to treat the disease or the blindness that followed, only poisons whose side effects were sometimes more horrible than the disease itself. Between navigating, steering the boat, and swatting mosquitoes, Slater was beginning to tire.

☙❧

By dawn, Perez was airborne in the Russian-made Mi-8. It was larger than his Mi-2 and carried a crew of three, in addition to being able to ferry twenty-four troops into battle. Along the way, he had downed several stiff belts of brandy, which steadied his nerves and reduced the pain shooting through his body. At the airbase, he had changed into a flight suit and hobbled to the waiting chopper while being briefed by Sergeant Trujillo. The suspect's car was heading toward Villa Domingo.

Perez's flight plan called for an interception along the route and he was ready for a confrontation.

"Abel Leader, this is Ground Force One." The voice crackled over the chopper's radio and Perez keyed his microphone.

"This is Abel Leader. Go ahead."

"Bad news, Colonel. We are at a bridge some twenty miles west of Villa Domingo and they've blown the bridge. Repeat. The bridge is out."

"Can you cross the river?" Perez asked over the loud drone of the chopper's engine. The pilot had navigated a course to intersect the road out of Managua and Perez watched the road as he spoke.

"Negative, sir. We have two jeeps and a truck. No track vehicles. Tanks could make it but the river is too deep for our jeeps. It's the end of the line until we can get help out here."

Perez slammed a gloved fist into the aircraft's console. As he did, a sharp pain stabbed his chest. "Damn!" He brought the microphone to his lips and continued. "Okay, Ground Force One. Get some help out there along with some tanks. They won't get there in time to be of help but get them there, nonetheless. Understand?"

"Roger, Able Leader. Will do. Will try to make contact once we are across the river. Good luck, sir."

Perez didn't respond to the final transmission but, instead, signaled the pilot to increase airspeed. The road to Villa Domingo rushed below him as the helicopter sped eastward. The final judgement to which he hastened was becoming a war of attrition. He took solace, however, in the fact that his heavy machine gun and RPG7 85 mm rockets would make fast work of the anarchists.

CHAPTER 33

At the rapids, the *panga's* motor sputtered and died before Slater and Maria could get it to shore. Slater uncovered a pair of oars wrapped in burlap, fixed them into oarlocks, and fought the current until he had brought the boat to river's edge. It would require a portage through the dense undergrowth past the rapids and they would have to make Cordoba without the use of the motor. After a quick inspection, Slater determined that the engine was history. Drifting with the current would slow their progress but they had no other choice. Fortunately, they were close enough to the village that if they had to abandon the river they could make a run for it through the rainforest, a thought that frightened Slater.

The abrupt, unexpected noise of the chopper zooming low over the river startled him. He jerked his head around in time to see the aircraft bearing down on them like a plump insect. He yelled and Maria shot a glance skyward. The chopper was a mere ten feet off the water's surface looming larger with each passing second. The noise from its rotors was deafening.

"Get the boat to shore!" Slater said.

The two of them struggled against the current to pull the *panga* to the rocky shoreline but the swift water made handling the boat difficult. The chopper zoomed past and fired a hail of bullets, missing them. The machine-gun fire crashed into the trees splitting large limbs from their trunks. Near shore, Maria managed to pull the bow of the boat under the protruding branches of a crooked hemlock. More bullets ricocheted off rocks, causing large splashes in the water. When the chopper shot past, its skids were a foot above the river's surface. Slater pulled Maria into a thicket of rubber plants where they waited for the chopper to abandon its strafing runs.

But the helicopter didn't give up.

With another pass, it rained a tirade of bullets into the brush, a ricochet barely missing Maria. Interspersed with the machine gun fire, Slater could hear the echoes of the heavier artillery as the chopper's cannon pounded the earth with terrible explosions. He grabbed Maria by an arm and stood to run.

"We've got to go on foot," he said above the helicopter noise. "Let's get out of here before it's too late."

The pair ran, crouched, through the dense underbrush. Slater unsheathed his machete and used it to hack their way through the tangle of vines and branches that obstructed their path, while overhead, the helicopter swept up and down the river, firing its machine gun and S-5 rockets into the jungle. The twin turbines of the helicopter screamed, producing a deafening noise which, along with the battering, caused a continuous cacophony that shattered his senses. The chopper continued to fly strafing runs in a crisscross pattern over the river and surrounding jungle. Slater figured it was only a matter of time before the rockets or cannon fire scored a direct hit. The jungle's thick canopy gave them a little measure of concealment but he feared the chopper would get lucky.

Another low pass by the helicopter brought it directly overhead and Slater pushed Maria to the jungle floor where they lay motionless, waiting. The aircraft hovered above them, the barrage of machine gun fire and rocket fire momentarily ended. Slater glanced skyward—the chopper was still overhead. He thought he saw someone in an army uniform peering out its window with binoculars.

"Don't move," he whispered in Maria's ear. "The damned bastard is right over us."

After several minutes, the helicopter moved on, firing blindly over the river. Fatigue rumbled through Slater's legs, rendering them almost useless, and he knew Maria was exhausted as well. Sharp branches, like thorny tentacles, tore holes in her blouse and her hair was matted with sweat. Slater calculated the distance to Cordoba. Fifteen kilometers more. He doubted she would make it.

Slater pulled her to her feet and pushed her ahead of him toward the coast. He tripped over a vine, sending him sprawling to the ground. Lying on his back, his chest heaving, Slater heard the helicopter still pummeling the jungle with its rockets. It felt good to rest a while. He brushed a foot-long centipede from Maria's blouse and she cringed in disgust.

"I hate those things," she said, standing.

"Surely, they are running low on fuel," Slater said, following her lead. "They can't stay up there forever."

"Listen, Jim. It's farther away. Do you think…"

Slater cocked his head to one side and nodded. "They're leaving," he said. "Like I said, they couldn't stay here forever."

"Where are they going? Cordoba?"

"More than likely. It's the logical choice. Put the chopper down to conserve fuel and wait for us. We can't outrun them and they know it."

"What'll we do when we get there? They have the upper hand."

"I dunno. We'll just have to wait and see. Maybe they won't see us. It's all I can offer right now."

Rested, the pair stumbled through the jungle toward Cordoba and their ultimate rendezvous with the Sandinista gunship. Once they arrived at Cordoba, they would have to make a stand.

They were running out of options.

ഇരുഇ

Colonel Perez was overjoyed when he had the pair of fugitives in his gunsights. But, to his disappointment, the bullets were off their mark and his pilot had to circle to try again with the rockets. By the time they turned and were closing in on the target, the man and woman disappeared into the rainforest.

The pilot maneuvered the chopper as close to the trees as he dared and hovered while Perez studied the terrain with his binoculars.

Nothing.

They inched their way down the river's bank, cannons pointed in the general direction the pair had vanished. Perez watched as a large alligator slithered into the muddy water.

"Sonofabitch! Get me down river. There's only two of them. They are hiding somewhere down there."

Perez pointed a finger at the spot where he had last seen the pair. The helicopter pilot flew in low circles while Perez continued his search of the jungle below. Unable to locate the fleeing pair, he pointed toward the village.

"Take me to Cordoba," he commanded the pilot. "We'll wait there. They're headed to the coast, I'm sure of it."

The pilot nodded and pulled on the cyclic, lifting the aircraft higher over the trees, then followed the river to the Mosquito Coast.

e/se/s

Maria was running as fast as her legs could propel her when she tripped over a hidden vine and careened through the air. She landed with a soft thud and plowed her face into the moist earth, a sharp pain stabbing into her right ankle. Slater knelt beside her, drenched in sweat. Their clothes were torn into tiny ribbons and when she pushed the hair out of her face, she felt a trickle of blood on her cheek. Her foot was twisted sideways at an odd angle to her leg. Shock waves of pain riddled her body and she cried uncontrollably.

Slater pulled her to her feet but when she tried to put weight on the foot, she screamed and fell to the ground again, chest heaving, head pounding.

"Shit," she said, her knee buckling when the pain raced up her leg. "I can't make it, Jim. I can't go on."

Her body was in agony from the pounding it had taken during their flight from Managua. Every muscle pleaded for rest.

So she did what every self-respecting woman did in similar situations, she wept once more. She knew she was on the verge of losing it, but she no longer had the strength or the will to prevent it. Slater sat beside her, put his arms around her, and held her close.

"It's fine, honey. We'll rest a while. You'll feel better in a few minutes. If I have to, I'll carry you the rest of the way."

"I can't," Maria protested between sobs. "I just can't go on. Go on without me. Save yourself. I have endured El Chipote before. It's not that bad. I can get back into Perez's good side. I know how to sway him."

She noticed the pained look on Slater's face and knew her remarks hurt him.

"Surely you don't mean that," he said. He kissed her forehead and brushed her tousled hair away from her bloodstained eyes.

"No, of course not. But the prison I have endured before. I can do it again. So, please, save yourself. I'm finished."

She nuzzled Slater's sweaty chest and buried her face into it. Closing her eyes, she drifted into a black void of total helplessness. The cold prison floor felt good against her bruised cheek. Rivas was standing over her, a menacing, foul look on his face. In her dark haze, she saw his face contort into an evil grin. He reached down with a dirty hand and pulled her to her feet, his eyes bulging. He smacked his lips while he tore her blouse away from her breasts and she wept as he ravaged her, snorting loud pants of passion. Maria fought to hold back the tears but the evil she felt was too much to bear.

When she awoke, Slater had fashioned a splint for her ankle out of palm leaves and thin vines. He held it up, grinning.

"Try this on," he said. "Let's see if it works."

Maria held out her foot and watched Slater cinch the splint tight on her ankle. When he jerked her foot back into a normal position she let out a scream. She thought she would pass out. When the worst of the searing pain had stopped, she smiled at his handiwork. He helped her to her feet and she found she was able to hobble.

"Sorry about that. Feeling better?" he said.

"Much."

"I thought about what you said a little while ago," Slater said. "You know, about giving up. You can forget it. If we go down, it will be together, you hear me? Never to see you again, well…"

Maria touched his lips with her fingers. "Shh," she whispered. "I know. In the end, I would never get over losing you, either. How long was I asleep?"

"About an hour." Slater looked at his watch. "It's 2:30. The seaplane will be landing around four so we still have plenty of time. Think you can go on if I help you?"

Maria nodded and started through the jungle. She stopped short and pointed to two, giant yellow centipedes that were under them. She was out of her element in the coastal rainforest with its variety of wildlife that could kill and eat a person in a minute. She hated the insects, alligators, and snakes. In addition to the nightmares, there was the nagging fear that they were not going to get to the seaplane, and she knew it worried Slater as well. If, by some miracle, they managed to get to Cordoba and couldn't get to the plane, what then? Perez, she knew, would be waiting.

Maria prayed that they would be delivered from their mutual nightmare while Slater hacked a way toward the village. The pain in her ankle shot into her thigh, which made walking difficult, but as long as Slater supported her arm, she was able to limp ahead.

"How far to the village?" she asked, pointing to a twenty-foot python hanging from an acacia tree, her mouth sticky and dry

"Another two hours or so," Slater said. He used the machete and hacked an opening past a rubber tree.

Maria grimaced but continued limping behind Slater. The splint worked well and her ankle was beginning to feel somewhat better, the pain not as bad as when she first awoke. Maybe at Cordoba she could find some water. She was getting dehydrated

❧❧

Perez and the three-man crew watched the children gather around the helicopter as they rested on the beach that stretched out behind the village of Cordoba. The curious observers looked like they aged from eight to fourteen and they laughed and giggled among themselves. Perez opened the chopper's side door, jumped to the ground, pulled his Stechkin 9 mm pistol from its holster, and fired three shots into the air. The children scattered to the safety of the village, while the adults of Cordoba peered from behind the drawn curtains of their homes. No one ventured near the helicopter.

He lit a cigar, took a few deep puffs, and blew the smoke into the salt-laden air. From his coat pocket, he pulled a flask of Napoleon brandy and took a drink. He savored the amber liquor and took another puff on his cigar. Beyond the beach, the Caribbean Sea stretched to the horizon and the blue-green waters shimmered like the beautiful emeralds of the necklace he gave Maria. He wondered what had happened to her since her escape from El Chipote. Had she been part of the terrorist attack on the National Palace? Or was she hiding in the mountains?

He paced the length of the helicopter, pausing now and then to gaze out at the Caribbean. The mosquitoes were out in full force but the smoke of his cigar kept most of them at a distance. The chopper sat on a tall, sand knoll behind the village, which provided a good view of the beach, only a few seconds from intercepting anyone trying to make the water.

Cordoba was geographically isolated from the rest of Nicaragua's population. Founded as a port for pirates in the early 1600s, it subsequently became an entry point for slavers bringing their captives from Africa. It was a lazy village with only a few restaurants and other businesses located on its adjoining bay.

The waiting bothered Perez. The infernal waiting for something to happen. As always, during these periods of inactivity, he felt helpless, no longer in control, and it stuck in his gut like a piece of rancid meat. He couldn't do anything until the man and woman arrived and, when they did, he would blow them away.

He continued to pace, finding that it eased the pain in his legs. He rubbed his aching chest. A soured stomach, brought on by a cigar that lost its savor, forced him to take another gulp of the brandy. He continued to pace and wait.

ເ⁄ວເ⁄ວ

Slater and Maria hid in a clump of tall grass at the edge of the jungle. In front of them was the vast expanse of the beach at the edge of Cordoba. By luck, they had exited the jungle south of the village. Slater shifted his M-16 onto his back and reached for his binoculars. Scanning the area, he saw the helicopter perched on a knoll and tried to make out the officer who was pacing in front of it. He passed the binoculars to Maria who jumped at the sight of Perez. Lines of *pangas* were anchored a few meters offshore. Being late in the afternoon and the fishing done for the day, the boats were empty and the beach deserted. Farther offshore, the shimmering island of Isla Grande rose from the calm, turquoise waters like a lush garden.

He took the binoculars from Maria, scanned the horizon.

"There it is, hallelujah," he said. "They made it. It's right where Casey said it would be. They're just sitting there, waiting for us." He pointed to the seaplane rocking slowly in the sea south of the island. He let out a soft howl and clenched his fist.

"They're here?" Maria said.

He pointed to the southern tip of the island and handed the binoculars back to Maria. "Just where Casey said they would be."

She trained the glasses back on the helicopter parked on the knoll. "Think we can get to the plane without them spotting us?" she said.

"I doubt it. Our best hope will be one of those boats. Maybe they won't spot us for a while. Are you up to it?"

"Are you kidding? If I've made it this far, I'm not about to give up now. Besides, we have a date at your mother's, don't we?"

Slater squeezed her arm. "You bet," he said.

He checked their weapons a final time, took the smoke flare from his pants pocket, and stuffed it into his ragged shirt. After kissing Maria on the cheek, he sprinted to the moored *pangas*. The soldiers didn't appear to have seen him. He glanced over his shoulder at Maria, then motioned for her to follow.

CHAPTER 34

O ut of the corner of his eye, Perez caught a quick glimpse of a man and woman running along the beach. At first he thought they were two lovers having a grand time on a beautiful day but the more he studied them, he realized they were the couple on the river. He threw the butt of his cigar on the ground, crushed it with his heavy boot, and jumped into the helicopter.

"There they are!" he screamed to the pilot and pointed toward the water. From his vantage point, he could tell that they had pulled a boat free. He felt his pulse rise in his temples. "Get this damn thing in the air! I won't lose them this time."

The chopper's engine whined and its rotors began to turn. The pilot checked his instruments and flipped switches while Perez tapped his knee with a gloved hand.

"Dammit, man. We need to be in the air. Can't you fly this thing?"

Perez's patience disappeared with the pounding in his head. Grabbing binoculars, he scanned the horizon and found the United States Navy seaplane afloat in the surf beyond the reef. The realization hit him that if the couple reached the plane, it would be all over. The distance to the plane, he estimated, was three thousand meters. They had plenty of time if the pilot could get the damn chopper airborne. He had to intercept the couple before they reached the plane—he didn't dare risk firing on the United States Navy.

"What's the problem?" he asked the pilot. "Why aren't we flying?"

"Can't fly without manifold pressure, Colonel."

The pilot flipped another switch on his instrument panel and peered out the cockpit. As the big bird rose in the air, Perez felt a wave of relief but kept his eyes riveted on the couple. They had the boat pointed out to sea and were climbing aboard.

∽∾∽

When Slater and Maria reached the boat, they threw their M-16s and grenade launcher into it. Standing in the crashing surf, Maria fought to turn the boat so that its bow faced the offshore island, while Slater cut the mooring line. When the boat was free of its tether, Slater pushed Maria over the gunwale and jumped in behind her. She scrambled to a seat in the bow while he labored to start the motor.

The motor was ancient, requiring few moments for Slater to familiarize himself with it and find the starter pull. From over his shoulder, he saw the helicopter's turning rotors and realized that any minute the chopper would be bearing down on them. Slater gave the motor a couple of quick pulls but it failed to start.

Nothing, not even a sputter.

He tried again but the motor refused to come to life.

"Let's try another boat," Maria said. She looked toward the noise of the helicopter and squinted into the sun.

"No time!" yelled Slater. He pulled at the motor again but it still refused to cooperate. He threw his hands into the air in desperation "Of course! The damn choke!"

He pulled the choke lever all the way and tried again. This time the motor coughed a few times then sprang to life with a high-pitched roar. He gripped the handle, took a seat in the stern, and shoved the motor into gear. The bow leaped skyward as the fishing boat shot toward Isla Grande. Pitching over the water, Slater looked back at the beach. The helicopter was gone. He yelled at Maria over the noise.

"Get a rifle! Be prepared to use it! The chopper's on its way!"

Maria turned and Slater knew she saw the aircraft banking toward them, skimming low over the water. It was on a direct line and its nose was tipped downward, the classic indication of acceleration. Amidst the boat's bouncing and careening, Maria reached for an M-16 and held the weapon between her knees. She gripped the boat's gunnels and fought to keep her balance.

Slater pulled the boat's rudder control toward him sending the boat lurching to starboard. To his left, he watched the helicopter alter its course to compensate for his sudden move. It climbed skyward behind them and banked, so Slater repeated the maneuver and the little boat careened to the starboard again. Once more, the helicopter adjusted its flight path and, in doing so, slowed its airspeed. It danced in the sky, barely a few feet off the water's surface as it tracked the tortuous course set by Slater. It was gaining ground and would be on top of them at any moment. Slater could almost make out the two men in the cockpit. Each sudden turn made the boat difficult to handle as it crashed into its own wake and nearly capsized. Maria struggled to keep her balance in the boat's bow.

The chopper screamed overhead and made a sharp turn. Machine-gun fire erupted from the aircraft and the bullets plowed into the water around the *panga*. When Slater altered the boat's course again, he took a deep breath and watched the aircraft bank for another run. When it was close enough for him to get a good look at Perez, the chopper opened fire with the guns protruding from underneath the cockpit.

"Shoot the damn thing!" he shrieked.

Maria raised the rifle and began firing at the helicopter as it headed straight at them. The weapon was on full automatic and she could see little white puffs from the bullets bouncing off the chopper's armored belly. When it was ten meters off their port bow, it opened fire again. Bullets hit the water in big splashes. Slater pushed the boat to port. Its bow hit a large wave produced by the chopper's prop wash. Airborne for a moment, the boat landed on the backside of the wave with a heavy thud. The maneuver threw the chopper off its line of attack. Heading toward the island, Slater began a series of zigzag maneuvers to stay ahead of the gunship. But it was no use, for they were no match for the chopper's speed and maneuverability. Each time he pitched the little boat in a new direction, the chopped altered its course accordingly and bore down on them anew. The waves that crashed over the boat's gunwale began to form a large puddle on its floor, and he worried that, soon, the boat would be full of water.

Slater shot a quick glance at the waiting seaplane and found that it was still bobbing calmly in the bay. He wondered if its crew realized the chopper was about to sink them but kept a zigzag course toward the plane.

Beyond the breakers of the reef, as they neared the island's southern tip, Slater could see the seaplane's side door open. Waves rolled against the boat pitching it forcefully from bow to stern.

Maria was on her knees in the front of the boat using her legs to secure her position. Her finger was still on the trigger and Slater could hear the bullets ricochet off the chopper. Once again, the bird swooped past them and banked.

Then the unspeakable happened.

The helicopter's machine-gun fire ripped through the boat tearing large holes in its side and water began to pour in. Maria ejected a clip from her M-16, shoved in a fresh one, and resumed firing, but the aircraft seemed invincible, the bullets from Maria's rifle either missing their mark or bouncing off the chopper's fuselage.

Water swirled into the boat over Maria's ankles. Now more sluggish in the water, the *pangas'* speed slowed, its maneuverability impaired. Control was impossible.

Slater kept the throttle wide open but he knew it was hopeless—they could never outrun the chopper. It was only a matter of time before the boat went down or the chopper's fire found its mark. Between the boat's slower speed and them fighting a current, they weren't making much progress toward the seaplane. The boat was barely moving through the water. They crashed into a big wave and Maria flew overboard—in an instant, she was gone. Panicked, Slater, scanned the waves, his eyes darting over the frothing water. He eased back on the throttle and prayed Maria would surface.

The helicopter banked for another assault but still no Maria. His heart was in his throat and his pounding pulse lashed at his tired brain. An arm bobbed in the water.

The chopper bore down on them, its noisy rotors cutting through the humid air. Bullets slammed into the motor sending a plume of smoke into the sky and a ricochet hit Slater in the shoulder. He fell to the boat's deck, into rising water. The helicopter now hovered off the boat's port side and he sensed a rocket blast was imminent. Without thinking, he shouldered the remaining M-16 and fired a fusillade at the chopper's turbine engines.

"Take that, you sonsofbitches," he yelled above the noise and emptied the clip.

The bullet wound to his shoulder made handling the M-16 difficult but Slater pushed the pain from his mind and continued firing. Water had filled the boat to its gunwales, rendering the small craft on the verge of sinking. Soon Slater would be out of ammunition and the battle would be over. Maria had stopped moving her arm and rocked, apparently lifeless, in the sea.

The helicopter arced around the boat and pointed its rockets at the helpless *panga*. Slater emptied the clip into its belly, oblivious to everything except his finger on the trigger. Flashes of the chopper flickered before him like an old-time movie in slow motion. As the last of the bullets hailed into the chopper, there was a tremendous explosion. Dark smoke erupted from the turbines of the aircraft. With a second explosion, the chopper disintegrated into an orange fireball and plunged into the Caribbean Sea. The spinning tail rotor shot past the *panga*. Another explosion and flash of light. Then quiet, the chopper a burning, charred mass of metal and debris sinking into the Caribbean Sea. Within seconds it sank, leaving behind a steaming surface and smoldering bits of wreckage. Only the sounds of seagulls pierced the air.

With his good arm, Slater paddled to Maria and pulled her

into the boat. She gasped for breath then noticed his wound.

"God, you're hurt," she said.

"It's nothing," Slater said.

Maria ripped open his shirt and inspected his shoulder. The blood had dried and the pain had returned.

"You poor dear. You need to see a doctor."

"There will be time later. Now, let's get to the plane."

Maria used the one remaining oar and helped row toward the seaplane. The smoldering wreckage was gone, leaving behind serene surf under an intense sun. Slater settled back against the battered motor while Maria brought them closer to the seaplane. Her muscles rippled under her torn, soaked blouse, and he admired her beauty—still obvious beneath the grime. A young navy seaman greeted them through the seaplane's door and extended his hand.

"Welcome aboard," he called. "We thought that chopper was for sure going to blast you both to kingdom come."

A young man with short, blond hair and an infectious smile helped Maria into the belly of the aircraft then reached for Slater.

"Thanks," he said. He scrambled up to the cockpit and patted the pilot on the shoulder.

"You guys all right?" the pilot asked.

"We're fine. And thanks for waiting."

"He's been shot in the shoulder," Maria said, waving a finger at Slater. "He needs medical attention. And I think my ankle may be broken"

"No problem," the young man said.

"Sorry we couldn't have been of more assistance but we're only carrying sidearms. Not much firepower on this bird."

Slater slumped to the floor of the plane next to Maria and put his arm around her. She was spitting seawater, drenched and chilled. The blond seaman found a blanket and covered her while Slater massaged her cold hands. With a loud roar, the plane pitched forward and was soon airborne, heading south to Costa Rica and freedom.

എന്റെ

Shortly after landing at the airport outside San Jose, Slater and Maria were ushered into their room at the Ambassador Hotel. They said goodbye to Casey's station chief who'd met them at the airport with a doctor and transported them to the hotel. They sat in silence until there was a knock on the door. A white-jacketed man delivered a case of bottled water and a large magnum of white wine. They each opened a bottle of the water and drank in quiet gulps. Maria's once damp clothes were dry but her hair was matted against her face in a disorderly confusion of tangles. There were scrapes and bruises over most of her body. She still wore the splint Slater had fashioned for her in the jungle near Cordoba. Her hands were raw pulp and caked with dried blood. Slater studied her for a moment then laughed.

"What?" she said.

"Nothing," he said. "It's the way you look. Like you've been through a war zone or something."

His laughter was infectious. Maria giggled and pushed Slater onto his back. He issued a high-pitched howl.

"We *have* been in a war, stupid." Maria touched his bandage while he continued to yowl. "You think you look like a king at a ball? Look at you. Your hair's mostly gone, there's blood all over you, your clothes are ripped to shreds, and you smell to high heaven. Besides, you've been shot. Yeah, boy, you're a real winner."

Slater studied the label on the wine and turned it several times in the ice bucket. He lay exhausted on the floor and soon fell asleep. When he awoke, Maria was gone and he heard the shower running in the bathroom. Revived, he pulled off his clothes, kicked off his boots next to the sofa—and, naked— ambled into the bathroom, and knocked on the shower stall door.

"May I join you?" he asked.

Maria opened the door a crack and stuck her head out. The room was filled with steam and the warm mist felt good on his aching body. "By all means," she said.

Standing in the shower with Maria, Slater marveled at her delicate but muscled hourglass figure. She rinsed the soap off her light-brown skin and his eyes wandered from her erect nipples down to her thighs. He let out a small gasp.

"Damn," he said. "I can't believe how beautiful you are, Maria."

He pulled her close and kissed her hard on her lips. She didn't back away. Instead, she put her arms around his neck and pushed her tongue deep into his mouth. They embraced for the longest moment until Maria pulled away. Her hands explored his body, sending shock waves of pleasure through his spine. Slater noticed her eyes were closed and that she was leaning against the shower wall, a smile on her full lips. Then she opened her eyes, looked at him, and laughed.

"Turn around," she commanded softly, "and I'll wash your back.

She began to scrub the grime from his body and Slater concentrated on the miracle of her touch. With tenderness, she cleansed the bullet wound in his shoulder and, between her touch and the hot water, he was transported to a place where time was meaningless. As Maria worked the tension from his back, he found himself in a trance, hypnotized by the suppleness of her body and the softness of her skin. Finished with his back, she turned him around and continued on his chest. Under her spell, he felt as if he might explode at any moment and fought to maintain his composure. Maria wore a smirk on her face and she teased him with her tongue until he couldn't bear it any longer. He pulled her to him. They embraced and kissed for a long while. When there was no hot water left, and they could not see for the steam, they toweled off with thick towels and headed for the bedroom.

Maria lay on the bed and Slater followed, admiring her all the way. Her ample breasts beckoned him and as he lay beside her, his hand found the spot where her soft thighs joined. She pulled him to her and moaned when he touched her.

It was better than he ever imagined it could be. Maria knew all the right places and he lost count of the times he thought he couldn't hold back. Then she would stop and wait until his erratic breathing slowed before finding a new location to fondle. Through the erotic haze, she tasted like lilacs and the per-

fume in her hair left him in ecstatic agony. Maria pulled him
on top of her and begged him to take her.

When the orgasm came, it felt as if his soul poured into
Maria. She cried out for him not to stop and they pleasured
each other until totally spent.

Afterward, lying next to each other, they gazed into each
other's eyes.

"Was it worth it?" Slater asked. "The wait, I mean?"

"You are the best, the absolute best. I do believe you're going to make a fine husband, young man. Just when I thought
my world was coming apart at the seams, you arrived and
gave me hope, hope of surviving the brutality and the government's attempt to exterminate us. You gave me something to
live for. I waited for this moment at the expense of my own
sanity but it was worth it. Every stupid, lousy, idiotic minute
of it."

"Will we have lots of children, Maria?"

"Plenty. And they will all look like you, my dear. My parents would be so proud of me, seeing me this happy. I wish
you had had a chance to meet them. I know they would have
liked you very much."

Maria curled up in the crook in Slater's arm and fell asleep
on his chest. For himself, he was in heaven, glad to be going
home with Maria. He pulled a blanket over her, closed his
eyes, and drifted into a black, velvet nothingness where Maria
waited with outstretched arms.

About the Author

Richard Edde was born and raised in Oklahoma. After graduating from Central State College, he attended the University of Oklahoma College of Medicine, where he earned his medical degree in 1971. After spending a few years in family practice in two rural Oklahoma towns, he completed a residency in anesthesiology. Following a long career in academia and private practice, he retired to devote time to writing. His first novel, *The Photograph*, was released in 2014. Dr. Edde resides in eastern Oklahoma with his wife.